Mindgames

Ellen I. Gorowitz

iUniverse, Inc.
New York   Bloomington

Mindgames

iUniverse books may be ordered through booksellers or by contacting:

iUniverse
1663 Liberty Drive
Bloomington, IN 47403
www.iuniverse.com
1-800-Authors (1-800-288-4677)

ISBN: 978-1-4401-4070-9 (pbk)
ISBN: 978-1-4401-4069-3 (ebk)

Printed in the United States of America

iUniverse rev. date: 5/14/2009

To Vanessa and Leora

Prologue

Ashahr sent its mind's eye into space, Searching for food.

It was always hungry. Even in the middle of devouring the life energy of its latest prey, the prey it had been dreaming about forever, it was thinking about its next meal.

It took time to set up the pattern that would bring Ashahr the life energy it needed. Mix a diverse population of sentients who didn't like or trust each other, stir in the seeds of dissatisfaction and dissent, and turn them into hatred and rage. Then wait while events take their course: maybe a simple snack like a revolution, or maybe something more tasty and filling like a war. The energy released from the self-destruction of a planet—or, if Ashahr was lucky, an entire star system—would provide a transcendent meal. The problem was that nothing sated it for long, and then it was time to start Searching again…

The Alliance and the Hegemony were intriguing food for thought. The Alliance of the Six spanned not one star system but three, connected by corridors through hyperspace. Six inhabited planets that were connected by only one thing: the inhabitants' desire not to be part of the entity calling itself the Zoryan Hegemony.

The Zoryans had started the Alliance/Hegemony War, and it lasted for twenty-five years. There were truces here and there, but they never lasted long; Zorya broke them whenever

3

it could come up with an excuse. The Hegemony needed Alliance resources to maintain its dominion; it needed war to justify its philosophy of life. The Hegemony originally was better prepared for war than the Alliance, but eventually the tide turned; one step short of total surrender, Zorya was forced to negotiate a real truce.

This put at least a temporary end to the conflict's potential as nourishment for Ashahr, and it burned with thwarted rage. It hadn't started this particular war, but over the years the conflict had provided decent sustenance. Gradually, though, as Ashahr thought about the situation, it saw some potential. The Zoryans were ripe for its presence already, and some of the Alliance worlds, with their own conflicts and contradictions, were definitely headed for problems. The more Ashahr thought about it, the hungrier it became, until the need and the hunger forced its thoughts into the proper forms for action.

And so, Ashahr began to create its pattern ...

Chapter 1

An island of light floating in the darkness of the nearly empty room, the holographic model of a human brain revolved slowly on its invisible axis. Glowing red lines extended from the silver lozenge that was the implant, snaking along neural pathways, following forks and branches, knotting and merging. How beautiful. How complete. How perfect.

Diana Zarev smiled at the thought. *It's done. My life's work, and for this moment, I can pretend that it's perfect. And who knows? Maybe it is.* She Shielded her mind more tightly from possible intrusion by other telepaths in the vicinity of her lab and dared to dream on. The implant was complete, or as complete as it would ever get by modeling and computer simulation alone. It was time for live testing. And once that was done—successfully, of course—the entire world of humanity here on Logos Prime would change. Forever.

She leaned forward out of the darkness to take one last close look at the model before shutting down the program. The light reflected back a halo of cropped, platinum hair and played along the small, delicate bones of her face; the red lines tracing through the brain were reflected in her ice-gray eyes. *And not a moment too soon,* she thought, noticing the fine lines at the corners of her eyes. *I'm not getting any younger.* She pressed a button, and the image faded into the surrounding darkness.

"Lights," she called, blinking as the room responded. Now the darkness was outside the room: third shift had begun without her being aware of it. Time to go.

Even though she knew she was late for the meeting, she didn't hurry. No point in arousing suspicion now, after having been careful all this time. She didn't even look at the S2 guard stationed at the transport tube—if she had nothing to hide, she wouldn't be expected to notice him. After all, Security Service existed to preserve order and protect Psi-Actives—especially PAs like her, a high-ranking staff member of the Think Tank.

"Good evening, Doctor Zarev," a quiet voice said politely. She turned to face someone she vaguely recognized as a first-year student. At first she was surprised at his use of spoken language; then she became aware that her mental Shields were still up. He'd spoken out of a wish to avoid invading her privacy. Her heart beat a little faster. Would the student wonder why she was Shielded here in the Think Tank, near the top of the Core where all the power on Logos Prime resided? She dropped the Shield, leaving a Block only around her knowledge of the implant, and Read the young man's name and true intention.

She Sent a thought to him in the form of a teasing question: *On your way to a late-night study session Sandro, or something more interesting?* She Sensed his embarrassment and Read from his mind his wish that he hadn't called attention to himself. He scuttled away from her, down a corridor branching off in the opposite direction. Diana wanted to laugh, more out of nervous tension than anything else. *The best defense is a good offense.* If anyone had something to hide, it wasn't Sandro and the Think Tank professor he was meeting for that late night "study" session.

Finally the transport tube arrived. This time she nodded at the S2 guard standing next to the metal doors. As the doors opened, she inserted her accessdisc in the slot, keying in the code for her alleged destination: her compartment ten levels below the Think Tank's psy-med labs. Once the transport tube started moving, though, she pulled a telltale out of her carryall and shoved it hastily into the same slot. The lift would record Diana Zarev's entry point as the psy-med labs and her exit point as her compartment that night, but it would keep traveling another two hundred levels without retaining any memory of her true destination.

She leaned against the wall, wiping sweating palms against the dark jumpsuit she'd also removed from the carryall and put on in the lift. It wasn't just the usual fear of getting caught; it was also anticipation and excitement at the movement toward her goal. At least that was what she hoped would happen tonight. Of course, things could still go wrong. Her work aroused strong controversy even amongst the few members of the Bridge who knew about it. What would the Challenge leadership think of the whole thing? Would they be willing to help her set up the live test? Would any of them be brave (or foolhardy) enough to *be* the live test? What if the Bridge members who thought that the non-telepathic Psi-Nulls would never want to be anything like their telepathic oppressors were right?

No, she thought fiercely. *They're wrong.* The implant would prove, once and for all, that the only real difference between humans amounted to no more than an extra sense, one that she could now create in her laboratory for anyone who wanted it. No, damn it, Psi-Nulls weren't mentally inferior to Psi-Actives, angry and impulsive, violence-prone by nature. It was human to be angry when you were told, from the moment you were old enough to think, that because you can't Read minds, your place in life was in the lowest levels of Logos Prime's inner Core.

Which wasn't where the transport tube stopped, but it wasn't all that far away, either. She wasn't going to the bottom, where the agripods, maintenance units, and recyclers were located, or even the warren of the lowest-level living quarters;

she was on her way to the mid-level PN compartments. She braced herself as the transport tube opened. Stepping out, she was assaulted by light, noise, and movement all around her. The air was cold and slightly damp, smelling faintly of human sweat. Third shift didn't mean much down here; people slept when they could and worked when they had to, at both legal and illegal occupations. They got away with the illegal ones because S2 didn't feel the need to bother with PNs hurting each other as long as PAs weren't inconvenienced.

She quickened her pace to match those around her, hoping that her speed and the jumpsuit would be enough to keep her from standing out in a place where everyone knew each other. A PA alone down here, without a guard—no one would bother waiting for her explanation that she was a member of the Bridge before sending her back upstairs where she belonged. In pieces. The corridor in front of her was blocked by a long line of people who looked like they'd been waiting there for a while, and she pushed her way through the crowd, trying to ignore the angry shoves she got in return. Rationing again; there must have been another agripod failure, though no one living in the Core's upper levels would ever know about it.

The hallway she was looking for was far less busy, and it didn't take long to find the compartment where tonight's meeting was taking place. She'd been given a code for the door, and she punched it in. After a minute, the door slid open, and she stepped inside, hoping she was strong enough to persuade these people to try her idea.

"You're late, Diana. Was there a problem?" Kieran asked. Good, some familiar faces. The speaker was a fellow Bridge member. Diana almost started to Send a thought in reply, but quickly she remembered the Bridge directive that no telepathy was to be used when they were with their Challenge colleagues.

"No, I'm sorry, I just got caught up in my work," she said, grinning. "In our work." She lowered herself to the remaining unoccupied floor pillow and peered at the others sitting in a small circle, surrounded by the blue half-light produced by an activated privacy screen. Besides herself and Kieran, the Bridge was represented by Monique Haverill, an older woman whom everyone trusted. Not that Challenge members shouldn't trust Bridge members—but often they didn't.

The relationship of sympathetic Psi-Actives and their organization, the Bridge, to the Psi-Nulls' underground Challenge was delicate. While the Bridge made clear that its members believed in complete equality between PAs and PNs, in real life no such thing existed, and often it was easy for Challenge members to forget that Bridge members were risking much—their lives, their freedom, and their sanity, given the ever-present threat of Reconditioning—in order to help create the possibility of a different future for humans living in the artificial structure of the Core on otherwise uninhabitable Logos Prime.

The Challenge was represented in the room by Jacob and Louisa, whom Diana knew, and by another woman she didn't know. As Diana focused her attention on the stranger, she was jolted by the familiar Sense of psychic energy. A Challenge member who was PA? Not only that, but her face looked vaguely familiar; she was not someone Diana knew personally, but maybe someone whose image she'd seen in the datanet. The woman watched her with a grave expression but said nothing. No one introduced her.

Finally, Monique spoke. "Diana, we've told our Challenge colleagues about what you've been doing. Why don't you brief them on your progress in developing your implant?"

Diana's eyes sparkled as she warmed to her subject. "It's done. I ran the final simulations tonight, and everything checks out. The latest design change continues to achieve the results I'm looking for while reducing the side effects to what I think would be more tolerable levels." She went on to describe what her tests told her would happen to a Psi-Null individual once the device was inserted into her or his brain, as well as how she would help manage the physical and psychological impact of the change. She studied her colleagues' faces eagerly, but was disappointed to see little enthusiasm. The unknown PA's thoughts were Shielded.

Finally, cautiously, she brought up her request. "I haven't done any live testing, for obvious reasons. From seven years ago, when this was just an idea, to today, secrecy has been a top priority. If the Think Tank ever found out what I was doing I would have been carted off and Reconditioned faster than—" She broke off as the unknown woman shuddered deeply, shaking her head. Jacob put his hand on her arm, and she straightened up, her face once again impassive. Yet Diana could see the fire behind her dark blue eyes now.

"Anyway, the next step is to identify an appropriate test subject and find a way to conduct the test without alerting S2. I'd have to stay with the test subject full time for several weeks, and I'd certainly be missed upstairs. But there's no way the subject would remain undetected up there." She looked closely at Jacob and Louisa. "I know the Challenge has off-world contacts, and I was thinking that might be an answer."

The two Challenge members glanced at each other. "Monique told us this was coming," Jacob said slowly. "We wanted to hear it from you for ourselves, though. And we wanted Coraline to meet you so she'd be able to decide for herself whether she wants to be part of this."

"What do you mean?" Diana asked.

"There's a lot of conflict right now within the Challenge about which way we should be going," Louisa answered. "There are those who think the type of resistance we've been practicing—making connections, educating PNs, creating underground literature, as well as the small acts of sabotage— hasn't accomplished much and won't ever accomplish much. They think we need a more radical approach."

"A more radical approach would result in First Circle bringing S2 down on our heads," Kieran interrupted.

"That's what Jake and I think, but like I said, not everyone agrees," Louisa replied. "The radicals don't believe the answer is for PNs to become PAs. They'd rather kill PAs than imitate them." She leaned back, gazing at Diana. Her voice had a defiant edge. "I don't believe in violence, but there are times when, I have to admit, I see their point."

Diana had been expecting this, and she kept her response quiet and calm. "I didn't create the implant so that PNs would all become PAs."

"Then why did you?" The woman Jacob had introduced as Coraline suddenly spoke. Diana wasn't sure why, but she realized that if she was to go any further with her experiment, it was this question she had to answer and this woman she had to convince.

"Because," said Diana, "I believe that the psi-sense is just that—a sense. Like sight or hearing or touch. We don't base our society on who has the sharpest eyesight or the keenest hearing, and we shouldn't base it on who has the strongest psi-sense, either. Psipower isn't intelligence, and it certainly isn't character. Yet all of our political, educational, cultural, and social structures are based on the notion that people who can Read minds are smarter and better than people who can't, and that they deserve to have more of this world's limited resources.

"If a device like the implant can substitute completely and effectively for the organ that activates the psi-sense in PAs but is missing in PNs, it would force them to open their minds to the concept of equality. And if First Circle, the Think Tank, and S2 still don't get it, it can give the Challenge a new and powerful weapon to continue the struggle."

She took a deep breath to steady herself. "There's another reason, though. I think that the evolution of psipower in humans has taken a wrong turn. PAs have become too homogenous and are continuing to evolve in ways that are unhealthy and sterile. A wider variety of telepathic humans might make it possible for us to achieve higher mental evolution." She smiled. "But that's just my private fantasy. For our purposes, I do think there's value in being telepathic, and I'd like to give PNs who want it the chance to experience it for themselves."

There was a long silence after she finished speaking. Finally, Coraline turned to her two companions and nodded. They stood up, and Jacob gestured to Kieran and Monique. "Coraline wants to speak to Diana alone." The Bridge members agreed, and the four of them left the room.

Would you like something to drink? Coraline Sent.

Diana nodded. *As a matter of fact, I haven't had a chance to celebrate the completion of the first phase of my project yet, so I'd like a glass of* d'lor, *if you've got any.*

Coraline laughed. *Sounds good to me.* She stepped out of the light, into the blurred darkness of the rest of the compartment. Diana found herself wondering what Coraline's home really looked like and why a PA was living down here in the first place. It wasn't generally permitted—unless the person in question was someone that Logos Prime's rulers couldn't really punish but didn't want to have around upstairs.

Exactly. Coraline had Read the speculation in her mind. She handed her a glass of red liquid. They saluted each other and touched their tongues to their drinks. The d'lor bubbled and fizzed, adjusting itself to their body chemistries. Diana studied her mysterious companion. Coraline was older than she was, she judged, but not by much. Diana's psi-sense told her of a hard life that made Coraline appear older than her years. Yet she'd retained a classic beauty, with bright gold hair pinned back to reveal sculpted cheekbones and eyes that were both thoughtful and haunted. She still looked familiar..

My mother was Astrid Saint-Claire, Coraline Sent, and Diana gasped. Before her disgrace and eventual suicide, Astrid Saint-Claire had been a high-ranking Think Tank geneticist as well as one of the founders of the Bridge. But the real reason Diana was jolted by the name was that Astrid Saint-Claire had tried, back when she herself was only a child and at the very beginning of the Challenge, to do something similar to what Diana was doing now: rejoin the divided human race.

Astrid had violated one of Logos Prime's most sacrosanct rules: the one concerning genetic selection. Specifically, only mental equals were permitted to have children together. She'd performed genetic experiments using herself as the subject and unregistered genetic material as the "fathers" of her children. Diana looked sharply at Coraline. Was she the product of one of those experiments?

No, Coraline Sent, again Reading her thoughts. *My father was also Psi-Active. He left when my mother started going crazy—at least that's the way he saw her attempts at curing this sick society.* Her mouth twisted, and Diana winced with the Sense of both contempt at his weakness and the rejection and abandonment Coraline felt when she thought about him. Her chest tightened as she recalled her own experiences with parental desertion.

Coraline continued, *My mother had two other children, my younger brothers, who both live off-world. When the Bridge told me what you were up to, I thought one of them might be a good candidate for your experiment. But I had to convince myself that getting them involved was a risk worth taking.* She smiled. *And you convinced me. The problem now is that I don't know whether either of them would be willing to participate.*

They're both PN? Diana Sent.

Yes. Neither has the organ for psi-sense, but one of them seems to have picked up genetically some unusual mental characteristics, which might make him a better test subject than the other. Coraline shook her head. *But he's not a Challenge member and has made it clear that he has no intention of getting involved with the Challenge. The other one is a Challenge member, but I can't imagine that he'd be willing to become telepathic. He's more the radical type.*

We'll just have to find out for ourselves. Can you get in touch with them and set up a meeting? Diana Sent.

Not here on Logos Prime. My brother Nick Hayden, the one who's a Challenge member, is a Free Raider.

Diana raised her eyebrows. Humans who had joined the Free Raider Force during the war and remained with it as inter-world mercenaries after the war ended were banned from returning to Logos Prime.

But I'm still able to contact him, and I can meet him on Praxis if there's an emergency.

What about your other brother?

Coraline was silent for a long moment, her eyes and thoughts elsewhere. The remains of her drink no longer bubbled. *I haven't seen my other brother since he left Logos Prime to join the war effort. That was seventeen years ago.*

He's also banned?

No, he can go wherever he wants. But he's never tried to contact me.

Diana was puzzled. She wasn't quite sure what to ask; this felt like dangerous ground. *Do you know why not?*

I think he just wants nothing to do with his past—and I'm part of his past.

What about your other brother, the Free Raider? Does he see him?

Sometimes they do business together. Nick's tried to convince him to join the Challenge, but like I said, Andrei won't have anything to do with it. Her bitterness was obvious. *I think he's just scared of jeopardizing his exalted position.*

What's that?

Coraline gazed at her. *My other brother is Andrei Savinov.*

For Earth's sake! Stunned, Diana responded before she had a chance to think. *The Alliance's Peacekeeper.*

Coraline shook her head with frustration. *For all the good it does Logos Prime's PNs, yes, that's right.*

Diana thought for a moment. *What makes you think he might be a good test subject?*

Because he's literally a genius. Astrid tested him when he was a child. Even though he's definitely Psi-Null, his intelligence is far outside what are considered norms for both PNs and Pas. His intuitive abilities registered off the charts.

Diana tried to Read further into Coraline's thoughts on the subject but found she was being Blocked. She switched to Sensing and blinked, startled by the sudden onslaught of conflicting emotion: frustration, resentment, love, pity ...

Andrei might well be the best candidate for the test . He was always much more like PAs than PNs anyway, which is why he was tortured growing up, by PAs and PNs alike. He even drove Nick and me crazy with that cold, impenetrable exterior. But Astrid adored him. I think they had a lot in common—emotionally, that is.

If he can't be persuaded to help the Challenge, maybe there's some way we can persuade him that trying the implant would help him in his position as chief negotiator for the Alliance. Diana Sent this suggestion. *Though I really don't know how well it would work for reading nonhuman minds.*

But even if he agrees to do it and it works, unless we can persuade him to join the Challenge, we might as well be throwing it away, Coraline Sent.

No, that's not true. Even if he won't join the Challenge, at least we'll have found out for certain that the implant works. Diana smiled. *And since I'll be with him for a while during the test, it'll give me a chance to try to change his mind about the Challenge.*

Coraline nodded, admitting that she might have a point. *How will you get permission to leave Logos Prime for the time it'll take to do the experiment?*

I've been thinking about that. I'll have to come up with some kind of study that Robert Jaxome will give me approval to pursue off-world. If we can get either of your brothers to agree to this, I'll find a way to make it happen.

Coraline nodded, standing up to signal the end of the meeting. She started to release the privacy screen to let Diana out of the room, then let her hand fall back. She switched to speech. "Do you have any family, Diana?"

A difficult question. Diana shook her head. "Not really."

Coraline looked weary. "I used to have a family. The way this world *is* blew it apart—blew us apart. But I remember when we were together. When we were happy." She pressed a button, and the room's opposite wall faded out to reveal a floor-to-ceiling, wall-to-wall viewscreen. Diana recognized the image of Lake Glass. The artificial lake glittered a brilliant cobalt in the rose-gold sky and real sunlight that only a favored few ever got to see, high up in the outer Core. Two golden-haired children splashed in the water, their mouths open wide with delight. A woman strongly resembling Coraline—Astrid Saint-Claire—stood on the shore, smiling as she holo-sketched them. Off to one side, another child, long and lean with a mop of dark hair, lay on his back on the artificial lawn with his arms laced behind his head, daydreaming. Diana put her hand on Coraline's arm, Sharing her longing and sorrow. She slipped out without another word, leaving the other woman alone with her memories and her dreams.

Chapter 2

It was the middle of the night, but you'd never know it in Seladorn, one of the planet Sendos's five Central Cities. The industrial-strength smog blanketing the sky blotted out whatever weak moonlight might have existed, and the canyons of skyscrapers lining the city's narrow, twisted streets made it look the same from the start of one cycle to its end. Nick Hayden inserted a silver disc into a plate in the featureless, soot-grimed wall of an anonymous building in the warehouse district. Part of the wall, the size and shape of a door, irised open, and he slipped through quickly.

Sendos: a brutal, overpopulated oligarchy, constantly beset by guerilla-style civil wars between the members and supporters of the Five Families holding most of the planet's resources. Normally each Family had its own pleasure palaces and didn't mingle, and humans weren't particularly welcome anywhere. But there were a few special places catering to special tastes and occupations—like spying and arms dealing—where an outsider might be tolerated. This place was one of those. Nick stared down the suspicious, hostile glares of the locals, which quickly subsided as they regarded his solid build, fighter's stance, and grey jumpsuit with the red bar on the sleeve. *There was no use messing with a Free Raider Captain,* they decided, and turned back to their own activities.

Good enough. He passed through the main room and into a warren of cubicles off a back hall.

Ravat was pacing nervously when he entered the room. A Karellian of the Niwahr class, under his black cloak and hood his skin was a mottled, pasty white—as far as one could get from the smooth silver-grey of the elite Citizen class. His large, dark eyes glittered madly, Nick observed, partly from nerves and partly from the aura suppressant he had obviously taken recently. In spite of the dangers of the drug, Nick understood his reasoning: how could he possibly be an effective spy with his aura giving away his every emotion?

Nick nodded a greeting and sat down at the polished black table, gesturing for Ravat to do the same. On top of the table was a steaming bottle of deep red liquid and two glasses. He poured a drink for himself and his hired spy, using a straw to pass the liquid through his breathing unit, and adjusted the translator in his ear.

"What's the big deal, Ravat? What've you got for me today that's so important I had to make a special trip here for it?"

Ravat drew in the drink through the tentacles waving delicately from his three fingers. He pushed the cloak aside slightly so that the hole in his throat used for speech emerged. "Some unusual information, Captain Hayden. It seems there are very strange things happening on Selas these days."

"The prison? What about it?"

"A friend of mine—a source—flew cargo there and back. Usually it's the same old supplies, the same old supply routes. But over the last several cycles—three of your months, I believe—the cargo has been a bit more unusual."

"Yeah? In what way?" Nick's curiosity was finally piqued.

"Arms shipments."

He knew Ravat was eager for a reaction, but Nick wasn't going to pay up for this intel if he didn't have to, so all the Karellian got was a pair of raised eyebrows. "Not exactly a place where you wouldn't expect to find arms shipments," he commented dryly. "I hope that's not your great discovery, that weapons are being transported to Selas."

Ravat's indignation showed itself as a slight wisp of red light appeared behind him, in spite of the aura suppressant. "Ah, but it's the type of weaponry that is so intriguing," he answered smoothly, recovering his composure. "Laser cannons, particle-beam torpedoes, wide-range disruptors ..." He smiled, having finally produced the desired reaction as Nick choked on his drink.

"War weapons," Nick said, once he could talk again. The kind his brother, the Alliance's Peacekeeper, had outlawed under the Settlement between the Alliance and the Zoryan Hegemony.

Ravat nodded. "My source told me they're being stored there."

"By who? For what?"

Ravat shook his head. "I'm sorry, Captain. That I cannot tell you. My source didn't know. But she made her own personal record of the manifests for those shipments, along with notations on the storage location. For sale to you at a very reasonable price."

Nick leaned back casually in his chair as he refilled their glasses. *Time to deal.* "Well, I can't deny that this interests me," he said thoughtfully. "We've always done well by each other, Ravat."

"So true, Captain Hayden." He took a palm-sized fileviewer out of his cloak, unlocked it, and handed it to Nick. "My terms."

Nick studied it for a minute. "So in return, I'd receive a black-coded disc with this information, plus a layout of the prison with the location of the storage areas."

Ravat nodded. "It's all there."

"I'm sure it is, and I see here your usual assurances that this information is as complete as you can possibly verify it, that you are not selling this information to any other party, blah, blah, blah. Your word is your bond, after all," he said with a touch of irony.

Ravat nodded gravely. "Of course, Captain. You have not had occasion to doubt me in the past. At least not over anything that really counted."

"True," Nick admitted. "But this is different—the intel doesn't come straight from you. How do I know your cargo pilot friend won't be selling this to anyone she thinks might be interested—or even just telling her tale in some bar, like this one?"

"You weren't listening carefully enough, Captain Hayden," Ravat answered. "I told you she *used* to fly cargo. She told me about this when she thought someone was after her, and she gave me the disc for safekeeping shortly before she was murdered."

"Too bad." Nick leaned forward, his voice quietly intense. "You sure you didn't kill her for it?" The thought of this annoyed him. It would go against his own code to buy secrets from someone who'd killed for them, and he really wanted this information.

Ravat looked indignant. "Absolutely not. How long do you think I'd last in this business if I went around murdering my sources?"

Nick nodded thoughtfully; the Karellian had a point. "If I find out you killed her and then lied to me about it, you won't last long, I assure you. And you know I have my ways of finding out, don't you, Ravat?"

The Karellian didn't answer, but the aura suppressant obviously wasn't working all that well: the grayed orange light spoke of sullen fear and compliance.

"Have you told anyone else about this?" Nick asked.

Ravat shook his head. "I haven't shopped the disc around, if that's what you mean. Though I will if you don't want it. I pride myself on knowing my clients well, and I thought this was something that would appeal especially to you. Given the

Challenge's need for arms and the difficulty of obtaining them under the Settlement—"

Nick waved a hand to cut him off. "Yeah, well, I'll take it, and I'm buying your silence as well. With no exceptions."

"But of course," Ravat answered cheerfully.

Nick reached into his pocket and pulled out a blue creditdisc. He rolled it end over end across the table toward the spy, who inserted it into the fileviewer and nodded his satisfaction. He took the black-coded disc out of a fold in his skin and handed it to Nick, who unlocked his own fileviewer and quickly scanned it, keeping his expression carefully neutral. "Looks like it's all there."

"A most satisfactory transaction," Ravat commented, draining his glass as he prepared to leave. "I don't suppose you'd care to share with me your plans for that information?"

Nick laughed. "You're kidding, right?"

Ravat shrugged. "I didn't think so. Best of luck to you, then, Captain Hayden. I have a feeling you're going to need it." He pushed the door shut behind him.

Yeah, yeah, Nick thought. Even though he knew he shouldn't stick around, curiosity got the better of him, and he turned back to the disc in order to examine its contents more closely. Whose weapons were these, and what the hell were they gonna be used for? Should he contact the other Challenge leaders on Logos Prime? Most of them were stuck there with no off-world clearance, so there was little chance they'd know anything about it. Staying with the Free Raiders after the war had limited his own access to Logos Prime, but there were ways around that—as there were ways around just about anything, as long as you weren't afraid of bending the rules.

It was going to take some rule bending to get to the bottom of whatever was happening on Selas.

Chapter 3

Get up, Andrei Savinov thought. *Now. Get. Up. Now.*

His body was unimpressed by this command from the Alliance's Peacekeeper. He wondered if he was actually beyond the ability to move at this point. There was a risk that if he really did manage to stand up and walk toward his Zoryan opposite number, he'd fall flat on his face. But since he'd already done that during this negotiating session—figuratively, at least—he was determined to end this never-ending day with dignity. Slowly he rose to his feet and walked toward the Zoryan negotiators, stopping in front of their new leader.

The Zoryan—more than a head taller than him and covered with the spiked natural body armor of kri's kind—loudly thumped kri's taloned fists across kri's chest. Andrei wasn't certain he could close his swollen fingers into fists, but he did the best he could to reproduce the salute. He was glad they couldn't see behind the dataglasses; he knew he couldn't keep the pain out of his eyes, and Zoryans went crazy if they sensed the slightest physical weakness—in each other as well as in their opponents. *For Earth's sake, let this be over already,* he thought.

Both sides' staff members took their cues from their leaders and also saluted each other. Guards lined up to escort the Zoryan delegation to the docking bay and off the Peaceship while bodyguards surrounded Andrei. Even though they needed him alive for Settlement negotiations, Zoryans had tried to kill him too many times for this to be a mere formality. Andrei wondered if they knew how close they'd come to succeeding in the last attempt, a year ago.

Finally they were gone, but now he had his own staff to deal with. They turned from the door and stared at him with various expressions of bewilderment, anger, and fear. He knew how they felt, as the horror of the last five days—especially this last double session, two days without a full-length recess—spun through his mind's eye. And failed negotiations replaying themselves in slow motion was not a pretty sight.

Danar-sar-Zhiral, the Peacekeeping Mission's second-in-command, didn't look as upset as the others. In fact, assuming Andrei was interpreting the pulsings of the Sendosian's bifurcated skull correctly, there was some malicious pleasure there. Danar had wanted to lead the Mission himself, and as head of the Alliance's Diplomatic Corps, he should have been able to, but the Zoryans had other plans. Zoryan Warleaders led peace talks, and so should Alliance Warleaders, they'd declared. It turned out to be one of those non-negotiable demands. And so Andrei Savinov, former Chief Strategist of the Alliance Military, had become the Peacekeeper.

"Run along now," he told them.

The skull pulses grew more intense. "What about debriefing, Commander?" asked Danar. "These talks did not go well."

"I'm aware of that," he replied dryly. "We've been at this for quite a while, Danar. I think we could all use some downtime before we try to assess the damage. Sylvain will contact you later to set up a debriefing session." Sitting down again, he gestured to dismiss the entire staff. Obviously still troubled, they filed out, leaving him alone with his Executive Assistant, Sylvain Dulaire, and two bodyguards. The other two were outside the door.

Sylvain's commlink chimed. "All clear. Zoryans are no longer aboard the Peaceship. Stand down from General Alert." Administrative Operations told him. He looked at Andrei, who nodded, and he dismissed the bodyguards. This left the room empty except for the two of them. *Still one too many people,* Andrei thought. If he was going to collapse, he didn't feel like having an audience.

"You can go, too, Syl," he told his Exec. "Go get some sleep."

"I did," he replied. "We all took a full-length recess here and there. Only one who didn't, as a matter of fact, was you."

Andrei shrugged. "You saw what happened. I didn't dare disengage." He waited, but Sylvain still wouldn't budge. "Did you want something?"

"I have something to show you." He pulled a black cube out of his pocket and handed it to Andrei.

He turned it over in his gloved fingers. "What's this about?"

Sylvain shook his head. "One of the junior Zoryan bodyguards slipped it to me to give to you. Checked it for concealed weapons, but I haven't been able to find anything. Can't find out much myself, though—it's black-coded for your eyes only." He gazed at Andrei questioningly. "You have any idea …?"

"Maybe." Andrei leaned back in his chair, giving up on the idea of being alone. At least the image of perfection didn't need to be kept up any longer. He held out his hands, and Sylvain pulled off the gloves and set them down gingerly on the table. The iridescent black hands of the gloves were tightly molded to his own hands' proportions, while the silver spikes that ran from above the wrist to the elbow gleamed heavily and menacingly. Part tool to access remote databases, part defensive weapon, and part display, the spiked gauntlets represented the Alliance's attempt to replicate Zoryan body armor, though the potentially deadly built-in flashpoints were inert at the moment. He sighed, flexing aching fingers and running deeply scarred hands through his hair. He took the translator out of his ear, then reached for the dataglasses and removed them. He was about to rub his swollen eyes when he felt Sylvain touch his shoulder.

"Mm-mm," Sylvain warned. "Use this instead." He handed him a bottle of restorative drops. Andrei nodded his thanks as he tilted his head back slightly to insert the drops. That done, he took up the cube again.

"Did you bring a spindle?" he asked.

Sylvain shook his head. "Didn't think you'd want to view it right away," he replied. "By the way, why are we still here?"

Andrei didn't answer him. Time to try again. He stood, his hands braced against the edge of the table as the conference chamber slipped in and out of focus. He couldn't raise his head without feeling dizzy; couldn't think of a part of him that didn't ache. Built-in body armor made the black uniform heavy and constricting. Though he'd had a year to get used to the fact that he was never going to be the same as before the accident, he was still frustrated by the betrayal of his body, ashamed of feeling so worn out, considering all he'd done for the past five days was sit at this table and talk. Debate. Argue. Try not to plead. And try not to lose, while coming as close to losing as he could have come without a new war breaking out. And he simply couldn't stand the thought of that, especially without Kylara at his side.

"Andrei, you all right? Maybe you should sit down again." From a distance, he could hear the anxiety in Sylvain's voice; could feel him moving closer.

"I'm fine," he answered, quietly resolute. "Let's find out what K'ril I'th has to say for kriself."

Gratitude that he'd finally reached his office was immediately overcome by the sight of a cold-box on the table in the corner. It definitely hadn't been there when he left.

"You wouldn't happen to know what that is?" he asked. Sylvain started toward it, but Andrei pulled him back. Yes, a year had passed, but he still thought of explosives, especially since they'd just had Zoryans aboard the Peaceship.

Sylvain looked surprised, and then he understood. "Sure do. Ordered it myself. It's vegetables. From Erlande." He grinned, obviously pleased with himself. "Fresh vegetables, Andrei. Thought you'd like them. Can't live on protein bars and nutrient drinks forever."

Really? Why not? Andrei sighed. He knew he should be grateful, but just the thought of eating made him slightly nauseous. For the last six months, food had tasted like sand.

Six months since Kylara's death.

"Thanks, Syl," he finally said. "I'm too tired to eat now. Maybe later." He felt a stab of guilt as his Exec's face fell, but he couldn't think about it for long—there was still the mysterious message cube to deal with.

"You have ninety-five messages, Commander Savinov," his desk told him. "None are priority black. Five are priority gold. Twelve are priority red …"

Priority black were his spies. He was disappointed that there was nothing from them that might help explain what had happened. Gold messages were from five of the six Alliance Heads of State; Logos Prime didn't care about Settlement negotiations. Red were from Council members. All clamoring to find out what happened. "Hold them all," he instructed.

"I believe you will find message fourteen particularly interesting, and messages eight and twenty-one are …"

Even his desk was ignoring him these days. "Hold them all," he repeated firmly. He took the cube from Sylvain and fitted it onto a spindle.

"Retinal scan is required to access this message and begin decoding procedures," the desk told him as the link from the spindle to desk was completed. He complied and waited while the decoding began. "Decoding complete. Special Alert! Use of recording devices will activate auto-destruct. Message will auto-destruct concurrent with transmission."

Andrei shook his head. If the sender went to so much trouble to see to it that nothing would be left behind, it was probably worth keeping. He took a small, white bottle out of his desk and gave it to Sylvain, who painted the black cube with a clear gel. That done, he instructed the spindle to begin showing the message.

A burst of black light appeared in the middle of the room, and it rapidly coalesced into a Zoryan figure. As he suspected , it was K'ril I'th's face that appeared first, followed by kri's body. Kri did not appear to be wounded. The Zoryan General's image stared directly at him and spoke.

"If you are watching this, Commander Savinov, then you must know that the events I predicted have come to pass. I am either dead or have gone so deep into hiding that I might as well be dead, for all the help I can give you now. Those of us who believe that peace might be possible between your people and mine no longer have the power to attempt to make that happen.

"Like a disease, the so-called religion I spoke of to you has grown in strength, to the point where we can no longer control it. Those whom you will be facing—or, perhaps, have already faced across the table—belong to the new leadership. They are the prophets of the new religion—those who have seen the true way and have been given the gift of sight by Ashahr …"

"What the hell?" interrupted Sylvain, completely mystified. Andrei shook his head for silence.

"Which will help the Zoryan Hegemony defeat the Alliance of the Six and rule the stars, the way the new religion says we should. It is our destiny, these new leaders proclaim. And the people of my world, enduring the privations that the long war brought us, still angry that we had to settle for a truce instead of outright victory, and anxious that our colonies have sensed weakness in the leadership and could be planning their own rebellions, are willing and eager to believe.

"War will come again, Commander, unless you can find a way to stop it. While the Settlement has outlawed the manufacture of war weapons, the new leaders have made statements to the effect that since conquest is our destiny, Ashahr will provide the means to accomplish it. The gift of sight is the first of those means. How the rest will come about is unknown to me.

"Commander Savinov, I regret my inability to help you right now. I regret the blood that will be spilled in this mad, meaningless venture. We were so close to finding a new way for our worlds." The figure bowed kri's head and faded away. Kri's eyes were the last to disappear; they had an unusually human look in them. *A look of despair,* Andrei thought. He shook his head to clear it; his imagination was clearly working overtime.

"Play it again," he told the spindle.

"Not possible. Message has completed auto-destruct." The data-formed microbes he'd let loose to the kill the virus had failed. A perfect end to a perfect day.

"Guess that's why the negotiating team changed," Sylvain remarked. "And why they were so hard to deal with."

Andrei didn't answer.

"Think they're really planning to go to war again?" he persisted.

Andrei still didn't reply; he was staring into the space where K'ril I'th's image had been. Though his face was expressionless, his eyes revealed a mind light-years away.

Sylvain tried one last time. "What in hell's name is the gift of sight?"

Andrei finally roused himself, though his voice was so quiet that Sylvain had to move closer to hear his answer. "Telepathy. The gift of sight is telepathy." The message was gone, and there were no witnesses to the secret meeting he'd had a few

weeks earlier with K'ril I'th. He sat back, remembering that
meeting…

* * *

Andrei made the switch from an official Peaceship cruiser to
an unmarked voyager parked in an old, unused spacedock
on T'rak, T'lar's second moon and a well-known Free Raider
outpost. He had an open account with the Raider who'd
procured the ship for him. Though he knew Nick would have
done it for free, he didn't want to involve his brother in a
doubtful venture like this—one with an unknown purpose
and unknown consequences.

He took the voyager out to Quadrant Three of the neutral
space between Alliance and Zoryan territory that was still
labeled the War Border by both parties. That K'ril I'th had
chosen Q3 for this unusual meeting wasn't too surprising:
it was the site of the asteroid belt they'd been arguing about
for months. If they were caught, it would be easy to say that
they were doing a joint survey to determine mining rights—
wouldn't it?

He landed the voyager on a vast plain of red, violet, and
black lava. The thick, glazed swirls of the stuff resembled frozen
waves breaking against a nightmare's beach as gouts of flame
the same colors exploded randomly around him. He leaned
back in the pilot's chair and waited.

K'ril I'th emerged from the other side of one of the nearby
hills and began walking toward him. Zoryans didn't need
atmosphere suits; their natural body armor sufficed in all
climates, at all temperatures, under all conditions, no matter
how hostile. The Alliance had found that out the hard way
during the war. Andrei activated the atmospheric screen within
his ship to protect himself, and then he opened the door and
let his former enemy inside. It was hard to make room, given
kri's size and bulk, and the deadly spikes of the Zoryan's body

armor seemed to fill the small ship's interior. Finally they were settled, and they sat for a minute, just staring at each other.

"I was not sure you would really come," K'ril I'th admitted.

Andrei smiled slightly. "A black-coded message asking for a secret meeting in neutral space, come alone … it seemed a bit too obvious to be a trap."

K'ril I'th grinned, revealing four rows of pointed teeth. Even Zoryan teeth were armored. "So true, Commander. Thank you for, shall we say, trusting me."

Kri fell silent again, and again Andrei waited. Waiting was a skill that his childhood had forced him to master, and his latest incarnation as Peacekeeper had further honed his ability.

"What do you hear of events on the Zoryan homeworld?" K'ril I'th finally asked.

Andrei raised his eyebrows. Was he actually supposed to admit to spying on Zorya? "This and that. What events are you referring to?"

K'ril I'th shook kri's head impatiently, ignoring his question. "No games today, Commander. There are cracks appearing in the Hegemony, starting with the homeworld itself. Conditions on Zorya have worsened—we work our colonies harder, but to less and less effect. There is talk of revolt on some of them. More than just talk, in one case." The Zoryan opened kri's mouth, baring kri's teeth, and flexed kri's talons. "Of course, it was immediately subdued. The rebels were eliminated. But the sentiments remain, and they grow stronger."

"And on Zorya itself?"

"The prevailing sentiment is to continue to suppress dissent and search for new worlds to control. There is talk that the Settlement needs to be, shall we say, renegotiated." Kri stared hard at Andrei. Andrei knew kri was waiting for a reaction, and as usual, he made sure kri was disappointed.

"Zorya and the Alliance are always renegotiating the Settlement, but that's not what you mean," he answered quietly. "You're talking about going to war again. Is that what the Central K'rilate wants, K'ril I'th? Is that what *you* want?"

The Zoryan shook kri's head vehemently. "No. I do not wish to go to war with the Alliance again. Some members of the K'rilate do not. However, there are others that do. They are followers of a new religion that has recently come out of nowhere to attain an astonishing popularity."

This was news to Andrei. His spies seemed to have fallen down on the job. "What kind of religion?"

"Followers call themselves the Children of Ashahr, the Dreamer of Darkness. You know how important the concept of darkness is to us—the darkness of space, the darkness of our too-short nights bringing relief from the blasting rays of our sun, the darkness of the recesses of the mind, where true knowledge comes from. This Ashahr supposedly came out of darkness to bring new knowledge to our people."

"What sort of knowledge?" Andrei asked, as if he couldn't figure out what was coming next.

"Knowledge of our true place in the universe," K'ril I'th replied.

"At the center, no doubt." Andrei's tone was dry.

"You sound as if you are familiar with this concept."

"It's not unique, but it's usually quite deadly." Andrei paused, but K'ril I'th didn't respond. "Please go on."

"Ashahr has appeared to some of our leaders in dreams and told them that as a superior race, Zoryans are the true rulers of the stars—and of the planets that orbit them. That it is our destiny to rule the Six as well as the Hegemony."

"A convenient theory, don't you think?" Andrei commented. "Zorya needs a continuing supply of off-world resources. Your colonies are being drained. That's how the war happened in the first place. The only difference this time is a new supporting ideology—a myth to make conquest seem legitimate." He paused, leaning back in his chair and looking out at the landscape again. "Your people lost much in the last war."

"As did yours," K'ril I'th interrupted. "As did you."

Andrei winced inwardly and continued. "Are they really ready to die again so soon, just because a few members of the Central K'rilate claim to have had a vision of manifest destiny?"

"It isn't just a few members of the Central K'rilate, Commander. Zoryans of a wide range of classes have experienced visions of Ashahr."

"Have you seen it? What does it look like?"

K'ril I'th shook kri's head. "I have not seen it. And that is another problem—the K'rilate is becoming divided into those who have heard and understand the dreams of Ashahr and those who have not. And those of us within the K'rilate who have not just happen to be those who are most in favor of making the Settlement permanent and opening up trade relations with the Alliance."

"Who are Ashahr's chief supporters within the K'rilate?"

"You are not going to like this," K'ril I'th warned.

Andrei laughed. "I already don't like it. And I'll bet you're going to tell me that my old friend K'ril S'lat is one of the new high priests of Ashahr's so-called religion, aren't you?"

K'ril I'th nodded. "S'lat recently introduced new legislation in the Central K'rilate redefining what is considered subversive to include any action that indicates a desire to pursue initiatives with the Alliance that go beyond the minimal requirements of the Settlement."

"Kri's resisted the Settlement from the start."

"That's not the worst of it, though," K'ril I'th warned him. "Kri has gotten G'al accepted as a member of the Central K'rilate. They have actually managed to stop trying to have each other killed long enough to form an alliance."

It was bad news indeed to hear that the head of the Hegemony's secret police was now an official member of Zorya's ruling body. Andrei took a deep breath and slowly let it out again without speaking.

"K'ril G'al has called for a complete review of the Settlement in order to identify what kri calls Alliance treachery in cheating us out of valuable territory that should be ours to rule." K'ril I'th paused. "I suppose this means our joint mining initiative will have to be postponed."

"I suppose it does." But Andrei's light tone belied increasingly bleak thoughts. *Not again, damn it. Not again. Not with Kylara gone.* Kylara Val, the Alliance's Prime Commander, had been killed at the end of the last war. No one could replace her—not in battle, and not in Andrei's heart. "… they call it the gift of sight."

Andrei suddenly realized that K'ril I'th had been speaking and that he hadn't been listening. "What does that mean?"

"Ashahr has told those who have experienced its presence that it will provide the means to destroy the Alliance. That is the gift of sight, which will allow us to Read and destroy the minds of others—including telepathic minds."

Andrei looked away as he felt a sharp stab of pain in his chest. The damned heart probably needed adjusting again. "I need to know more about this," he said finally. "If Zoryans can Read our minds—and turn our minds against us—Ashahr and its followers might have a chance of success after all." He struggled to maintain a calm appearance through a second chest pain. Dropping dead from heart failure right now would save him from having to deal with this mess. But the pain finally eased, and he turned back to face K'ril I'th directly.

"You're in trouble now, aren't you? They're not going to leave you in charge of Settlement negotiations anymore. Not unless you can fake being a member of their group of Ashahr-worshippers. And if they can Read minds … you won't be able to fake much of anything."

"Nor will you," K'ril I'th replied.

Andrei didn't react. "What's been happening to those who oppose these new ideas? Has G'al—pardon me, K'ril G'al—had them arrested? Executed? Have you been threatened?"

"I am touched by your concern," K'ril I'th commented dryly. "And I am well aware of its origin. If you do not have me to deal with anymore, you are going to have someone much, much worse."

Andrei grinned. "You've been quite enough of a challenge, K'ril I'th."

K'ril I'th hissed softly. "I, too, have found you an honorable opponent." Kri stood up suddenly. "It is time for me to go. To answer your question, no one has been formally arrested and executed—yet. However, there have been a few questionable disappearances. Perhaps those of us who are still able to see reason will be able to put a stop to this before it gets any further out of control. We have negotiations scheduled for the coming decon, yes? I hope I will again be the one sitting across the table from you at that meeting."

"I hope so too." They saluted each other with crossed fists as K'ril I'th left. Andrei watched kri cross the plain to kri's waiting ship. He spoke softly at the retreating figure.

"Watch your back, my friend."

* * *

"But that would mean this Ashahr, whatever it is, is a real entity of some kind," Sylvain said. "One that can make Zoryans Read minds."

Sylvain's voice snapped him back into the present. "It would appear that way," Andrei answered, keeping his tone neutral.

"Telepathy's outlawed for use in Settlement negotiations."

"We'd have to prove they really have it," Andrei replied. "Which won't be easy, with K'ril I'th's message erased." He shook his head. "I wonder why kri did it that way. Maybe kri was afraid it would fall into the wrong hands and could be used against kri later …"

Sylvain's eyes took on a look of panic. He obviously wasn't thinking about the message. "If Zoryans can really Read minds, we're done for! How will you negotiate with them if they can get into your mind and pull out your thoughts?"

Andrei felt a brief flare of anger. "You mean like PAs do back on Logos Prime? I'd fight it the same way I always did—try to out-think them. Think faster than they Read, add more levels of reasoning, use the Disciplines, be devious, be deviant." He broke off, opening hands that had curled into involuntary fists, reflecting long-buried anger. He didn't want to think about Logos Prime, the homeworld he'd left seventeen years ago to go to war. He winced with pain as he opened stiff fingers, his hands still swollen, and clumsily reached into his desk and brought out an analgesic spray. Sylvain took it from him and sprayed both hands. Relief came instantly, but it never lasted long.

At the time of the accident (if anyone could call an almost-successful Zoryan assassination attempt involving a flashbomb exploding in his personal cruiser an accident), medlab surgeons had tried regeneration, and it had failed. Andrei was one of those rare humans whose bodies adjusted poorly to regen technology—even his minor injuries healed slowly and with difficulty—but never before had it failed completely. His doctors told him that he could either live with partial regen with its pain and scarring, or he could have his hands replaced with mechanical prosthetics. Because regen was almost always successful, there had been few advances made in prosthetics. Artificial hands would work, and they would be strong, but touch would be purely the function of a microscopic sensor web.

He and Kylara had thought about it. The artificial heart was one thing (especially since he hadn't been given a choice about that), as were the regenerated lungs, but artificial hands were something else. Nothing would feel the same—not to him or to her, not touching or being touched. She didn't want him to do it, and he agreed to partial regen. But she was dead now, and he doubted he'd be touching a woman again for a long time. Maybe it was time to have them done.

He rubbed burning eyes, suddenly remembering how tired he was. He leaned over to rest his head on his arms, on top of the desk. "Mm-mm," Sylvain admonished. "Bed." Numbly, he obeyed. He'd figure out how to save the Alliance after a few hours' sleep.

Chapter 4

Nick had an outstanding marker with a member of the Karellian Protectorate, and he decided that it was time to call it in. "Permission to enter Dome Four at coordinates 2.0.12," a mechanical voice announced, and he took his cruiser in through the newly opened panel in one of the translucent silver domes that covered much of the planet's inhospitable surface.

Karellia was somewhat of a enigma to the rest of the Alliance. Its sentients wouldn't say where they had come from or why they had left their planet of origin. They had just claimed this icy ball of poisonous gases countless years earlier and put up the domes that housed their entire population— the lower classes living on the planet's surface, with the higher-ranking Karellians living underground.

Even though it was the Alliance's most technologically advanced world, the source of much of Karellia's technology was, like its inhabitants, shrouded in mystery. There was just enough strangeness in their "inventions" to make you wonder … like the items he was looking for today, thought Nick, stepping out of his cruiser.

A figure twice his height, half his weight, and completely shrouded in blue cloth stood waiting for him at the spacedock's door. Nick walked over to him but didn't bow—not to a member of the Personal Service class. The servant gestured for

Nick to follow, and they took the long elevator ride to where the highest-ranking members of the Citizen class lived deep underground.

The elevator door opened into darkness. The servant pressed a button on the wall, which illuminated a narrow tunnel, and then closed the elevator, leaving Nick alone. Muttering to himself irritably, he crawled the tunnel's length. It ended in a silver-white room, empty of furniture except for a few islands of light. A gray-shrouded figure, with its little amount of exposed skin burnished to reflect silver as bright as mercury, slid gracefully out of one of them. This time, Nick bowed deeply. The figure bowed in return and gestured to one of the islands of light. Nick eased himself gingerly into it—he always half expected to land on his ass when getting into one of the things—but the "chair" held him firmly.

"Hey, Protector Virad," he said finally. "Nice to see you again." With that, he'd used up the extent of his repertoire of social courtesies.

"I'm not sure whether I can say the same, Captain Hayden." Virad's answer was cautious. "Surely this is not a social visit."

Nick smiled broadly. "Y'know, you're right about that. Truth is, I'd like your help with a little project I'm working on. I need to borrow a lightship."

Virad slid out of his chair and floated around the room. His silver-white aura had darkened to a deep gray, reflecting a combination of dismay and annoyance. "Captain. I was— am—deeply grateful for the assistance you've rendered to the Protectorate—"

Nick cut him off. "I think it was you, specifically, that got the benefit of our arrangement, Protector Virad. This isn't between me and the Protectorate. It's between me and you."

Virad sighed. "Point taken, Captain. I guess, as you Raiders say, I owe you one. But your request is not a simple one. Lightships are prohibited according to the conditions of the

Settlement." His aura became tinged with red. "Commander Savinov bargained away one of Karellia's finest weapons."

Nick slid out of his chair and in two strides was in front of him. He tried with his usual limited success to control his temper. "Yeah, and you got nothing back, right? How many K-cycles were you at war before the Settlement? Your precious Karellian technology wouldn't have won the war, Virad, and you know it. By the time lightships were outlawed, the Zoryans had already figured out how to detect 'em. I'd say you didn't lose much of anything compared to the last five K-cycles of peace." While he had his own criticisms of his younger brother, he wasn't willing to put up with hypocritical whining by the treaty's beneficiaries over his handling of the Settlement.

Virad took a step back. His aura shifted colors wildly, then stabilized to a sullen grayish blue. "You do have a point, Captain." He emphasized the title sarcastically; Nick recognized the warning to remember Virad's own title the next time he addressed him. "The Settlement has brought order and peace back to Karellia after a very long, very costly war, and we do appreciate the Peacekeeper's efforts. However, the fact remains that lightships were classified as a proscribed weapon under the Settlement and are not permitted out of restricted warehousing. Even if you assume that I am willing to let you, as you put it, *borrow* one, how am I supposed to gain access to it?"

Nick laughed. "Oh, come on now, Protector Virad. A top-ranked member of the Protectorate and the Citizen class? I'm sure you'll come up with something." He folded his arms. "Of course, if you know for sure you'll never need me or any other Free Raiders again for anything, I guess you could turn me down, and there wouldn't be much I could do about it." He shrugged. "Though I could probably come up with something if I thought about it hard enough."

Virad held up his long, thin hands, translucent tentacles waving gracefully. "There's no need to be so dramatic, Captain

Hayden," he said smoothly, in control again. "I believe I can accommodate you after all—in the interest of future relations between ourselves as well as between Karellia and the Free Raider Force—"

"Yeah, sure. I'm also gonna need a lightsuit."

Resigned, Virad nodded. "Of course you realize, Captain Hayden, that if you are caught with this equipment, I will claim that it was stolen from us—and demand the full punishment allowed under Alliance law. And if you don't return it at the time we agree on, I will come looking for you."

Nick nodded his acceptance. "Fair enough," he replied. "Because frankly, Protector Virad, if I get caught with this stuff, *you* will be the least of my problems."

Chapter 5

"Commander Savinov, we are still having difficulty understanding the nature of your request."

Andrei sighed. He looked over at Darya Ardelle, Logos Prime's Representative on the Alliance Council. She shook her head with exasperation. He looked back at Lantera-A, part of the Glendine binary who were the current Council Chair. "I'm asking you to go to the Institute for Advanced Telepathic Studies on Logos Prime and present this request for the use of their personnel in order to find a way to combat Zorya's new mindweapon."

"Are you sure there is such a thing?" Lantera-B asked.

Hadn't they read his report? Had they been asleep for the past hour while he was explaining all this? He hated to think he'd made the long trip to Glendine, the current Council headquarters, for nothing, but it was beginning to look that way. "It's the only conclusion I can draw from what happened during the most recent negotiations," he replied. "K'ril I'th is gone. Those who replaced kri refused to tell me why. They just came in and repudiated everything we'd done for the past six months, without a word of explanation. Whatever I said, they had an answer—in fact, they had an answer before I said it." How could he make them understand?

He continued, "They weren't being clever, Lanteras. They knew what I was going to offer. They knew what I was going to counter-offer. There was nothing I could say to reach agreement with them or to get around them. I recognize the use of mindreading because I've been in that position before—had my thoughts pulled out of my head, studied, and disregarded. That's what it's like dealing with the Psi-Actives of Logos Prime. The Zoryans at the negotiating table now have telepathic capabilities. I'm sure of it. And we need to fight fire with fire."

Lanteras looked at each other and shook their heads simultaneously. Lantera-A spoke this time. "None of this explains why you want us to do this instead of you, or you and Councilor Ardelle together."

"You and Councilor Ardelle together!" Lantera-B said. "After all, she is Logos Prime's Senior Representative, and you are from Logos Prime yourself—in addition to being the Alliance's Peacekeeper and a Special Representative to the Council."

"The Alliance's Peacekeeper and a Special Representative!" Lantera-A continued. "Why in six worlds should the leaders of the Institute for Advanced Telepathic Studies give higher regard to a request coming from off-worlders than it would from two high-ranking members of their own people?"

"Because we are not their own people!" Darya interjected, losing her patience. "Neither Commander Savinov nor I are telepathic. We're what they call Psi-Nulls. They are Psi-Actives. Come on, you know this already! They're like the Citizen class on Karellia, or the leaders of the Five Families on Sendos—or like binaries here on your own world of Glendine, Lanteras. They're the folks at the top of the heap—"

Translators started humming, searching for the meaning of the bizarre-sounding phrase.

"—and we're on the bottom. The PAs running the Think Tank—the Institute—don't care that the Psi-Nulls fought their war for them. That PNs died out in space so that their way of life would be preserved."

"Darya …" Andrei's voice was a quiet warning.

"They don't care that Commander Savinov is a war hero and is leading the effort to keep the war from starting up again. They see him as a Psi-Null, and that limits his credibility with them. *Immensely.* The Think Tank is the most isolationist institution on isolationist Logos Prime. Its leaders don't want anything to do with the rest of the Alliance. They're not going to listen to a PN tell them that they have to come out here themselves and dirty their hands with Zoryans."

"Then you should go to your central governing authority on Logos Prime and have them order the Institute to comply with the Commander's request," Lantera-B said severely.

"The Institute must comply with the Commander's request!" Lantera-A added. They were obviously getting fed up.

Darya sighed noisily and rolled her eyes at Andrei; she was fed up too. "The Think Tank *is* the government. Robert Jaxome is both the Director of the Think Tank and the Governor of Logos Prime. The governing authority, First Circle, takes its orders from him."

Silence. Andrei leaned back in his chair, running his finger along the rim of his glass to reheat his tea. He didn't look at Darya again. He didn't have to be telepathic to know how the Lanteras were going to respond, or to know what would happen next. He would have to go to Logos Prime and make the case himself. This certainly wasn't one of his better weeks.

Finally, they gave their answer. "It is inappropriate for the Acting Council Heads to get involved at this level of protocol. Either Councilor Ardelle should speak with the governing authority of First Circle and have them order the Institute to comply, or Commander Savinov should present the request to the Institute himself," Lantera-A said.

"Present the request to the Institute himself!" Lantera-B added. "The argument that he would not be well received, simply because he is not telepathic, is difficult to accept.

Commander Savinov has proven his superior abilities in service to the Alliance time and again. These Institute leaders are supposed to represent the intellectual elite of your planet. We are sure that Commander Savinov will be able to make them listen to reason."

"Commander Savinov will be able to make them listen to reason—we are sure of that!" Lantera-A had the last word. With that, they ended the session.

"You sure you don't want anything stronger to drink?" Darya asked Andrei as she headed for the dispenser.

He laughed, shaking his head. "Come on Darya, were you really expecting anything else? You know how legalistic the Lanteras are. The Alliance Council Charter says that each planet's Council Representative deals with matters involving their own homeworlds. Besides, I'm sure the whole thing doesn't make much sense to them. Logos Prime is the only one of the Six that didn't send members of its own elite as Council Representatives."

"Shows what the PAs think of the Council," Darya muttered.

Andrei shrugged, resigned. This was an issue that no longer had any meaning for him.

"So what now?" she asked.

"There's no point in your going to First Circle," he replied. "I'll go to the Think Tank and make the case as best I can. Maybe they'll see it as some kind of intellectual challenge. Who knows – maybe they'll even be frightened of the potential consequences." He sighed. "I know I am."

***

There wasn't any other option, Andrei thought, not for the first time. He stared unseeingly at the viewscreen of his cruiser as Sylvain flew them toward Logos Prime.

Not for the first time, he inventoried the telepathic capabilities of the Six. Sendosians and Erlandians were Psi-Null, as were Glendine singletons. Glendine binaries could communicate telepathically, but only with each other. Karellians projected their feelings outward in the form of an aura but were unable to Read the thoughts of others. T'larians … what possibility did the inhabitants of T'lar represent? Many of them could Read vital signs and possessed certain types of empathic and healing abilities. But even though they were an unusually sensitive and perceptive race, he didn't have any evidence that they could Read minds. But what about the Disciplines?

He thought about the instruction he'd taken with the Zh'ladar. T'lar's spiritual leader had taught him a great deal about how to open his mind to higher levels of consciousness as well as how to discipline his mind against disorder. He'd thought of going back to the Zh'ladar for help, but the truth was that the Disciplines wouldn't be enough. They might give him some limited protection against mental assault, but that wouldn't help him gain the kind of negotiating advantage he'd need to forestall another war.

Which left him back where he'd started: the PAs of Logos Prime. He had no idea whether or not they could Read Zoryan minds, especially Zoryan minds affected in some way by the alien entity Ashahr. Maybe they wouldn't be willing or able to help, but they seemed to be the only possibility he had right now.

Andrei's position—and the PAs' lack of interest in interstellar affairs—had insulated him from having to deal directly with them for a long time, and he was dismayed at the strength of his resistance to encountering them now. He wasn't so much afraid of them as he was of himself—his reaction to them. He'd deliberately repressed his hatred of them for so many years, and now he was starting to feel it again. Hatred for what they'd done to his mother, to his family.

His family. Because Free Raiders had participated in the war effort, he'd stayed in touch with Nick, though the relationship was strained by his chosen lack of involvement with the Challenge. Coraline he'd simply left behind. Like the rest of his life on Logos Prime, at first it had hurt too much to think about, then numbness had set in, and he'd convinced himself that they were better off without each other. He shook his head, banishing the memories hovering at the edge of consciousness. He couldn't still care about all that. He'd walled it all off years ago, and he'd be damned if he'd let this mission put the slightest breach in that wall.

Logos Prime came into view, and he swallowed hard at the sight of the Core structure. The top was a translucent dome surrounded by a circular docking ring for spacecraft. Below this, the structure was also circular; it was blinding white to help throw off atmospheric heat, with a completely smooth and featureless exterior. Inside the Core, on both the PA and PN levels, were viewscreens on almost every wall. Some of them showed images created by the inhabitants of the Core, while others showed images taken from the few intact records of Earth remaining from the generation ship that had brought humans to this star system. Without viewscreens, humans would have been driven insane from the claustrophobia of living their entire lives indoors.

The Core's living areas were carefully divided by class and function. The top was occupied by the governing authorities and the Think Tank with all its labs, offices, and classrooms. The upper levels were PA compartments. Then came mid-level PN compartments for PNs with some status—those whose occupations were the most valuable to PAs. Finally, the lowest levels were where everyone else lived and worked.

In his eighteen years on Logos Prime, Andrei had lived on both PA and PN levels. He hated all of it.

Chapter 6

One thing you can say about Psi-Nulls—they know how to work with their hands.

Diana looked over at Lauren, a lab colleague and casual friend, who'd Sent this remark. She suppressed her distaste so Lauren couldn't Sense it, busying herself admiring the length of cobalt cloth shot through with silver threads that Lauren was holding up. Lauren pointed at another bolt, this one sky-blue. *You'd look wonderful in that, Diana, and you could use something new to wear outside the lab on the rare occasions that you leave it.*

She smiled, pretending to acknowledge the good-natured teasing while her mind was elsewhere. She took the cloth up from the table and held it below her chin in front of a full-length mirror placed in front of the stall. Through the mirror she saw Coraline at a jeweler's cart, trying on a bracelet. Without turning around, Coraline acknowledged her mindtouch.

The cloth's owner began to look impatient. "I can have it made up for you in any of the latest styles," he cajoled.

"I'll think about it," Diana promised. She nodded to Lauren, who was busy working with the stall's tailor on her own outfit, and drifted off.

This weekly trading post was one of the few places in the Core where PAs and PNs could mingle. Handmade clothing, jewelry, furniture, and decorative objects were designed by PAs and created by PN artisans. Though they wouldn't want to be noticed in serious conversation, it was occasionally possible for Bridge members to use the trading post to pass on smuggled goods to Challenge members. Luckily, Diana and Coraline didn't need to be face to face to have a serious conversation. They circled the large, crowded room, keeping a few stalls between them.

You're a medtech. Diana couldn't keep the surprise out of her thoughts at seeing Coraline's uniform. PNs weren't entitled to individual medical care by human doctors; they were diagnosed and treated by medlab computers and dispensers. PNs also weren't allowed to train to be doctors. But someone had to run the machines and perform the few treatments that the machines couldn't do by themselves; hence, PNs could be trained to be medtechs. But Coraline Saint-Claire wasn't PN.

I couldn't stay upstairs after Astrid died, she Responded. *Not to live, not to work. But thanks to the fine work of the Bridge, I've been acquiring stolen medical knowledge for a long enough period of time that I think I know as much as the average PA doctor—yourself excluded, of course.*

Of course. Diana stifled a grin as she ran her fingers along the edge of a beautifully carved artificial-wood bowl. *But the implant isn't a piece of ordinary medical technology. I don't know if you'll be able to understand all the specs.*

I'd like to give it a try anyway. Coraline hesitated. *I'd also like to be kept informed of your progress once the experiment is underway.*

That could be very risky.

Nick's taught me how to set up a black-coded channel. Diana Sent nothing, and Coraline persisted. *These are my brothers, Diana. If I'm going to put one of them at risk, I need to be informed and involved. Otherwise I can't go through with it.*

Diana paid for the bowl. "I'm still looking around," she told the stall's proprietor. "I'll pick it up on my way out." The woman nodded, and Diana turned her attention back to

Coraline. *I don't like it, but I guess I understand,* she Sent. *It's a shame Nick's banned from Logos Prime. We wouldn't have to meet them on Praxis, since Andrei is coming here tomorrow.*

WHAT?!

Diana winced with the intensity of the thought hurled at her. She gave Coraline a quick glance; she was frozen with shock but still had the good sense not to look in her direction. Diana Sent, *Commander Savinov is going to address the Think Tank's department heads tomorrow morning. None of us knows what it's about. People are surprised Jaxome is permitting it—letting a PN into the top levels of the Think Tank.*

It must be some kind of Alliance crisis. Coraline had regained her composure. *I know Andrei wouldn't choose to be on the same planet, much less the same room, with a bunch of Think Tank PAs if there was any way for him to avoid it.*

Well, maybe whatever it is will be something we can use to our advantage, Diana Sent. She Shared regret and sympathy. *I'm sorry you had to find out from me that he was coming here, and not from him.*

Bitterness so strong she couldn't help but Sense it, but Coraline didn't Send a direct response. *I'll study your specs. Assuming everything looks all right, I'll get in touch with Nick and set up a meeting.*

Should I meet you back here next week? Diana Sent.

Unless you hear from me sooner than that. Without looking in her direction, Coraline crossed the room to the stall where Diana had bought the bowl. Nodding to the proprietor—a longtime Challenge member—she picked up the bowl and took it away with her.

Diana didn't watch her leave, but she couldn't help but worry about the pouch filled with black-coded discs that she'd left under the lining at the bottom of the bowl. What if Coraline's compartment was searched? Shaking her head slightly to dispel her fears, she headed back to the stall with the sky-blue cloth. Maybe a new outfit wasn't such a bad idea after all.

* * *

Andrei knew that wearing body armor on his so-called homeworld would have been a breach of protocol. Nevertheless, he missed it as he stood before the assembled Think Tank department heads. His black uniform was unadorned except for the silver bar on the right sleeve—designating a rank that meant nothing to them. This was in sharp contrast to the multicolored costumes of Logos Prime's elite, who prided themselves on individuality and originality in dress and put considerable time and effort into their appearances. The uniform was one of the things he'd liked about the Military right away; no more trying to force himself to think about what to wear. Now even his off-duty clothes were black.

He tried not to think about his lack of protection for both body and mind. He tried not to think about anything but the problem at hand. He'd used the Disciplines to shut down his emotions, distancing him from his memories. None of it mattered; he just had to get the job done.

He looked around the small, tiered amphitheater, careful not to meet anyone's eyes for more than a heartbeat. The Think Tank department heads seated in front of him were looking at him with curiosity—the curiosity of scientists examining a particularly unusual specimen. As he continued his surveillance, his attention was caught by a small, striking woman with a halo of spiky, silver-white hair; she was staring at him intently from the last seat in the second row. No one was sitting next to her. Her eyes might have been light blue or gray, with just a spark of silver. Finding himself curious, and maybe even attracted to her (was that possible? a PA?), he returned her gaze. He imagined speaking to her. What nonsense. He abruptly turned away, annoyed with himself for the lapse in concentration.

All heads swiveled to the back entrance as Robert Jaxome came into the room and headed down toward the podium. "Ah, good, we're all here. On time, for once," he remarked with a hearty cheerfulness that Andrei found disturbing because of its false quality. He reached the front of the room and gestured for Andrei to come forward.

"It's not every day that the Alliance's Peacekeeper chooses to pay a visit to the Institute for Advanced Telepathic Studies. Commander Savinov has convinced me that the matter he brings to our attention today is of serious concern and worthy of our most intense consideration. You may begin whenever you're ready, Commander."

"Thank you, Director," Andrei replied. Earlier that morning, he'd had breakfast with Jaxome in his office to explain what he would be talking about. Even though he'd tried to keep it as straightforward as possible, he already knew, based on Lanteras' response, that it was a hard story to believe. Not the least of his problems was that Logos Prime humans didn't believe in religion, so the idea that Ashahr was a mindweapon disguised as a religious symbol of some sort would be completely foreign to them.

He was surprised and pleased that Jaxome had listened to him so carefully, and he dared to hope that this session would go as well. He fixed his eyes at a point beyond their heads and launched into it.

"What I request from you, therefore, is any knowledge you have of alien physiology and psychology—obviously with particular attention to Zoryans—and mind-control techniques, both how to use them and how to combat them." He paused for a moment as he came to the hardest part. "In addition, what I could really use is someone telepathic to join me in conducting negotiations. Whatever knowledge you can provide will help me develop a negotiating strategy, but that strategy may not hold up if Zoryans can Read through it. That's where the actual presence of a PA could prove invaluable. The Alliance is hoping for your support to prevent our hard-won Settlement from coming apart. I'm sure none of you want another war. You have the power to prevent that from happening."

He heard a cough, then a noisy yawn, then a ripple of amusement, ostensibly at the sound of the yawn. The unexpected sound startled him and broke his concentration, and for the first time since he'd started talking, he looked closely at his audience.

Bad move. *Very* bad move. As he saw the boredom in most of their faces and the amusement in others, he felt sudden despair at what a lost cause this was. They were laughing at him. A Psi-Null trying to talk to them as an equal, trying to tell them what to do. Trying to get them to waste their precious time on some trivial pursuit light-years away from their life of the mind on Logos Prime.

Memory hit suddenly and hard—the memory of Kylara pacing their quarters as she shook with rage at her failure to recruit PAs into the war effort, at a time when defeat seemed close at hand …

* * *

"They wouldn't listen to a word I said! Damn it, Andrei, they're supposed to be the greatest minds on Logos Prime! How can they be so stupid as to think that an interstellar war won't affect them? Do they truly believe that Zoryan weapons can't kill Logos Prime telepaths?" Suddenly her eyes filled with tears; she blinked them away quickly, but he had seen them. Eyes that never cried even as she lost comrade after comrade as the war raged on, seemingly into eternity. He took her in his arms and held her tightly, trying to give her strength and comfort with his touch.

"They were laughing at me," she whispered. "A PN trying to be someone. It never changes, does it? No matter what we do, we'll always be nothing to them."

* * *

"Commander?" Jaxome was looking at him curiously. "Are you finished?"

Andrei blinked rapidly, forcing himself back to the present time and place. "Yes," he said coldly. "Are there any questions?"

No one said anything. More than anything, he wanted to get out of that room, but once again his attention was caught by the woman in the second row. She was obviously troubled; she bit her lip and shook her head with frustration. It seemed as if she wanted to speak to him but something was holding her back. She didn't look like the kind of person who'd be afraid to speak her mind, but maybe he was making that up. He waited, but nothing happened. He nodded politely to Jaxome as he finally left the hall.

"Commander, wait!" He turned and stopped at the sound of Jaxome's voice. "You spoke well."

"Not well enough, I'm afraid," he answered. "The response was somewhat less than favorable."

"I think people here believe that the Alliance survived without our services before, so there's no need to get involved now." Jaxome's voice had a strange tone to it, almost a tone of warning.

Andrei turned to face him, not trying to hide his curiosity and confusion. "Perhaps I didn't make myself clear, Director. This is different. If Zoryans can Read minds, they will win the next war."

Jaxome abruptly stopped looking benignly paternal. The broad, friendly smile was replaced with cold contempt. "Young man, listen to me. I was curious about what a PN who'd managed to achieve such a high position would be like, so I agreed to speak with you. Since you seemed intelligent and sincere, I gave you the benefit of the doubt in arranging your talk with these very important, very busy people to suit your convenience.

"But while you were speaking, I was conferring mentally with some of my key department heads. They told me that we do not have the slightest shred of evidence that Zoryans have ever been, are at present, or could ever be, telepathic. Perhaps you're concocting this story in order to cover up your own failures as a diplomat … a highly unlikely profession for a Psi-Null in the first place."

Andrei didn't hear the rest of it. He didn't dare. If he hadn't walked away, he knew he would have taken Jaxome apart with what was left of his own hands.

* * *

Sure enough, Coraline did know how to set up a black-coded channel. "What did he do?" she asked at the end of Diana's story.

Diana sighed. "What could he do? He left. I didn't dare try to speak to him when no one else would."

"It sounds awful."

"It was awful. Because he knew. So many PAs think PNs don't know how they think about them, but there's no doubt in my mind that he knew that the people in that room—the so-called great minds of Logos Prime—thought he was talking complete nonsense."

"Do you think it's truly possible that Zoryans could be telepathic and that they could be ready to start another war?" Coraline asked. "Not that he's crazy," she hastened to add, "but is it possible that he misinterpreted something that happened…?" Her voice trailed off, reflecting confusion and doubt.

"Just the fact that you, his own sister, can ask me that question shows why they were able to dismiss him so easily," Diana snapped.

"You're not even willing to admit that it sounds bizarre?" Coraline sounded embarrassed and annoyed at the reproach.

Silence.

Coraline sighed. "All right, Diana, I get the point. So you want to give him the implant?"

"I don't see that we have much choice," she replied. "What good would it be to the Challenge if we're all under Zoryan occupation?"

"Do you think he'll agree to try it?"

Diana thought again about what had happened in the meeting; once more seeing Andrei Savinov in her mind's eye. She remembered Coraline telling her that her brother was cold and unfeeling. Of course, her own feelings of loss and rejection at his hands might make her unable to see him for what he really was ...

Throughout his talk, he'd kept his mind as carefully guarded as a PN could, but at the end he'd been tripped up somehow, and she had used the opportunity to slip behind those defenses. She'd Sensed desperate passion, layered with soul-deep grief and weariness born of endless years of war. She'd also Sensed humiliation, both old and new, as well as rage—not just at them, but also at himself for failing to convince them of the life-or-death importance of his request. A person who didn't feel anything?

"He'll agree. He has no choice, either."

* * *

"Come on, Corie, I'm working on something pretty big right now. I don't have the time for another bullshit Challenge meeting where we sit around and pretend we're gonna do something major this time."

Coraline sighed. "Nick, this isn't just some little scheme. It's really important that you come. What I've got to talk to you about could change everything on Logos Prime."

Silence. "Care to be more specific?" he finally asked.

"You know I can't do that. You'll just have to trust me."

He laughed. "You're always so dramatic. All right, all right. Anything for my big sister. I'll be there."

Now comes the hard part, she thought. "There's something else I need you to do," she said.

"What could that possibly be?" he asked, still sounding amused.

"You have to contact Andrei and get him to agree to join us."

This time the silence was much longer. Coraline chewed on her lip as she waited. How could she convince him if he said no?

"I guess if I ask you why, you'll tell me it's connected with whatever it is you can't tell me about." Nick's tone was flat.

Coraline let her breath out again. He would do it. "You're right. I'm sorry," she answered.

"Do you really want to see him again, Corie? I'm not sure he'll want to see you."

"I know that," she answered, pushing away her feelings as hard as she could. "He might not choose to have a family reunion, but that's not what this is all about. Just tell him that I know that he has a problem where the future of the Alliance is at stake, and this could help him solve it."

"What problem? What the hell are you talking about?" Nick demanded.

She didn't answer, and she heard him muttering angrily as he cut the connection. She wasn't upset, though. Nick said he'd be there and that he'd get Andrei to come, and she knew he'd keep his word.

It was then that she realized that she hadn't answered his question about whether she wanted to see Andrei again. She hadn't answered because she had no idea what the answer was.

Chapter 7

One of Coraline's lovers was a popular PA artist who was also connected to the Bridge. He had a small hideaway on Praxis where he designed and built his holo-models and enviropaintings. Coraline and Nick used it once in a while for secret meetings, as security on Logos Prime's moon was considerably easier for Nick to penetrate than on the planet itself.

Diana looked around curiously at the half-finished things hanging in midair and poking half in, half out of the walls and ceilings of the one-room dome. She saw shapes that were colors and colors that were shapes. There were a couple of portraits, and Diana thought she recognized Coraline's profile in one of them. One corner of the room held an image of an aquarium—the way it would look if you were a fish. In another corner, snow fell softly from the ceiling and disappeared as it hit the floor. She sat down on what appeared to be a large blue-green mushroom, and the chair molded itself around her.

She watched Coraline pace the room, not looking at the artwork. She could Sense that her anxiety wasn't related to the threat of being discovered by the authorities.

"What was it like growing up in a mixed family?" Diana asked, using words instead of thoughts, both for distraction and for distance. Even though she knew Coraline wanted to talk about it, she didn't want to get tangled in her emotions.

Coraline sighed. "Stressful at times. When my brothers were born, Astrid still had a good position within the Think Tank, so we were all allowed to stay upstairs together. The boys went to a PN school, of course, so they lived their lives in both worlds. But we were very close as children. It was the outside world that tried to make us think that we were different from each other, Astrid told us. What truly mattered was that we were family."

Her eyes flashed with anger. "When S2 took the boys away, it destroyed her. She was never allowed to see them or even speak to them again. She'd gone through some serious episodes of depression before that, but afterward she just continued downhill until finally she couldn't stand it anymore."

Diana was startled. "Your brothers were taken by the Security Service? For what? What did they do with them?"

"They put them in separate PN Group Homes. I guess, in a way, Nick was to blame. He just couldn't stop getting into trouble. He was bright and restless, and there was nothing for him to do in that useless PN school that my mother was forced to send him to. Then he turned sixteen, which was when he was supposed to get his work assignment. Of course, he was no one's favorite—not docile and subservient enough. So he didn't have anyone looking out for him, trying to get him a good assignment. He ended up in MRO."

Diana winced. "It doesn't sound like Maintenance and Repair Operations would be a good fit for someone like that."

"No, it wasn't. The Order to Report arrived, and he disintegrated it in a fit of rage. When it hit the disintegrator, it sent out a signal to the school, which reported it to S2, of course. They came to our compartment to pass judgment on him—and on Astrid. Since Nick was too young to be Reconditioned, they decided that she was responsible for his behavior, that she was an unfit mother. They told her that because she was a deviant PA, she'd been unable to instruct her

PN sons about their proper place in society. They decided that Nick and Andrei needed to be with their own kind." Coraline's eyes had filled with tears as she spoke, and she wiped them away with an angry brush of her hand. "It wasn't Nick's fault. It was the system, the damned system, rotten through and through."

"What about Andrei?" Diana asked.

"He was thirteen when it happened. He had problems with school too, but in a different way. At the start of each year, he'd download the curriculum and the assignments for the whole term. He generally finished it in less than a week, and the school wouldn't give him anything new. He'd go to class as often as he could tolerate it—they made life difficult for Astrid if he didn't—and he'd sit there reading litdiscs, playing chess with the computer, or hacking his way into the datanet in search of whatever bit of knowledge he was interested in that day. He didn't complain or act out in any way, just lived in his own world, in his own head.

"It drove them all crazy," Coraline continued. "PNs weren't supposed to be either particularly intelligent or intellectually inclined, and PN schools are all about providing basic skills to prepare Psi-Nulls for whatever trade they will be assigned to. Being smart was considered trying to be PA, so teachers and kids alike made fun of him. Nick sometimes helped him fight them off, but he was usually busy with his own adventures. S2 decided to take him away too, because they assumed that if Astrid had failed with Nick, she wouldn't do any better with Andrei—who in some ways represented even more of a threat to the status quo. No one could figure out what to do with him."

The Alliance had known what to do with him, Diana thought, recalling the little she'd been able to pull from the datanet about Andrei Savinov. He'd blasted through the ranks, from Captain to Force Leader in record time, becoming the Alliance's Chief Strategist sometime in his late twenties.

Somehow, though, he hadn't ended up as Prime Commander. In fact, eight years after his appointment to that assignment, his career had taken a different turn entirely. As Peacekeeper, he was the architect of the vast, interconnected set of negotiations and treaties called the Settlement, which was responsible for making sure that the war didn't start up again.

Coraline stared at Diana with troubled eyes, bringing her back to the original conversation. "When S2 came, Nick fought them so hard that they had to tie him up to carry him out. Astrid was hysterical, and I was trying to keep her from launching herself at them. But Andrei ..." She shook her head. "Andrei just silently packed up his things, kissed Astrid and me on the cheek, and left. I couldn't believe it. A year later—when they let me see him and Nick, to tell them that Astrid was dead—I asked him what he'd been thinking that day. He just shrugged and said there'd been no use making a scene. He didn't even cry when I told him his mother had killed herself."

"You thought he should have fought them," Diana prompted gently.

"Don't you? Nick and I were both hurt that he didn't seem devastated by our family's destruction."

"Thirteen is pretty young to be taken away from your family and stuck with a bunch of kids who hate you for being smart. Do you really think he didn't feel it?"

Coraline sighed. "I'm sure he did, but ..." She shook her head. "I saw him once more after that, the day he went off to join the war effort. We were polite, wished each other well ..." Again, she couldn't finish the sentence, and Diana easily Sensed her helplessness.

"Why do you think he's never tried to see you?"

"I don't know," Coraline replied. "I hope he didn't turn out to hate PAs so much that he couldn't stand the thought of being related to one. Even Nick isn't that bad, but I suppose it's possible."

Diana was skeptical. "Do you really believe that?"

Coraline shrugged.

Diana thought for a moment. "You know, you could break the Bridge directive against Reading PNs just this once. I certainly wouldn't tell anyone. It might help you understand him better, which might give you some peace of mind."

She didn't tell her that she'd already done this herself when Andrei appeared before the Think Tank. She still couldn't figure out what had ever possessed her to do it—except that he had fascinated her. A Warleader, whose life experience was completely alien to her. The way he spoke indicated a very powerful intellect at work. And she admired the courage it would take for a PN to face the intellectual elite of a world that despised him. Not to mention the way he'd looked at her … She quickly put a Block around this last thought so Coraline couldn't Read it.

"No, I couldn't," Coraline replied. "Astrid Conditioned me never to Read my brothers. She thought it was only fair, since they couldn't Read me."

An interesting way to balance the scales, Diana thought. She was just about to continue the conversation, but at that moment the dome warned them of an approaching intruder. Coraline activated the one-way viewscreen and punched in a code to let Nick through the security grid.

Nick Hayden was an attractive man, Diana thought, *if you liked them on the large side.* Tall, blond, and muscular, he and Coraline shared the same aristocratic features. She found herself feeling jealous as she watched them greet each other happily. She was an only child whose parents, like most Logos Prime PAs, hadn't had much interest in family life. She'd paid the price for that, spending her early childhood passed back and forth between her mother and father and finally ending up in a PA Group Home. It was not an uncommon occurrence, as many PA children spent time being raised by others, but that didn't make it any less painful a rejection. She hadn't heard from either of them in more years than she could remember.

Coraline and Nick's warm, easy manner with each other made her feel lonely, too. Because of her Bridge activities, she was wary of getting too close to her colleagues, and she felt alienated from most of the PAs she knew. Her Bridge associates, the few PAs who shared her beliefs, didn't dare spend too much time together. Even though there'd obviously been hell to pay, she could see that Coraline had benefited from belonging to her very unusual family.

Nick was examining the artwork. He frowned, shook his head in disgust, and turned his attention to Diana. "This is Doctor Diana Zarev," Coraline told him. "She's a member of the Bridge. She's also the head of the Think Tank's psy-med labs."

He shook her hand, grinning. He had an infectious smile and a crushing grip. "There should be some way for the Challenge to benefit from having someone so high up in the Think Tank hierarchy working with us," he said.

Diana nodded. "There is—at least, I hope so. But I think I'll wait until we're all here to explain what this is about." She looked over at Coraline, who nodded.

"Andrei is coming, isn't he?" Coraline asked Nick. "What did he say when you told him I was going to be here?"

"Not much," Nick answered. "He asked whether I thought it was safe."

"For me or for him?" Coraline snapped.

Nick's answer was a shrug. "You sure you're ready for this, Corie?"

"Yes, of course." But no special mindpowers were needed to see that she was upset. They chatted idly as they waited. Finally, the perimeter alert sounded again. Nick reached reflexively for the disruptor pistol at his belt as Coraline activated the viewscreen. He let his hand drop as he recognized Andrei, and she punched in the codes again to let him in.

Andrei entered the room, still pushing his hair back into some semblance of order after removing the atmosphere suit and helmet in the outer passageway between the security grid and the dome. His head came up, and he froze in place, staring at Coraline. Even though his expression was impassive, Diana Sensed that he was shocked. Why, considering he knew that she would be here? But he didn't say what he was thinking, and neither of them moved or spoke for what seemed like an eternity.

"Hello, Andrei," Coraline finally said. Her voice was quiet and hesitant.

"Hello, Coraline."

Quite a display of control, Diana thought, feeling a touch of admiration. *I guess you learn that in diplomacy.* Or was it part of his personality? He didn't say anything more as he unclipped a search/neutralize wand from his belt and held it up.

Nick held up his own s/n wand, looking annoyed. "I've already taken care of that, Andrei," he snapped. "No one's watching or listening."

"Good," Andrei replied, apparently undisturbed by the lack of welcome on his brother's part. Diana knew that he'd seen her when he came in, but he didn't say anything to her. Instead, he wandered around the room, looking at the artwork. "Some of these holo-models are impressive," he remarked, looking at Nick. "Is the artist a friend of yours?"

"Hell, no. This stuff looks like crap to me," Nick answered. "Friend of Corie's owns this place. A Bridge guy. This is her meeting, Andrei. I told you that."

"So you did," he answered. He turned his attention to Diana, and she found herself feeling unexpectedly nervous as his watchful, disturbing green eyes studied her. Green eyes were extremely rare in Logos Prime humans; it was some kind of genetic anomaly. She tried to cover her confused feelings with logical thinking, but the effort wasn't working all that well, for some reason.

"I remember you from the Institute," he said. His normal speaking voice, when he wasn't giving a lecture, was quiet and calm. For some reason, she'd expected the voice of a Warleader to be loud and strident, more like Nick's. "I assume this isn't a coincidence."

She shook her head. "No, of course it isn't. I'm Diana Zarev, head of the Think Tank's psy-med labs."

"And a member of the Bridge," Coraline interrupted. "As am I." Her initial reaction seemed to have worn off, and she sounded angry at his lack of response to her.

"I'd heard that you joined the Bridge," Andrei remarked.

"Do you care?" Coraline asked. "It's been a very long time since we've been together, Andrei. Isn't there anything you want to say to me? Isn't there anything you want to know?"

"I want to know why I'm here," he replied coolly. They all watched in silence as he crossed the room to the dispenser and got a cup of tea. Diana covertly studied him as he programmed the dispenser and waited for his drink. He wasn't as tall as Nick or as solidly built. His thick, wavy, black hair was unruly; he needed a haircut, but it didn't seem like something he spent any time thinking about. His appearance was striking, as were those of his brother and sister, but he didn't look anything like them.

What she most noticed, though, was how tired he looked. There were dark smudges under his eyes, and his complexion had a grayish cast to it. But her medical intuition was alerted, and she looked closer. Maybe it was something worse than being tired. She struggled to keep herself from Probing him.

It seemed that Nick was thinking the same thing. "You look kinda worn out, Andrei," he remarked. "Running the galaxy all by yourself must be hard work."

Diana winced at the sarcasm, but Andrei merely shrugged. "Some weeks are better than others," he answered. "This hasn't been one of the good ones." He reached into the dispenser and fumbled with the glass of tea.

That was when she noticed his hands. They were horribly scarred, and it took effort for him to get his fingers around the glass. He'd been wearing gloves on Logos Prime, so she hadn't noticed it then, and he hadn't offered to shake hands with her when they were introduced. Coraline also noticed, and she gasped. "What happened to your hands?"

For the first time, he looked annoyed. "An accident," he replied briefly. He took the glass over to the nearest chair and sat down, gesturing for them to do the same. *Used to giving orders – and having them obeyed,* Diana thought. He turned back to Coraline. "I don't want you to think it doesn't mean anything to me to see you again after all these years, but this meeting is dangerous for all of us. So could we please get started?"

"Fine with me," Coraline shot back angrily. "Diana, why don't you tell Andrei and Nick about your project."

She nodded and launched into a description of the implant. She explained that it was a biochemical and bioelectrical device that would serve the function of the missing psi sensory organ in PNs. It would affect all neural pathways, expanding a person's consciousness to the point where he would become telepathic. A PN fitted with this brain implant could Read minds, Sense emotions, Send and Receive thoughts, and Shield and Block thoughts and feelings from being Read and Sensed by other telepaths. "Of course, these skills would have to be taught, as they are to PAs from the time they are young. But I believe adults will be able to pick them up very quickly, with proper training."

"What do you mean, proper training?" Andrei asked.

At first she was surprised by how unsurprised he sounded, but she was beginning to see that controlled surface as part of his style. There was no question that it could be irritating. No wonder Nick and Coraline had found him hard to understand. "The work has all been done using computer modeling and simulations. The implant hasn't been tested on anyone yet.

When I insert it, I'll be running a live experiment. Whoever gets it will have to cooperate with the requirements of the testing I'll need to do, as well as accepting instruction from me on how to use it."

Both men were silent as they absorbed what she'd told them. Coraline spoke up. "Don't you get it, Nick? This could change everything on Logos Prime—the whole structure of society! We'd finally have a real weapon against the Think Tank."

Nick did not look impressed. "Hold on a minute. You think the way for us to fight the ruling power structure is to become PA? For Earth's sake! What the hell kind of idea is that?"

Diana opened her mouth to try to answer him, but Andrei interrupted. "Did you bring any documentation of your research?"

"I finished the final set of simulations last week, and I've got a complete probability matrix defining all of the outcome permutations."

"Can I see it?" he asked.

She raised her eyebrows. How could she answer without sounding like she was insulting his intelligence? "It's very complex, Commander Savinov. It covers the effects of the implant on every neural pathway. I'm not sure it would be meaningful to you without a lot of explanation that, as you pointed out, we don't have time for right now."

"I'd just like to take a first pass at it, see what it's all about." Andrei turned back to Coraline. "Have you reviewed Doctor Zarev's data and experiment logs? What do you think?"

"What makes you assume I'd have the technical knowledge to understand them?" she countered.

Andrei smiled at her for the first time since they'd seen each other. "I doubt you would have brought Doctor Zarev together with Nick and me if you didn't have some idea that this would work."

Coraline nodded. "Yes, I think it will work." She turned to Diana. "Why don't you let him see your records, Diana? Andrei's a quick study."

Diana got up and went over to the case she'd brought with her. Reaching inside, she pulled out a fileviewer and a stack of discs and took them to him. As he reached for the fileviewer, once again she noticed the scars covering both hands

"Is this coded and initialed to your eyeprint?" he asked.

Diana nodded, activating it for him. He scanned the discs rapidly, saying nothing, then turned off the fileviewer and handed the package back to her. "That looks pretty bad," she remarked, trying to sound casual. "Why didn't you have your hands replaced? Do you object to bio-enhancement?"

She knew she'd caught him off guard, because he actually looked surprised for a second. Then he drew a sudden breath. "You want me to test the implant for you."

"We're not sure," Coraline quickly replied. "Diana created this for the Challenge to use, which is why Nick's here. But since she heard you talking about Zoryans becoming telepathic, she thought you might have a more immediate need for it."

Andrei's gaze was penetrating, but Diana met it. "So someone heard me after all," he said softly.

"I heard you," she answered. "I just couldn't say anything without giving myself away."

"I understand. I could tell you were different…" His voice trailed off; he seemed startled by what he'd said. They stared at each other, confused and fascinated. Two outsiders …

"What in hell's name are you talking about? Telepathic Zoryans?" Nick cut in. Andrei turned away from Diana as he launched into a description, for Nick and Coraline, of what he'd told the Think Tank.

"That's quite a story," Nick remarked when he was finished. "Assuming it's true, stopping those bastards is gonna be even harder this time around. If this implant really works, it might at least buy some time to figure out a way to deal with them."

"My thoughts exactly," Andrei said.

"On the other hand," Nick continued, ignoring him and addressing Coraline, "your pal here developed this for the Challenge, not the Alliance."

"What makes you think the Challenge will survive long enough to accomplish anything if the Alliance falls?" Andrei countered.

"So even if the Challenge doesn't get first crack at it, once this Alliance crisis is over, we'll expect it to be turned over to us." He finally turned toward Andrei, eyes and manner defiant.

A smile played at the corners of Andrei's lips. "That would be fine with me. I have no desire to be telepathic—"

"You don't?" Nick interrupted.

"No, I don't, in spite of whatever you think of me. Assuming we manage to neutralize the danger, Doctor Zarev can remove it from my brain and implant it in yours." His eyes sparkled with amusement. "I'm looking forward to that already. I can't wait to see you turn into a PA."

Nick's tone in return was grim and mocking. "Sorry, little brother. That's not the deal I'm willing to make. I'd rather be out there"—he gestured toward the viewscreen showing the poisonous, swirling mist that was the atmosphere of Praxis— "without an atmosphere suit than be turned into a telepath by some artificial device implanted in my brain. No, if it works— assuming you don't die or go crazy in the process—you'll use it to help us defeat the PAs. You'll join the Challenge." He shrugged. "Though technically, I guess, since you'll be a PA, you'll be Bridge."

"Wait a minute," Andrei snapped. "I'm sure there are Challenge leaders who would be willing to do this in order to advance their cause, even if you're not."

"Maybe there are, but they aren't you, Andrei. I want the Alliance's Peacekeeper on the Challenge's side—partly for the propaganda and morale value, and partly for the use of your mind. Whatever I think of you, as you put it, after all these years, I still haven't met anyone smarter—or more dedicated or successful, once you sink your teeth into something. I want you to use that brainpower and willpower to help your own people for a change."

Diana Sensed Andrei's anger. "We've had this discussion before, more than once." His tone was flat, his voice tightly controlled. "Even if I became telepathic, PAs wouldn't be my people. But that doesn't mean PNs are my people either. I have no interest in labeling myself anything that has to do with the meaningless mind games and class struggles of the Core. As far as I'm concerned, Logos Prime is just another Alliance world. As the Alliance's Peacekeeper, my job is to deal with external threats. I don't interfere in the internal affairs of member worlds unless specifically requested by their governments to do so."

"Damn you, Andrei, this is your homeworld we're talking about! What kind of game are you playing with yourself, pretending that what goes on there doesn't matter to you? Weren't you furious when those Think Tank bastards treated you like a nobody? Isn't it time you stopped hiding out there in space and stood up for yourself?" Nick was on his feet, red-faced, voice raised as his hands curled into fists. Diana couldn't tell whom he was angrier at, the PAs or his brother.

"Stop. Please, both of you, in our mother's name. Stop." Startled, Diana looked quickly at Coraline. She was curled over in her chair, shaking her head, her face buried in her hands. Nick and Andrei stared at her, stunned into silence. Nick quickly crossed over to her and put his arms around her, stroking her hair and murmuring in her ear.

Diana turned to look at Andrei. His mask of control had slipped, leaving a mixture of pain and helplessness winding around a core of exhaustion. He closed his eyes for a second, massaging the bridge of his nose with his fingertips. He took a step toward Coraline, but then he froze as she and Nick turned toward him again, and his face returned to guarded impassivity.

"Corie," he began slowly. "What do you want to do?"

Coraline looked at Diana. *What do you think?* she Sent.

Diana knew what she thought. *Of course I want Andrei on our side. But I'm not willing to say he shouldn't have the implant just to get revenge for his not joining the Challenge.*

But Nick will think I'm siding with him—that I don't care enough about the Challenge. Coraline's thoughts were desperately torn.

"All right." The sound of Andrei's voice cut through their mental conversation. He sounded both resigned and determined. "I can't promise you anything specific, but assuming I survive this experiment and we're not at war, I'll do what I can to help the Challenge." He turned to Nick, anger finally showing in his face. "Will that satisfy you, Nick? Or do I need to take an oath that I'll lay down my life for your precious Challenge; for the people who never spoke a single word of kindness or respect to me when I was growing up on their pathetic little world?"

Nick and Coraline looked at him in shock. He laughed bitterly. "You thought I hadn't noticed? You thought I didn't care about being considered an outcast by both sides? If not for the war, I would have lost my mind trying to exist among *your* PNs on *your* homeworld—the people for whom you now expect me to risk everything I've worked toward."

No one said anything in response. He stood up abruptly. "We're wasting time. I have to get back. Can I keep this set of discs to study them? What's the next step?"

"Yes, you can keep them," Diana replied. "Go through them, and figure out what questions you've got. Also, I need access to your medical records. In the meantime, I'm going to persuade Jaxome to send me to the Peaceship as a special advisor on the Zoryan problem. I'll install the implant once

I'm aboard, and I'll stay on to run the experiment and help you with the adjustment process."

"Access to my medical records?" Andrei asked. "Why?"

Out of all the questions he could ask, why this one? "Because I need to know how it'll affect you, specifically— not just a simulation of a so-called average PN." She studied him. He didn't seem angry, just uncomfortable—even more guarded than usual. "Is there a problem?"

"I don't know if I can get into those records," he answered.

He was lying. What was he trying to hide? "Your sister claims you were a pretty good hacker in your younger days," she said. "I think you can handle it." He didn't answer, and she pressed him. "Commander, I can't do the procedure if I don't have those records. It's your decision."

He sighed. "You'll have them, Doctor."

"How about Diana, if we're going to work together?"

"Fine. Please call me Andrei."

"Fine."

They looked at each other, then looked away in embarrassment. He gathered her discs and she gave him the case, which he slung over his shoulder. Ready to leave, he turned again to Coraline and Nick. "Nice seeing you again," he murmured with just a trace of irony in his tone. Neither said anything, and he headed for the door.

"Wait!" Coraline cried out suddenly. "Andrei, we haven't said anything to each other! After all these years … I've missed you. There's so much I've wanted to ask you—so much I want to tell you. I never even got the chance to tell you how sorry I was about Prime Commander … about Kylara … Have you thought of me at all?"

He stepped backward as though she'd struck him. "Yes." His voice was a near whisper. "I've thought about you. I've missed you. It's just that …" He shook his head as if trying to clear it. "You must be about forty by now. Only eight years younger than Astrid was when she died. Do you have any idea how much you look like her? Seeing you again …" His voice trailed off.

Coraline looked stunned. She went over to him and gently drew him close to her. At first he stiffened; then he tentatively returned the embrace. Diana could Sense his fear, bordering on panic. Fear of getting too close to her—as if it could unlock a door he'd have too much trouble closing again. As he finally released her, he almost bumped into Nick, who'd approached them from behind. They stood close together, awkwardly, not knowing what to do next.

"Hey, Andrei, I'm sorry …"

"No harm done, Nick. We all do what we think we have to do to get the job done." He turned away. Nick's mouth was open; he obviously had more to say, but Andrei's attention was focused on Coraline. "Another time, Corie. We'll try again another time." He left without looking back.

"What the hell was that supposed to mean? 'We all do what we think we have to'?" Nick demanded. "Delivered in his usual smart-ass way, like he's talking to a kid." Shaking his head with exasperation, he started moving restlessly around the room again.

"I don't think he meant it like that, Nick," Coraline answered wearily. "I think he meant that he knows you aren't trying to hurt him. That the Challenge is so important to you that you'll say whatever you think you have to say to get him to see things your way."

Nick sighed, and Diana could Sense his anger dissipate, replaced with frustration and hurt. "You're right—and so was he. I do care about him. But he's so damned hard to understand … to get through to. It's only gotten worse as time's gone by. I think that after Astrid died, he's only ever been really close to one other person—Kylara Val."

"The former Prime Commander?" Diana asked. This was the second reference to her in the past few minutes.

Coraline nodded. "They were lovers for the past seventeen years, from the time Andrei joined the war effort until her death about six months ago."

"She was really something," Nick added with admiration in his voice. "The Alliance couldn't have asked for a better Prime Commander. If she'd lived long enough to turn her attention to the Challenge, PNs would be a free people today."

"What makes you think she wouldn't have decided to stay out of it, the way Andrei did?" Diana asked. "After all, she was a Warleader too."

Nick laughed. "Because she was more like me than he is—she couldn't resist a good fight."

"She must have had more self-control than you. After all, she didn't end up joining the Free Raiders after being kicked out of the Alliance Military," Coraline remarked. Nick looked embarrassed, then shrugged, grinning.

Diana was still thinking about Andrei Savinov and Kylara Val. "How did Andrei react when she was killed?"

Coraline looked at Nick, who shook his head. "He's never been willing to talk about it," he answered. "At the time it happened, I tried, but he did the same thing he always does when you ask him a personal question—he blew me off. Same as he did when you asked him about the so-called accident with his hands. Which looks to me like what would happen if you were dumb enough—or unlucky enough—to touch something, without armored gloves, that had been irradiated by a Zoryan flashbomb. But I'm not sure, because I don't know anyone who's ever survived one of those. During the war, there were lots of assassination attempts on key Warleaders."

Diana and Coraline stared at him, appalled. He shrugged. "He's all business whenever I see him, which isn't that often. Mostly he avoids me. He says it's for our own good that we don't reveal our connection, and he's right."

"Is that why you all have different last names? To keep anyone from knowing that you're related?" Diana asked.

He nodded. "Andrei also altered our personal history files in the 'net." He stood up abruptly. "I have to go too. It really isn't safe for us to spend too much time together. Besides, I'm busy with a little project of my own." He told them briefly about the cache of arms on the prison moon of Selas.

"And you have no idea who's stockpiling the weapons or why?" Coraline asked.

"If I knew who, I'd probably know why, but I don't know either," he replied. "At the least, I'm hoping that my little visit to the place will answer one or both questions. At the most, maybe I can get hold of some powerful methods of persuasion for the Challenge to convince First Circle—and S2—that we're serious contenders for power on Logos Prime."

"But that would broaden the struggle considerably," Diana cut in. "It might lead to outright civil war."

Nick grinned. "My thoughts exactly."

Chapter 8

"Come in, Diana, my dear. I can't remember the last time your name appeared on my calendar." Robert Jaxome was beaming, his hands extended to clasp hers in welcome. "I don't suppose you're just dropping by to renew our friendship?"

Diana was amused at the choice of words. She and Jaxome had never been anything resembling friends. The Blocks that she'd built around her Bridge activities were firmly in place, as usual, and in addition she'd Shielded her mind against any general mental inquiries. This was common practice among PAs in social settings, so it wouldn't cause suspicion. In fact, it was easy to Sense that he was equally well guarded. So much for friendship, PA style.

"No, I'm not, Robert, though it's certainly a pleasure to see you again," she lied cheerfully. She might despise it, but she knew how to play the game. "You're looking quite well."

He laughed. "For an old man, you mean."

She shook her head, still smiling. "For a man in the prime of life."

"Indeed," he responded dryly. "Be that as it may, you are as lovely as ever."

Now it was her turn to laugh. "For a woman tiptoeing toward middle age."

"As lovely as ever," he repeated gallantly. They took drinks from the dispenser. She moved toward the chair in front of his desk, and he shook his head, gesturing toward two plush, oversized armchairs by the window across the room. "There's no need for so much formality. Come, sit here, and enjoy the view."

Ah, yes, she thought, *the famous view.* While Diana had an outer Core compartment with one wall of windows to herself, it still wasn't high enough to see much through the red and black mist clouds rising from the bubbling volcanoes and steaming seas that made up most of the planet's surface. In fact, she preferred her viewscreens.

Up here was a different story: there were no windows, because there were no walls. The office of the Institute Director and Governor of Logos Prime was the domed top of the Core, providing the impression that the room was poised in midair. Here, the mist thinned out, leaving the sky a pastel, golden-toned pink. For a brief moment, Diana thought about the bleak darkness of life for PNs at the bottom of the Core, hundreds of levels below. She quickly stopped, though; she didn't dare risk having him Sense her anger. "Magnificent," she murmured.

Jaxome nodded his agreement. "Yes, even after all these years, I still find it inspiring. But I'm sure you're not here to admire the scenery."

"I'm afraid not. And I know you're busy, Robert, so I'll get on with it." She took a deep breath. After all the years of secrecy, it wasn't easy to ask for something that would reveal something about herself to the single most dangerous individual to her cause. With this request, she felt like she was risking everything.

"You know, I was at the meeting the other day when the Peacekeeper spoke." A cautious opening.

He raised an eyebrow. "I requested the presence of all department heads, Diana. It would have been odd if you hadn't been there."

She nodded. "I find myself somewhat concerned over the information he presented to us. In spite of his Psi-Null status, he was the war's top strategist, as well as the Settlement's chief negotiator. So he's dealt with them quite extensively. He says he has inside information that Zoryans have developed telepathy, which matches his own evaluation of the results of their most recent negotiating session. Why are we so sure that he doesn't know what he's talking about?"

Jaxome shrugged, his jolly, paternal expression changing to annoyance. "You know as well as I do that telepathy is an inborn sense, Diana. Lockwood and Reynard explained it quite clearly to me—there isn't the slightest evidence that it has ever existed in Zoryans, and there is no evidence that it *can* exist in Zoryans. I shouldn't have wasted our time with Commander Savinov. He was merely making excuses for his own failure."

Diana persisted. "But Robert, we have records showing that there was a time when telepathy didn't exist in humans either. On the homeworld."

He shook his head, waving his index finger to make his point. "Incorrect, Diana. There was a time when humans didn't understand how to identify or use the psi-sense organ. Telepathy existed as potential before the awareness of the psi-sense had evolved sufficiently for superior humans to access it." He frowned. "That potential was so frightening to the Psi-Nulls of Earth that they practically had us burned at the stake."

She raised her eyebrows. "Excuse me?"

"Witches, my dear. Sources of otherworldly evil, according to what we know of Old Earth mythology. Fools who were afraid of powers they didn't understand tormented and even set fire to the innocent holders of those gifts. Oh, this wasn't done by the time telepathy was understood, but the fear and hatred that emerged as our powers got stronger weren't so different, and they drove our people away. Into space, to create our own society where the life of the mind is paramount." Again he frowned. "Such a pity they brought their Psi-Null lovers with them. Damned near ruined the breeding stock."

Diana didn't say anything. There was no point arguing with him. He was like most PAs—the pretense of open-mindedness concealing rigidity of thought and viewpoint. She could easily see him burning someone at the stake, whatever a stake was.

She sipped her drink and gazed out the window. If they hadn't brought their Psi-Null lovers along and hadn't had Psi-Null children, who would have maintained their home on Logos Prime? After all, who knew that the descendants of the artists, professors, pure research scientists, and other intellectuals who'd left Earth in a generation ship wouldn't end up on the uninhabited paradise they'd thought they were headed for?

Well, they did find paradise. It just happened to be inhabited by Erlandians, who didn't have room for them. In fact, none of the five inhabited planets in these star systems wanted them. The Alliance of the Five, as they were then called, gave the humans this worthless ball of fire and brimstone, and the Karellians designed and helped them build the massive structure now called the Core.

Since the ship was too damaged to repair and move on, the humans grudgingly accepted the situation. But in a sort of passive-aggressive retaliation, they'd fought tooth and nail against sharing the burdens involved in fighting the war. After all, the Zoryans would have to go through all of them before they got to Logos Prime, and what would be there that they'd want?

She gave up and returned to her original subject. "So you believe it's been proven beyond doubt that the potential for telepathic communication doesn't exist in Zoryans."

"It hasn't been the most researched topic here, but the evidence is fairly solid."

"Is 'fairly solid' good enough, when getting it wrong might mean another war?"

Jaxome looked at her curiously. "We remain as far from the War Border as we ever were, Diana. Why does this concern you?"

Here it is, she thought. "Two reasons. One, if it's true that telepathic power is developing amongst Zoryans, it represents an interesting phenomenon, one that I believe is worthy of further study. Two, from what little I know about interstellar affairs, the Alliance is still resentful of how little Logos Prime did for the war effort."

"We gave them our best PNs, didn't we?" Jaxome chuckled. Time and again, the Alliance Military had begged for PAs, but since none of the other worlds was drafting its elites for the front line, they couldn't force the issue. A few had gone, but not enough to make a difference.

Diana continued, "And it would be to our credit if we could contribute some research that might avert another war. If the enemy is now interested in telepathy, we could be in more danger than we were the first time around."

"I'm not impressed with your second reason, but your first has some merit. If, by some off chance, psipower is evolving amongst Zoryans, it could be a chance to examine an unusual historical juncture in the growth of a civilization—if one could call the Hegemony a civilization." He looked thoughtful. "Is this an area of study you would like to pursue? Do you wish to send someone to the Peaceship to work with Commander Savinov? I'm not sure who would want to go."

She took a deep breath. "I'd like to do it myself, Robert." He didn't respond, and she continued. "Most of our people have no desire to go into space, and since it's my idea, I don't see why anyone else should be forced to do it. Besides, studying the brain of another species close up could prove fascinating."

His look of curiosity changed to amused speculation. "Are you sure that it isn't studying Commander Savinov that might prove fascinating, Diana? I would think, with his dashing good looks and that air of grim determination he has about him, women would find him quite attractive."

Alarmed, she checked her Shield. Still firmly in place. "Oh come now! He's Psi-Null."

"Never been interested in one of them before? Never stepped out of class to try something new and different?"

She met his eyes with a mocking smile. "I'm sure that's easy for you to check, Robert. If you go to the trouble to do so, you'll find that I've never been involved with a Psi-Null. And I'm not about to start now. I'm interested in the situation from a purely professional perspective." She waited for his response with as much calm indifference as she could project.

He nodded. "My apologies. It's just that you have an excellent position here. I wouldn't want to see you do anything you might have cause to regret later on."

She knew she had to act like she cared about that. "Do you think examining Commander Savinov's claim will cause problems for me politically?"

"It doesn't have to, my dear, as long as you handle it properly." He paused, and it seemed to her that he was deciding how to phrase his next comment. "But there is something that might taint your record if you don't handle it properly."

Feeling weak with sudden fear, she forced herself to remain still, to register an expression of only polite concern. "What would that be?"

"Our records indicate that you have not had any children yet, Diana. You are aware that given your superior genetic endowment, you are required to produce at least one. We know that you are dedicated to your work, and you know that you would not have to raise the child yourself. Is there a problem preventing you from fulfilling this civic responsibility?"

Silence. She knew this would come up at some point. Why wasn't she better prepared? Because she hated thinking about it, that's why. Yes, she'd like to have a child of her own one day, but she couldn't stand the idea of bringing one this sick society. She licked dry lips, swallowed. "I still have time, Robert."

"Yes, you do. I just wanted to remind you…"

"I remember." She fervently hoped he wouldn't inquire further, and breathed a sigh of relief inside when he smiled his broad, false smile and crossed the room to his desk.

"Good, good, Diana, my dear. Just doing my job, you know. Let's get back to the business at hand, shall we?" He spoke to his filewriter. "Create an official permit for long-stay off-world travel for Doctor Diana Zarev, effective…" He turned back to her. "When would you like to leave?"

She smiled. "Now."

***

"No."

Sylvain had been silent while Andrei told him about his visit to Praxis and his plan to try the implant. When he was done, Andrei leaned back in his chair and waited, allowing his Exec time to absorb the news. He'd just about gotten re-immersed in the text he was reviewing when Sylvain uttered his one-word response. He looked up, surprised at the intensity in his voice. Sylvain's face was a study in outrage as he stood at rigid attention in front of his desk. Andrei raised his eyebrows, amused by the dramatics.

"Commander Savinov, I must strongly protest this reckless, dangerous …" With a deep, exasperated breath, Sylvain gave up on formality. *"Really bad* plan!"

"I thought you would," Andrei replied. When his Exec didn't even grin, he started to feel impatient. "Sit down again, Syl. You know I don't like it when you hover over me like this. What exactly do you see as the problem? Or, for that matter, the solution?"

Sylvain sat, looking stunned. "The problem? You have no idea what'll happen to you! You could lose your mind—hell, you could lose your life! I don't care if she's done all kinds of fancy studies that say it's going to work—this is your brain we're talking about. Best brain the Alliance's got! How can you even think of going forward with this?"

Andrei's temper, always carefully held in check, began to flare in response. Too many people were picking at him these days. It didn't help that he had his own doubts and worries about the implant but wasn't able to express them to anyone. "How can I not go forward with it? What's the alternative? Wait until the Zoryans take my brain apart, find out all our weaknesses, then wage war on us?"

Sylvain was quiet. He had no answer to this.

"I don't see one either. I have to try to fight them on their own ground. It's our only chance." Andrei sighed, rubbing the bridge of his nose. "I know I'm taking a big risk. I can only hope that Diana Zarev knows what she's doing—that she'll be able to recognize the signs of something going wrong early enough so that she can remove it, if she has to, before there's any permanent damage."

"How about letting one of the Mission staff do it instead? After all, you use bodyguards to protect your body. Why not get someone else to do this, to protect your mind?"

Andrei shook his head, his thoughts focused inward as he once again battled his guilt over the four bodyguards that had died during different assassination attempts. More than once, he'd tried to get rid of his bodyguards, but the Alliance Council and the Peacekeeping Mission staff—not to mention Sylvain—always overruled him.

Sylvain was still thinking. Finally he raised his head and gazed steadily at Andrei. "Let me do it. I can tell you what they're thinking, and you can figure out what to do about it."

Andrei was touched by his loyalty. "It's nice of you to offer, Syl, but it doesn't make sense. Part of the deal is that the implant will allow me to Shield my thoughts from them. If you had it, they'd still be able to read my thoughts." He shook his head again, dismissing any way around the situation. "It's my game, and I've got to play it out."

Sylvain sighed with exasperation. "Not a game, Andrei. That's part of what I'm worried about—your attitude. You decide something needs to be done, and only you can do it right, and you won't look at what it's going to cost you. Kylara was that way too, and it got her killed in the end. There was no reason for her to be on board that cruiser when it was destroyed. She just couldn't leave the actual fighting to the soldiers, even after she became Prime Commander. Had to be there herself, in the middle of everything—"

"Which was why we won the war," Andrei cut in. But Sylvain was remembering it wrong. She hadn't gone out there to fight; she'd gone out to search for the Zoryan baseship supplying the war effort, following a lead that they'd paid for in blood. And she'd found it, too. She'd managed to relay the coordinates just before her ship was destroyed.

He didn't want to talk about this; he didn't want to think about it. Didn't want to hear again his own voice insisting that she leave this spy mission to others to complete. They'd argued, she'd gone, and she'd died out there. So had ten thousand Zoryans on board the baseship he'd ordered destroyed: enough of a loss that, when added to the others they'd recently absorbed, it finally forced them to the negotiating table. It was no consolation at all that just before she'd left, they'd made up and told each other of their love, for what turned out to be the last time.

He couldn't afford to feel this right now. "My mind's made up, Sylvain. Are you going to help me make it work?"

Sylvain shook his head sadly. "Course I will. Don't I always?"

Chapter 9

Nick had forgotten how uncomfortable a lightship could be. He was stretched out in the long, narrow cylinder, unable to even sit up. Invisible, it floated like a proverbial ghost, lying in wait for the cargo ship that was due to pass by on its way to Selas. He focused on the starfield in front of him, watching and waiting. Trust the Karellians to come up with this weird thing—some technology no one understood, which they'd developed into something so useful and so damned uncomfortable at the same time. Like the Core on Logos Prime ...

Finally the lightship sensed the approach of its target, and he began maneuvering it into position. Since the war had ended, lightship detectors weren't standard issue on cargo ships, and without one, the lightship could neither be seen nor sensed by the large, approaching cruiser. He deftly landed on the cruiser's surface. Selas, Sendos's third moon, loomed in front of him as the cruiser unwittingly carried its unknown passenger through the sensor net and into the heart of the prison complex.

Once inside the landing dock, he waited again while the cargo—supplies for the prison—was unloaded. It seemed like an eternity before the cargo bay finally emptied out and he could get out of the lightship.

He left the cargo bay and proceeded to the first of myriad checkpoints on the way into the prison. The black-coded disc had provided access code schematics, and he raced through the combinations, fingers flying on the keypad, until the doors opened with a hiss. The second and third sets of doors also fell before him, and finally he landed in the central corridor.

The central corridor was flooded with white light that burned with searchlight intensity. The air had a metallic smell, and Sendosians in uniform hurried past him, not reacting to the invisible intruder. He immediately started moving with the crowd, dodging and weaving to avoid the risk of being touched accidentally. It was too easy to bump into someone who couldn't be seen. As he retreated from the main hub of the prison, traffic thinned out, and the hallways grew narrower and darker.

Seeing the transport tube at the hallway's end about to close, he hurriedly dove inside; without the access codes to the transport tubes, the only way to get from level to level was to follow others into them. The transport tube dropped so suddenly and rapidly that he felt a wave of nausea. It passed the level he wanted and continued its descent. Waiting until the Sendosian passenger got out and no one replaced him, Nick pressed the keypad for his target level.

Stepping out of the transport tube, he continued moving fast, occasionally checking the map programmed into his dataglasses. The path twisted and turned, making him feel like he was trapped in a maze. A couple of times, guards almost ran into him, and he hurriedly scrubbed at a trickle of sweat at his hairline, caught by the mask. It was difficult to keep from looking at the time counter in the far left-hand corner of his vision supplied by the dataglasses. He was all too aware of the limits of both the suit and ship: if he wasn't back by the time the cargo ship took off again, or out of there before becoming visible again …

He finally came to a set of double doors that was different from the others. Made of a dark blue, shimmering metal, they came from the floor and ceiling, meeting in the middle. A thick band of light covered the seam where they met. Security measures were at their most elaborate here, reinforcing his certainty that he'd reached his destination.

He checked the time again. If the schedule on the disc was correct, someone was due here today, around now. Who, and for what purpose, remained a mystery.

Not for long—at least with respect to who. A gray-robed Sendosian, large even for his race, swept past Nick, close enough to brush him with the wide sleeves of his garment. Nick stared at him intently, trying to catch a glimpse of his face as he turned his head. Not a chance, as the Sendosian had a featureless mask of chromed silver covering his entire head. The robe had nothing on it that would identify the status of the wearer. Though the guards nodded recognition, the Sendosian still went through the various identification and status verification procedures set up at the checkpoint. Nick stood next to him as the door opened, and they went in together.

He found himself in yet another transport tube. This one had three lights on the keypad: red, blue, and black. The Sendosian pressed the blue light and settled back, arms folded. The transport tube moved sideways and backward, though at a pace that wasn't as jarring as the regular prison transport tubes. Finally, the doors slid open, and Nick stepped out with his new friend. Assuming he was going to leave before the Sendosian did (and hoping no one else would show up, use the elevator, and find it), he left a telltale attached to the door.

The door opened directly into a small, entirely featureless conference room, empty of furniture except for a small, round table and two chairs. There were no windows and no other entry or exit point besides the transport tube. On the table were two pairs of dataglasses and two sets of datagloves, meaning that the information was stored in a remote database, accessed through a virtual reality program. The Sendosian pulled a blue accessdisc out of his pocket and slipped it into a slot in the table's reflective surface. It shimmered and the words "Cleared For Entry" appeared in Alliance Standard – luckily not in Sendosian. *Which means this isn't just a Sendosian plot,* Nick thought. The Sendosian put on the gloves and the dataglasses and went to work.

Nick was dismayed, but only briefly. He'd thought he might need to handle a situation like this, and he had planned accordingly. He stood behind the chair so that when he took the sleep spray out of a pocket in his lightsuit, the Sendosian wouldn't see the canister hovering in midair. He released the spray into the air around the Sendosian. Since Sendosians and humans didn't breathe the same air,the spray wouldn't affect him.

The Sendosian kept working for about a minute, and then he looked up, head turning from side to side as his skull pulses became more irregular. Not seeing anything, he settled back again. For a couple of minutes he continued working, but gradually his hand and eye movements grew slower, and he shook his head from side to side. The skull pulses slowed. Finally his head rolled back on the padded headrest of the chair.

Nick breathed a sigh of relief and waited another two minutes to make sure that the Sendosian was completely unconscious. Then he sat down in the other chair and put on the second set of equipment. He had a brief mental picture of someone entering the room and seeing the unconscious Sendosian slumped in front of one chair and one set of equipment hanging in midair with nothing under it in the other. Shrugging it off, he accessed the program.

He immediately found himself inside what appeared to be a long, softly glowing, white corridor snaking off into eternity. It looked just like the prison hallways, and Nick was momentarily confused by the double image. Set into the walls on either side of the corridor were doors. Where the hell was this? Nick peered intently at the doors, which as far as he could see had no labels on them and no handles, switches, locks, or buttons of any kind with which to open them.

As he continued staring down the hall, he noticed that there was one thing different about one of the doors. It had a silver-blue light ringing it like neon tubing, and he walked up to it. This must be where the Sendosian had been working. *Let's try the direct route,* he thought. He knocked on the door with the dataglove. One word formed against the surface of the door: TREATIES. The door slid open.

He stepped inside and looked around. All four walls were black and covered with writing that was the same silver-blue that lined the doorway. The writing seemed etched into the wall, and though it was Alliance Standard, it was hard to read. Nick strained his eyes upward to see where it started. Turning in a tight circle, he finally found the document's title above the doorframe—and he wished he hadn't found it after all, as he read the words NONAGGRESSION PACT BETWEEN THE ZORYAN HEGEMONY AND THE LIGHBAHT. The *what?*

He returned from his state of frozen shock as he felt his eye stinging from a drop of sweat that had found its way from his hairline and down his forehead. He started reading frantically, then stopped, fighting panic. It was in some damn kind of legalese. *Andrei could read it,* thought Nick. *Andrei probably writes stuff like this for the Settlement. But Andrei isn't here right now, is he?* Time was bearing down on him as heavily as the dataglasses pressing against his face; there was no way he could get through this document and find out what other explosive devices were in this particular data matrix before the Sendosian regained consciousness … not to mention find the cache of weapons and get out in one piece.

Nick left the room—closed that file—and started down the virtual hallway, knocking on one door after another without entering any of them. He wished he could copy the data or send it to his ship so he could examine it at leisure, but this was out of the question. Even if he'd had the kind of computer power that could store and read this program—which he didn't, since a Raider wouldn't need it—there was no way it would go undetected. The names that lit up at his touch were different on each door: KEY ALLIANCE CONTACTS, HEGEMONY CONTACTS, ARSENAL INVENTORY, BATTLE PLANS, ALLIANCE COUNCIL, MINDWEAPON, LOGOS PRIME ACCESS, PEACEKEEPER … He stopped at this last one, feeling anticipatory dread. He was about to open the door when he heard the Sendosian moan.

Damn. Still in the matrix, he sprinted back down the hall to where he'd started, undoing all of the entry points he'd accessed, logged out, pulled off the dataglasses and gloves, and jumped out of the chair. He found his head reeling from the sudden re-immersion in reality. The Sendosian was stirring uneasily and had just lifted his head when Nick finished putting things back the way they were.

He watched tensely, barely breathing, as the Sendosian looked around the room. Nick couldn't see the expression on his face under the mask. What would he think had happened? Nick positioned himself next to the door as the Sendosian took off the dataglasses and stood up, prowling around the room. He took out a search/neutralize wand and held it up, but of course it registered nothing. Nick gritted his teeth to keep from grinding them. The time counter filled his consciousness, driving out thoughts of deadly conspiracies—at least temporarily.

After what felt like an eternity, the Sendosian sat down again and put on his dataglasses. Nick waited a couple of minutes, then activated the telltale. The transport tube's door slid open silently, and he jumped in.

Three buttons: red, blue, and black. The blue light went with the room he'd just left. He didn't know about the other lights. One of them went with where they'd started, but what about the other? And what about the guards at the transport tube's doors? What happens when it opens and there's no one in it? Desperate, he took a guess: black, the universal designator for military secrets. The transport tube responded, and moments later, the doors opened.

Nick stepped out cautiously. The room was empty. He looked around, puzzled. There was no other entry or exit point but the transport tube. There was no furniture, no windows, nothing on the walls except a small silver square at the opposite end of the room. The walls themselves were a soft, glowing white in color. They appeared hazy, as if his vision was blurred. Curious, he reached out his hand to touch the closest one, but instinct stopped him, and he pulled it back. He started to take a step forward, toward the opposite wall, but abruptly he changed his mind again and pulled his foot back. He stood rooted to the floor, trying to decide on his next move.

He reached into his pocket and took out his s/n wand, keeping it carefully covered with his hand in case someone was monitoring the room from another location. There was something about this place.... As he extended it outward, sweeping in a wide band across the walls and floor, he breathed in sharply as the lines of purple light jumped out at him, revealing a security grid covering the entire room.

He checked the time again and switched the wand from search to neutralize, pointing it at the floor in front of his feet. The blue lines abruptly went dark. Using a narrow bandwidth, he made a temporary path through the grid, letting it switch back on behind him. If someone was monitoring the room, the on-off pattern might look like a system glitch—at least for a minute or two.

Using a zigzag course, he finally reached the opposite wall. Turning the wand on the wall, he again created a random-looking pattern until he finally got to the silver square. After making another path through the grid around it, he tapped on it once, gently. The upper right-hand quadrant of the adjacent wall slid open. Eyebrows raised, he tapped twice, and the bottom right-hand quadrant of the same wall also opened. Nick grinned; he'd broken into safes like this before, but never one that took up an entire room.

He made his way cautiously over to the two openings in the wall and peered inside. Sure enough, the weapons described on Ravat's black-coded disc were right here, inside these walls. He couldn't judge the depth of the safe, but it seemed to extend back for some distance—a very long distance.

He quickly crossed back to the access device on the wall and began using different combinations of taps to open the other panels, trying not to keep more than two open at the same time, in case of monitoring. Now that he was in, he needed to use the little time remaining to try to analyze what he saw. What was unusual was the way that the weapons were grouped. While there were many of each kind, they weren't all stockpiled together, and each quadrant of the wall seemed to have a different assortment. In some cases, the differences were slight; but in some, it was more significant. But what kind of pattern did they form?

And then there were the weapons even he didn't recognize.

It seemed to take forever to get back to the landing dock and longer than forever for the cargo ship to finish loading. It was due to leave in a couple of minutes—and the lightship was due to become visible not long after that. If the cargo ship got too far off schedule, he was done for. Nick waited tensely, watching as the cargo ship's pilot finished signing off on the manifests. She finally keyed in her signature on the last one and got into the ship. As the cargo ship powered up, he drew his first real breath in what felt like hours.

He now had two tasks: monitoring the lightship's systems and controls while tapping into the cargo ship's communication system. So far, so good—no suspicious actions on the part of the pilot, and no instructions given to be suspicious. The cargo ship left the landing dock and headed toward the sensor net. Once again he held his breath as the cargo ship cleared the sensor net and continued on into space. Not a moment too soon as a pale, flickering shadow briefly appeared where his hands were hovering over the instrument panel. He would soon become visible again, as would the lightship.

Streaking away from the cargo ship, the walls of the lightship slowly materializing around him, he sighed deeply and closed his eyes, trying to fix in his memory everything he'd seen, and trying without success not to agonize over what he hadn't seen. All that information behind those doors … what the hell did it mean? So much for a simple weapons score. This was much bigger than he'd ever imagined. He thought about the door marked PEACEKEEPER and sighed again. He'd pulled Andrei into his business, and now, without even knowing it, Andrei had returned the favor.

Chapter 10

"Welcome to the Peaceship, Doctor Zarev. I'm Sylvain Dulaire, the Peacekeeper's Executive Assistant. Please allow me to escort you to your quarters."

This clipped little speech could have been mistaken for formality, but Diana couldn't help but Sense the not-too-subtle undercurrent of cold hostility. Startled, she searched his face for a clue, but the wide-set hazel eyes gave nothing back—a trick he'd probably learned from his boss. Yet the anger was there, no question. It seemed like more than just the resentment many PNs held for PAs in general. What had she done to merit this reception? "Thank you," she replied.

He nodded and turned away. She didn't see her bags, and she assumed that someone else had taken them. That was all right: she had the implant tucked away in the carry-on she had over her shoulder. He didn't wait for her to catch up to him as he strode down the corridor, controlled anger apparent in the tight set of his back and shoulder muscles. She tried pausing along the way to look at the viewscreens showing images of the homeworlds of the Six or the starfield, but he wouldn't wait.

She'd seen images of some of the various types of sentients who were part of the Alliance, but that wasn't the same as seeing them for real. Up close, the variety of colors, sizes, and shapes was dazzling to her inexperienced eye. It was disconcerting to observe that humans were only a small minority on the

Peaceship, but it made sense, as the Core's population was tiny compared to the other inhabited worlds of the Six.

The biggest surprise came from seeing T'larians, even though the other alien races were stranger looking. Though much taller and thinner than humans, midnight black, and completely hairless, their features were actually humanoid: they had the same number of arms and legs and the same arrangement of facial features. She wondered if it was possible that, sometime in the distant past, they'd also come from Earth, or someplace like Earth. There was no reason to assume that in the whole universe, there wouldn't be sentients that were similar to each other.

The others couldn't possibly have been related to humans. Glendine binaries were as small as T'larians were large. Completely identical twins, even their movements and gestures were the same, and they were always together. She wondered what this did for their sex lives. It was hard to see exactly what Sendosians looked like, because of the breathing apparatus they wore, as well as their dramatic clothing, but she found their huge, blocky bodies and massive, double-skulled heads intimidating. Erlandians looked vaguely like images she'd seen of an Earth creature called a lion; they were orange-gold and walked on six appendages, but their most unusual feature was the bushy manes of writhing tentacles surrounding their heads. Finally, there were the Karellians, but it wasn't possible to see what they actually looked like past their long cloaks and deep hoods, just flashes of white, gray, and silver.

She couldn't stop staring, but the aliens barely spared her a glance. Sylvain nodded to various sentients but didn't stop and introduce her to anyone. They stepped into a transport tube, and he murmured a command. He turned toward the door and stared straight ahead, his arms folded in front of him. She opened her mouth to speak, then changed her mind. The strained silence lengthened until the door opened again. The corridor at this level had no decorations and no windows to the outside world, and she was struck by the sterility of it as she followed him. Even though the Core was also a closed environment, its massive size and the ever-present viewscreens allowed its inhabitants—at least its PA inhabitants—to feel like they were, well, somewhere.

"I guess the Peacekeeper doesn't believe in decorating non-public areas," she remarked.

"Commander Savinov's not involved in the maintenance of the Peaceship," Dulaire shot back. "Administrative Officers Lithras A and B and their staff take care of the ship. But if you need anything, the Commander has instructed me to respond to your requests." He spoke using the same formal tone, emphasizing his hostility rather than masking it.

"Otherwise you wouldn't have anything to do with me, would you?" she said softly. He stiffened slightly but otherwise pretended that he hadn't heard. He finally stopped in front of a door and keyed in an access code. It slid open, and she followed him inside. The quarters were actually two rooms: a small one for working and a smaller one for sleeping. They were as devoid of personality as the Peaceship's corridors. *How could anyone stand to live here for any length of time?* she thought.

He handed her a disc. "Here's a copy of basic information you'll need for your stay here, Doctor," he said, still struggling to sound courteous, and still failing at it. "Access codes to your quarters, the lounge, the observation deck, and medlab. Map of the ship, with off-limits areas marked in red. Information on shipboard procedures and routines." He turned to go. "We are on Alliance Standard Time here. Commander Savinov requests that you meet him at his quarters in one hour. I'll be back to escort you."

Though she still felt slightly groggy from the K12 she'd taken to deal with the effects of the two long pass-through points, she decided to confront him and find out what was going on. "Please wait a minute, Mr. Dulaire," she said. Her voice was calm but determined, and he froze, turning back toward her. "You seem to have decided before we'd spoken two words to each other that we weren't going to get along," she continued, trying to sound pleasant. "What seems to be the problem?"

For a moment he looked like he was going to deny it, but instead he finally let his emotions appear as his eyes flashed with anger. "Why are you bothering to ask me anything, Doctor? Why not just Read my mind?"

"Because it's not respectful and, therefore, not acceptable for a PA to Read a PN without explicit consent." It was standard Bridge phrasing of their policy.

"That so?" He looked at her speculatively.

She nodded, taking her chances. "I'm a member of the Bridge."

"Andrei told me," he replied.

She was briefly surprised at the switch from 'Commander Savinov' to 'Andrei'. It convinced her even more that she needed to get him on her side. "Did he tell you why I'm here?"

He scowled, turning away from her as if he were ready to leave again. She suddenly understood. "He did tell you. And you don't approve of what we're going to do."

He turned back again. "That's right, I don't!" His voice got louder as he spoke. "Just so far the workings of the human brain can be simulated by a computer. After that, it's unknown territory. And you're going to run an *experiment*"—he spat out the word with contempt—"on the one person in the Six who can possibly prevent the Alliance from being destroyed."

Diana sighed. "That's why he wants to do it, Mr. Dulaire. He thinks this will help accomplish that goal. He's afraid he won't be able to do it any other way."

Sylvain shook his head. "He could end up dead, or hopelessly brain damaged."

"Not according to the simulations I've run."

"I don't give a damn about simulated results! Why can't you find someone less ... valuable to try this on?"

She thought about the files she'd read on Andrei Savinov's career, both as a Warleader and as Peacekeeper. She thought about the honors the Alliance had given him, and what he'd done to merit those honors. "From the little I know about Commander Savinov, I'm not sure he'd appreciate your reasoning."

"I don't care!" Suddenly his anger seemed to collapse. "I've spent years trying to keep Andrei safe," he said wearily. "Times when I've been good at it, and other times I haven't done so well. Worst is when it's something like this—when he insists on doing something I know is going to be trouble. He's walking right into dangers I can't even understand, much less protect him from." He shook his head. "And he won't protect himself, that's for sure."

"Why not?" she asked.

Sylvain sighed. "Because he doesn't. Andrei thinks he should be able to do anything he needs to do, whatever the cost to himself. If something goes wrong with your damned experiment, he'll think it's because he isn't trying hard enough."

She felt alarm. This was definitely not a good trait for an experimental subject. She didn't need to Sense or Read Sylvain to be aware of his feelings of defeat, frustration, and worry, and she felt sorry for him. "Listen, Mr. Dulaire. I know you'll have a hard time believing this, but I don't want anything to go wrong either. I've done whatever I could to make the implant safe, and I'm here in order to monitor him closely enough to shut the whole thing down if it seems necessary."

Diana touched his arm gently. He didn't move away. She said, "You and I are going to have to pull together on this. Since you work so closely with him, you'll probably be the one who will notice first if something's wrong. Not to mention that with all the changes he'll be going through, he'll need someone to confide in."

Sylvain shook his head. "As much as Andrei ever confides in anyone. The worse things get, the less you'll hear about it."

That wasn't helpful either. "He certainly doesn't confide in his family. I know that," Diana remarked. "It's been very disappointing to Coraline." She hesitated a moment. "Do you know why he doesn't want contact with her? Is it because she's PA?"

"No, not at all," Sylvain replied. "He'd never take that out on her. I think part of it is that there so many painful memories connected with his family. Coraline just reminds him too much of his mother. Has she told you about her?"

"A little."

"Don't know all the details, but I guess Andrei and Astrid were pretty close. Even when he was very young, Astrid confided in Andrei—he knew all her plans, her secrets, her fears. It was hard on him, I think. To be a kid and stuck with all that stuff." He shrugged at her look of surprise. "He promised Nick, for their mother's sake, that he'd protect Coraline if he could. He's got people keeping an eye on her, but he's always been worried that if the Zoryans or their collaborators knew she was related, they might try to use her against him. Or she might have a hard time on Logos Prime if he got in trouble with the government there."

Yet another surprise. "She thinks he's afraid that if she gets caught for her Bridge activities, the Peacekeeper would be connected with the Challenge, and his position would be undermined," Diana said.

Sylvain laughed, and she could hear contempt in his voice again. "Andrei, afraid of losing his *position?* You can't be serious. First of all, he's not built that way. And second, the Alliance Council's terrified of losing him."

"Why?"

"The job's impossibly stressful. No one else can do what he does. And the Zoryans want him as Peacekeeper. Or at least the previous Zoryans did—who knows what this new group wants? Most of all, because he's already tried to resign his commission once before, and I know he'd do it again if he thought someone could take his place."

Diana shook her head, lost. "I don't understand."

He studied her. "What do you know about the war? About the end of the war?"

"The Alliance won a big battle, didn't we? The Zoryans were forced to surrender …" Her voice trailed off as she realized that was all she knew.

Sylvain sighed. "That's it? Typical Logos Prime PA who thinks nothing going on outside the Think Tank is worth bothering with."

She wasn't going to argue with him, especially since he was right. She was suddenly ashamed of how little attention she'd paid to the war, of how easy it had been to believe the propaganda that was fed to PAs—that it was too far away and had nothing to do with them. "You're right, Mr. Dulaire. I don't know much. Are you willing to explain it to me?" She smiled at him. "It seems I have the next Standard hour free."

He looked at her sharply, searching her face for signs of mockery. She waited. He nodded abruptly and began.

The Alliance was finally closing in on Zorya, he told her; a lot of important battles had been won, and Zorya's resources were stretched to the breaking point. Andrei and Kylara had gotten a lead on the location of a key Zoryan baseship, and she went out to investigate. She got caught—but just before her cruiser was destroyed, she managed to transmit the coordinates back to Andrei at Command/Control. He sent out a fleet right away, hoping that the Zoryans didn't know that Kylara got the message through. They engaged with a Zoryan fleet sent out to defend the baseship, and both sides took heavy losses. With what the Alliance lost in the battle, it wasn't likely that the remaining ships could take and hold the baseship, so Andrei ordered it destroyed. There were ten thousand Zoryans on that baseship, which was more than they could afford to lose and keep fighting. So they agreed to a truce.

"He ordered the deaths of ten thousand sentients?" Diana asked, unable to keep the shock and revulsion out of her voice.

"Ten thousand *Zoryans!*" Sylvain snapped back. "Small payment for twenty-five years of war! Small payment for the murder of our Prime Commander!"

She didn't reply, and he continued with his narrative.

The Alliance won and brought them to the negotiating table, he told her, but the cost was huge to both sides. Over twenty-five thousand were killed in that final battle, including the Alliance Prime Commander. Everything was in chaos. After all those years of fighting, no one was set up for the next step: trying to make and maintain a Settlement. Among the warleaders, there was a lot of political maneuvering as to who would take over the Prime Command. Since Andrei was the Chief Strategist and had planned and directed the deciding battle, of course the Alliance Council chose him.

Sylvain shook his head, remembering. But Andrei didn't want it. He was crushed by Kylara's death and felt guilty about the baseship, though everyone agreed it had been the right thing to do. He'd spent his whole life fighting the war, and it was over; and he'd been with Kylara all that time, and she was gone too. He couldn't stand the thought of taking her place as Prime Commander. He was working hard to help secure the War Border and find places for all the Logos Prime PNs who didn't want to be repatriated, and finally he couldn't take it anymore and resigned. He moved to T'lar—

"Why T'lar?" Diana asked.

Andrei had become friends with the Zh'ladar—T'lar's spiritual leader—and was offered a place in Sanctuary, even though it was ordinarily closed to off-worlders, Sylvain told her. Sanctuary was T'lar's most sacred space. The native name, translated literally, meant "place of soul-refuge." Andrei took instruction there with the Zh'ladar in the Disciplines: meditation and mental practices that focused the mind and gave the practitioner some control over body functions like respiration, heartbeat, and circulation.

There wasn't much left of T'lar after the Zoryans broke through the Alliance Defense Grid and attacked it with planet killers twelve years ago, and after years of trying to terraform the place, the Alliance Council finally decided that it was hopeless. They were going to evacuate the remaining inhabitants and let the planet go.

But the Zh'ladar—and the T'larian people—wanted to stay. Andrei was the Force Leader assigned to oversee the evacuation, but after meeting the Zh'ladar, he designed a plan to keep it going until a new solution could be found. T'lar was no vacation spot now—except to Andrei, for whatever strange reason—but at least it still existed as a homeworld.

"Anyway," said Sylvain, "the Zh'ladar understood how he felt at the end of the war, and helped him disappear."

"Leaving you behind?" Diana asked gently.

Sylvain looked surprised and embarrassed, then angry. "Did you Read that?"

"No," she answered. "It's just that from the way you talk about these events, it sounds like you lived them yourself."

He stared hard at her, his eyes blazing with the intensity of his feelings. "I did live them myself, Doctor Zarev. I was born and raised in one of the lowest levels of the Core—middle of nowhere. Big-shot PA, you've got no idea what that's like. The war was the only way out for people like me. Working for Andrei … you couldn't possibly understand what that's been like, either. He taught me how to use my mind. Gave me a purpose in life." He looked away. "Did I feel bad when he left? Sure, but I understood why he did it."

He shook his head, changing the subject. "Anyway, Zoryans don't separate their military officers from their diplomatic corps. They were in an uproar that the Alliance would send negotiators to the Settlement who hadn't fought in the war. They knew Andrei—knew how he was responsible for handing them the closest thing to defeat they'd ever had. Weird, but they respected him for that. They demanded that he negotiate the Settlement for the Alliance. The Council actually violated the Sanctuary and persuaded him to come back."

"How did they manage to persuade him?"

Sylvain's lips tightened. "Used Kylara, of course. Said that if he didn't do it, there'd be no Settlement, the war would be on again, and Kylara would have died for no reason. You can guess the rest of it. And of course, once he'd started, there was no backing out. Andrei's like that. Things consume him." He stared at Diana, once again back in the present and remembering what he'd been angry about. "Your experiment's just more of the same."

Diana met his eyes. "You think I'm just going to make everything worse."

"Don't you think so?"

"I hope not, Mr. Dulaire. I hope that the implant makes his job easier."

Sylvain smiled grimly, mocking her. "There, see? You're talking about his job, while I'm talking about his life. His life will be harder, no doubt about it."

Once he was gone, she still had some time to herself before she had to meet Andrei. She looked around again, but there still wasn't anything to see. She thought about going out to examine the Peaceship further, but decided to wait until later. Instead, she organized her desk and pulled up Andrei's medical records on her fileviewer to study them again.

What he'd been trying to hide had jumped right out at her, and she'd been appalled at the mess she found. The artificial heart he'd been given was an inferior model, with a defect in the way it conducted electrical impulses to the heart muscle. This caused the sino-atrial node, the heart's pacemaker, to function abnormally. The result was arrhythmia—a potentially fatal fluctuation in the heartbeat's rhythm—followed by heart failure.

And the heart had failed twice in the year since he got it. Heart failure had led to cardiac asthma, with fluid collecting in his regenerated lungs, damaging them as well. Even if he could force the authorities on Logos Prime to give him a better heart, at this point he wasn't strong enough to get through the surgery. But if he didn't get a new heart, any future episode of heart failure could kill him. She didn't know how long he had to live, but she doubted it would be more than a few years. And surely he knew it.

She thought again about whether she could, in good conscience, continue with her plan to use him as her test subject. She was sure that the implant itself wouldn't damage the heart any further, but there would definitely be some painful side effects. What really bothered her were the psychological issues. If the experiment proved to be stressful on a psychological level—and she assumed it would—the strain on his mind would put more strain on his heart.

She shook her head in frustration. Aside from the initial testing done on all new military recruits, there were no psych records attached to Andrei's medical profile. She didn't think he'd tampered with it. PNs didn't get psychological counseling on Logos Prime, and she doubted that they did off-world either. So there was no record of his being treated for post-traumatic stress disorder, which would be necessary, in her opinion, for anyone after a disaster of this magnitude. Especially since, six months after this so-called accident, the lover he'd spent half his life with had been killed. Did he really need another traumatic event right now?

Maybe not, but even without the implant, he was facing the challenge of dealing with a telepathic enemy. At least this way, he'd have a chance of avoiding a defeat that would be a disaster not just for him, but for the entire Alliance.

When Sylvain came back to get her, she was ready.

* * *

Andrei stared intently at the figure floating in front of him: a holographic model of the human brain traced with red lines emanating from a silver lozenge representing the implant. He'd created a visual representation of the data on the discs that Diana had given him. The brain was lumpy and misshapen, and the lines tracing neural pathways were tangled, some of them leading nowhere. But he thought that he'd managed to get some idea of what Diana was trying to do. He wanted to make sure he understood everything.

Sighing, he shook his head. He wasn't going to understand everything. He wasn't a scientist, and besides, he didn't think even Diana understood everything. *We're not going to know exactly what will happen until the thing's already in my head,* he thought, turning off the model and getting up to get a drink from the dispenser. He took it over to the sofa. Sighing again, he stretched out, trying to relax.

Relax, hell. You're about to be turned into your own worst enemy. What is there to relax about? No. PAs aren't the worst. There's always the Zoryans …

He gazed at the holo-model of the War Border on the opposite wall. Pressing a button on the remote control unit he'd left on top of the coffee table, he watched as Kylara's face materialized, floating ethereally between the stars and planets. *Love of mine,* he thought, *I'm doing the right thing, aren't I?* Needless to say, there was no answer.

He was deeply lost in thought when the door chimed. Another button on the remote caused a circle in the top half of the door to turn transparent, revealing Sylvain and Diana. He pressed it again to open the door and stood up to greet them, turning off Kylara's picture. Diana entered first, looking around his office with obvious curiosity.

His desk dominated the room. Not exactly a desk, it was more a control center: a half circle with his chair in the middle. A number of networked and free-standing servers were linked together, the expansive matte-black surfaces winking and glowing with numerous layers of embedded open files. A large, highly detailed holo-model of the Six and another of the Zoryan Hegemony hovered in one corner of the room, while an equally elaborate holo-model of the War Border stretched across the opposite wall. The remaining wall space above the sofa was taken up with the Peacekeeper's Seal and the Alliance Council's Seal. The door to his bedroom was closed.

"Home, sweet home?" she asked, with a touch of irony in her voice.

He shrugged, at a loss for a clever reply. What in six worlds was "home" when he'd spent the last seventeen years living in one metal box or another out in space?

Sylvain and Diana got drinks for themselves and sat on the sofa, while Andrei sat in the chair facing them. "Your trip was all right?" he asked.

"Fine," she answered. "I'll admit I was a little nervous going through two long pass-through points. I've only ever been through the short-hop pass-through point between Logos Prime and Praxis before. But there were no problems."

Her reply puzzled him at first. What kind of problem was involved in passing through the hyperspace tunnels known as wormholes? Moving at speeds faster than light, a ship traveled through the coordinates of the entry black hole and came out at the exit hole. Neither the Alliance or the Hegemony would exist without the pass-through points, as few of the planets in either system orbited the same star. There hadn't been many PAs serving in the war effort, and there were none attached to the Peacekeeping Mission, but he suddenly remembered that PAs had some kind of sensory distortion problem when passing through hyperspace. "How do you deal with it?" he asked.

"As long as we take a dose of K12 before entering each pass-through point, everything's fine," she replied. "It has a very mild tranquilizing effect. That's all."

Sylvain and Andrei glanced at each other. "That's all?" Andrei repeated. "Mildly sedated isn't an ideal state to be in when you're going into battle, especially if you're the one piloting a cruiser." He looked at Sylvain again. "Did we have any PAs piloting cruisers?"

Sylvain grinned and shrugged. "Little late to worry about it now."

Andrei suddenly looked startled as his perspective shifted. "This is going to happen to me when I have the implant, right? I have to pass through all the time. Even though I'm not usually doing the flying, I can't afford the disruption."

"You'll get used to it very quickly, and you won't notice it at all after a while. The only reason I felt it is that I never go anywhere." She smiled reassuringly as she took a small, silver injection tube out of her bag. "Kinepherine. K12. Your own personal supply."

He took it from her and crossed to his desk to slip it into the small top drawer where he kept the spray he used on his hands. He was silent as he returned to his chair. Not for the first time, he struggled against the desire to call the whole thing off.

"Since we seem to have gotten onto the subject anyway, why don't you tell me what concerns you most about this project?" Diana said. "You must have a number of questions."

Was she Reading him? He thought that Bridge members didn't Read PNs. Maybe his control was slipping, or maybe it was just the next natural thing to say, or … *Come on,* he thought impatiently. *Get over it.* "I've studied your data, and I think I know what you're trying to do," he began.

Her eyebrows rose. "I didn't think you'd be able to make much of those discs."

Sylvain turned in his seat toward her, eyes flashing, ready to resume hostilities. "Don't you underestimate Commander Savinov's—"

Andrei cut him off with a slight shake of his head. Returning to his desk, he activated the model of the brain. Diana's amused expression changed to astonishment as she came over to study it. "How did you manage this?" she asked.

He gestured to the other holo-models. "I prefer thinking in pictures," he replied. "I know I haven't got it completely right ..."

"It's close enough," she answered. She looked again, more closely this time, at the holo-models around the room. "You designed these too? They're amazing. They make the models we saw on Praxis look like they were done by a novice."

He felt embarrassed. What was he trying to do, impress her? "Even the Peacekeeper needs a hobby." He pointed at the model again. "Could you sketch out for Sylvain and me how this works?"

She did. The implant itself would be located in the neocortex, the highest, most developed area of the brain, located in the upper right corner. The part of the brain where intuitive abilities originated, it also served as the home for the psi-sense organ. Nerve impulses would travel from there to the nerve cells arranged in six layers that formed the cerebral cortex, the outer surface of the cerebrum. This was the region of conscious thought and sensation. From there, the information carried in the nerve impulses would travel to other parts of the brain: the cerebellum, responsible for controlling balance and coordination, and finally, the brain stem.

"Which is where the problem will be," Diana said.

He wasn't surprised. The brain stem controls vital signs—breathing, blood pressure, and heartbeat. When stimulated by the additional activity of the implant, his heartbeat would speed up. The last thing he needed. "How will I experience this?" he asked.

"The adjustment process will be more difficult," she answered. "For the first few days, it'll probably feel as if you've taken an overdose of stims. I take it you know what that's like?"

He nodded. Yes, he certainly knew what central nervous system stimulators felt like. Sometimes it seemed as though he'd spent almost as much time fighting sleep as he had fighting the war. But since the accident, they were off limits to him. He felt a touch of fear as he thought of what this could do to his heart, but since she hadn't called off the experiment, she must have concluded that even if it was painful, it wasn't going to kill him.

"Your heart rate and blood pressure will rise abruptly, and you'll experience chest pain and shortness of breath. But your body will get used to it after a while. I can't tell you in advance whether you'll be able to control the pain with chemical intervention or not."

She gave him a measuring look. "I've been pretty frantic, trying to redo all my physical status simulations. I might have gotten a head start on the process if, when we met on Praxis, you'd told me that you had an artificial heart ... and a lousy one, at that."

"I didn't think it was that important," he replied coolly.

"You're kidding, right?" Diana snapped. "Of course it's important. Why didn't you say anything?" She drew a quick breath as the answer came to her. "You didn't want Coraline and Nick to know."

No, he didn't want them to know. The various attempts on his life had always been hushed up, both for morale purposes and to keep others from getting any ideas about his vulnerability. He could have told his brother and sister, of course; he could have shared with them what it felt like to be the only survivor of a flashbomb going off in his ship, planted by an officer he'd trusted, who had turned out to be a Zoryan collaborator. He'd certainly relived it often enough in nightmares to be able to tell them about the whole thing in great detail. But what for? So they could feel sorry for him? So they could worry about his safety?

Abruptly, he turned off the model of the brain and went back to his chair. Diana and Sylvain followed.

"Your medical record doesn't explain how, as a PN, you managed to get a new heart at all," she said.

Andrei looked over at Sylvain, and they both grinned. "The Alliance Council gave Logos Prime a direct order, with threat of sanctions if they didn't comply," he answered. He'd found out about the whole thing only afterward, of course—how Kylara had threatened to bomb the Core personally. And she would have done it, too. "I guess you could say I was lucky."

"I guess you could, but it wouldn't be true," she replied. "What a horrible experience it must have been. Did you have any counseling? Were you given mood stabilizers?"

Amusement at the memory of Kylara's theatrics was immediately replaced by fury, and he had to struggle to get his temper under control. "I would never have anything to do with that," he answered coldly. "You're a member of the Think Tank, Diana. Those are PA control devices—the type of things they used on my mother to try to get her to conform."

There was silence, and Diana looked upset. "They can also be used to help people who have difficult issues to deal with," she responded. "Your mother suffered from depression. They might have been able to help her—"

"Let's not discuss my mother right now," he interrupted. "Back to the business at hand."

She nodded. "I'm sorry. I didn't mean to disturb you," she said quietly. "Why don't you tell me your concerns about the implant."

He felt guilty for jumping on her, and grateful that she was willing to let it go. "The biggest problem I see is that even if it works for Reading human minds, you haven't done anything in the way of investigating how effective it will be in helping me Read Zoryan minds. Which, of course, is what I need it for."

She nodded. "PAs, as a whole, have had little contact with nonhumans. But as you said, there were a few who served in the war. They did report being able to Read Zoryan minds to a very limited extent—only in direct contact with them, of course, like in an interrogation. We can't Read minds across space, you know."

"That was the excuse First Circle made in refusing to contribute PAs to the war effort. I always wondered whether it was actually true." Andrei commented. She looked at him sharply, but there was no anger in his tone; he was just stating a fact. "Do you know anything about the structure and functioning of nonhuman brains?"

"Not much, but I could learn," Diana answered. "I'd need access to information on Zoryan brain structure. The implant was designed to be used by humans, on humans. I can't guarantee that you'll be able to use it to Read Zoryan minds, but it's certainly worth a try." She shrugged. "At the very least, you'll be able to keep them from Reading your mind."

"That's worth a lot," he replied. "Sylvain and I will help get you whatever you need in the way of information on the Zoryan brain and Zoryan psychology. As a matter of fact, I've done some work on the latter myself, from a strategic point of view."

He leaned back and took another sip of his drink, thinking. "I guess that brings us to my second question. Aside from feeling groggy when passing through hyperspace, how exactly is this going to affect me? On a day to day basis, I mean. How fast is it going to take effect, and how much instruction will I need in order to manage the process? No one on my staff is going to know about this, except Sylvain. Am I going to start behaving differently, in ways that could cause suspicion?"

"Not if you don't want to," she replied. Her tone of voice surprised him, and he turned back to her again. She looked thoughtful; he seemed to have hit a nerve. "You aren't going to experience a personality change unless your beliefs change, Andrei. You aren't going to become any smarter as a result of the implant, but you will be able to take in more information more rapidly. If you start feeling impatient that the sentients around you can't make connections the way you do, can't use information the same way or draw the same conclusions you do, because they can't Read minds, you might change your way of relating to people.

"But it wouldn't be because the implant is releasing some electrochemical impulse that makes you arrogant and self-absorbed, like so many PAs are. The personality traits are the end result of a distorted way of thinking about others. For example, if you were to start thinking that you were entitled to treat others with less respect because of the types of minds they have ..."

He shook his head, attempting to mask his feeling of revulsion. He was going to become one of these people? "I don't think that will be a problem."

"I'm sure your Exec will let you know if he thinks you're getting out of line," she said.

He looked over at Sylvain, who grinned. "I have no doubt of that."

"You should have an understanding of what you're going to experience when we first begin," she said. "As the implant starts to work, everything will seem much sharper and clearer, but at the same time disorienting because of the changes in the way you'll be processing information. You'll feel like you're having both visual and auditory hallucinations, but the imagery won't be solid. It'll be more like seeing and hearing ghosts. This will improve—they'll disappear—as I train you to make sense out of what you're perceiving. You won't be able to get much sleep for a while, I'm afraid."

Fear again. Andrei pushed it aside. "That sounds pretty disruptive."

"Assuming your ordinary day isn't just busy but also has a lot of contact with others, you'd be best off having an imaginary illness of some kind for the first week after insertion. That would allow you some time to get used to the implant without an audience. As I said, I'll be working with you to help you learn how to control the sensory input you'll be Receiving, which will be pretty overwhelming at first. As you get the hang of it, we'll work on actively using your augmented senses to Read minds and to Block others from Reading your mind."

"The next Alliance-Zoryan negotiating session starts in six Standard weeks," Sylvain cut in. "Will he be ready in time?"

Andrei and Diana gazed steadily at each other. "I'll have to be, won't I?" he said softly.

She nodded, her eyes not leaving his. "You will be."

Chapter 11

"Are you sure this line is secure?" Through the hissing sound of the black-coded channel, Coraline sounded worried.

"Andrei's Executive Aide set it up, so I assume it's all right," Diana answered. She was taking the call in her quarters. "Though I must admit, it would be nice if thoughts could be Sent through pass-through points."

"How's it going out there?"

"All right, I suppose."

"Can you be more specific?" Coraline sounded less than patient. Diana sympathized with her—she had to be worried that she'd done something that could end up hurting her brother. She tried to organize her thoughts.

"I put in the implant ten days ago. There were no complications with the insertion procedure itself …" She stopped herself abruptly from finishing the sentence as she remembered her promise of silence to Andrei. She'd been about to tell Coraline about the chest pains that were so severe that he could hardly move for the first two days. Painkillers had been ineffective, as had sedatives, but at least the heart didn't fail. "We've been working together since then, pretty much day and night, on basic techniques for mastering the psi-sense. I finally decided we needed a break—or at least I needed a break. So we are supposedly resting right now."

This last remark was heavily ironic, as at this moment she was attempting to sort out her assessment of her patient's condition, and her patient was most likely still going through his mental exercises while bouncing off the walls. He couldn't sleep; he couldn't even really relax. Even as he was gasping for the breath he couldn't catch, he'd insisted they keep working.

Andrei Savinov had turned out to be a far from ideal test subject. He was so used to being in charge of everything that he couldn't give up control, even when it came to something he wasn't in control of—specifically, her experiment. The fact that he usually knew what he was talking about made this even more annoying. Sylvain had been right—he didn't complain about symptoms, which made it hard to keep accurate records. And he was obsessive about his Peacekeeping Mission; he would keep pushing until he collapsed, for the sake of the Mission. Diana's colleagues and friends had teased her about being obsessive from time to time, but she felt like a dilettante compared to him.

"How is Andrei holding up?" Coraline asked.

Diana sighed. "I can't exactly tell," she answered carefully.

"I beg your pardon?"

"I'm not sure ..."

"What are you saying?"

This time the sigh was so loud that she was sure Coraline could hear it, even over the channel's hissing noise. "Much of the time, he's Blocking me from Reading him, though he hasn't been able to create a complete Shield. The Blocks aren't very sophisticated, but they're surprisingly effective. Relying on visual observation and bioscanner readings I can conclude that..."

"Why did you start off by teaching him how to Block? And how did he master it so quickly?" Coraline sounded as shocked as Diana had felt when she'd first encountered his Blocks.

"I didn't!" She'd promised herself that she'd be calm and retain her professional demeanor, but the voice that came out was louder than she'd intended, and her frustration and anxiety came through. "It appears that the implant's providing some kind of natural—or unnatural—ability." She paused. "I didn't design it that way."

Coraline swore, probably under her breath, but Diana heard her anyway. "If you didn't design it that way, why is it happening?" When she didn't get an answer, she laughed. "How ironic. Trust Andrei to have come up with a way to do the one thing he was already good at—hiding his thoughts and feelings."

Diana had nothing to say to this. Coraline continued. "You said he was Blocking you much of the time. So what happens during those times when he's not? What's going on behind the mask?"

As she sighed again, Diana realized she had to calm down. She was so tense that she was forgetting to breathe normally. "Pretty much what you'd expect."

"And what's that?" Diana could hear Coraline struggling to keep from yelling at her.

"Chaos," she replied. It was the most accurate description she could think of.

Now it was Coraline's turn to sigh. "All right. You knew that everything couldn't possibly go exactly like you thought it would. Is everything else all right?"

"Not quite," Diana admitted.

"Oh?"

Diana winced at the hostility in Coraline's voice. "He's having trouble distinguishing between speech and thoughts."

"You mean he's not learning how to Receive thoughts directed at him?"

Diana closed her eyes for a moment. "I mean he's Receiving thoughts without trying, and, according to him, the thoughts he Receives sound like spoken words. Sometimes when we're not face to face and I Send him a thought, he answers with words, and he claims that he heard me say something."

Silence. Diana tried again. "He says he can hear sentients thinking from all over the ship, at random, which should be impossible."

"Have you set up any tests to verify that he's really Receiving thoughts from outside the room?" Coraline asked.

"I tried Sending him thoughts from my quarters to his, but he didn't Receive them," Diana answered. "He says that it's like background noise. Sometimes it gets louder, sometimes it's not there, and he can only distinguish whole thoughts now and then."

"Is he disturbed by it?"

"Yes, the noise bothers him. He's tried to have two staff meetings since I put in the implant, and he had to leave them both because he couldn't keep the spoken words and thoughts separate from each other." Diana shook her head in exasperation, then remembered that it was an audio-only channel. "I've been going over and over my data, trying to figure this out. The thing that bothers me is that on rare occasions, I've seen things like this in PAs I've treated who've had nervous breakdowns."

They could both hear the hissing of the channel in the silence that followed. "So what now?" Coraline finally asked. "Will you abort the experiment until you can figure it all out?"

Diana had thought about this and made a decision. "What happens now is that we proceed as planned. I don't think Andrei's in any danger, and the reasons we gave him the implant are still there. We've started putting together a model of the Zoryan brain in order to develop techniques for Reading one. Some of the data is stored in records from PAs who returned from the war—we're trying to access them through the Think Tank without causing any suspicion. That's the top priority right now. The talks start in less than six weeks."

She heard Coraline chuckle. "Since when did your top priority become the Peacekeeping Mission, Diana? My kid brother got to you pretty fast."

Diana's tone was defensive; she couldn't help it. "We made a deal with him, remember? We help him fight the Zoryans, and he helps the Challenge. His work just happens to have more time constraints on it than ours, that's all."

"Are you sure that's all?" Coraline still sounded amused. "I can't say I really know you, but I saw how you reacted to Andrei when we were on Praxis, and I hear how you're talking about him now. I think you're interested in more than his mind."

"Coraline, what are you talking about? Andrei is—"

"Yes, I know. Your patient. Your test subject. You're totally dedicated to your work. You have no time for extracurricular activities. And so on and so forth." The channel became silent for a moment, and when Coraline spoke again, her voice was serious. "It's probably not a good idea, Diana. To care for him. You Shared with me how your parents walked out on you, how they were only interested in pursuing their own goals. Well, Andrei has his own goal, too—final victory for the Alliance. Astrid's struggle, even her death, didn't motivate him to care about the Challenge, and neither did Nick or I." Her voice sounded strained. "I'm fairly sure that I never would have heard from him again if I hadn't contacted him. A man who could turn his back on his family like that isn't a good choice for a lover."

Diana struggled against a wave of anger. *She has no idea what she's talking about,* she thought. *She really doesn't know him—or she knows him as someone who has long since become someone else. But why would Coraline know him? He's never told her anything about himself or his life. And what makes me think I know him any better?* "What about Kylara Val?" she asked.

"I've never met her, and I don't know what his relationship with her was really like, but I do know that they were

Warleaders together—with the common goal of winning the war," Coraline answered. "Look, don't get angry with me. I'm just trying to warn you that if you are interested in him in that way, you shouldn't count on getting anything back."

Diana took a deep breath. "Coraline, Andrei's assistant told me that Andrei's been watching you for years through his spy network, that he knows all about you. He's stayed away from you so you wouldn't be affected by his actions. He promised Nick that he'd protect you ..."

The silence stretched out. Diana shook her head wearily. Had she done the wrong thing by even bringing this up? "Are you all right?" she finally asked.

"Yes. I'm fine." Coraline's voice sounded distant. "I'll try to help you with your Think Tank research and get you some answers as quickly as possible." Without another word, she severed the connection.

Diana leaned her head back in her chair and closed her eyes, again trying to slow her heartbeat and regulate her breathing. *This is how he feels right now,* she thought, then stopped herself abruptly. Identifying with her patient, her subject, wasn't going to help either of them. It didn't matter what she thought of Andrei Savinov; it didn't matter that he most likely didn't think of her that way—or think of her at all when they weren't working together. What mattered was the experiment: getting it done, getting it right.

She got up from the desk and went into the bedroom. *First the insertion procedure, then the long hours of struggling with its operation, then processing it all. No wonder I'm not thinking straight. I'm done in,* she thought wearily as she pulled off her boots and lay down on the bed. *Just an hour or two's rest ...*

She woke hours later to the sound of the door chiming repeatedly. "Come in," she called without bothering to see who was there. Still dazed from sleep, she stared with a puzzled frown as Sylvain stalked into the room, looking worried—very worried. She had to force herself not to Read his thoughts. "What's going on?" she asked.

"Did Andrei tell you he was going somewhere?" he demanded.

She shook her head. "Why? Where is he?"

"I have no idea," he replied. "Administrative Ops says he took his personal cruiser out about two Standard hours ago and didn't leave a destination on file." He paused, staring at her shocked expression. "What is it? Do you know where he's gone?"

Diana didn't answer him. She jammed on her boots and ran out the door, Sylvain close behind her. She continued running all the way to Andrei's quarters, dodging the sentients in her way. "Open it," she demanded. He punched in Andrei's access code. Immediately she went to his desk and jerked open the small top left-hand drawer.

She and Sylvain looked at each other with horror as the silver injector tube of K12 caught the light.

Chapter 12

Chaos.

Barely under control, finally, through a combination of willpower, some imperfectly executed T'larian Disciplines and Diana's surprisingly patient instruction. At least that was surprising to Andrei; but the one person in the Six he'd never had any patience for was himself. He found her intelligence, her energy, and her sense of humor attractive when she wasn't driving him crazy asking him the kind of questions he didn't dare ask himself.

He certainly couldn't control the chaos through the use of intoxicants. Diana had warned him not to try, that at this stage of the game it would be fruitless, but after she left, he'd held the glass of Erlandian *livrash*—his usual drug of choice when he'd had enough of everything going on in his life—in shaking hands and drank it down all at once. Except for a violent feeling of nausea, it hadn't had the slightest impact on the whirling, high-speed chaos going on inside him.

He needed rest, but there was no sleeping. He darkened his bedroom, lay down, and closed his eyes, but all that accomplished was to focus his attention even more sharply on the feelings of disorientation and the pounding of his heart. He sat up again and looked around. Every object in the room stood out in sharp, glowing relief, so brightly that he had to remind himself that the room was dark. "Lights," he called, hoping the illusion would fade.

Instead, it intensified. Everything was alive: the walls, the floors, the furniture. The molecules they were made of danced in front of him, and every surface was transparent. Holding up his hand, he could see the veins branching through it, sending dark blood on its way; electric charges of nerve endings sparkled. He swore under his breath, shoving his fists into his eyes. When he opened them again, the room was back to some semblance of normalcy, and he sighed with temporary relief.

The maelstrom of thoughts chasing each other through his brain was interrupted by the tone announcing an incoming transmission. How long had that been going on? He got up and made his way out of the bedroom and back to his desk, rubbing his shoulder where it had smashed into the doorframe. There was a steady pulse of black light glowing on the screen as he turned it to face him: black-coded channel. Suddenly he swayed, closing his eyes as he leaned against the desk. "Nick," he murmured. It wasn't a guess.

"What the hell took you so long?" Nick demanded, with no words of greeting.

"Sorry," Andrei replied, distracted. The message wasn't programmed with a visual component, but he could distinctly see Nick sitting in his cruiser. He looked tired and worried. How was it that he could see him? *Damn these hallucinations.* "What's wrong?" he asked.

"I ran across some pretty strange goings-on I think you need to take a look at," Nick answered.

Sendosians. Nonaggression Pact. War weapons. Andrei wiped a thin film of sweat off his forehead. His pulse throbbed in his temples, and his breath ran ragged. What had Nick said, and what had he thought? How in the name of the Six could he hear what Nick was thinking over all this distance and without even trying? What was real, and what was not?

"Andrei? You still there?"

"Sorry," he said again. "How did you find out about a plot against the Alliance?"

Silence. "I didn't say anything about a plot against the Alliance." Nick finally spoke. His voice sounded edgy with irritation but careful, as though he were dealing with a madman. *Perhaps he is,* Andrei thought. Before he could answer, Nick spoke again, his voice thick with anger. "That fucking implant. You've got it now, don't you? And you're Reading my mind."

"Yes. No. I guess so, but I don't see how. Thoughts can't be Sent through pass-through points, right? Isn't that right? I'm sure that's right. I'm not trying to Read your mind, Nick. I don't understand how this works. I thought I did, but ..." Andrei realized he was one step away from complete incoherence and stopped talking as he tried to organize his thoughts. Impossible. The channel hissed in the ensuing silence.

"Okay, Andrei, okay. Calm down. I believe you. You sound terrible. Take a couple of deep breaths or whatever the hell it is you do to relax. Disciplines or something. Take it easy." Was that Nick being nice to him? Hard to believe, but he could Sense his brother's concern even without the words. He shouldn't be able to do that either, from here to there.

"We need to get together," Nick continued. "There's too much I have to tell you for just a black-coded transmission. Do you think you can get out of there and meet me at the usual place?"

"I don't know. Yes, all right." Andrei didn't dare refuse; the stakes were too high. "See you in three hours." He signed off, then tried once again to pull his mind together. As he left his quarters, pulling on a flight jacket and keying in the access codes on his commlink for remote start-up of his personal cruiser, he wasn't entirely satisfied with his efforts, but he figured he'd have the hours that the trip would take to keep working on it. It was only as the ship locked into position for the first pass-through point when he remembered the injector of K12 in his desk drawer.

***

Andrei dreamed that he was swimming through space as though it were water, watched by countless pairs of golden eyes in place of stars. The feeling was one of complete tranquility, and he had no desire to rejoin the outside world at all …

Cold. Consciousness returned in a dimly lit space with the sensation of something cold brushing his forehead. He reached up to touch it and realized it was just that: sensation. *Coldwand,* he thought groggily. Blinking to try to clear his vision, he found himself staring into a face hovering above him. At first, all he could see was a blur of pale hair and blue eyes, the deep, sparkling blue of an Erlandian winter ocean. He and Kylara had imagined having a house on the beach on Erlande after the war was over; he probably still had the plans he'd made somewhere. Hair like spun light, cobalt eyes … "Coraline," he murmured, still dreaming. *I'm sorry, I'm so sorry.* Did he say it or just think it? He needed to say it, needed to tell her …

Nick laughed. "Not by a long shot." Andrei blinked, his vision cleared, and it was his brother's face above him. He shook his head, winced at the fresh jolt of pain that went through it, and started to sit up. He was dizzy, so dizzy that he felt sick to his stomach. He was starting to remember. Nick's strong hands pressed against his shoulders to stop him from rising.

"You've tried getting up twice in the past hour, and you passed out again both times. Just in case the third time isn't the trick, why don't you stay put for now?" Though Nick's tone was light, he didn't let go of Andrei until he nodded and leaned back in what seemed to be the passenger seat of his cruiser, fully reclined. He could feel his heart skipping beats, feel blood pounding behind his eyes.

"We're on my ship?"

Nick nodded. "I got your distress call."

'My distress call?"

"You don't remember signaling me?"

"Not offhand. Where are we?"

"Nowhere," Nick answered. "You never made it to the old spacedock on T'rak. I waited a while, then tried to raise your ship and picked up a narrowband distress signal. Followed it back to the first pass-through point from the Peaceship to T'lar and found you drifting. So that's where we are."

"Did we set up a ship-to-ship link?"

Nick grinned. "Not exactly."

Andrei was confused for a moment, then groaned. "You broke in."

"The damage is minimal and easily fixed, Commander, Sir." Nick gave him a mock salute.

"That's encouraging." Andrei closed his eyes, but it was too tempting to just drift away, so he opened them again and tried to sit up. Moving slowly this time, he was successful. Without trying, he Sensed the anxiety that Nick was trying to cover. "I'm all right," he murmured. "Just a little groggy."

"Yeah, sure," Nick answered.

Andrei winced as he Read from Nick's thoughts what Nick had found when he'd forced his way into Andrei's cruiser. He drew a sharp breath as he took in Nick's panic, thinking he was dead, that he'd been killed by ... what?

"No, really, Nick, I'll be fine. You called Sylvain, didn't you?"

"Still doing your mindreading act, hmm?" Nick's tone was sharp. "Yeah, I contacted your trusty assistant, who's on his way here right now with the drug you somehow managed to leave behind. Did you think that even though real PAs can't pass through hyperspace without K12, you'd follow your usual pattern of doing whatever you damn well please and getting away with it?"

Andrei sighed. "I'm not getting away with much of anything these days." Usually Nick couldn't get the better of him, but his mood had turned abruptly dark. He was stunned by how difficult this whole experiment was turning out to be; how in six worlds could he have thought it would work out exactly the way they'd planned? "No, I wasn't thinking anything. I just forgot about it. Pretty stupid, hmm?" Embarrassed, he couldn't look at Nick.

Nick watched him with a thoughtful expression; again without trying, Andrei could Sense his feelings turning from annoyance to something dangerously close to pity. "Yeah, I guess so. But it sounds like you had a lot on your mind. From what Dulaire told me about the adjustment process, you probably shouldn't have gone anywhere anyway." He shook his head. "After all these years, you still haven't figured out how to take care of yourself. Just like Astrid."

At the sound of their mother's name, Andrei drew a sharp breath and struggled not to respond. He was not going to fight with Nick. "You led me to believe it was important that I come. Which brings us to the point of this trip. Tell me why I'm here." He tried to get up, but the floor and ceiling started changing places, so he sat back again. "Could you get me a glass of water, please, before you start?"

Nick shook his head. "Not a good idea, considering how sick you've been. I'm not cleaning up after you again."

Andrei was puzzled. "What are you talking about? The ship has an autocleanser."

Nick looked embarrassed—an unusual expression for him. "Yeah, well, when I hacked into your ship-to-ship link, I trashed some of your auxiliary systems by accident. I was in a hurry, damn it! So here I am, on my hands and knees, scrubbing …"

Andrei laughed. "Serves you right."

Nick also grinned. "So no water for you. Now be quiet, and listen."

Andrei listened, with his ears and with his mind. He heard Nick describe his trip to Selas in the terse words and phrases of a debriefing, but the psi-sense added levels of meaning that ordinarily he might only have guessed at. He followed Nick through the arid, white corridors, dodged the menacing guards. Through the dataglasses, he saw the words glowing on the virtual door fronts and the security grid glowing in the floor and walls of the room holding the weapons cache.

Nick's emotions threaded through the words and images. His horror at what he'd discovered mixed with his fear of getting caught and his attempts at figuring out how to turn the situation to the Challenge's advantage. The Challenge, always the Challenge. How far would Nick go to eliminate PA control of Logos Prime? What would be left of Logos Prime after Zorya and its collaborators got through carving up the Alliance? Pain stabbed viciously through Andrei's temples, and he began feeling nauseous again.

"Andrei? What is it?" He heard Nick call him as if from far away, and he shook his head to try to clear it. Impossible. Images continued battering his consciousness: the virtual corridor stretching to infinity, the files unread, the weapons stacked in strange piles. Whose weapons would be fighting whose private war? "Talk to me," Nick insisted. "What does it all mean? What're we going to do about it?"

Andrei forced himself to respond. "We? This is an Alliance problem, Nick. What do you mean, we?" Andrei finally lifted his head and stared at him. "You want those weapons for the Challenge."

Nick opened his mouth to protest, then shrugged. "I won't deny that's true, especially since you probably pulled it out of my mind. But like you said, this sounds like something bigger than the Challenge. Your name was on one of those doors, and I didn't get enough information to know what kind of danger you're actually in. So I'm part of this, whether you like it or not. Now I'll ask you again—what the hell d'you think is going on?"

"It's obvious, isn't it? Zoryans have used collaborators wherever and whenever they could find them. They seem to have found someone—or some group—large enough to serve as an entry point for their next incursion. An entry point from inside the Alliance. Sendosian, I assume, though probably not exclusively."

"What's the Lighbaht?"

"Sendos's Ruling Family."

Nick frowned. "What're you talking about? Sendos doesn't have a Ruling Family; it has five."

"The Five Families have been jostling for position for centuries," Andrei replied. "Partly for control of Sendos's wealth, but even more from a desire to prove which of them is the true Ruling Family. The Family Leader who can claim the title of Lighbaht will be able to claim, by right, the allegiance—and the resources—of all the others."

"So you think the Zoryans are going to help one Family become the Lighbaht in exchange for what? Arms? Access to the Alliance?"

"Both." He turned to watch Nick. "You're sure there was nothing about the masked Sendosian that was familiar?"

Nick shook his head, shrugging his shoulders with regret.

"Can I take a look? Inside your mind, that is. Maybe I'll see something that will help me recognize him. I don't think it'll hurt."

Nick snorted. "Just my dignity."

"Nick, please. If I was one of them, I wouldn't ask, would I? I'd just take what I wanted."

"All right, all right. Just get it over with, already."

Andrei took a deep breath and focused his thoughts. He had no idea what he was doing, really. He'd been telepathic for a week, and what a mess he'd made of it. "Think about the Sendosian," he directed. He closed his eyes and Reached into Nick's mind. The large, gray-robed figure stood before him, chromium mask gleaming. There was something familiar

128

about him, but as hard as he tried, Andrei couldn't get a fix on it. *Damn.* He Reached out again.

His eyes flew open as his mind caught the cruiser that was still too far away to be detected by his ship's own sensors. PAs couldn't do that either. *Sylvain … and Diana.* He swore softly under his breath. "Why did he bring her out here?"

"What are you talking about?" Nick asked.

"Syl's on his way, and Diana's with him."

"Diana?"

"The PA doctor running the experiment, remember?"

"I do now." Nick stared at him intently. "Exactly how do you know they're there? The implant?" Andrei shrugged. "I didn't know PAs could do that. It's a skill that would have been worth something during the war—if the Alliance Military had done a halfway decent job of forcing First Circle to send PAs into the war effort."

"I don't think they can do it. It's probably a property of the implant," Andrei answered wearily. He wasn't going to rise to this bait either, as though there were something he and Kylara could have done to force Logos Prime to give up its most valuable citizens for a war that was too far away for them to believe in. He'd been Searching for Nick's Sendosian, and instead he'd found a spaceship that hadn't even passed through hyperspace yet. The implant was out of his control.

"Wait a minute! I thought this thing was supposed to give you the same mindpowers as a PA, not more."

"It's an experiment, remember?" Andrei sat back, closing his eyes as he finally gave up the struggle of portraying self-confidence. "I don't know if I can handle this, Nick. Maybe it's a mistake to try. Maybe Sylvain was right, and someone else on my staff should have tested it first. But how could I hand off that kind of risk?"

"You were a Warleader, Andrei. You handed off risk all the time."

His eyes flew open again. "Yes, I did, didn't I? I sent Alliance soldiers out to die while I sat in Command/Control and watched."

Nick snorted. "Watched? Is that what you call it? Is this some kind of false modesty bullshit? Wasn't it you who invented the Battle Mind, or did you just take the credit for it?"

By turning the streams of data coming into Command/Control during a battle into real-time virtual reality simulations, Andrei's Battle Mind program allowed strategists to adjust their battle plans to current conditions. It had helped turn the war around. He knew this, but in his current state of mind, it didn't matter. He hadn't been there on the front line at the end. He'd *watched*—and listened to the reports of the casualties, the lists of ships destroyed—until one day, finally, his worst nightmare came true when one of them was *Windrider*. Kylara's ship. He leaned over, elbows on knees and head in hands as current pain blended seamlessly with old pain.

He felt Nick reach out a tentative hand toward his shoulder, then draw back as he pulled himself out of the way. Pity was intolerable—especially this repulsive self-pity. He was furious with himself as he fought back another wave of nausea. Nick shrugged, got up, and backed off. He paced the deck while Andrei sat with his eyes shut. The silence was awkward as they waited for Sylvain and Diana to arrive.

They both started as Sylvain's signal came through, and Nick returned to the cruiser's control panel. "They'll be within range pretty soon," he said. "I'll set up a ship-to-ship link." Andrei nodded, pulled himself to his feet, and made his way toward the back of the cruiser. "What are you doing?" Nick asked.

"Since I have nothing better to do right now, I think I'm going to be sick again." The bathroom door slid shut behind him just in time.

He stayed in the bathroom for a while, trying to pull himself together, and came out just as the docking ring irised open and Sylvain and Diana appeared. The Sense of anxiety from the two of them, closer to fear than mere worry, permeated the small space. He couldn't help but feel it, just as he seemed unable to keep from hearing their thoughts. Did all PAs have so little control over what they Sensed and Read, or was it the implant, or was it his lack of training? Was their world always this noisy and confusing? Maybe it explained their personalities. He stared coldly at them, finding it easier to be angry than vulnerable. "I didn't realize it took two people to carry one small injection tube."

"Are you all right, Commander?" Sylvain asked.

Andrei Read his guilt-ridden thoughts, and his anger strengthened. "You didn't even know I was leaving, Sylvain. It's ridiculous for you to feel responsible for this." Sylvain looked confused; he opened his mouth to speak, then closed it. Andrei turned away suddenly, his gaze fixing on Diana. Suddenly he gasped, hands raised to his temples, as he felt something invading his mind, coming from her. A reflex he didn't know he had kicked into action, and she cried out and reeled backward as though he'd slapped her. They stared at each other in mute shock.

Nick stepped in. "All right, whatever you PAs are doing, that's enough already."

What little was left of Andrei's self-control at this point finally broke. He wheeled toward Nick and gave him a hard shove, his eyes blazing with rage. "What the hell did you call me?" he yelled, leaping toward him. Nick dodged him easily. Andrei pulled back his fist to strike, and Nick leaned forward, caught both his arms, and held them tightly.

"This is ridiculous. You've forgotten everything I ever taught you about how to fight," Nick said. "Now calm down, and I'll let you go."

Andrei tried once to break his hold, but he had no strength left. Nick let him go, and he struggled with himself to keep from trying to hit him again. "I'm not a PA, Nick, and if you ever call me one again, I'll fit you with this damned thing myself. We'll see how well you deal with it." He turned away from Nick and back to Diana, who hadn't said a word the entire time. "And you! I don't care if this is your experiment. Stay the hell out of my mind, unless I agree to let you in."

She was still staring at him, and the pain in her eyes brought him back to his senses. He collapsed into a passenger seat, utterly miserable and humiliated. "I'm sorry," he whispered. "I'm sorry. I don't know what I'm doing anymore. I can't do this. I can't make it work."

"I know how you feel." For the first time since entering the cruiser, Diana spoke. Her calm voice melted the tension in the air. "Andrei, listen to me. You're not losing your mind. Remember, I told you it might feel like that at the beginning, and you've added a lot of stress by passing through unmedicated. Let's just go back to the Peaceship and continue working on controlling the implant. I know you can control it."

Control. He opened his eyes and pulled himself out of the seat. "You're right. Besides, Admin Ops is going to have personnel out looking for me if I don't get back soon. Syl, give me some lead time. Get a briefing from Nick on our latest crisis in the making."

"Commander, you sure you're well enough to pilot this ship?" Sylvain asked.

Andrei nodded. He had to be, so he was. Diana reached into the pocket of her jacket and pulled out a bioscanner. She showed it to him, and he shrugged his acceptance as she clamped it to his wrist and waited while it took readings and displayed them holographically. "I think you're okay, but I'd like to come with you," she said quietly.

"Does AO know she left with you?" Andrei asked Sylvain. Sylvain shook his head. "All right. I'll tell them I was just giving her a tour of the neighborhood." He sat down again, eyes closed, while Sylvain and Nick made repairs to the cruiser where Nick had broken in. He wasn't trying to sleep; he just didn't want to deal with any of them.

He opened his eyes again when he felt Diana watching him. "Do you feel like you can really do this?" she asked.

"Of course," he snapped. "If you're worried about your safety, go back with Sylvain."

She shook her head, looking exasperated, and didn't reply.

When the repairs were complete, Nick came over to him. "We're done. But we'll need to talk again soon, come up with a plan of action."

"Right." Andrei smiled to himself. He knew Nick's plan of action already: find a way to steal those weapons for the Challenge. And why not, as long as Andrei didn't need them to destroy the Alliance's enemies. While he welcomed this truce, he suspected that their conflict was far from over.

* * *

"The damage is minimal and easily fixed." Andrei's voice was no louder than a murmur.

Diana raised her eyebrows, puzzled. "What are you talking about?"

"Just something Nick said. Will you please stop worrying, Diana? It's getting on my nerves."

Diana ignored his second remark. "Something Nick said about what happened to you?"

"About what happened to my ship when he broke in to respond to my distress call."

She tried hard to be patient. "So were you talking about your ship or your mind?"

Andrei didn't answer. Diana sighed. It was almost like he was deliberately trying to make everything more difficult.

"No, I'm not," Andrei snapped. "It was a stupid mistake, all right? Stupid, thoughtless, irresponsible ... do you have anything to add to that description? Anyway, you got something out of it—you know the implant works. For all intents and purposes, Nick was right. I'm Psi-Active now, just like you."

"Not exactly like me," she muttered.

"Oh?"

"You tell me, Andrei. You tell me how you've managed to Block me from Reading you when I hadn't even started teaching you how. You tell me how you managed to neutralize my Probe."

"What's a Probe?"

"When we first came aboard the ship, I tried to Probe your mind to determine what kind of psychic damage your little adventure might have caused. You weren't supposed to be able to feel it, but I never even got close before you shut me down. Hard."

"I'm sorry if I hurt you." He didn't sound sorry at all.

"I'm over it. But that's not all. You've been answering thoughts people haven't been Sending you." She continued watching him, less angry now and more thoughtful. He wasn't looking at her; his eyes had a feverish glaze as they moved over the cruiser's control panel. The bioscanner told her what had happened to him physically, and she was gradually putting together pieces of the mental aftermath.

Even though she knew it wasn't her fault, she found herself feeling guilty. She'd only once mentioned the K12 to him; she hadn't really drilled it into him that he needed it. But she hadn't thought he'd go anywhere without telling her, while they were running the experiment, and that's when she would have reminded him about it. There wasn't a lot of experience with this problem, but the literature was quite clear: aside from the physical effects, it was also possible for a PA who'd gone through a pass-through point unmedicated to experience a psychotic break. At least his mind seemed to be intact …

"Thanks for the vote of confidence." His tone was acid.

You know, she Sent, *the least you can do, if you're going to be rude enough to respond to thoughts that aren't addressed to you, is to practice Sending thoughts instead of speaking.*

"I don't have anything else to say."

For a long time, neither one spoke. She watched him out of the corner of her eye as he rubbed the bridge of his nose with his fingertips, obviously still upset. She hated to add to his troubles, but she didn't have a choice.

Andrei, there's a problem—the K12.

Don't tell me you left it with Sylvain.

Very funny. The problem is that the sedating effect, which normally would be slight, will be magnified by what you did.

Are you saying I'm going to black out when I take it?

I'm saying it's going to be hard for you to stay awake for a while, while your system makes the adjustment.

"That's just great," he said wearily. He was silent for a minute, working on something on the control panel. She took out the injector and pressed it against the inside of her wrist, then turned to him and waited.

All right, then, Andrei Sent. *If I fall asleep, just press this button. It's hooked up to send a distress signal to Sylvain. These three buttons, on this panel over here, will put us on autopilot until he can come and link up with us, take us in tow. This is the sequence you'd activate them in.* He showed her.

I had no idea we could have been towed, Diana Sent. *I never would have agreed to let you fly this thing if I'd known there was another way to get it back to the Peaceship.*

Andrei laughed then, making her even angrier. She grabbed his wrist, pushed up his sleeve, and pressed the tube in. Hard.

They were silent as they went through the pass-through point. Diana could Sense Andrei's fear, both that the drug wouldn't work and that it would. A blink of an eye, a drawing of breath—the universe twisted over and back again for a moment, and they were through. She leaned back in her chair, shrugging the tension out of her shoulders. Finally, she turned to face him.

He was slumped in the chair, eyes partly closed, breathing slowed. She reached over to press the first button in the sequence, the one that would activate the linked distress signal, but he pushed her hand out of the way and struggled to right himself. "No," he murmured. "No, I'm all right. It's all right." He was taking deep breaths and rubbing his face with both hands. "Nick had a coldwand. Maybe he left it in the first-aid kit."

"I'll look," she replied, also reverting to speech. For someone who wasn't telepathic by nature, speech would be easier to handle than the process of Sending and Receiving thoughts, which he was still learning. She found the coldwand and brought it back to him. He nodded his thanks and adjusted it to the highest setting, then touched it to his temples and the back of his neck, wincing at the sensation. It seemed to help, though. He sat up straighter and started monitoring the boards again.

Diana tried to control her anxiety, resisting the urge to use either a bioscanner or a mental Probe on him. It wouldn't accomplish anything except to annoy him. She watched him out of the corner of her eye. He could maintain a certain level of efficiency for a few minutes; then he would start to fade. After the initial effect, the coldwand didn't seem to be much help. His hands were trembling slightly as he made a course adjustment. That done, he leaned back his head. His eyes seemed to close of their own accord, and he gasped as they snapped open again.

"I'm going to get us both killed if I can't wake up," he said. "Isn't there something you can give me?"

"I can try a restorative," she answered. She injected it into his wrist.

"I don't feel any different," he said after a few minutes had passed. "Try a stronger dose."

"No," she answered. "I don't dare. Your heart won't be able to take it. Be patient. It may just be working more slowly than usual."

"Mmm," he murmured. She wondered if he'd heard her, or if he even remembered his own question. His eyes looked like green glass, bright and drugged, in a face with no color. What would his people think when he got back to the Peaceship?

"Talk to me," he said.

"What about?"

"Anything that would keep me awake. Tell me about yourself. Your job. Your family. Do you have any family? A lover? Why did you join the Bridge?"

She tried to cover her sudden nervousness with logic. "You'd keep your mind busier if you talked to me."

He laughed slightly. "I couldn't string two sentences together at this point."

This was probably true, she thought. She couldn't decide whether she was flattered or frightened by his request. In all the time they'd spent together over the last ten days, he'd hardly talked about anything but the work they were doing. She'd occasionally tried to start a personal conversation, but in spite of his polite replies, his resistance was obvious. But occasionally she could Read and Sense from him that he was interested in her, almost in spite of himself. Like him, she was a very private person, reluctant to share her secrets. But if she wanted the chance to get to know him better, she knew that she had to be more open, herself.

She fiddled with her hands and looked out the viewscreen— looked anywhere but at him. "My parents are still alive. I don't have any contact with them, though. My mother wasn't at all like Astrid, from what Coraline's told me."

"Not too many like Astrid," he said, his voice lifeless.

She opened her mouth to ask him about his mother, but changed her mind as she Sensed the barriers going up again. Drawing a breath, she continued. "My parents, like most PAs, didn't live together very happily or very long. They only had a child together because of the rule that very high-functioning PAs have a duty to the race to produce at least one citizen who will carry their superior genes."

"Are you?" Andrei asked.

"Am I what?"

"A high-functioning PA?"

"Yes." She took a page from his book and didn't elaborate.

"Very high functioning?"

"Yes."

You were in a Group Home, too.

She was startled by the unspoken interruption; she hadn't felt him Reading her. That in itself was strange: a property of the implant? "I don't want to talk about that."

He nodded, and she caught a fleeting thought of his own Group Home experience. *Neither do I*, he Sent. He took up the coldwand again and touched it to the backs of his hands this time. She'd noticed that they were red and swollen but had decided not to mention it. Now she took his analgesic spray from her pack. "You think of everything, Doctor," he remarked. "Must be those superior genes."

Even though she knew that he was annoyed at himself for this second lapse in judgment (forgetting the K12 was the first) and just taking it out on her, she was irritated. "I thought you wanted me to talk to you."

"I do."

"Well, using what I tell you against me isn't exactly the way to make me feel like doing it."

"You're right," he replied, surprising her. "I'm sorry." He rubbed his face with his hands again. "I'm having trouble thinking clearly."

She stifled a laugh. "I can imagine."

"I'm sorry about your parents."

"It's all right. It was a long time ago."

There was yet another awkward silence. She knew he saw through the lie, but he didn't say anything. She wanted to know why he was here in the first place, but it would take him too much mental effort to reconstruct what had happened, even if it wasn't some secret mission he wouldn't allow her to know about anyway. She wished she knew how to fly this thing so he could get some sleep.

That's thoughtful of you. I wish you could too.

Andrei, I've been trying very hard not to Read your mind. Would you please do me the same courtesy?

"What are you talking about?" She looked over at him. Again he was struggling to keep his eyes open. He thought she had spoken. Damn, what was wrong with the implant?

"Never mind. Let's talk, like you said. What else did you ask me? My family, my job. I manage all the psy-med research going on at the Think Tank. I also have a small staff of doctors working for me to treat the physical effects of psi-related illnesses."

"I didn't know there were any."

"There are many of them. PAs believe in separating the life of the mind from the needs of the body, but I've seen for myself that it doesn't make sense in real life. In real life, the mind and the body form a feedback loop, each affecting the responses of the other." She looked over at him; he was rubbing his eyes. "I'm afraid I'm going to put you to sleep if I keep this up."

"I'm sorry," he repeated. "I guess I'm not taking in anything too complex at the moment." He was quiet for a minute, then he grinned. "I asked you if you had a lover. Or lovers. I know most PAs don't settle down with one person."

She raised her eyebrows. "Neither do most PNs, Andrei. It's a proven fact that monogamy isn't characteristic of human nature."

His smile broadened, but he didn't say anything.

She felt embarrassed. He was making fun of her, but she couldn't figure out the joke. Licking dry lips, she continued.

"To answer your question, no, I don't have lots of lovers—not even one right now. Between my regular job and my work for the Bridge, I'm too busy for that sort of thing." *Leave it alone,* she added.

PAs don't treat each other much better than they treat us, do they? he Sent. *Inhumanity breeds inhumanity. Easy to see why you'd think starting a new a relationship isn't worth the pain the old ones have caused you.*

This was much worse than the Group Home revelation. She was horrified. *For Earth's sake, I didn't even feel that coming. I thought you were supposed to be a diplomat, know something about discretion. You can't go around digging in people's psyches like an S2 interrogator!* She jumped out of her seat, her face burning with fury and embarrassment, and stalked to the bathroom. The door slid shut behind her; she wished she could have slammed it.

What now? Stay in here until they got back to the Peaceship? And what then? *I overreacted,* she thought. He'd hit her dead on with the truth, and she hadn't been able to handle it.

She splashed some water on her face and opened the door again. She hadn't felt him Read her. The implant was processing information in a different way than she had anticipated. She had to use logic and reason to identify what was happening, to analyze the results. *You're hiding,* she told herself. Hiding from what he said; hiding from him. Squaring her shoulders, she returned to her seat. He was studying the control panel, and he didn't look at her when she sat down. Silence hung heavily between them.

"What about you?" she asked quietly. "Has there been anyone since Prime Commander Val?"

She heard him draw a sharp breath. His eyes still wouldn't meet hers. "No."

"While she was still alive, didn't you have any other lovers to turn to once she was gone?"

Now he was wide awake. The glassy look was gone from his eyes, replaced by anger. "No. That's not the way it was for us."

"What do you mean?"

"Just what I said. There was no one else. We had everything we needed with each other."

"That's unusual," she replied cautiously. Actually, it sounded unreal—idealized, perhaps, over time. But the emotion that the conversation evoked seemed to weaken his Blocks, and she was assaulted by an intense wave of raw grief and aching loneliness. The feelings, at least, were as real as they could possibly be.

She felt awful. *I'm so sorry,* she Sent. *I shouldn't have brought it up.*

He said nothing.

She sighed. Try again, try something else. "This isn't going well, is it? Let's talk about the Bridge instead. You asked me why I joined the Bridge. Actually, my work had a lot to do with it. I'd always felt that there were things about our way of life that weren't healthy."

"What do you mean?" Andrei asked. He was waking up. His voice sounded much more alert, though odd in some way—strained and tense. She decided that it was just emotion left over from the previous conversation, and went on with her story.

"The mind/body problem that I mentioned earlier. PAs believing that intellect is everything. Dividing people into intellect versus emotion, and claiming that PAs are the only ones capable of higher thought, that PNs are too emotional, too stuck in their bodies to think clearly and do jobs that require logic and reason." Her voice expressed her anger and contempt. "This is the excuse our society uses for all of its repression and pathology.

"The longer I've spent treating PAs and studying psi-related illness, the more I've come to believe that the society we've based on the life of the mind is itself sick. I started wondering what the psi-sense really means. Does it create a certain type of person, or is it just an excuse to preserve the status quo? I think it's an excuse. Logos Prime, the way it is now, is decadent and static, and I decided I wanted to be part of something that would create change.

"I know the Challenge hasn't done much yet. It's still mostly forming connections, educating people, creating theory and underground literature, and trying to gain support at this point. But if the implant really works, there's a chance that we can really accomplish something."

Andrei didn't answer. Instead, he was coughing and gasping for breath. He leaned forward in his chair, clutching his left arm with his right hand. Heart trouble, for sure. Alarmed, she pulled out her bioscanner again.

She swore at the readings. The restorative turned out to be too strong after all.

"Can you do anything?" His voice was a hoarse whisper.

"It depends. Are we too far away now to set up the distress signal to Sylvain?" He nodded, and her heart sank. "Then there's nothing I can do. If I could, I'd give you a sedative. I think by now it would work. You need to rest, right now."

Andrei shook his head. "Not right now, I'm afraid. But I might be able to create some type of temporary balance." He set the ship on autopilot. Closing his eyes, his whole body went still. After a while, his breathing slowed into an easy, even rhythm, and his hands, which he had balled into fists with the pain, slowly opened. She watched, puzzled. He finally opened his eyes and looked at her. His expression and body language reflected complete calm. She ran a quick scan and studied the readout with curiosity.

"What was that all about?" she asked.

"T'larian Discipline. Meditation techniques that control heart and respiratory functions—at least for a little while. I've been reaching for this level since this whole thing started, but this is the first real success I've had. Maybe it'll hold for the rest of this trip. We're almost there." He nodded at her, but she didn't feel as reassured as she knew he wanted her to be.

"You were saying that the implant would accomplish something," he said, picking up where they'd left off, as though nothing had happened. "What are you hoping for?"

"I'm hoping that when PAs find out that the key thing that separates them from PNs—the psi-sense—can be reproduced artificially, it'll open their minds to the concept of equality. I prefer to see that accomplished peacefully. But if the powers that be still don't get it, the implant will also help us come up with a more effective offense."

"Let's hope you get the chance," Andrei answered.

"Was this trip connected with the Zoryan situation?" Diana asked.

He nodded and started pressing buttons on the main control panel. She could feel the ship bank slightly as he opened a relay. "Savinov to Peaceship. Entering ID codes. Permission to come aboard."

"Permission is granted, Commander. Please use docking ring G2." Ten minutes later, they were stepping out of the cruiser and through the ship-to-ship link. She was right behind Andrei, and she bumped into him as he stopped abruptly.

"Lithras," he said in a pleasant tone of voice. "To what do I owe this special attention?"

"You know full well why we're here, Commander Savinov." One of the two Glendine females—Lithras A and B, Heads of Administrative Operations, Diana finally remembered Sylvain telling her—spoke sharply at him. "While there are no rules that dictate when you may leave the Peaceship and where you may go, there are strict rules governing the use of bodyguards at all times."

"Bodyguards at all times!" the other one echoed. They both blinked their disapproval. "You have violated this rule in the past, Commander, and you have violated it again today."

"Violated it again today!" the first one, Lithra A, continued. They shook their heads at the same time and in the same direction. Diana tried not to gape at this performance. She shot a glance at Andrei. His expression was politely attentive, but she knew his mind was elsewhere.

"As you well know, there have been attempts against your life on more than one occasion," Lithra B continued. "The Alliance Council is fully within its rights to insist that you take at least one bodyguard with you whenever you leave the ship."

"One bodyguard with you whenever you leave the ship!" Lithra A said. "You informed the officer on duty that Mr. Dulaire would be accompanying you. We were most surprised and distressed when Mr. Dulaire contacted us inquiring as to your whereabouts."

Syl usually covers for me. One more thing I screwed up. Diana didn't react as she Received this message from Andrei.

"I don't suppose you'd be willing to count Doctor Zarev as a bodyguard," Andrei said.

Lithras A and B just stared at him. "Commander, we have recorded this incident in your file. The Alliance Council may choose to issue a reprimand, as they have before, but we have recommended that they consider more serious action to convince you to change your behavior."

"More serious action to convince you to change your behavior! We hope they will listen to us this time."

The hell you say, Andrei Sent to Diana. He nodded politely at them. "Very well, Lithras. I apologize for any disturbance I may have caused. I'll try not to let it happen again."

Lithras' heads snapped toward each other, then in unison toward him. "You'll try …?"

But it was no use; Andrei was out the door, Diana following close behind him. She caught up to him, and they headed for his quarters in silence. She could Sense the tension as he deliberately turned his mind to getting on with whatever had sent him into space, without a bodyguard—or anything else he'd needed.

"You have twenty messages, Commander Savinov," his desk reported. "One is priority black—"

"Decode the black, and hold the rest," he snapped. He activated his desk's holo-screen. It glowed with black and purple iridescent light, and columns of gold numbers appeared as the desk started decryption procedures.

Diana looked at him with astonishment. "What do you think you're doing? I told you, you have to get some sleep."

He shook his head. "I have too much to do right now."

She was infuriated. "You'll be out of commission a lot longer if you don't listen to what your body is trying to tell you. I guess this is why your sister said you're more like a PA than some PAs we know!"

He didn't even look at her. "Doctor. The flight was interesting. Thanks for your help. You're dismissed."

Smug bastard, she thought. *The hell* you *say, Commander.* Pulling up her strongest Blocks, she slipped a spray unit out of her bag and programmed it with a fast-acting sedative, her hands in her lap to disguise what she was doing. "I need to talk to you, Andrei. Can you turn that off for one second and listen to me?" she asked.

He sighed, then turned off the screen. "What is it?" he asked, finally looking up. She reached across the desk and sprayed the sedative she'd prepared directly in his face. It was just a puff of air, really, but he gave a cry of shocked outrage, as if she'd sprayed ice water at him.

"That was a mistake," he snapped. "You have no idea what's going on here—what I need to do." He got up and went around his desk toward her. "Give me the antidote, and we'll discuss this like reasonable—" He broke off, squeezing his eyes shut and pressing a hand against his forehead. "What was I saying?"

"You were telling me how tired you are, and that you're going straight to bed," she replied sweetly.

"I was not," he snapped. He swayed and rubbed his eyes. "You're sneaky."

"And you're stubborn. I know better than you what you need right now. Are you going to get into bed yourself, or am I going to have to drag your unconscious body in there?"

Muttering under his breath, he made his way into the bedroom. As he sat on the edge of the bed to take off his boots, she wondered if he was going to fall on his face. Finally, he lay back. "I can't believe you did this …" The sentence trailed off, and his breathing steadied and deepened as his eyes closed.

She sat on the edge of the bed and scanned him. Satisfied with the readings, she lowered the lights. For a moment, she just sat there, watching him. Slowly, she reached out her hand and brushed it lightly across his forehead. There was no reaction. She smoothed the hair away from his face, then gently traced the line of his cheekbone with her fingertips. Just as she was about to take her hand away, she felt his fingers touch her, and she froze. His hand covered her own, and his fingers tightened on hers. After what felt like an eternity, they got heavier and slipped away.

She was shaken. What had she been thinking of? Hopefully he wouldn't remember, or if he did, he'd think it had been a dream. She left the room quickly, not daring to look back.

* * *

The sensation was one of falling, but not quickly. Drifting. Diana's fingers slipped away as he moved; he couldn't hold onto them. Drifting gently down … to where?

Slowly, ever so slowly, he turned onto his side. He felt again the warmth of a woman's fingers in his, but they were much larger, stronger fingers—hands he knew as well as he knew his own. He tried to open his eyes, but they felt glued together. "Shh, it's all right," she reassured him. It was a calm, strong voice with a slight musical edge; he could hear laughter in the grace notes of that voice. His heart contracting, he was finally able to open his eyes and stare into Kylara's face ...

Which was so close to his that he could kiss her without moving a muscle. Afterward, as he drew back, he stared into the glowing, blue-green eyes that he'd lost himself in for so many years—that he'd felt lost without for the past six months. Putting his arms around her to draw her closer, he ran his hands through her hair, his breath a moan as he drew the long, red-gold strands out around him. Her arms tightened around him, kissing him again until his breath was gone, then slowly drawing away. So slowly; everything was still happening in slow motion. He leaned back against the pillow, staring at her with wide, stunned eyes and trying to think through the drug-induced fog in his head.

"I've dreamed about you so many times," he whispered. He couldn't get his voice to work. "This feels different somehow. Very different. I don't understand."

"Maybe this isn't a dream," Kylara offered.

"It's got to be. But it feels so real." Something about this was deeply unsettling, almost frightening. Something wasn't right.

"What are you afraid of? Do you think you're going crazy?"

"Short trip that would be," he muttered. Then he said, "What makes you think I'm afraid?"

"Because I still know you, love of mine. Nothing can change that." Her smile was gentle, heart-stopping—the smile he knew so well, that no one in her Command had seen. None of them had known her, like no one knew him. The only recognition they'd ever had for their true selves had come from each other. The old term of endearment burned, the way her fingers burned as they touched his face. He couldn't hear her mind working; he was grateful for that.

"You know about the implant? That I'm telepathic now?"

"Yes. Is that what's frightening you?"

"Among other things." His eyes closed briefly, and he struggled to open them. He didn't want to lose even a moment of this dream. "The Settlement ... do you know about the Settlement?"

She nodded. "I wouldn't have seen you choosing a second career as a diplomat."

"It wasn't my choice."

"But you're good at it. Of course. Like anything else you decide to take on."

"That doesn't matter now. They're getting ready to start it all over again, Kylara." It hurt to say her name: a sharp, twisting pain. "They have an ally of some kind, called Ashahr. I don't know where it's from or what it wants. But it appears that Ashahr is working with militant Zoryans who've managed to get control of at least part of the Hegemony's government, in order to undermine Settlement negotiations." Why was he telling her all this nonsense, instead of how much he missed her, how hard it was to live without her? It seemed to come out without thought.

"How does Ashahr operate?"

Why was she asking him this? "I'm not sure, but I know telepathy is involved. Either Ashahr is telepathic and has a mindlink with its Zoryan allies—or its servants; I'm not sure who's doing what to whom here—or has provided a way for them to become telepathic themselves. Hopefully the implant will help me figure it out and defeat it." He sighed. "If it doesn't defeat me first. But that's not the whole story. There are collaborators at work—"

"Really? What are they doing? What is their goal?"

"They're stockpiling weapons for Zoryan rearmament, in exchange for ... well, I'm not sure yet who they are and what they've been promised. But I have some ideas, and I know what direction to look in—"

"Do you really?"

"What do you mean?" He blinked with confusion. What a strange thing for her to say, and what a strange way to say it: as if she was challenging him. He shrugged it off; who could explain a dream, and why was he wasting their precious time together talking about this stuff, as if she could still help him? He reached for her again, his pulse quickening.

"So you think you understand what is happening, Andrei. What do you *think* you know?"

This stopped him cold. The fear he'd forgotten about slammed back into him, full force. Something was wrong— more than wrong. He pulled his hand away as if it had been burned. "What should I understand?" he asked carefully. "Who are you?"

There was no answer. The air around him seemed to have thickened. His vision wavered, and his breathing became more labored; it seemed as if he were underwater. As he watched in horror, the color of Kylara's eyes started to change: the irises dissolved, leaving only black pupils that expanded to fill the eye sockets. Her eyes turned into pits of darkness. Speechless with fear, he tried to move away, but he couldn't even lift a finger.

She smiled. Four rows of Zoryan-style razor-sharp, chromium teeth glinted against a background of gaping blackness. *Commander Savinov.* The whisper-voice sounded like metal scraping against metal. The lips didn't move. *I am pleased to meet you at last. You are much feared amongst my newest people. Yet now that I can see into your mind, it is not what I anticipated. Your military strategies were bold, brilliant, and ruthless, yet I do not sense triumph. I sense remorse and a great weariness, a darkness, poisoning your very soul. Perhaps you will be defeated this time, or perhaps you just need a new goal.*

He couldn't find his voice, but he could still use his mind. *What did you have in mind, Ashahr?*

The metallic scraping sound accelerated for a second, giving Andrei the impression that it had actually laughed. *You can rule the Six, Commander, and the Hegemony as well. You can do with them what you choose. Your power could be unlimited.*

As long as I play your game, Andrei Sent. *What game is that, Ashahr? What will you do? Rule them all through me?*

You can have her back, you know. You know how it feels. You see how real this dream can be. You can have whatever it is you want most. Andrei gasped, his back arching reflexively with the sudden piercing sensation of pleasure singing along his nerve endings. There was no question that it was Kylara's touch and that the last six months had been the bad dream, not this, not this …

He struggled to regain his senses. *What's your dream, Ashahr? Who are you? What are you going to do with all this power, once you have it?*

The feeling of pleasure abruptly vanished, replaced by equally sharp pain and terror as Kylara/Ashahr raked her/its hand through his hair and pulled back his head so that he was staring into the void of its eyes. It was much stronger than he was, and the constant shifts of emotion left him off balance, making it harder to anticipate its next move and plan his response. It was a mindgame that would be hard to win— maybe even impossible …

Or you can have hell in the form of a madness that will never leave you. The gift of sight will destroy your mind, Commander. It has already begun to do so. Only I can save you.

Anger helped Andrei Send thought through his fear. *And what's your price for this so-called salvation? Betrayal of the Alliance?*

Ashahr appears in dreams, he remembered. He needed to wake up. Struggling to regain consciousness, he finally managed to move again, and he pushed himself away from it, toward the edge of the bed. Damn, he was slow. Kylara/Ashahr was watching him, mouth twisted in what seemed to be a smile of malicious amusement. He groped under the mattress for his disruptor pistol.

Who will you destroy with that? Andrei, you cannot hurt me. But oh, how you can hurt yourself!

Despair. Crushing despair. He was five years old again, realizing fully for the first time how different he was from everyone around him, PA and PN—that he truly belonged nowhere. He was thirteen, listening to Astrid and Coraline sobbing as he packed his case under the mocking eyes of the S2 officers who had come to destroy his family. Then Coraline was standing in front of him at the Group Home—the first time he'd seen her since he'd been taken away—telling him that Astrid was dead by her own hand. The few secret visits he and his mother had managed had shown him the depths of Astrid's despair, but his lack of surprise didn't ease the pain. He saw the faces of friends and comrades who'd died during the war; he remembered the death vigils he'd kept. He was twenty-eight, moving among the dead and the dying—what was left of the fleet he'd sent into space two days earlier. And now, seven years later, it was six months ago, and he was watching the replay of *Windrider's* destruction, the explosion burning from his eyes through his brain and into his heart like the flashbomb that had burned through him. He felt each moment with first-time intensity.

And now he was doomed to repeat it all: to live it over and over as the banked flames of war flared again. Because he wouldn't be able to stop it. He wasn't smart enough, strong enough. The implant would twist his brain into some unrecognizable thing, and his mind would be useless, useless …

He pushed himself backward off the bed as his hand closed around the weapon. Suddenly, he couldn't see her/it. He turned in a tight circle, trying to aim at something.

"Andrei, no!" a voice yelled. "Lights on full!" White light blasted him, and he swore, still trying to find a target. When he could finally see through the haze, Sylvain was gaping at him in horror, and the disruptor pistol was pointed at his own head.

Chapter 13

The observation post on Praxis was not First Circle's idea. No one on Logos Prime believed that the Zoryans could get that close to their homeworld, but the Alliance Council had ordered Logos Prime's governing body to put it there as part of the war effort. Thus the small, barren moon held a small, barren monitoring station. Small as it was, the station was the largest structure on Praxis. Clustered around it were a number of one-room domes. These were private residences for the station's workers, and studios or retreats for the few high-level PAs who didn't mind traversing a short-hop pass-through point and thought there was some novelty in having their own private spaces on the moon.

Nick slipped through the security grid on Praxis with his usual ease, thanks to his fellow Challenge member, Marek Lugano. Marek worked the third shift, monitoring Octant Four of the grid. It was the perfect position as far as the Challenge was concerned: he knew who was coming in and going out, and he could turn his attention away from the boards just long enough for a Free Raider cruiser to sneak past him.

Nick had arranged for his arrival to coincide with the end of Marek's shift. He'd set down his cruiser on the inner edge of a crater beyond the monitoring station's perimeter, and he watched through his remote viewscreen as Marek exchanged a nod and a few words with his replacement, put on his atmosphere suit, and headed out to his hovercar. He continued to watch as the vehicle made its way toward him. When it got close enough for short-range sensors to pick it up, he gave his own atmosphere suit a final check and stepped out of the cruiser to meet him. Marek grinned in greeting, and he gave Nick a mock salute as the little hovercar adjusted itself to his weight and floated off again.

Marek's dome wasn't nearly as luxurious as Corie's artist friend's had been, Nick thought, but the absence of weird art made it far more comfortable. He pulled out an s/n wand, which immediately glowed blue. He was just about to draw his disruptor pistol when an amused female voice drawled, "Nicky, Nicky, put that pointy thing away."

"You're early, Fiona."

"Early bird catches the worm, my friend."

"I've seen birds on Erlande, but what the hell's a worm?"

"Something to do with hydroponics. It's just some old saying." Fiona Callahan stood there in the middle of the room, arms folded, grinning at him. Still beautiful, he thought, remembering with wistful fondness the affair they'd had years ago. They hugged briefly—with friendship now, nothing more—and all three sat against the low cushions in the middle of the room as Marek activated a privacy screen around them.

Like all PNs who were Challenge members, Fiona had two identities. The one that allowed her to make this run to Praxis was a shuttle pilot ferrying supplies and passengers to the moon at regular intervals. Her other, real identity was both smuggler and teacher. The items smuggled were her tools for teaching: litdiscs and technology provided by Bridge members that was sometimes easier for her to acquire when they were left on Praxis than they would be from hundreds of levels above her in the Core.

Nick knew that, unlike himself and most of the other Challenge members he knew, Fiona didn't care much for the adventure—the challenge—of smuggling. No, what she cared about was her teaching. She cared about opening the minds of PNs whose limited knowledge and lack of meaningful life experience had resulted in limited understanding of their circumstances and even less hope of change. If enough of them were able to learn and grow, eventually they would have to believe that they didn't deserve to be the servants of Psi-Actives—and the Challenge would spread like wildfire.

Just in case information wasn't enough to win their war, she also smuggled weapons used for acts of sabotage, which were procured by Nick or other Raiders who sympathized with the Challenge—or who merely had something to sell. "So, Nick, where are the goods?" she asked.

"On Selas," he replied, smiling at Fiona's and Marek's puzzled looks. "I had Marek let me know when you were making a run, so I could talk to you, Fi. I don't have anything for you to take back right now, except information. And a proposal for the others." Quickly he gave them an edited version of his trip to Selas, concentrating on the cache of weapons. As always, he didn't mention his contact with Andrei. None of his fellow Challenge members—or fellow Free Raiders, for that matter—knew that his brother was the Peacekeeper. One of the few things he and Andrei agreed on was the need to keep their connection as hidden as possible. He also decided to leave out the Nonaggression Pact—after all, that was Andrei's problem.

"So you don't know who these weapons belong to," Marek remarked when he had finished. "Or what they're supposed to be used for."

Nick shook his head. "Assuming none of the Six is getting ready to go to war against each other, there are two choices.—either a group like us trying to start something, or Zoryan collaborators."

"You know of anyone, or any group, that fits either description?" Fiona asked.

"I've got some ideas, but not really. I've still got some fact finding to do," Nick replied. "But that's not the point. The question for us is, do we try to get these weapons for ourselves?"

"You mean try to buy them from whoever is doing the collecting, or try to steal them?" Fiona asked.

Nick nodded, grinning. "Yes."

"Well, which do you mean?"

Marek laughed. "I think he means whichever works. Right, Nick?" His face turned sober then. "Yeah, well, the problem with that approach is that whoever's capable of putting together a stash like that is probably a pretty dangerous opponent. And it's not likely we can scrounge up enough credit to buy them, either."

Nick shrugged this off. "If we could pull it off, think of what we'd have! Real weapons, and enough of them to make a difference."

"So we'd have hardcore war weapons, Nick—so what? What would we do with them, destroy the Core? We live there too, remember?" Fiona was angry. "It's one thing to blow out a computer and shut down a work assignment station for a day, or liberate a Reconditioning facility, but to make war on part of the population of Logos Prime … I want to see them change, not see them die."

"Some may have to die in order to see change, Fiona. You know that as well as I do."

"No, Nick, I don't. You may find this hard to believe, but not everyone thinks like you."

They glared at each other as the impasse lengthened. Finally Marek broke the charged silence. "What about the Peacekeeper?" he asked.

Nick was startled by the question. "What about him?" he asked. He was annoyed. Why had he bothered asking these people anything? He should have just put a raid together and presented them with it as a done deal.

"Stockpiling war weapons is illegal under the Settlement. I've heard that the Peacekeeper has his own spy network. Do you think he knows about this?" Marek asked.

"If he does, why hasn't he confiscated the weapons?" Fiona asked in turn.

"Maybe he doesn't know whose weapons they are either," Marek suggested. "Maybe he's leaving them where they are just long enough to try to trap whoever is accumulating them. So if we went for them, he'd trap us instead."

"Savinov is a Logos Prime PN—" Fiona started.

"Who's never expressed the slightest sympathy for the Challenge," Nick reminded her. "Marek's right. We have to be careful of him too." He turned to Fiona, gazing steadily at her. "Fiona, I know we don't all agree on how to get there, but we do agree on where we're going—freedom for PNs to live our own lives, make our own choices, and own our fair share of the wealth of Logos Prime. Maybe just having these kinds of weapons would be enough to force them to listen to us."

Fiona sighed. "All right, Nick. You find out who they belong to and figure out how we could get them, and I'll talk to other Challenge leaders and find out what they want to do." She ran a hand through her short, auburn hair and looked at her chronometer. "Time to go."

Marek got up, nodding. "For you too, Nick. There's going to be a glitch in the security grid's main computer in"—he looked at his chronometer—"twelve minutes. The backup system should come on just after you clear the grid."

"As long as it doesn't come on just before," Nick muttered, still feeling frustrated. He got to his feet and found Fiona standing in front of him, her dark eyes searching his face. Suddenly she smiled and kissed him on the cheek.

"Don't go away mad, Nicky," she murmured. "I promise I'll relay your idea fairly. Who knows? You may yet get a chance to blow something up."

Chapter 14

"How did you get a visual black-coded channel?" Diana asked.

"I'm on Praxis right now, with Rowan, and the woman working the security grid is a Challenge member," Coraline told her.

"Rowan?"

"The artist whose studio we used to meet Andrei and Nick."

"I hope Rowan's not there right now, Coraline." Diana's voice was still guarded.

"No, he's not." Coraline studied the image in front of her. "You look exhausted, Diana. Is that an occupational requirement out there on the Peaceship?"

Diana sighed. "I think it is. The last couple of weeks have been very stressful."

"From studying the data you've been sending me, I'd imagine so." Coraline paused, thinking. "To be truthful, I'm not exactly sure what to make of it all—whether the experiment is a success or whether it should be aborted. Or both."

"I've been thinking the same thing," Diana answered. "In some ways, it's been successful beyond what I imagined. Andrei can Sense feelings, Read minds, and Send and Receive thoughts. He can build and maintain Blocks." She broke off, shaking her head. "In fact, that's his obsession—building stronger and stronger Blocks. I know you think of him as self-protective, Coraline, but this goes way beyond that. I'm sure he's doing it with a goal in mind, but he won't tell me what that is."

She shook her head again, but this time Coraline got the impression that she was trying to clear her head rather than express frustration. Diana continued, "So he has all the PA abilities, but he can't seem to bring them under complete control. Which at first I thought was a training issue, but now I believe the reason is that he's experiencing the thoughts and feelings of others with much greater intensity than most PAs have to deal with."

She turned directly toward the viewscreen, and Coraline was surprised at how troubled she looked. "Coraline, you know how we're raised and trained to deal with the psi-sense. Our emotional temperatures are deliberately lowered. We're taught from birth to screen out multiple sensory inputs, especially emotion-based inputs. That's why so many PAs are such robots. But we've both known—and I've tried to either study or treat—PAs who can't handle their psi-sense, who were vulnerable for some reason and went mad with the pressure. There are times when I'm really afraid this'll end up that way if I don't stop the experiment."

Coraline was dismayed but unsurprised. The data Diana had sent her from her work on the Peaceship with Andrei was filled with anomalies; there were too many outlier variables where there shouldn't be, too many places where tolerance levels clearly had been exceeded. She asked, "What does Andrei think?"

Diana swore under her breath, making Coraline smile to herself. As if she didn't know the answer to that one. "You were right about one thing concerning your brother—he's impossible! He won't talk about how he feels, won't talk about the experiment, and like I said, he's building this elaborate Shielding mechanism that effectively shuts me out of his mind.

It's only when I threaten to abort the whole thing that he lets me run my tests or answers any questions at all." She looked away from the screen then, her voice and posture revealing her feelings of defeat. "I think he's avoiding me. Sylvain's been helpful, though."

"Who?"

"Andrei's Executive Assistant, Sylvain Dulaire. He's been with him a long time, and he's worried enough about the whole thing that he's been willing to talk to me."

"And what's he telling you?"

"Andrei's experiencing physical symptoms that aren't part of the program. Severe headaches that come and go quickly and with no warning. Dizzy spells. Mood swings, irritability, poor concentration. But Sylvain says this could all come from overwork, stress, and lack of sleep. He says Andrei's been sleeping even less than usual."

Coraline shrugged, partly to get the tension out of her shoulders and partly from frustration. "But since he's being so evasive, you can't determine the origin of the symptoms."

"That's right." Diana hesitated. "I've thought about pushing harder on the threat to end the experiment, but neither Sylvain or I think that will work. My feeling is that if he Read my intention to remove the implant, he'd totally cut off my access to him."

"Couldn't you Block him from Reading you?" Coraline asked.

Diana looked grim. "Not anymore, I'm afraid. I don't think Robert Jaxome could Block Andrei from Reading him at this point."

Coraline sat back in her chair, not knowing what to say. An image suddenly flashed in her mind of Andrei as a solemn little boy, holo-sketching and daydreaming alone in his room. But his face had always lit up when he saw her. Suddenly she was overwhelmed with guilt: what had she done to him? If something went really, permanently wrong, how would she be able to live with herself? She struggled against her fears. "I'm sorry, Diana, I missed that. What did you say?"

"I asked if you thought it would do any good for you to talk to him, since he isn't willing to listen to me."

"I'm certainly willing to try, but I'm pretty sure it wouldn't help," Coraline answered. "Unless you assume he's already crazy, he has a reason for acting like this. Even though I haven't known him as an adult, as a child Andrei always had a reason for what he did. It just wasn't obvious to the rest of us. Are you sure you're getting all the information you can out of that assistant of his? If they've worked together closely for a long time and he's completely loyal to Andrei, he may know more than he's letting on."

Diana was silent for a moment, obviously thinking it over. "You may be right, but he's already pretty conflicted about going behind Andrei's back. That doesn't mean it's not a good idea, though. I'll see what I can do."

Coraline watched her closely. "What about you, Diana? Is there any possibility that you could get Andrei to trust you any better?"

Diana looked away from the screen again. "I don't know," she finally answered. Coraline could hear the weariness in her voice, even through the coding. "I sent you data from the trip he took through a pass-through point unmedicated, but what I didn't tell you was that when we got back to the Peaceship, I thought he needed to rest, and he wouldn't listen, so I sedated him against his will." She ran a hand through her bristle of hair and sighed. "He never said anything about it, but I don't think he's trusted me since then ..." Her voice trailed off.

"It hurts," Coraline prompted gently.

"It hurts," Diana agreed, "because you were right about something else besides him being impossible to deal with—I do care about him. Not too smart, right?"

Coraline tried to think of something to say, but she couldn't. Still mulling over a response, she started as a red light began flashing on the board in front of her. "We're out of time, Diana. Just one more thing. If Andrei's shutting you out, I doubt it's because you forced him to get some sleep that he desperately needed. He's not the grudge-holding type. Look in another direction for the answer."

"What do you mean?"

"I mean that you were the one who told me that Andrei stayed away from me all those years in order to protect me. Maybe he cares for you too. Maybe he's trying to protect you in some way."

Diana froze, her eyes widening with astonishment. Coraline could tell that this truly hadn't occurred to her. "From what?"

"From whatever he's trying to Block."

Chapter 15

The Settlement still held, but to Andrei, the next war had already begun. Inside his head.

The Disciplines didn't help. Neither did the kind of drugs he had access to through his medical dispenser. Access to, that is, without consulting with either Djagdisj, the Peaceship's T'larian doctor (who knew nothing about the implant), or Diana. He'd tried some of the favored PA intoxicants but found them sweet, light, and worthless. Luckily, after a while he'd discovered that he could drink *livrash* again without feeling sick, and some of it now and then helped quiet the interminable noise from what felt like the thoughts and emotions of everyone in the universe reverberating inside his head. But he didn't dare do it too often or drink too much; he knew that Ashahr was waiting for him if he let down his guard.

Ashahr was real; he was sure of it. The thought that it was capable of penetrating his subconscious mind was so terrifying that at times he wanted to believe that the encounter had really been a dream—or a delusion caused by the implant. But he couldn't convince himself that it hadn't happened.

He was beyond tired; he had left tired behind an eternity ago. He was too frightened of the consequences to allow himself to sleep deeply anymore. His work took twice as long as it should have, as he struggled to focus on the tasks at hand.

This was a big problem, as the workload would have been daunting even if he'd been in peak condition to begin with.

For one thing, there was little question that the War Border was heating up: too many "incidents" were being reported to be mere coincidence. He and Sesna-Goveril, the Erlandian Prime Commander who'd replaced Kylara, clashed repeatedly about how to handle them. Sesna-Goveril wanted to strike back, hard; Andrei was running out of arguments in favor of waiting. Besides hoping to avert war through the negotiations, he had Nick's news to consider: the Alliance was vulnerable to attack from within as well. He'd decided not to tell Sesna-Goveril about this until either he or Nick finished uncovering what was really going on—a decision that didn't help him make his case, but one he felt was necessary. If the Alliance Council and the Military heard about this, they'd declare war immediately, and Andrei knew they weren't ready.

For another, he had less than four weeks left to prepare for negotiations with Zorya, and for what he now knew would be a direct confrontation with Ashahr as well as with the Hegemony. Addressing the demands of the new negotiating team was only part of it, and the easier part at that. The hard part was figuring out how to Read Zoryan minds. Based on the little information they had about the structure and functioning of the Zoryan brain, he and Diana had put together what they believed was a fairly accurate model of how Zoryans thought. It ended up looking like an interlocking set of spirals, with thought patterns that were layered and combined in ways that seemed impossible to Read through. Worst of all, there was no way to test whether their theories made any sense at all in the real world.

It won't work. It won't work. He wasn't used to thinking about failure. Yes, there'd been battles he'd directed that had been lost; yes, there were negotiations he'd conducted that hadn't accomplished what he'd hoped for. But real, true failure, the kind that couldn't be fixed? Even though the war had not been won, at least it had been brought to a draw after all those years of fighting. So with the exception of Kylara's death, the answer was no. But thoughts of failure—and its consequences—kept passing through his mind, sometimes so intensely that they paralyzed him. Was this his own doing, or the implant, or Ashahr?

He tried not to think too often about what the implant was doing to him: whether the physical, mental, and emotional symptoms he was experiencing with frightening intensity were telling him that it was time to let Diana take the thing out before it killed him. At least knowing it was there, he had a chance of dealing with Ashahr—assuming that the Shield he was building worked the way he hoped it would. If it worked, it would give him half a chance of meeting the Hegemony on its own ground.

He especially tried not to think about Diana. He didn't want Ashahr to become aware of her existence; he didn't want to pull her into his battle. In spite of all her efforts, he knew how she felt about him. And his own feelings? Confusion, mostly. His attraction to her—once he'd stopped denying it to himself—felt disloyal to Kylara. The truth was that it didn't matter how he felt; it was too dangerous even to think about it.

Quickly he shifted his thoughts away from her and back to the task at hand. Besides fighting with his psi-sense and preparing for war, there were the everyday tasks of the Peacekeeping Mission to deal with. He'd reassigned as many of these as possible to his staff (much to their astonishment, as delegating was not one of his strong points), but there were a few things no one else could do. Chief amongst these were intra-Six disputes that came before the Alliance Council for resolution. As Special Representative to the Council—and its most accomplished negotiator—he was often asked to do arbitration of various Intra-Six disputes. He'd been able to postpone a number of hearings by telling the Council that he was too busy with upcoming negotiations, but this business with T'lar and Erlande just wasn't going away.

He gazed at the holo-model of the Six across the room. T'lar was closest to the War Border, with Erlande its nearest neighbor. Erlande, untouched by Zorya, was a lush blue and green paradise. T'lar, on the other hand, had been nearly destroyed by the Hegemony. Fireballs created by nuclear blasts had incinerated most of the surface, leaving a layer of soot and ash that smothered whatever plant life remained from the initial destruction. Alliance technology had managed to patch together a livable atmosphere and remove the toxins from the soil, but the place was now a chain of deserts studded with mountains of rock. The large bodies of water had all dried up, leaving dust storms in their place.

Even before the catastrophe, T'lar's technology base had been limited. An austere, religious people, T'larians had some unusual empathic and visionary capabilities, which they used primarily for healing. Having lived off the land, they could do little to support themselves in the absence of their planet's natural resources. For many years, the Alliance gave them whatever they needed to survive, but as the war dragged on and the economies of the Six became strained with the effort of supporting it, support for T'lar's plight dwindled. Finally it was agreed that T'lar had to earn its way, or the population would be resettled on one or more Alliance worlds.

Erlande—and water—held the keys to solving the problem. T'larians had been able to develop some desert plants into the sole cure for several common Erlandian diseases. T'lar had them pay for those medicines with water, with enough left over after the drugs were produced to allow the small settlements representing what was left of the population to move toward self-sufficiency again.

This barter arrangement worked well until recently, when Erlande discovered ways to manufacture the most important class of drugs synthetically. T'lar still needed the water, but

Erlande now wanted to be paid in credits rather than in barter, and T'lar had few credits to spare.

The Alliance Council basically washed its hands of the situation. No one wanted to support T'lar anymore. Both T'lar's and Erlande's leaders requested arbitration. In working on a solution, Andrei had been trying to persuade Erlande to accept a short-term combination of credits and barter, and to persuade T'lar that it had to accept testing of the Alliance's more radical technologies for reusing water (even though there was evidence that they might further damage what was left of the planet's fragile ecosystem) and find new ways of making money to buy the water it needed. Erlande was reluctant to change its mind, and T'lar was reluctant to change its ways.

And now they'd submitted a second request for binding arbitration, and he needed to respond. They wanted a hearing this week. Shaking his head with a sigh, he started writing up another order of postponement. Perhaps he could get the Council to provide another extension of emergency funding to T'lar. Perhaps he could hire some Free Raiders to steal water from Erlande. Perhaps he could just put his head down for a minute or two and rest his eyes without actually sleeping …

He was startled by a tone on the desk's comm board. "Visual message coming through, priority gold," it told him.

"Origin?"

"Sanctuary."

Damn. He hauled himself to his feet just as the image of the Zh'ladar materialized before him. A tall, imposing figure three times his age, the Zh'ladar radiated vitality. Wearing a red robe: male, this cycle.

"A pleasure to see you again, Commander Savinov."

'Commander Savinov'. Not a social call. "The pleasure is mine, Your Grace." Andrei executed the complicated bow due T'lar's spiritual leader as best he could, but dizziness overtook him, and he ended up on both knees instead of one.

"That was somewhat less than graceful, Andrei." Somehow the Zh'ladar managed to sound both amused and concerned at the same time.

"I guess I'm out of practice," he replied, dodging the unasked question. "This is a coincidence, Your Grace. I was just reviewing T'lar and Erlande's request for arbitration."

"That is why I am contacting you, Commander." Back in formal mode again. "Qerej has informed me that you are considering another postponement. This would represent significant hardship for the T'larian people."

Andrei didn't react. "I understand that, Your Grace. But if T'lar and Erlande were willing to consider letting the full Council decide the matter by vote instead of relying on me to arbitrate, it would go much faster." How could he force him to change his mind? He folded his arms across his chest. "I sincerely hope, Your Grace, that you haven't chosen Peacekeeper arbitration because you believe that our personal relationship will cause T'lar to receive a more favorable decision than if the Council were to vote. I assure you, it wouldn't be to T'lar's advantage if I were to act with special favor on your behalf."

"I am well aware of that, Commander Savinov." The Zh'ladar's voice was disapproving. "Frankly, I am surprised you would even bring it up. I know that performing arbitration is not your favorite pursuit, but the reason your services are in such demand is that your intellect, your judgment and, your objectivity are highly valued. I am also surprised that you seem to have forgotten that Erlande, who knows full well of our friendship, has joined with us to request your services. They believe that you will do the right thing, and so do we."

Andrei swallowed a dull, sinking feeling that was a mixture of embarrassment and despair at being trapped into accepting the Zh'ladar's request. How could he possibly handle another negotiation right now? How could he possibly turn his back on T'lar after all the work he'd done to keep the planet alive? He massaged the bridge of his nose with stiff fingers. Words jammed in his head, preventing him from crafting an articulate response. And in back of it all, he heard echoes of Ashahr's laughter mocking him …

"Andrei, please tell me what is wrong," the Zh'ladar said gently. "If you are ill, in body or in spirit, perhaps I can help you."

As usual, the cool voice was hypnotically relaxing. He pulled himself together and made an attempt to resist it. "I'm just tired," he finally managed to respond.

"I can see that you are completely exhausted rather than just tired, but I do not believe that is the whole problem," the Zh'ladar answered. "Something has happened to you. What is it? Do you no longer trust me to keep your confidence?"

Andrei vaguely wondered whether the Zh'ladar could Read his mind. "I wish I could tell you, but I can't," he said. "Please, don't ask anymore. Maybe later, when it's all over, we can talk about it." He straightened up and pushed his mask of formality back in place. "All right, Your Grace. As always, you've been most convincing. I will review documents and hold a formal hearing at the end of the week. Sylvain will inform the Council today and collect the files."

"T'lar is grateful, Commander Savinov," the Zh'ladar replied. He didn't push Andrei for further explanation, for which Andrei was relieved.

Andrei stared at the order of postponement he'd been writing. The words blurred in front of his eyes. He deleted it with a savage stab of his finger and summoned Sylvain.

"What? A hearing on the water dispute now?" Andrei Sensed Sylvain's incredulous dismay at Andrei's bad judgment, laced with doubt about his ability to handle it. "But there's no time to spare. Too much else going on! What about the—?"

Andrei smashed his fist down on the top of the desk in fury. "I'm not interested in your opinion, Sylvain! I don't need you to remind me of my responsibilities—I'm far more aware of them than you are. Just do what I say, damn it, and don't question me anymore!"

They stared at each other in shock. Andrei couldn't remember ever losing his temper with his Exec like that. When he felt that angry, his habit was to say as little as possible, as quietly as possible, until he had his feelings under control again. But old habits didn't seem to count for much these days. He didn't know which was worse, the pain in his hand or the sharp, sudden pain stabbing his temples. He swore under his breath. Sylvain took a step toward him, but Andrei waved him away as he fought to pull himself together.

"Forgive me, Syl. I didn't mean to shout at you like that. It's just that ..."

"It's all right, Andrei. I understand." Andrei Read the lie behind the comforting words. Sylvain didn't understand; he was frightened.

He wasn't the only one.

It was only after Andrei was alone again that he thought he should have asked the Zh'ladar if he knew anything about Ashahr. He and Diana had searched the datanets of five of the Six to see if there was any mention of the entity in the history or mythology—religious or otherwise—of any of them. So far, they hadn't uncovered anything, but T'lar didn't have a datanet for them to access remotely. Either he or Sylvain would talk to Qerej when they saw her at the hearing.

For all the good it would do. After all, did it really matter where Ashahr had come from? It was here now, and it wasn't about to leave him alone—at least not until it finished the job that the implant had started, and drove him insane.

Chapter 16

The light above Andrei's door blinked red, and Sylvain pressed his palm against the door. As it slid open, he found himself on T'lar.

He gaped at the size and level of detail of the holo-model that had taken over Andrei's office. He was in a shallow, bowl-shaped plain surrounded by mountain ranges. The plain would have been a lake at one time; he didn't know which one. The mountains, their bald surfaces pitted and scarred, faded off into the middle distance. Reddish-gold light flecked with dust motes didn't go far in making the scene any less stark, probably because Sylvain had been there himself and knew what a desolate place it had become.

He turned away from it and looked around the room with dismay. Andrei's office was generally somewhat cluttered, but this was chaos. In addition to the holo-model, fileviewers of all sizes and flat-rendered T'larian maps and documents covered every surface, including the floor. He shook his head in distaste at the barely touched, congealed dinner, which was still exactly where he'd left it for Andrei. He picked it up and tossed it into the recycler. Sighing, he started to dial up breakfast from the dispenser but realized that it would be futile and selected a nutritional supplement instead. When his boss was in this frame of mind, completely absorbed by something, there was no point in fighting it.

He was completely absorbed, but by what? Yes, the T'lar/Erlande problem was complex. Even more so were the impending negotiations with Zorya. But neither of those were the real problem right now. The real problem was the implant—and maybe Ashahr.

Maybe Ashahr. He recalled, with a shudder of horror, coming in on Andrei during his "dream" of the mysterious entity. What would have happened if he hadn't? Neither of them shared any speculation with each other about how it might have ended, and neither told Diana what had happened. Sylvain had come close once or twice—the woman seemed to genuinely care about Andrei—but Andrei had made it clear that he didn't want her to know. Most likely he was afraid that she'd assume that the implant was responsible for a near-fatal hallucination and abort the experiment. Sylvain wanted this desperately, but he didn't feel like he had the right to make it happen against Andrei's wishes.

Had it been a hallucination? Andrei insisted that it was real. This was the way Ashahr operated, through manipulation of the subconscious. The implant's role hadn't been to give the entity access to his mind, but to give Andrei access to awareness of what Ashahr was doing. Suddenly the idea of removing it was out of the question. Would you take your cruiser into battle without any sensors?

"Good morning, Syl." Andrei was just pulling on the jacket of his formal uniform as he came through the bedroom door. Sylvain took a peek into the bedroom and noticed that the bed hadn't been slept in.

"What's this all about?" he asked, gesturing at the holo-model.

Andrei gazed at it without speaking for several moments. As the silence drew out, Sylvain studied him covertly. Shadows cut lines into Andrei's gaunt, drawn face, darkening the rings under his eyes. Just as he was preparing to repeat the question,

Andrei spoke. "I'm not exactly sure, but I think I'm looking for water."

"What do you mean?"

"Just that. No matter how hard I try to figure out all the angles, my instinct is telling me I've overlooked something." Andrei turned toward him. Sylvain was startled; Andrei's eyes had a strange luminescence, as if he were running a fever. "I'm not sick," he said sharply, and Sylvain winced, trying to swallow his anger at having his mind Read. Damn it, this was what he'd left Logos Prime to get away from! They glared at each other, then each looked away. Stalemate.

"The thing you think you've overlooked is water on T'lar?" Sylvain asked. "What about all the surveys that have been done? Hasn't been any new supply of water discovered in forever."

"I know that," Andrei answered, gesturing to the mass of documents around the room. "I don't have any concrete evidence that anything's been overlooked. Like I said, it's a feeling, more than anything else." He stared at the mountains again. "But it's such a strong feeling, I can't ignore it."

Sylvain felt a pang of fear. "Could it be a suggestion planted by Ashahr?"

"For what purpose?" Andrei asked.

Sylvain shrugged helplessly. "Don't know. Just that it seems so unrealistic. Maybe Ashahr's trying to distract you."

He didn't have to have the empathic Sense to feel Andrei turn cold; he might as well have accused him of being crazy. He decided to change the subject before either of them said something they'd regret. "Andrei, how about some breakfast? You need to eat—keep up your strength."

Andrei shook his head and pressed a button on the desk. The image of the holo-model shredded, and the pieces faded away. He started gathering the fileviewers and flat-renderings. "The Representatives have both arrived, Syl. Let's get this stuff together and get on with it."

Sylvain sighed, exhaling his frustration as he took everything out of Andrei's arms and gave him the nutritional supplement. Andrei drank it in one long swallow, then helped him finish organizing the material. As they got to the door, Andrei stopped. "You go ahead, Syl. Tell them I'll be there in a couple of minutes. And don't forget to ask Qerej if she's ever heard of an entity that calls itself Ashahr."

* * *

The extra minutes didn't help. Andrei sat on the couch, head in his hands. He could feel invisible hands dragging at him, trying to pull him down into the strange dream state he'd struggled against as he worked through the third shift. The Disciplines helped somewhat, but it was like pushing back the tide. Finally he couldn't put it off any longer, and he headed toward the Conference Chamber. He felt lightheaded; the edges of his vision blurred, and the walls of the Peaceship threatened to close in.

He stopped abruptly just outside the door to the Conference Chamber, his heart rate speeding up an instant before his mind could fix on the cause. Fear. No, it was *dread* he Sensed, more than just plain fear. It was as though someone had awakened and found her nightmare to be real. Qerej; the emotion that chilled his blood belonged to Qerej. He focused his mind on her and quickly found what he was looking for.

The source of her fear was Sylvain's question about Ashahr.

Straightening his jacket, head up and eyes forward, he strode into the room. "Greetings to you, Representative Aladair-Turil. Greetings to you, Representative Qerej. I apologize for keeping you both waiting."

The eyes of both Representatives and their assistants were on him as he took his place at the head of the table and gave each of them a quick, perfect bow. Qerej gave him a polite nod of welcome. Her expression was impassive, with no sign of inner turmoil. Aladair-Turil's mane of tentacles unfurled gracefully in his direction. All of the staff members bowed to each other.

That over, Andrei sat down in front of the two piles of documents that Sylvain had left in front of his place. Pushing the pile of fileviewers to one side and moving the flat-rendered maps closer, he started looking for the one he'd used to make the holo-model. After a moment or two (though it could have been longer, as his sense of time was shot to pieces), he felt like he was being watched and looked up. He *was* being watched, by the entire room. He looked back down at the map in bewilderment and dismay. What the hell was he doing?

"I'd like to start by recapping the most recent negotiations," he said, trying to sound more stable and in control than he felt.

"The most recent negotiations failed. That's why we're here today. End of recap." Aladair-Turil's voice boomed, and Andrei winced internally at the sound, though he was careful to show no expression. He was used to the volume of Erlandian voices under normal conditions, but these weren't normal conditions. These days, everything bothered him.

"I understand that, Representative, but I'd like to hear in your own words, and in the words of Representative Qerej, what you tried to accomplish and why you think you were unable to come to an agreement."

'Waste of time," Aladair-Turil growled.

"Nevertheless, it's how we're going to proceed if you want me to arbitrate. Would you care to go first, Representative Aladair-Turil, or do you cede the floor to Representative Qerej?"

"All right, Commander Savinov, have it your way." The Erlandian quickly forgot his objection as he spun out his side of the story. Andrei tried hard to concentrate, but his mind started wandering back to the maps. All night he'd stared at them, trying to match them with geologists' reports that had been made over the years. He'd also gotten hold of some archeologists' reports on lost tribes throughout T'lar's history, matching their projected locations to points on the maps.

The map that had captured his attention was an old topographical study of the Djelat Range. While there were rumors in the texts of an ancient city on the edge of Djelat Lake, there was no evidence that water still existed there. The lake was dead, and the mountains were dead … or were they?

Aladair-Turil's voice faded to meaningless background noise as Andrei took up the flat-rendered map once more. It was large. He pushed everything else aside and spread it out in front of him. "Spotlight," he said softly, activating a light under the table. The map glowed. "Overhead lights off." He didn't even hear the exclamations of the others in the room as the lights obeyed. He stood up and stared down at the map. Breathing deeply, he focused all of his attention on it, traveling the landscape with his mind. Finally he closed his eyes and saw …

He was in a narrow underground passageway: cool, dark, and silent. The walls glowed dimly, and stalactites hung down from the ceiling almost to the top of his head. He reached up; they were slickly wet to his touch. Dimly in the background he could hear some kind of religious chanting in another part of the cave. He followed the sound down the passageway, his hand brushing the wet walls for guidance. Finally the passageway opened into a huge, high-ceilinged cavern. Weaving its way through the sound of the chanting was the sound of rushing water: a waterfall somewhere further into the cavern.

He walked to the edge of a wide, deep pool that was blacker than the darkness surrounding him. Staring into its depths, at first he could see nothing; then, gradually, he noticed faint lights glimmering under the surface. They were bright, golden, oval-shaped lights in pairs, with darker gold centers. Pupils and irises—eyes, he realized. He'd seen this somewhere, sometime before … in the dream he'd had on his trip to meet Nick. Bending over, he dipped his hand into the ice-cold surface of the water. *Who are you?* he Sent.

Welcome, Andrei Savinov. We are glad that you finally heard our call. Many eyes; one mental voice.

I didn't hear anyone call, at least not consciously.

Nevertheless, you are here. You can hear us now.

Whose voice is this?

You are hearing the voice of Unity. There are many of us, as you can see, but we are many in one. We speak with one voice. We think with one mind.

Do you live in the Djelat mountains of T'lar?

No, this is but a point of contact between our star system and yours.

What do you mean?

We are Sending our thoughts, and this image of ourselves, to you from a place too far away for any other type of contact.

How can you send thoughts that far? And how can I receive them?

We can Send them because of what we are, and you can Receive them because of what you are becoming.

Oddly, he felt no fear—no emotion save that of curiosity. *Am I becoming something that can hear you because of the implant?* he sent. *If that's correct, then when it's gone, I won't know you anymore?*

The implant helped you take the first step toward transformation, but you won't need it to complete the work.

What work? he asked. *What transformation?*

Time is short. You are not yet capable of maintaining contact for much longer, and we need to talk about Ashahr.

His heart quickened. *What do you know about Ashahr? Can you help me defeat it?*

Ashahr, the Mind-Killer, is from our star system. Its goal is chaos—eternal, perpetual chaos. It feeds on the energy released through the self-destruction of its victims.

How does it accomplish this? Where does it come from? How does it operate?

Through its ability to invade and manipulate the minds of others, Ashahr lays out a pattern that destroys the natural life it touches. Ashahr set its pattern on our world millennia ago and killed it. We are the sole survivors. We became Unity in order to survive and to fight Ashahr wherever and whenever we can.

How do you fight it? he asked.

No, Andrei, the question is, how will you fight it? You will be our weapon.

He smiled to himself. *To think I just came up with the idea that you would be my weapon.*

We will work together.

Yes, all right, he Sent. *But how?*

The scene faded, and the Conference Chamber took its place. He looked around, dazed, feeling as if he were waking from a very deep sleep. The room spiraled around him as he gripped the edge of the table. As it finally stabilized, he let go of the table. Too soon. Luckily Sylvain, who was standing next to him, grabbed his arm and eased him into a chair. He tried to think through the noise of his heartbeat hammering in his ears, as well as the shock and confusion he Sensed from the various sentients staring at him from around the conference table.

What happened? Diana Sent. She moved toward him quickly, bioscanner in hand. He tried to remember if he had called for her.

No, Sylvain called me.

How long was I …? He paused. How long was he what? Unconscious? Asleep? In a trance state?

I'm not sure, she Sent. *Sylvain called me about five minutes ago. I don't know how long he waited before that. Andrei, what happened to you? Were you hallucinating?*

He didn't know how to answer. Having finally gathered his senses, his eyes swept the conference table, verifying the emotions he'd Sensed. Aladair-Turil was conferring furiously with his aides—this was a breach of protocol, after all. Qerej was on her feet, but she hadn't moved or said a word. She was watching him to see if he needed her healing skills. *Qerej, I've found water for you!* he wanted to shout, but he restrained himself. Surely they'd all think he'd lost his mind. At this moment, he couldn't even explain to himself what had happened, much less to two Alliance Representatives in a public forum.

"Representatives." He put as much calm authority behind his voice as he could muster under the circumstances. "I extend my strongest apologies, but I must recess this hearing. I seem to be having a relapse of my recent bout with the flu."

"Floo?" Qerej asked. "What is floo?"

"It's a human sickness, Representative Qerej. I picked it up when I was back on Logos Prime recently. Nothing serious, just slows us down a bit."

"Human sickness? Is it contagious?" Aladair-Turil's mane quivered with alarm.

"Not to nonhumans, I assure you, Representative Aladair-Turil." Andrei stood up carefully. To his relief, the room remained stable. "But I need some time to rest. Again, I apologize."

"When shall we resume the hearing, Commander?" Qerej asked.

Good question. "I'm not sure, Representative. I'll try to give you an answer in one Standard hour. Please enjoy the Peaceship's hospitality in the meantime." He bowed to each of them and left, Sylvain and Diana behind him, before they could voice any further protest.

"What happened in there?" Sylvain demanded. "Was it Ashahr again?"

Diana gasped. "Have you been contacted in some way by Ashahr?"

"In some way," he agreed, raising an eyebrow at Sylvain in silent reproach. His assistant glared back at him. He gave it up and opened a channel to Qerej, requesting her presence in his quarters. That done, he leaned back and shut his eyes. Whatever had happened in there, it hadn't been sleep, which he was beginning to crave almost desperately. Maybe if he slept, he'd be contacted by Unity again, he rationalized. Though there was no forgetting that Ashahr was still out there.

When he reluctantly opened his eyes again, Diana and Sylvain were watching him with renewed concern. He had a brief fantasy of some future time when he could just live without being under surveillance—sentient or supernatural. Maybe in his next lifetime. "It wasn't Ashahr this time. I was in a cave under a mountain in the Djelat Range. Mount Dhaslan. An entity that called itself Unity Sent thoughts to me from a pool in the cave." He didn't dare look at them, afraid of their reaction. "It—they, I guess—told me they were some form of collective consciousness, and that Ashahr was an enemy from their star system. That Ashahr would try to replace our civilizations with its own pattern of existence, which happens to be violent, self-destructive chaos. They also said that they'd help me fight it." He grinned, suddenly realizing the implications of what he'd told them. "Maybe we finally have a real chance at beating Ashahr at its own game."

"Assuming this Unity is real," Diana said gently. She hesitated, probably Sensing the defensive withdrawal he could hardly control. But one of the things he admired about her was that she would press on when she thought it necessary, even when she knew that what she had to say wasn't welcome. And so she did. "Andrei, this may be real, and it may not be. It all sounds very unusual. It's been obvious, since the implant experiment began, that your response to the activation of the psi-sense has been highly atypical. In some ways, your mindpowers are much stronger than that of even a very high-functioning PA, but that doesn't tell the whole story."

Andrei didn't want to have this conversation in front of Sylvain, but she'd given him no choice. "What does that mean?" he asked.

"Your adjustment to these mindpowers has been highly atypical. It's possible that the stress of coping with this overwhelmingly powerful psi-sense may be altering reality for you. But the truth of the matter is that I can't make a legitimate judgment about what's real and what isn't, because you seem determined to thwart my attempts at studying what's going on in any detail and helping you cope with it."

She put up her hand to silence his protest. "No, please don't insult my intelligence by continuing your routine of 'nothing's wrong, I'm just tired.' You've been fighting something. I thought it was the implant—and maybe it still is—but now that you tell me you've been contacted by not one, but two alien entities Sending thoughts across an unimaginable distance, I'm not sure what to think."

He didn't have a good answer for this. Luckily, Qerej was at the door, putting the subject to rest for the moment. He ushered her in, and they sat in armchairs across from each other while Sylvain and Diana took the couch.

"The Zh'ladar sends greetings," she told him.

"Thank you," he replied. Gazing into her fathomless eyes, he couldn't help but smile at the thought of what he was about to tell her. "I have good news for you to bring back to him. Qerej, there is water in a cave under Mount Dhaslan. I know this for a fact."

There was silence as she absorbed his statement. "How do you know it, Andrei?" she finally asked.

"I saw it. I had a vision of it, there in the Conference Chamber." He waited, but she didn't say anything. "I'm sure you find this hard to believe."

"No, not really," she replied. "As you know, we of T'lar believe there is much truth to be found in dreams." She gazed steadily at him. "Is that what it was, Andrei? A dream?"

"I'm not sure," he answered slowly, addressing his and Diana's question as much as hers. "If a dream can be defined as a message from the subconscious mind, I suppose that's what it was. I guess we won't know for certain whether it was a fantasy originating in my own subconscious desire for that kind of solution, or whether it was a message from an independent entity, until we send out a survey team to the Djelat Range." *Or until it contacts me again,* he thought.

"How do you plan to convince the Alliance Council to send out another survey team, when previous teams discovered no water there?" Qerej asked. "Do you think they will believe you?"

"I won't go through the Council. I'll send out my own team," he replied. He looked over at Sylvain, who nodded.

"I know who to contact," Sylvain said. "But what are you going to tell Aladair-Turil and the Council? And what's T'lar supposed to do for water in the meantime?"

He'd thought about this. "We'll tell the Council that T'lar has agreed to try the bio-reform project the Karellians have developed, and that it requires an emergency loan to keep things going until the process starts working."

"But we have already rejected that project," Qerej reminded him.

"Let's just say I talked you into it," Andrei replied. "It's what the Council wants to hear. They're not going to wonder too hard why T'lar changed its mind. We'll cancel it as soon as the team finds water."

Qerej nodded her agreement.

"Good. We'll begin immediately. Now, to more important matters. I wanted to ask you what you knew about Ashahr."

He Sensed the same shiver of dread from her at the name as he had before. "Ashahr is a name from mythology," she replied. "An immensely powerful agent of destruction, made powerful by the way it could use the minds of its victims against them. The legends said that it was able to inflict madness on individuals and groups, planet-wide. That civilizations fell when Ashahr wanted them to. There are some that say that the destruction of our planet's ecosystem was the will of Ashahr manifesting through Zorya's attack." Her eyes were wide as she stared at him. "Tell me, Andrei, why are you interested in Ashahr? Have you evidence that it truly exists? That it is something real?"

He sighed. "I'm afraid I do."

* * *

It took a while to convince them to leave him alone. Qerej wanted to talk about his visions, or whatever they were. Diana wanted to talk about the role the implant was playing in allowing him to reach out with his mind further than any human telepath had ever done—or whether Ashahr and Unity were the creations of a mind that had abandoned reality and turned in on itself. Levelheaded Sylvain only wanted to discuss the implementation of the survey, but even this was beyond him after a while. When he couldn't stand it anymore, he pushed them all out the door, making elaborate promises to continue the various discussions after he'd gotten some rest. Whether he'd really keep those promises was another matter.

Alone, in silence, he finally tried to face what had happened. What had Unity meant about a transformation beyond what the implant had already accomplished? But he couldn't pursue this line of reasoning very far without feeling the cold edge of panic waiting to overtake him. The implant was a temporary condition, not a transformation. In fact, the only permanent transformation he could visualize was death, and he wasn't particularly eager to see what was on the other side of that. Well, most days. Of course, some days were worse than others. When he thought about Ashahr's threat of eternal madness, death looked like a bargain.

He found himself pacing—something he hardly ever did. Nick did enough pacing for both of them. He could feel the muscles in his legs trembling; sleep deprivation was finally catching up with him. The moment he let the thought of sleep enter his conscious mind, it was impossible to resist. Stretching out on the sofa with the hope that being less comfortable than in a bed might limit him to dozing, he dimmed the lights to half strength and closed his eyes.

He immediately plunged headlong into deep sleep. A door in his mind closed; another opened …

Wake up, my darling. Time for another little chat.

He stared into the cold, black pits where Kylara's eyes used to be—would have been, should have been. *Such a cowardly trick, Ashahr, using the image of my dead lover to hide behind. Why don't you show me what you really look like?*

No, Andrei, I think I'll leave things the way they are for now. I like this body. You did too, remember? Remember what she felt like in your arms? Remember what it felt like to be inside her?

He wouldn't feel it this time. His mind whited out with rage, leaving him mentally speechless. Ashahr used Kylara's mouth to form a mocking smile. It took him some time to achieve a semblance of rationality. *What do you want this time, Ashahr?*

Something has happened. She/it reached out mentally, trying harder than the first time, and he felt warm pleasure, like a drug relaxing him into submission. *Tell me about it.*

Tell me about it? He used the sudden flare of hope he felt to push away Ashahr's attempt at seduction. *Are you telling me you can't figure it out for yourself?* He was mocking it, pushing for a reaction.

Kylara/Ashahr scowled and reached out. Back to fear again. *Show me what is in your mind.*

No, I won't. Go back to whatever hell you came from.

He was ready for this—he hoped. He used the Disciplines to focus his mind: a single focus, a laser beam of purposeful concentration. He visualized his Shield as thick, sheer canyons of ice, so cold it would burn anyone—anything—that touched it. Surrounding his consciousness with the Shield, he gathered all the mental energy he had at his command and waited.

Something touched his mind—something sharp. He shored up the wall of ice at that spot. It pressed harder against the barrier but couldn't make an impact. He looked out from behind the walls at Ashahr. Kylara's image was leaning forward, watching him intently. Now they were her eyes again, but they were full of hatred. Seeing Kylara looking at him that way caused him to lose concentration, and the next mindstrike almost broke through. He felt a sharp pain in his head and gasped, quickly averting his gaze and renewing his focus.

Ashahr Sent nothing through his mental barricade; it couldn't. He felt a stab of triumph almost as sharp as pain. *Give it up, Ashahr. Leave me alone. Leave the Hegemony and the Alliance alone. We won't accept your pattern.*

You think so? Ashahr Sent a fireball of rage and terror at him, made up of the emotions it had stolen from him. The memories associated with the emotions battered his defenses. "*No!*" he yelled, and it exploded harmlessly against the icy walls. With a mental cry of fury, Kylara's image broke apart in exactly the same way her battlecruiser had broken apart in the final moment of her life—and at the same time, he heard Ashahr promising him that his mind would disintegrate in much the same way. "*No!*" Andrei cried out again, drowning in the backwash of memory as the remains of the explosion sparked white and red in his mind's eye. He moaned, no longer able to separate physical from mental agony. "No, no, no, no …"

* * *

Diana left Andrei's office reluctantly. There was so much to discuss—so much work for her to do.

She couldn't say she understood what had happened. She couldn't yet bring herself to believe in telepathic entities from far-off star systems, but did that mean they weren't real?

She wanted to talk to Sylvain, but he was already preoccupied with his assigned task of putting together a survey team and sending it off to T'lar as fast as possible. It was obvious that he wasn't speculating about his boss's sanity. She thought about contacting Coraline, but she didn't even know what to say to her. *Do you think it's possible I might have accidentally configured the implant to pick up very, very long-distance mental communication?*

Which brought her back to Andrei. He was the one she really wanted to talk to. Try as she might, she couldn't Read what he thought about the whole thing or Sense what he was truly feeling. It seemed like he was pleased: the enemy had exposed itself, allowing him to design an appropriate defense, and an unexpected ally had appeared, with powers potentially equal to those of the enemy. It was like some kind of strategy game. But what could it mean to him to have this battle going on inside his own brain?

She briefly Sensed something wrong just as she reached her quarters, but there was no one there. She stood frozen at the door, trying to decipher what she'd felt. Nothing. Shrugging, she keyed in her access code and stepped inside …

… and landed on her hands and knees from vertigo so sudden and complete that for a moment, she felt as though she'd gone through a pass-through point unmedicated. Emotions followed the dizzy spell with nightmare intensity: fear; hate; severe, bitter despair. Each moved through her consciousness so quickly that she couldn't determine its origin or cause. She clung to the floor, trying to get her breath.

It ended as suddenly as it had begun. She hauled herself to her feet and tried to stop shaking. Then she ran.

She pressed the keypad in front of Andrei's door over and over. No response. She couldn't Read him through the door.

Pressing her lips together, she made a decision. After he'd begun to trust her, Sylvain gave her an access override code for Andrei's quarters, "to be used in an emergency." Somehow, she thought this qualified.

She walked tentatively over to the sofa. Andrei's dark hair and clothes were shadows in the half-light. His hands covered his face. She called his name quietly, then again with more force. He stirred, moaned, and sat up. When he moved his hands, his eyes were wide open, staring into the distance. She sat down next to him.

"Andrei, it's me, Diana. What happened?"

There was no response. She found herself feeling paralyzed. She was afraid to Probe him, or even just Read him. What could she do to help, if he was fighting mental demons?

What she really wanted to do was hold him. She brushed her hand gently along his arm. Afraid he'd be angry, push her away …

He pulled her roughly toward him and held on tightly, so tightly that it was hard for her to breathe. Shivering as if he was cold, he wrapped her in his arms. His mental barriers were down, and she could Sense his desperation. Desperate for warmth, for touch, for an end to being alone. She pulled her arms out of his grasp so she could put them around his neck, and he kissed her.

When they finally ran out of air, he drew away from her. He shook his head, looking stunned. She Sensed his guilt and confusion, and she felt her heart sink.

"I'm sorry. I don't know what I was thinking," he said wearily.

"You did what I wanted you to do," she answered. "And you know it."

He just shook his head again. She waited, but it was obvious that he wasn't going to approach her again, and she wouldn't get anywhere by pushing him. She decided to let it go.

For now.

"You want a drink?" he asked. She shook her head. To her surprise, instead of getting something from the dispenser, he went into his bedroom and came back with a bottle of *livrash*.

"PAs can't drink that," she said.

He laughed; it sounded unreal. "Practice makes perfect." He toasted her, draining his glass almost at once. "How did you end up here, anyway?"

"I Sensed ... something terrible. I don't know how, but I did. Can you tell me what happened?"

"Ashahr," he answered. "Was that what you Sensed?"

She shook her head. "I didn't Sense anything specific or Receive any thoughts. It was just emotion. Andrei, what did it want? What did it do to you?"

He refilled the glass. She opened her mouth, ready to make a doctor-type remark about intoxicants not solving anything. Then she thought about how she'd felt after a few seconds of exposure to the emotional minefield that was interaction with Ashahr (at least, that was his interpretation—or was it some type of psychotic episode that she'd Sensed?) and decided to keep quiet.

"It wanted access to my subconscious mind," he replied. "During the last set of negotiations, the Zoryans were able to Read my surface thoughts. Ashahr can access emotion, but not every level of thought. It not only wants to be able to Read everything, but also to control my mind—but I think it can't do it without my cooperation. This time, I was able to Block it from Reading me, but just barely. It finally gave up."

"For good, do you think?" she asked.

He shook his head. "No. I can't believe that." He looked away from her; staring again at horrors she couldn't see. "It lost a battle. It's gone away to regroup—to figure out a new strategy. Winning one battle won't give us the war."

"But you can fight it," Diana insisted.

He smiled grimly. "We'll just have to see what it comes up with next, won't we?"

Chapter 17

Nick was back in Seladorn again. It hadn't been so long ago, but given what had happened since then—given what he now knew—the place seemed changed. Menacing. It wouldn't have occurred to him to be afraid here in the past, but now he was braced for unknown danger.

When Ravat had contacted him, he wouldn't explain why Nick had to return to Sendos. After he said it had to do with the information he'd sold Nick last month, he didn't have to. Once again, Nick inserted the silver disc into the wall and slipped through the opening that appeared.

There was no one there. The bar was empty, the room was semidark, and Ravat was nowhere to be seen. *What the hell?* Nick thought, briefly wondering if he'd made some type of mistake and, if so, whether it was the fatal type. "Ravat?" he called, his hand hovering next to the disruptor pistol clipped to his belt.

"Right here, Captain Hayden," Ravat answered, stepping into the room from the adjoining corridor. "Please follow me." Unlike the front room, the corridor was lit. Ravat's face was in shadows, the aura suppressant masking his reactions. Nick hesitated. Then curiosity overcame caution, and he obeyed.

The small back room they entered—the same one as the last time they'd met—wasn't empty this time. Nick took a reflexive step backward, hand tightening on his pistol as he stared at the three sentients gazing back at him. There were two Sendosians and a woman from Logos Prime. One of the Sendosians stood in back of the table where the others were seated, an energy rifle held across her chest. The other Sendosian and the human were both wearing nondescript civilian clothes, yet Nick somehow had the impression that they weren't actually civilians. He mentally fitted a grey robe and a chromium mask over the figure of the Sendosian and came up with the same one whom he'd drugged and stolen information from on Selas. The older woman took her time measuring him with her eyes. Apparently satisfied with what she saw, she smiled. It didn't make her seem any less dangerous.

"Captain Nick Hayden, of the Free Raider Force and the Challenge," she said. "Which has your first allegiance, Nick? The Raiders or the Challenge?"

He sat down opposite them, even though they hadn't invited him to, and decided that it wouldn't be worthwhile to pretend he didn't know what she was talking about. "Why do you assume there's a conflict between them? My work with the Raiders pays for the intelligence—and when I'm lucky, the weaponry—that I supply to the Challenge. By the way, I didn't catch your name." He turned his head slightly to take in the Sendosian. "Or yours. Or your allegiances, for that matter." He grinned. "I'm assuming you're not here to arrest me for something. Something I didn't do, of course."

"No, we're not here to arrest you for anything. I'm Darya Ardelle, and this is Saalovaarian-sar-Ilyat."

"Senior Alliance Council Representatives." It wasn't a question, though it was a surprise.

"That's right, Nick. And I'm also a Challenge leader."

Nick shook his head, puzzled. "I know all the Challenge leaders. At least, I thought I did."

"I'm a very, very well-kept secret, for obvious reasons."

"What about him?" Nick gestured to Saalovaarian. "You're not gonna tell me he's a member of the Challenge too."

"No, I'm not. As his name states, Representative Saalovaarian is a member of the Ilyat Family."

Nick shrugged his lack of comprehension.

"The Ilyat has the longest, most illustrious history of all the Five Families," Saalovaarian said. "Yet we are the smallest in size, and we have suffered from this. Other Families have been able to take resources that are rightfully ours, resources without which our ability to achieve our true destiny has been unjustly curtailed—"

"Which is?" Nick asked.

'To rule all of Sendos."

Nick took a chance that admitting he knew what Saalovaarian was talking about would win him some points, instead of making him suspicious about where the information came from. "Your Family is the Lighbaht?"

Not a bad call; Saalovaarian's bifurcated skull pulsed with what Nick knew from his experience with other Sendosians was pleasure. "Just so."

"I hope it won't offend you if I ask you why you're so sure about that."

Saalovaarian's voice was cool in response. "Not at all, Captain. Our teachers have received knowledge of our true place in the scheme of things, in their dreams—dreams that I have recently had the privilege of sharing with them."

Dreams? What did dreams have to do with anything? It wasn't as if the Ilyat were slaves the way PNs, for all intents and purposes, were. The so-called dreams were obviously an excuse: an attempt to justify taking a shot at conquering the other Families. But where did the alliance with Logos Prime fit into the picture?

Silence. Nick wished he'd paid more attention that time when Andrei had tried to explain T'larian Disciplines to him. He could have used the control at that moment, as his heart and mind competed in a race with each other. He swallowed, trying to moisten a dry throat. If they were planning to kill him, they wouldn't be bothering to explain all of this—which meant that they were probably planning to recruit him. But he needed to play it out, get as much information as he could. "I still don't know what this is all about," he finally said. "Why I'm here. What you want."

Darya and Saalovaarian both turned to look at Ravat, who was standing in the corner of the room and seemed to be trying hard to be somewhere else. "What did you do with the information I sold you, Captain Hayden?" he asked.

"I don't see how that's any of your damned business," Nick replied. He looked briefly at the others, then back at Ravat. The look he gave the Karellian was quietly murderous, and Ravat looked away. "Did you sell Representatives Ardelle and Saalovaarian the same information you sold me, you miserable little creep?"

"He didn't have to," the Sendosian answered. "We knew the weapons were on Selas, because we put them there."

Nick chose not to answer, and Saalovaarian continued. "The tale this creature told you was true, as far as he knew it. His source eventually got careless, giving us the opportunity to discover her spying. By the time we found out that she'd given the information to Ravat, he'd already sold it to you." His skull pulsed again; this time, Nick recognized the threat. "How did you break into Selas without being discovered, Captain Hayden?"

Nick managed to maintain an appearance of unconcerned calm. "What makes you think I did?"

"Because at the same time Ravat was telling Saalovaarian that he'd sold the information to you, I was listening to Fiona Callahan's report to the Challenge's Inner Council about an unusual cache of weapons found on Sendos's prison moon by a Free Raider Captain who was also a Challenge member," Darya interjected. "I'm also curious about how you pulled it off. Did you do it all yourself, or did you have some help from outside or inside the prison? Oh, yes, one more thing—did you get into our files?"

Nick thought about lying and decided it wouldn't accomplish anything. "I got into the prison myself, using a lightship and a lightsuit. But I had help getting into the files." He grinned at their shocked expressions and let them sweat for a minute before gesturing to Saalovaarian. Several moments passed until the Sendosian remembered and understood what had happened. The deep skull pulses reflected barely controlled rage.

Darya, on the other hand, didn't seem particularly concerned. Perhaps she was just better at hiding it. "We appreciate your honesty. We obviously need to improve our security. So what did you make of it all?"

Here comes the tricky part, thought Nick. He decided to let them tell him about the Nonaggression Pact. "I didn't have time to read the files, so I'm not sure what to make of it," he answered slowly. "I would like to know how you guys got hold of such a wide variety of prohibited war weapons, especially the Zoryan ones." Darya and Saalovaarian glanced at each other, obviously startled, then looked back at him again. "I'd seen most of what was in your stockpile before, but there were a few that really had me stumped. It took a couple of illegal forays into the Alliance Military datanet to identify them as Zoryan. And now you're telling me they're yours. Well, either you've stolen some of the damaged Zoryan pieces captured by the Alliance Military during the war and held in storage, or you're doing whatever it is you're up to with Hegemony cooperation."

He paused for a moment, folding his arms as he thought out loud. "Which has me confused as hell. We spent all those years fighting them off. What could you have that they'd want, and what could they have that you'd want—besides the weapons?"

"The Alliance weapons were acquired through a variety of sources," Darya answered. "Many were bought from Free Raiders who smuggle and deal in arms. Others were diverted from military warehousing by our allies within the Alliance Military." She smiled as she caught Nick's raised eyebrow and continued. "The Zoryan weapons came to us directly from the Hegemony."

"For the purpose of …?"

"For the purpose of assisting the Ilyat and the Challenge with their struggles for freedom."

Back to that again, and it was beginning to annoy him. "The Ilyat's struggle is for power, not freedom," Nick snapped. "Your situation isn't the same thing as the PNs' on Logos Prime."

"As long as the Ilyat's claim to the Lighbaht is not acknowledged by all Sendosians, the Ilyat is oppressed," retorted Saalovaarian. Once again, his skull pulsed with his anger, and Darya gave Nick a look of warning.

"Nick doesn't understand yet," Darya said smoothly.

"What the hell is there to understand?" Nick asked.

"The kind of changes we are talking about here. Once the PNs are in control on Logos Prime and the Ilyat are in control on Sendos, the oppressed on other Alliance worlds will be encouraged by our example to rise up and fight for their freedom as well. Think of it. The singletons on Glendine, the Niwahr on Karellia … everything will change." Darya's black eyes were glowing with excitement.

Nick did think about it. Singletons were considered an aberration by Glendine binaries and cast out of the huge, interlocking clans that made up the hive-like structure of Glendine society. The Niwahr were servants to the Servant class on Karellia. While neither represented large proportions of their worlds' populations the way PNs did, they certainly could make trouble for the ruling powers, given support by outsiders—particularly Zoryan outsiders.

He suddenly felt a sick chill. "You're gonna let the Zoryans in, aren't you? You're gonna give them the codes to access the defense grid on our side of the War Border, and in return they'll help you neutralize the other four Families." That had to be part of the picture. But why so many different kinds of weapons, and why were they set up the way they were? Could he get away with asking?

Saalovaarian nodded, answering his spoken question. "Do you have a problem with that, Captain Hayden?"

"Yeah, I think I do," he replied. "The Hegemony was a pretty brutal, pretty effective enemy. What makes you think that once you let them in, you'll be able to control 'em? A treaty? A couple of coded discs, nicely initialed by all concerned? What's in it for them, anyway?"

"Of course they want something in return," Saalovaarian answered. "The war started in the first place because Zorya long ago exhausted its resources, and the colonies (slave worlds, Nick mentally corrected him) that are part of the Hegemony haven't been able to make up the deficit. The war only made things worse for them. Sendos will share its strong industrial base and mineral and energy resources with the Hegemony."

"All right, that explains the Zorya/Sendos connection, but what the hell does any of this have to do with Logos Prime? I suppose we've got some technology we can give them, but the planet itself isn't worth much of anything." His voice trailed off as he tried to think it through, and he shrugged as he reached a dead end.

"You're right, Nick. Logos Prime has no physical resources to offer, and our technology isn't that big a deal," Darya answered. "They want something different from us." She hesitated for several seconds, then shrugged. "They want our PAs."

For a moment Nick didn't speak, thinking she was going to continue. When she didn't, he caught her gaze and held it.

"They want our PAs for what, Darya? What're they gonna do with 'em?"

She blinked and looked away. "I'm not exactly sure what they have in mind. The Peacekeeper told me he thinks they're developing telepathy, with the help of some type of unknown entity. The Zoryans confirm this. They say they want to use our PAs to further develop their understanding of psipower. They want access to the Think Tank's research ..." Her voice trailed off, and he could easily hear her unvoiced confusion.

"Are they going to round up all the PAs and take them back to Zorya?" he demanded.

"I don't know. Maybe."

"Are they going to kill them after they've found out whatever it is they want to know?"

"I don't know."

"Do you care, Darya?"

She lifted her chin in sudden defiance. "Logos Prime will belong to free PNs. The horrible crowding and poverty of the lower Core will end. We will be able to decide how to live, what kind of goals we as a society want to pursue. No more wasting our lives and our talents for our self-styled masters!"

"And the Zoryans will be okay with this self-determination you think we're gonna have once the PAs are gone."

She nodded. "A deal's a deal. They don't want us or our planet anyway."

He struggled against feeling paralyzed with horror. It was one thing to demand that PAs share power with PNs. It was one thing to resent them—all right, hate them. But it was another thing altogether to round them up and ship them off to the Alliance's worst enemy. And what was it that she'd said about Andrei?

"Did you say the Peacekeeper knows about this? I don't think either he or Prime Commander Sesna-Goveril will be too thrilled when they find out what you've done."

"By the time the Alliance Military finds out what's happened, it'll be too late for Sesna-Goveril to do anything. Like I told you, we have our friends inside the Military. As for Savinov ..." Again she hesitated. Nick found his fingers tightening on his arms, which were crossed over his chest. "They'll deal with him themselves."

"They're gonna assassinate him? How many times have they tried to pull that off and failed?" He covered a fresh wave of horror with contempt as he forced himself not to wipe his sweating palms. *Watch it,* he warned himself. *Show you care too much, and they'll know you'll never join them.* He uncrossed his arms and leaned back in his chair, as if all of this was merely interesting.

"They claim that their telepathic ally will destroy him."

"How?"

"I don't know. What does it matter how?"

Darya sounded annoyed; he'd gotten too close to the line. Maybe she felt just a little bit guilty that she was going to let someone she knew and worked with get wiped out. He hoped so, otherwise she didn't quite belong to the human race herself anymore. Nick said, "I'm just curious how this whole thing is gonna work, that's all. It's a pretty big plan. Lots of bases to cover. Lots of work to be done, if you want to make it happen anytime soon. Speaking of which, what's the time frame?"

"Soon, Captain," Saalovaarian replied. "It will all happen quite soon."

"Care to be more specific?"

"No."

"Care to tell me what you want me to do?"

"Does that mean you're willing to go along with this, Nick?" Darya asked. She studied him closely. "You have a reputation for hating PAs, but you also have a reputation for hating the Hegemony. We know you were involved in guerrilla actions against them during the war. Are you sure you can tolerate the idea of having them as allies?"

Nick didn't answer right away. He thought it would arouse their suspicions if he appeared eager, especially after his comments about both the Ilyat and the war. He turned and looked directly at Darya. "You and I know the Challenge isn't getting anywhere. We wake up some people, play some games with the half-assed weapons we've managed to scrounge up. None of that amounts to real power. If this is what we have to do to take power, to buy our people the freedom they deserve, I can live with that."

He turned to Saalovaarian. "And speaking of buying, I may be a PN whose loyalty is to the Challenge, but I'm also a Free Raider, and I expect to be paid for my services, whatever they may be."

Saalovaarian nodded, and Darya laughed. "Sure, Nick, we'll pay you."

She didn't say anything else, and he grew impatient. "You'll pay me for doing what?"

"We'd like you to recruit a strike force for us," Darya answered. "A small group of trustworthy Raiders to help coordinate our side's operations with the Zoryan operation."

That was all she said. "That's not very specific," said Nick. "What would you want this strike force to do, and when do you need them to be available? The Raiders'll ask, you know."

"Raiders don't always get the whole assignment at once," Saalovaarian snapped. "They understand 'need to know.' And you and your Raiders don't need to know yet."

There was silence after that. Nick couldn't think of how else to get information from them without seeming like he was going to use it for any purposes other than their own. Finally, he shrugged, acknowledging that they had the upper hand. "So I wait to hear from you?"

Darya nodded. "That's it, for now."

"No, Darya. Actually, there is one more thing." Saalovaarian leaned back in his chair, his skull pulsing challenge. "We have what I believe the Free Raiders would call a 'loose end'." He gestured to Ravat, whose aura suppressant had worn off. His aura glowed bright orange with terror. "There is no place for him in our plan."

"He's a Niwahr. Why not set him to work mobilizing them?" Nick asked.

Saalovaarian shook his head. "He has neither the capability or the motivation." He gestured to Nick's disruptor pistol. "Kill him, please. Now."

Nick looked over at Darya, who shrugged her shoulders with an elaborate gesture and turned away. Ravat chose that moment to make a run for the door, but Nick was too quick for him. He grabbed him by the neck and twisted it sharply. The Karellian gave a high-pitched shriek and collapsed.

No one spoke. Nick flung Ravat's body over his shoulder. "I know a back way out of here. I'll get rid of him." He stared coldly at Saalovaarian, whose expression hadn't changed. "This goes on my bill, Representative."

Saalovaarian's skull pulsed with amusement. "Indeed, Captain."

Nick looked at Darya, who nodded. "I'll be in touch," she repeated. He nodded in return, slipping out the door.

It didn't take Ravat long to revive. Nick had counted on a Logos Prime PN and a Sendosian not having a clue that the neck hold wouldn't do anything but cause the Karellian to pass out. The scream was a nice touch on Ravat's part. Of course, the Karellian really thought he was going to die. *Oh, well,* Nick thought. *He'll get over it.*

"You're in my cruiser, and we're on our way to Tiflet," Nick told him by way of orientation. Tiflet was one of the two Free Raider outposts right inside the War Border. "From Tiflet you can buy passage wherever you like. But you'd better go as deep underground as you can possibly get, because if those two find out you're still alive, you won't be for long. And neither will I."

Once that was done, he immediately forgot about Ravat. He couldn't raise Andrei on their black-coded line. What the hell was going on? His frustration magnified by fear, he tried reaching Sylvain. Also no answer. In desperation, he contacted Coraline.

"What's happening?" she asked. He could hear from the groggy tone in her voice that he'd woken her up, but there wasn't time to feel regret.

He didn't answer her question. "Is Diana Zarev still with Andrei aboard the Peaceship?"

"Yes, why?"

"I need to talk to Andrei immediately, and I can't raise him. Do you think you can get hold of her?"

"Yes, but what's happening …?" she repeated. Her voice trailed off into his silence. "All right, Nick, I'll see what I can do for you. Wait for my signal."

He waited, feeling each minute pass with increasing anxiety. Finally her signal came. "Well?" he asked.

She was wide awake now, and she sounded both upset and angry. "I didn't get to speak to her, but she left a message for me." There was a pause. "I can't believe she did this. We'd agreed on a course of action …"

"On what?"

"The implant. We had a plan, which she's obviously decided to ignore."

He didn't give a damn about the implant, and he wasn't able or willing to hide his impatience. "Corie, where the hell is Andrei?"

"They're gone."

"Gone? Gone where?"

"I'm not exactly sure. Have you ever heard of a place called Sanctuary?"

Chapter 18

Ashahr didn't look like Kylara anymore. In fact, it didn't look like anything he could put a name to. Tentacles of writhing darkness; the complete absence of light. No, the death of light … Andrei watched from behind his translucent walls of ice, hoping they were strong enough for whatever came next, as the tentacles began to blur and mutate into a new form: shining blades of black light. He heard Ashahr's laughter—the sound of tortured, dying souls—as the blades sliced long, clean lines into his Shield. The pain was excruciating, and he watched in helpless horror as blood dripped from the rents in the wall. Nothing left; there was nothing left to do but die …

Andrei awoke gasping, clutching at his chest as one stab of needle-sharp pain was quickly followed by another, equally intense. *Easy,* he told himself as he struggled to bring his racing heart rate back to something resembling normal. Just another run-of-the-mill nightmare in which Ashahr destroyed him, and everyone he cared for and everything that had meaning for him perished in the flames of Zoryan war. It was something that Ashahr Sent when it was too busy elsewhere to actually interact with him—something to wear him down to the point where he was no longer strong enough to maintain his defenses.

He leaned back in his chair, pushing sweat-soaked hair off his face and rubbing kinks out of the back of his neck as he worked on his breathing. *Slow, deep, even breaths,* he thought. *Easy. Come on, now.* He shook his head in disgust at the mechanical, meaningless phrases, as well as the fact that once again he'd fallen asleep at his desk. *This has got to stop,* he told himself, but these words had as little power as the last batch to command his respect, and no power at all against the waves of exhaustion and depression that kept threatening to engulf him. Was it Ashahr's doing, or his own character flaws finally getting the best of him? Both, most likely. He swore under his breath, but he wasn't sure at whom.

Time was running out, and he still hadn't been able to reach Unity again. He'd tried everything he could think of over the past few days, and at times—more and more frequently, as a matter of fact—he'd thought he was getting somewhere. He remembered the feeling of dreaming-while-awake that he'd had both the night before and at the time of his encounter with Unity, and whenever he thought he felt it again, he tried projecting his consciousness outward to meet it. Nothing had happened, and after a while, his head hurt too much to continue. He needed another approach ... but what?

The door chimed. That was one nice thing about being telepathic, he thought idly; you not only knew who was at the door but also what they wanted, making it easier to decide whether or not to be available. In this case, the caller was Diana Zarev, with what she believed to be bad news. Andrei didn't try to Read what type of news; he just swore again and let her in.

Bad news aside, he was happy to see her whenever she showed up. He enjoyed looking at her and listening to her, even when she was lecturing him about one or another of his failings as an experimental subject. Her appearance was so different from what he was used to perceiving as beautiful for all the years of his adult life: tall, muscular Kylara with her long, red-gold hair. Diana was so small and delicate in comparison, but mentally, emotionally, where it counted, he knew that the strength was there. Her warm compassion combined with cool intelligence and a dry sense of humor that matched his own so well. He needed to forget what had happened between them; it had been a lapse in judgment, a mistake on his part. He didn't dare get involved with her—not with the future so uncertain.

Actually, he didn't believe his future was all that uncertain; his time, he thought, was almost up. Aside from the occasional diversion of Diana, death was more and more in his thoughts. He imagined it all being over, and at times it felt as seductive as fantasies about lovemaking. This was Ashahr's doing, no doubt, but even knowing that, he was still captivated. The agony of Kylara's death had briefly given him thoughts of suicide, but the idea that Zorya would have gotten both of them was too much to bear. Kylara would have been furious. But she wasn't here, and Diana wasn't real. But Ashahr was, and Ashahr was feeding him thoughts of death, and they tasted so damned sweet …

He shook his head, his breath a hiss of rage and pain. Ashahr would most likely destroy him. The only hope he had at this point was that he could summon up some last reserve of mental energy to take down the entity with him.

* * *

The door slid open, and Diana slowly entered Andrei's office/ quarters, clutching a large fileviewer in front of her like a shield. He nodded a greeting at her and gestured to the seat in front of him, but she stayed on her feet. She wondered if he'd Read her intentions. Probably not, or he wouldn't be so calm. She flashed a tight, false smile at him, her fingers gripping the fileviewer even tighter as she tried once more to prepare herself for the encounter ahead.

A long, painful conversation with Coraline had resulted in agreement between them that the implant had to come out immediately. They would have to figure out another way to stop Zorya, she thought. She would gladly use her own telepathic powers to help Andrei do that. After all, she reasoned with herself, he would have had to get along without the implant if it didn't exist or if they hadn't given it to him. The only remaining question was how to get him to agree to give it up.

"What can I do for you, Diana?" The words were too formal, and the tone of his voice was distant. *He knows something's up,* she thought. He didn't need to Read her; the expression on her face probably gave her away.

"How are you feeling today?" she asked.

He shrugged. "All right," he answered. There was no expression in his voice. She wondered if he had any idea how far from 'all right' he appeared: eyes narrowed as if even the normal light of the room was too bright; the ridged lines of pain between his eyebrows; the careful way he held his head, as if a wrong move would be unbearable.

"All right?" she pressed.

"All right," he repeated. Impatience colored his tone this time. "Is this a social visit?"

"No, it's not. I've finished analyzing the most recent thirty-hour brain scan," she said briskly, trying to sound businesslike. Trying to act detached. "I'd like to discuss the results, if you have some time right now."

He shrugged. "I have time for a brief summary."

"While standing on one foot?" When he didn't reply, she sighed her exasperation, sat down, and activated the fileviewer.

"The picture at the top of the screen is the thirty-hour brain scan I did when I first got to the Peaceship," she began. The brainwaves pulsed gently across the screen. In addition to that first time, he'd worn the monitoring disc behind his ear for an entire Alliance Standard day once a week for each of the three weeks she'd been aboard the Peaceship. "The second one is the one I did right after I inserted the implant, and the third is last week's," she continued, activating the center of the screen with a touch. She was watching his face, but his expression didn't change. They'd gone over this scan already, with her noting the changes that had appeared. By the next test, she told him, she should have an explanation for the abnormalities.

She didn't.

Taking a deep breath and licking dry lips, she tapped the bottom portion of the screen. "Here are yesterday's results," she said quietly.

For some reason, it didn't help that she'd spent hours and hours looking at these results already—she still felt the same jolt of horror each time she saw them. The smooth waves had become jagged peaks that occasionally crash-dived toward the bottom of the screen, where they flatlined for anywhere from five seconds to almost a minute, then resumed their frantic upward trajectory. "Now I'm adding markers at the points where you noted having that feeling you described as being pulled into a trance state. You'll see what happens." Tiny red lights flashed at the flatline points.

"Andrei," she said softly, sorry she couldn't ease the shock. Sorry she couldn't put her arms around him ... *Stop it,* she told herself sharply. "You're having seizures, and they've been increasing in frequency and intensity. The implant is damaging your brain. I'm so sorry. I've made a terrible mistake. The implant isn't safe. I shouldn't have given it to you, and I need to remove it immediately. I believe that the damage is repairable, but if you don't let me take it out right away, it will kill you."

She finally dared to look at him again. He was staring at the screen as if hypnotized. "I don't understand," he finally said in a strained voice. "I'm not having seizures."

Diana answered with careful patience. "You're thinking of the kind of seizure where a person rolls around on the floor, foaming at the mouth. That's not what this is all about. This type of seizure is called an absence seizure. You just go blank for anywhere from a couple of seconds to a minute. That's what your so-called dream states are all about."

"No," he whispered. His voice strengthened with conviction. "No. That's not the right answer."

"Why? Because it's not the answer you want to hear?"

"Because it doesn't take into account either Ashahr or Unity," he answered, sounding frustrated.

She shook her head. "Andrei, after seeing this, I can't believe that contact was real. Look at these brainwave patterns. They don't even look human."

"My point exactly," he interjected.

"Because your brain's being damaged! This kind of destruction of normal brainwave patterns has to indicate severely impaired functioning. In fact, it's a wonder you've managed to keep going as well as you have."

He didn't respond, and she fell silent. How frustrating it was to be totally unable to Read him or even just Sense his emotions. Once again she wished she could comfort him, and she no longer cared that he probably knew it. He looked like he was still in shock, staring blankly at the screen. Finally he seemed to shake himself mentally. He turned off the fileviewer and focused on her.

"Diana, please. The meeting with Zorya is just three weeks away. Surely you can wait that long." His voice was quiet and calm again, but she'd gotten to know him well enough to feel the tension behind his words.

"I wish I could, but I can't. The damage appears to be progressive, meaning it's getting worse at an increasing rate of speed. It isn't likely that in three more weeks you'll still be able to think at all, much less conduct negotiations. I'm not sure that you'll be alive in three weeks."

"If I'm not telepathic, it will hardly matter whether I'm there or not." He stared intently at her, green eyes burning. She could feel his desperation even without Sensing it. "What if I say I want to take that chance? I'll take full responsibility for any negative outcome."

"The negative outcome you're so quick to accept could be cerebral hemorrhage, death, or something even worse than death, like turning into a vegetable! Besides, who do you think you are? It's not your experiment—the responsibility isn't yours to take!" To her horror, Diana found herself yelling at him.

"When you stuck this thing in my head, it became my responsibility, just like the Alliance's future is now my responsibility," Andrei shot back, his voice also rising. "Do you think I'm going to let it go to hell, after everything I've done to save it? I won't let you ruin my only chance—" He stopped abruptly, letting out an exclamation of pain. He clutched his head in his hands, his fingers digging into his scalp as he pushed the chair away from the desk and lowered his head to his knees.

Shoving aside the jolt of fear that went through her, she jumped up and circled the desk, bioscanner already out of the pouch at her belt. Checking the readings, she readied an injection tube with a painkiller … only to have him reach up, snatch it out of her hand, and throw it with such force that it landed on the other side of the room.

"No more of that, Doctor." Though his voice was barely audible, she could hear the rage in its jagged edges. "There's nothing more to say. I'll let you remove the implant after the negotiations are concluded. In the meantime, you're dismissed. Get out of here, go away, and don't bother me again, or I'll have you removed from the Peaceship and sent back to Logos Prime."

"You can't dismiss me, Andrei," she said, moving away from him and retaking her seat. Anger gone, she felt sad and weary. She knew he would view what she was going to do next as the most profound betrayal, and by doing it, she would eliminate any chance of him returning her feelings for him. *Doesn't matter,* she thought, *as long as he's alive in the end.*

"Coraline and I have decided that unless you permit me to remove the implant today, we will report this experiment to the Alliance Council and advise them that you are unfit to carry out your duties as Peacekeeper," she said mechanically. His eyes widened with shock, and she continued. "If you try to stop me by confining me to my quarters, Coraline will carry out our plan herself. It's very easy for you to check whether I am telling the truth or not. I suggest you do so."

He didn't answer for a minute, and she could feel him Reading her mind. Finally he shook his head, wincing with residual pain. His voice was hoarse with urgency. "For Earth's sake! Why are you doing this? You'll destroy all of us. The Challenge won't get the implant, we'll all be Reconditioned, and Zorya will win. Ashahr will win. What purpose can this possibly serve?" She saw him shudder. "Coraline ... how could you do this to her?"

"Your sister agreed to this plan, Andrei. How else could we convince you to let me take it out?" Her heart ached with feeling that she'd lost him. Under that emotion, though, was fear. What if he didn't give in?

Silence hung between them. Finally he stood up. Everything about him was completely closed off to her. He didn't look at her as he spoke. "I once told you that you would have been an excellent strategist, Doctor Zarev. Not only do you have the intelligence, you also have the nerve. I suppose I have no choice. This has to be done today?" She nodded. "Could you at least give me a couple of hours to get a few things done before you do the surgery?"

Alarm bells went off, and she wanted to refuse. But what could he do to change things in a couple of hours? Why antagonize him any further? "All right," she replied, leaning back in her chair and folding her arms. "Go right ahead."

His eyebrows rose with astonishment, and he burst out laughing. "You're going to stay here and guard me?" She nodded, her lips twitching as she tried to keep from smiling.

She failed, and their gazes locked. She kept her eyes on his as he walked around the desk, and she stood up. She finally closed them when he took her in his arms and kissed her. As he pressed closer to her, she leaned into his embrace, and as her body opened to him, his mind opened to her.

And the walls came down, and she Shared ... everything.

Chapter 19

The only thing that surprised Sylvain about Andrei's decision to go to T'lar was that he was taking Diana with him. But once he saw them together, he understood. The touch of his hand on her back; the way she looked at him like she didn't have to pretend that she didn't care anymore. The way they looked at each other. Sylvain was pleased. At least one good thing had come of all this.

Kylara Val and Andrei Savinov. Fire and ice. Even though she was ten years older than Andrei, Sylvain had never met two people who matched each other the way they did. He'd never completely understood their insistence on monogamy—even though he'd dutifully explained it to the various women who'd approached him over the years, trying to find a way to get to Andrei—but what he did know was that they'd meant it. He knew he'd never felt anything like that for the women who'd passed in and out of his life through the years, and at times he'd envied Andrei and Kylara their certainty. They were not just lovers; they were life partners.

But of course it had backfired when Kylara was killed. Andrei missed her so much, and being alone wasn't good for him at all. And now this nightmare with the implant and Ashahr ... Sylvain shook his head, trying not to dwell on his fears. He resolved just to be glad that Andrei had found someone new. If, of course, he survived her crazy experiment.

It was third shift, but Andrei didn't want to wait until morning to leave. This didn't surprise Sylvain—his boss never had been accused of paying attention to what normal sentients did at normal times of day and night. At least this time Andrei had given him enough warning so he could get some sleep during second shift, before they took off.

Since it was only three weeks before Settlement Negotiations, Lithras were characteristically tense about security, and the cruiser had two voyager escorts. They would join the survey team when they got to T'lar, until Andrei was ready to return to the Peaceship. *Who knows when that'll be?* Sylvain thought. *Depends on what gets done with this trip.* Andrei was searching for Unity. What if they were only a figment of his implant-deranged imagination?

The lights were low, and he could see on his interior viewscreen that Diana had fallen asleep. Andrei gently removed one of his hands from hers and used the other to remove a pair of dataglasses. He stood up and stretched. Sylvain smiled to himself as Andrei got two glasses of tea from the dispenser and came up front, slipping into the co-pilot's seat and handing him one of them. They'd had some of their best discussions on trips like these. They sat in companionable silence for a while. Finally Andrei put aside his glass and sighed deeply, massaging his temples.

"Headache back?" Sylvain asked.

Andrei shrugged. "It doesn't bother going away anymore … just gets slightly better and slightly worse." He grimaced, rubbing his forehead this time. "Sometimes more than slightly worse."

Sylvain was surprised and disturbed—not by what he'd said, but because he'd actually admitted to being in pain. *It must be pretty bad for him to come to that,* he thought. He gestured to Diana. "Ask her to give you something."

"I don't want to disturb her. She deserves a few minutes of freedom from worrying about my problems." He sighed again. "Besides, her potions stopped working a while ago."

"You're just afraid she'll knock you out again and take that damn thing out of your head." His light tone suddenly turned intensely serious, almost bitter. "Would be all for the good, if you ask me."

Andrei didn't answer for a while. Sylvain watched him out of the corner of his eye as he gazed out the viewscreen. His mind was light years away. "It doesn't matter, Syl. It's all going to be over soon anyway, one way or the other."

"What do you mean?"

"I mean that unless this works, either the implant or Ashahr or some combination of the two is going to stop me from fighting the Zoryans off this time."

"Unless this works?"

"Unless I can get back in contact with Unity again."

"But Unity has to be strong enough to fight Ashahr, even though they don't seem to be strong enough to contact you."

Andrei looked over at him. "We don't know that for a fact, do we? Maybe there's some other reason they haven't made contact again. Maybe I'm not strong enough to Receive them from as far away as the Peaceship. At least, that's the answer I'm hoping for."

"But you did once."

"Yes, I did. Once. But Diana says the implant's damaging my brain at a pretty rapid pace, so maybe I'm not as strong a telepath as I was even a few days ago."

Sylvain choked on the tea as it burned his mouth. It was way too hot. What had Andrei been thinking when he programmed it? The cruiser's cabin felt hot too, and he tapped the insignia on his jacket to activate its cooling mechanism. Even after all their years together, Andrei's ability to speak so matter-of-factly about impending disaster still unnerved him. "She thinks the thing is killing you, but she went along with this trip. Funny, she doesn't strike me as someone who can be *seduced* that easily into doing things that go against her professional instincts."

For an instant, he caught a trace of a smile at the corner of Andrei's mouth; then it was gone. "Not seduction."

"What would you call it?"

He shrugged. "Persuasion. I removed the Blocks I'd built and Shared with her what had actually happened between Ashahr and me."

Sylvain raised his eyebrows. "That's all that happened?"

This time, Andrei grinned. "No." He sighed, leaning his head back and closing his eyes. "You know what happens when you don't get enough sleep? You start imagining things."

No kidding, Sylvain thought. "Like what?"

"Like a little while ago, I thought I saw Kylara. Not Ashahr's sick, twisted version of Kylara, but mine. The way I knew her."

Sylvain looked sharply at Andrei. "She say anything?"

"She told me if I ever touched another woman again, she'd kill me far more horribly than Ashahr could. I tried to explain to her that she was the one who was dead, but she didn't appreciate my logic." Andrei's tone was dry.

Sylvain had no idea what to say to this. For a while, they were silent as he made a course change. When he next looked over at Andrei, he was adjusting the cruiser's temperature controls again. "What's wrong?"

"It's freezing in here, and my jacket's heating mechanism doesn't seem to be working." Andrei sounded unusually irritated, almost angry.

Sylvain scanned the board, puzzled. It showed ten degrees above normal. He wiped some sweat from his face and looked at Andrei, who was rubbing his temples again as well as his eyes and forehead. Sylvain decided not to say anything.

"I've been thinking about Logos Prime a lot lately." Andrei's voice was quiet and pensive as he changed the subject.

"Because of her?" Sylvain gestured toward Diana.

"Because of Coraline. And because of Diana and maybe even because of Nick. Syl, do you think I was wrong about not helping the Challenge? I've spent my entire adult life fighting this war ... so PAs could perpetuate their rule over PNs."

Sylvain shook his head vehemently. "It was never that simple, Andrei. The future of the whole Alliance was at stake, not just Logos Prime. Besides, I think it'll be easier for PNs to win their freedom from PAs than it would've been for them to try winning it from Zoryan conquerors."

"But maybe we could have done both."

"When? You think you could've led the Challenge in your spare time, when you weren't fighting an interstellar war? C'mon, boss, even you're not that good." He laughed, waiting for Andrei to join in. He didn't. "What's gotten into you tonight? You've always been so sure—"

"Of what? That what I was doing was right? Well, even if I was then, I'm not anymore. What the hell do I know about alien entities fighting battles over control of my mind?" His voice rose. "Here's something I'll bet you never thought you'd hear me say, Syl. I don't know what to do next. If going to T'lar to find Unity doesn't work, I'm out of ideas. And here's something else that's new—I'm not even sure I still care. I never knew anyone could be this tired and still be alive ... I guess I'm still alive. I wonder if I'd even know if I wasn't. If death were some kind of eternal dream, would it mean I was stuck with Ashahr forever? Could I really be that unlucky, do you think? Maybe I'm responsible for so much death that it would be a fair punishment. Maybe that's what Old Earth religion meant when it talked about hell."

He paused for a second to catch his breath and then went on, his voice sharp with frustration. "Damn it, Sylvain, can't you fix the heat in here? I thought hell was supposed to be hot, not this cold." He laughed: a choking sound. "I guess this is what that phrase means. You know, the one about hell freezing over."

Sylvain stared at him, horrified, as his worst fear—that the implant would drive Andrei mad, or kill him, or both—seemed to be coming true before his eyes. Andrei had started shaking violently and gripping his head in both hands. His breathing was shallow and rapid, punctuated with an occasional moan as he tried to curl into a ball in the chair. "Diana!" Sylvain yelled. She started, looked around for a moment, then leaped up and rushed toward them. He briefly told her what happened as she scanned Andrei. "What's going on?"

"He's spiked a high fever," she answered briefly. "I don't understand this. He was fine a few hours ago. Help me move him, so he can lie down."

Sylvain set the ship on temporary autopilot, and they got Andrei back to his seat, fully reclining it until he was lying flat. She dialed a drug into an injection tube and pressed it against the inside of his wrist, then wrapped an insulating blanket around him. After a few minutes, he stopped shaking, and his breathing quieted. Sylvain watched anxiously through the interior viewscreen as Diana continued monitoring her patient. Finally she came over to him.

"What's happening?" he asked again.

She seemed surprisingly calm, but then he remembered that she was a doctor. She shook her head. "I'm not sure. It could be that his body's finally rejecting the implant—treating it like an agent of infection—or it could be some kind of outside interference, like Ashahr."

"Or Unity?"

Diana shrugged, looking helpless with her lack of knowledge.

"You going to take the implant out?" Sylvain asked hopefully.

She shook her head again, and he heard frustration and despair in her voice. "I promised Andrei I'd wait until we got to T'lar and he made one last attempt to reach Unity. I hope I'm not condemning him to death with that promise."

* * *

Cold turned to suffocating heat, then back to cold again. Diana's drug worked only briefly; then the torture resumed. Andrei struggled to calm himself, to remember that once he got to T'lar, there'd be a chance to get help from either the Zh'ladar or Unity. But as the fever continued to climb, he found that rational thought kept slipping away. He fought against losing consciousness, fearful of meeting Ashahr in such a weakened state, but sleep meant a release from pain, and it was hard not to long for it. To long even for death, sweet release …

His mind drifted. Sometimes he knew where he was and what he was doing there, and sometimes he was completely lost. A woman's voice, calmly reassuring, whispered inside his head; he felt her cool hand on his burning forehead. Sometimes he knew it was Diana; other times he thought it was Kylara or even Astrid. His mother had killed herself when life became too unbearable—when she knew she couldn't win. Maybe that was the right answer for him too.

He thought he was hallucinating when the golden eyes appeared at the corner of his vision, and he tried to ignore them. Gradually, though, the ship and its passengers began feeling less and less substantial, while the eyes filled the space their unreality left behind.

Unity, is that you? he Sent.

Yes, Andrei. We are sorry about the pain that this transformation is causing.

Explain.

The closest we can come to an explanation—that you are capable of understanding—is that we are using the device in your brain as the point of contact between your mind and ours. But it was not intended for that use—thus the physical symptoms you have been experiencing. The process is almost complete. When you get to T'lar, you must find a way to achieve a suspension of consciousness and bodily processes, a suspension that is stronger than sleep. It must present a barrier to interference by Ashahr while we complete the transformation.

Something shifted within him: a whisper of fear, which he attempted to push away. Part of him desperately didn't want to continue the mental conversation; he was afraid, almost to the point of terror, of understanding what Unity was Sending. Nevertheless, he couldn't back away—not when he'd gone this far. *Exactly what type of transformation are you going to complete?*

We are going to establish a mindlink with you.

The feeling of panic got stronger. He wrapped his arms across his chest, trying to stop the shaking that had started again. *Explain.*

The mindlink will create instantaneous two-way communication between you and us, but that is only part of what will happen. It will allow us to amplify your mindpowers to a degree that is unavailable to the strongest human telepaths.

What will that look like in real life? Andrei Sent, not sure if he really wanted to know.

There are many types of mindpowers in addition to telepathy—telekinesis, for example. And a sentient who is mindlinked with us can literally change the minds of others.

Can someone mindlinked with you hurt people, mentally or physically?

Yes. We cannot destroy Ashahr by ourselves. Others we have created mindlinks with have failed as well. We are hoping that a mindlink with you will be more productive.

Andrei felt sick just thinking about this. *What makes you think that a human can adjust to that level of mental functioning?*

While you are in suspension, we will finish restructuring your body as well as your brain.

He had so many questions. He started to Send something to Unity, but the pain his body was experiencing shut off his mind for … he didn't know how long. When he could focus again, the golden eyes were fading. *Wait,* he Sent. *You can't leave me now! I have questions you have to answer before I even think of letting you take up residence inside my head. What makes you so sure I'm going to survive this procedure?*

We are not completely sure. We will take what precautions we can to protect you.

What's happened to the sentients that you have attempted this with?

There have been a variety of outcomes.

Andrei waited, but Unity didn't Send anything else. Pressed for time, he changed the subject. *How do I know you're not just another version of Ashahr that will use me to create a pattern for your own concept of existence? How do I know there will be anything left of me when you're done?*

We will not use you for any purpose, Andrei. You will use the link with us to accomplish the goal that we share—the destruction of Ashahr—as well as any other goal of your choosing.

Ashahr said I could pick my own goals too. How do you know my goal isn't to be ruler of the universe or something? Set out my own pattern of order that would involve its own path of destruction? You don't know me.

We know you better than Ashahr does … better than you can imagine. We have faith in who and what you are. We have faith that you are the right caretaker for these abilities—the right caretaker for the fate of your worlds.

He couldn't decide whether to laugh or howl with despair. *I'm a lousy caretaker,* he Sent. *My mother killed herself. I couldn't save her. I abandoned my sister and the others of my kind on my homeworld. My life partner died in space, carrying out my battle plan. Not a good choice at all for that role.* He could feel the pain fluttering like dark wings in his head; he gripped his hair between his fingers, wanting to pull it out by its roots. Unity Sent a reply but the pain spiraled out of control, and he couldn't Receive it. Far off, he heard a voice moaning, whispering incoherent pleas for mercy, and he was horrified to recognize it as his own. He focused on his breathing, counting breaths until the wave of agony passed through him, and tried Sending again.

Couldn't you stop what you're doing for a while? Give me a chance to decide what to make of all this, what I should do next?

We cannot stop the process now, unless you refuse the mindlink. But we can help you find a path toward the decision.

How?

If you search, you will find someone who can help you decide.

Who? How do I do that?

Extend your conscious mind outward as far as you can, until you find the right person. It has to be someone with a mental signature that you can Read.

I don't understand.

At this point in time, you can only do this type of Search and Read a mind that you have Read before. You will not be able to Send or Receive thoughts. You will Search and Read what you find, and you will know what you must do.

Who? What am I looking for?

Silence, and emptiness. The golden eyes were gone, and he couldn't Sense Unity's presence in his mind anymore. Instead, he found himself looking into the silver-gray eyes of Diana.

Do you know where you are? she Sent.

Here with Unity, but it's gone now. Did you Sense it?

She shook her head. *How bad do you feel?*

Pretty bad. Almost worse mentally than physically, he kept to himself. He felt lost, damaged, scared of dying, tempted by the idea of dying—it seemed like such an easy way out of this mess. He was terrified of becoming something other than human. What would happen if he thought the wrong thing and somebody died? Is that what Unity really meant? He changed the subject. *Do you know how to Search?*

Very high-functioning PAs have some limited Search capacity, she Sent. *For example, we can Sense whether someone we're looking for is in a particular location, as long as it isn't too far away. But we're out here in the middle of nowhere, Andrei. There's no one to Search for and nowhere to look.* She studied him, puzzled. *What does this have to do with Unity?*

It told me to Search for someone who could help me decide.

Decide what?

He stopped Sending abruptly, throwing up a Shield over his thoughts and turning away from her, pretending that he was too weak to continue the mental conversation. How much should he tell her about the entity's mindlink proposal? He knew he'd have to fight her objections, and he didn't have the strength. He wasn't sure enough himself that he was willing to go through with it.

There was no point in thinking about that now. Who was he supposed to contact? Mental signatures. While he'd Read more minds than he cared to remember since this whole thing started, virtually all of that mindreading had been accidental; thus, he had no idea of anyone's mental signature except those he'd consciously Read. Diana was one of those, but she'd been with him the whole time and couldn't know anything he didn't know about the Zoryan crisis. In fact, there was only one person who might know something he didn't and whose mind he'd Read ...

Nick. He focused his mind as intently as possible on his brother's mental signature and projected his consciousness as far outward as he could, from the various Free Raider outposts to Praxis, to Seladorn and Selas, toward T'lar ... *He's looking for me,* Andrei thought with astonishment at the laser-like clarity of Nick's intention reflected in his mind. He started to Send him a message, then remembered what Unity had told him. *I've got to go into his mind without his knowledge or his permission,* he realized, feeling sick at the thought. *Violation. Everything we despise in them, but I guess I'm them now.* He had the same feeling of being torn apart that he'd had when Unity Sent the thought that he'd be the Alliance's caretaker: wanting to dissolve into crazed laughter with the absurdity of the situation.

There's no time. Don't think about it now. He concentrated on gaining access to Nick's thoughts, got in, and sifted through them rapidly, looking for the ones he needed. Seladorn. He gasped, stunned, as Nick's memory-eye faced Darya Ardelle and Saalovaarian-sar-Ilyat across the table; went beyond shock to cold horror as he listened to their plan to loose the Zoryan Hegemony on an unsuspecting Alliance. Treachery from within … but how was this connected with Ashahr's pattern?

He felt razor-tipped fingers caressing the back of his brain. Ashahr? No, he wasn't asleep. At least he didn't think he was asleep; it was getting harder and harder to tell for sure. *Hallucination. Ignore.* But the pain was returning, and he knew he had little time left to think it through. So Ashahr had gotten to the Ilyat as well, convincing them with dreams of a glorious destiny to play a role in the entity's own dream of destruction. *The oppressed take the place of their oppressors … the oppressed take the form of their oppressors. Community breakdown. Self-destruction. And the Zoryans, having been let in, will have little problem finishing the job. So is that it? That's the pattern? Ashahr wins because the Hegemony wins?*

There was a burst of black light inside his skull as one of the razor-tipped fingers of pain gave him a playful jab. *Zorya can't hold us. The Hegemony will be overextended, and we won't go down without a fight.* His thoughts sped through scenarios of attack and counterattack—one battle after another in wars without end. It sounded like a good meal for an entity that feeds on self destruction. Ashahr didn't want Zorya to win;

Ashahr didn't want anyone to win, because if anyone won, the banquet would be over.

Time up. Game over. A hard wave of fresh pain broke the thread of connection with Nick. After it ended and he was fully conscious again, he reached out to Diana. She put her arms around him, and he held her tightly.

"I can't do it," he whispered, desperate.

"Can't do what?" she asked. Her quiet, calm voice made him cling even harder to the promise of sanity she represented.

"I've got to do it. No choice … there's no choice. I can't live with what I know and do nothing to stop it, can I? But it's so hard …" His voice trailed off. He could feel Diana trying to Read him. He Sensed her frustration and the fear that she hid so well. He envied her that, especially when he felt as though Ashahr—and now Unity as well—had peeled away all of his own layers of self-protection and left him with nothing but his own panic, raw and exposed.

The walls shimmered with layers of heat, and he could feel the fever waiting to consume him again. He caught up Diana's cool hand and pressed it against his burning cheek, then kissed her fingers. "I'm sorry," he told her dreamily. "There wasn't enough time for us." He sighed, closing his eyes.

It looks like you're having a very bad day.

The ironic, amused voice inside his head sounded familiar, but it took him some time to place it: Robert Jaxome, head of the Think Tank. What was he doing here? With a sinking feeling, Andrei realized that at some point, he'd slipped into sleep and he was Receiving a visit from Ashahr. He struggled to pull himself together and make sure his Shield was still in place.

Well, some days are just—

Yes, yes, I've heard this before. You know, you've become terribly predictable, Andrei. The contempt in Jaxome's voice rang true; Ashahr knew exactly what it was doing.

So why bother talking to me?

Because I enjoy watching you fight your futile battles in the little time you have left—all that energy wasted, when you know that what you really want is to be done with all of this. What you really want is to sleep forever. Jaxome/Ashahr's voice was edged with malicious pleasure.

What do you mean, the little time I have left? You think you can kill me?

I don't need to kill you. You are killing yourself with that device in your head.

Without that device in my head, you'd be able to manipulate my feelings and thoughts without my even being aware of it.

I can do that anyway. But the infection your body has created to fight the changes caused by the implant is overheating your brain, cooking it. Cerebral hemorrhage is imminent. Ashahr projected an image of rabid hunger at him. *I usually eat the brains of my victims raw, but I'm willing to make an exception on your account.*

Sorry, but I'm not giving up. You'll have to go hungry this time.

Nonsense. You can't last much longer. The pain has become unbearable.

Feeling some relief that Ashahr didn't know what was really causing the changes—Unity—he projected contempt at it. *Unbearable, you think? You haven't got a clue what I'm capable of tolerating in order to defeat Zorya and destroy you.*

What a pathetic little display of bravado. Do you think you're fooling me, or are you really fooling yourself? Perhaps you need better access to what you really know—to your true thoughts and feelings.

It was as if floodgates had opened and all the pain and terror and bottomless depression he'd been forcing himself not to feel suddenly poured over him like a tidal wave created by a storm-tossed Erlandian sea. He didn't want to be telepathic, he didn't want to join with Unity, he didn't want to fight any more battles with himself or anyone else. Being dead would solve it all. Why should he have to go on this way?

UNITY! Ashahr's mental voice screamed inside his head: a scream that was a combination of rage and triumph. *So that's your secret! Unity is trying to use you to get at me! You think contact with me is so loathsome, Andrei. Do you really think you will be able to tolerate having a whole group of alien minds permanently implanted in your brain, thinking your every thought, controlling your every action? You will be a dead thing, grotesquely reanimated to suit the purpose of another! What makes you imagine that existence in that state would have any value?*

He couldn't answer. The flood tide of emotion continued to batter him. Distantly he heard Ashahr's voice in his head again. This time it was soft and quiet: seductive in its gentleness. *I can make it stop,* Ashahr Sent.

What's your price? The Alliance on a plate?

No, all I want you to do is listen to me.

Andrei gave up. *Yes, all right, I will listen to you.* The screaming in his head stopped. He wanted to weep with relief.

The truth is that you don't have to listen to me. You just have to listen to yourself. If you do, you will know that you cannot be part of Unity's plan. But I understand that you cannot be part of mine, either. I won't try to change that anymore.

Andrei was puzzled. *So what are you saying?*

It's over, Andrei. You are so tired, and you deserve a rest. You have tried your best, and you have accomplished so much. But now it is time to listen to your body.

Which is saying what?

How long is your heart supposed to last?

What was this about? *Not as long as a real one.*

The heart is ready to fail again. All you have to do is let it happen. It won't last long, and then there will be peace.

Peace. Andrei felt a wave of hope. *What do I have to do?*

Diana is infusing H2P-R into your arm.

He didn't remember feeling any chest pains, but something must have gone wrong with his heart for her to give him an antiarrhythmic. *So what?*

Take off the patch.

Andrei thought about this. He had a blanket over him, so he could do it without her noticing. *She's monitoring me. She'll know when the readings go wrong.*

Distract her.

Peace. Ashahr's voice in his head faded, leaving him to blissful quiet and darkness. At some level, he knew he should stop this. This was wrong thinking. Ashahr, the implant, Unity, had all driven him over the edge. He knew it, but somehow it didn't matter all that much. He saw Diana in his mind. She was special, but she was really only a pale copy of Kylara, who herself was only a pale copy of the ultimate seductress, Death. He knew what it would be like to have his heart fail again—this time, for good—and it would be awful, would hurt like hell, but it wouldn't last long, and then he would be in the embrace of Death, and it would feel better, stronger, sweeter than the most powerful climax. Transcendence …

Andrei could feel the shift in consciousness as he woke up, but he kept his eyes shut and his breathing slow and even. He Shielded his thoughts carefully from Diana, then opened his eyes and looked around. She was sitting next to him, and the bio-monitor was perched on the broad, flat armrest. If he knocked it to the floor, would it break? Unlikely but possible.

He looked inside her mind. She was afraid he wasn't going to make it to T'lar. She thought he was dying. She would fight to save him; how could he stop her? Why was he thinking of stopping her? What did he really want?

She had turned in her chair and was smiling down at him. "Welcome back."

Moving as little as possible, he felt for the infusion patch attached to his arm. He reached under his sleeve and pulled it off, Blocking her from Reading his intention. He tried to smile back but felt too wretched to make it real. "What's been happening?" he croaked. His throat was raw, as if the screaming in his head had been his own, but there were no chest pains—yet.

"You've had a very high fever, which put a strain on your heart," she answered quietly. "I think it's under control now. You lost consciousness. Did you see Ashahr?"

"Yes." He didn't say anything more.

"Do you remember what you were trying to tell me before you passed out?" she asked. "You said that something was too hard to do, but that you had to do it. What was it?"

He shook his head. "I don't remember. I must have been delirious." He felt a brief flicker of pain in his chest. It was hard to keep from wincing. When he went into full arrest, how was he going to hide it from her? This plan made no sense at all. Suddenly, he laughed under his breath. A master strategist, and he couldn't engineer his own death? He pushed down the blanket and struggled to pull himself to a sitting position.

"What are you doing?" Diana asked, looking alarmed.

PAs couldn't Sense or Read through closed doors. The only place with a closed door on board the cruiser was the bathroom. "I want to go to the bathroom," he answered. "Help me up."

She was a lot smaller than he was, and as she struggled to get him to his feet, he staggered, grabbing at the armrest for support. His flailing arm sent the bio-monitor flying. It smashed into the wall before falling to the floor. "Damn," Diana said under her breath. She turned to go after it, but he caught her arm.

"Don't worry about it," he said. He swayed on his feet, trying to get his balance back. Another chest pain, stronger than the last. The bathroom looked too far away. Did he really want to die in there, alone in space? He began limping toward it.

Andrei, wait, Diana Sent.

He stopped but didn't turn back. *What do you want?*
She held up the patch. *I want you to choose life.*

* * *

They landed on a long, wide plain, dry and barren except for clouds of tawny dust kicked up by their feet into the empty sky as they walked toward the only building in sight, the golden-domed Sanctuary. With the exception of her brief trip to Praxis—where she wasn't outdoors for more than a minute, in an atmosphere suit—Diana had never been on a planet's surface before. She turned around in all directions, fighting a sense of panic at the sheer endlessness of it. It was a wasted, scarred landscape, empty except for a distant mountain range, dark against a dark sky. The air was dry; it smelled wrong, tasted wrong, felt wrong. She coughed, struggling to breathe naturally through the filtration mask.

She felt a hand on her shoulder, and she looked up at Andrei. *It's all right,* he Sent. *The air is safe. It's just different from what you're used to. Don't be afraid.* He squeezed her hand, smiled. She nodded, trying to appear calm again. They waited while the two voyagers touched down and two soldiers got out of each of them. They came up to Andrei and saluted, then took their positions flanking him. The T'larian honor guard showed up a few minutes later, and formal greetings were exchanged. Finally, they were on their way.

Diana tried not to look around too much. She focused her attention on Andrei. He was amazingly steady on his feet, considering what she had pumped into him: an anti-inflammatory agent for the fever, a painkiller that was calibrated to a delicate balance between being strong enough to work but not so strong that it put him to sleep, plus the antiarrhythmia medicine for his heart. He'd retreated behind his usual mask of reserve, authority, and control. She had no idea what he was thinking.

When they finally arrived at Sanctuary's doors, Andrei sketched a bow to the large, dark figure silhouetted against the entranceway and smiled. "It's an honor and a pleasure to return to Sanctuary, Your Grace," he said.

"It is a pleasure to welcome you here again, Commander," the Zh'ladar replied, "though I must say you look … What is the human expression? Somewhat the worse for wear."

"The expression is correct. Not only that, but the situation has deteriorated since we last spoke. I'm short of time now."

"Very well. Come in." They started down an austere corridor lit by shafts of dull sunlight filtering through the long, narrow windows. The walls were a dark, polished material, the floor covered by intricately patterned red and gold rugs. At the first door they came to, the Zh'ladar stopped. "We have prepared refreshment for your party, Commander, and a place to wait until the survey team arrives." Andrei nodded at his guards, and they left with the T'larian honor guard. Diana and Sylvain turned to go with Andrei, but they were blocked by the Zh'ladar. "You may wait here also," he instructed. "Off-worlders are not permitted inside the Sanctuary. Someone will contact you when the Peacekeeper is ready to leave."

Surprised, Diana looked over at Sylvain and then at Andrei, who didn't seem to have heard. "Your Grace …" Sylvain began. The Zh'ladar shook his head and gestured toward the door.

"Hold on just a minute," Diana interjected, trying to control her anger, with little success. "Mr. Dulaire is the Commander's Executive Assistant and I'm the Commander's physician. We need to go with him."

"No, you do not," the Zh'ladar answered pleasantly. "I do not believe that Commander Savinov will be requiring his Executive Assistant for the time being, and I too am a healer, Doctor Zarev. I will be personally responsible for the safety and well-being of the Peacekeeper while he is a guest here at Sanctuary."

She opened her mouth to protest again, but Andrei interrupted her. "No, Your Grace." He was leaning against the wall, rubbing his face; obviously the drugs were wearing off, and it had taken him a minute to understand what was happening. His breathing was jagged, but he spoke with determination. "Not my aide and my doctor. My closest friend and my ..." He hesitated. "My lover. I don't know when I'll see them again, or what I'll be when I see them again. Please let them come."

The Zh'ladar studied him silently, then nodded. He touched Andrei's arm, helping him move away from the wall, and the two continued walking while Diana and Sylvain followed. Andrei started out walking a straight line, but his steps soon became erratic, and every few minutes he stopped, pressing his palms against his temples. She hadn't thought the place was so big from looking at its unprepossessing exterior—the iridescent dome was the only sign that the building had any significance at all—but now it seemed to stretch on endlessly. She had just about decided to tell the Zh'ladar that they had to stop—that Andrei couldn't keep going, and they needed a medfloat for him—when the corridor reached a dead end. The Zh'ladar opened the only door and ushered them inside.

The room was small but appeared warm and comfortable. Nests of large red and gold pillows were placed around a low table that held two small plates of food Diana didn't recognize, two glasses and a pitcher, and a long-stemmed golden goblet set off to one side. In the corner of the room was a low platform bed with a thick scarlet coverlet, also covered with red and gold pillows. There was a skylight above the bed, and on the opposite wall hung a tapestry—T'lar as it used to be, glowing green and blue with lush foliage worked in jewel-like colors on an intensely black night-sky background.

Andrei's glazed eyes seemed to clear a little, and he smiled, looking genuinely pleased. "My old room," he murmured. He went over to the bed and picked up a red robe lying on it, then crossed to a doorway in the opposite wall that Diana assumed was a bathroom and shut the door behind him.

The Zh'ladar finally looked at them directly for the first time since they'd met. "Please sit down," he said. "Have something to eat. I thought Andrei and I would have time for a meal together, but that does not appear to be the case." She looked over at Sylvain, who was still watching the door that Andrei had closed behind him. He shrugged, lowering himself to the floor, and she followed.

She picked at the strange-looking food in the awkward silence that followed. She didn't know much about T'lar and she knew even less about T'larian religion, of which this *person* was the head. She studied him covertly. He was hairless, with smooth, perfectly formed facial features and long, sculpted bones; she couldn't discern any difference between him and Qerej, whom Andrei had called female. They were both male and female, Sylvain had informed her, alternating in cycles. T'larians could tell gender by pheromones, but the only clue off-worlders had was the color of their clothing: gold for females and red for males. The Zh'ladar sat motionless, his features still. He looked ageless, timeless. It was hard for her to shake off the heavy silence and address him directly.

"Your Grace, Andrei says he needs to go into a state of suspension—temporary cessation of bodily processes—in order to create a barrier against Ashahr—"

"I know."

She was surprised. "How do you know?"

"It is part of our knowledge of Unity."

"Your knowledge of Unity? I don't understand."

"Unity and Ashahr are part of the mythology of our world," the Zh'ladar answered.

She shrugged. "Well, I didn't know Andrei would need to go into suspension, so I don't have the equipment with me to set up a stasis field. From what I've heard, T'lar is rather, well, primitive technologically. Are you going to be able to …?"

The Zh'ladar gestured to the golden goblet. "These herbs, compounded into a drug, will produce suspension."

She stared at the goblet. He didn't understand—suspension wasn't the same as sedation. No drug alone, without a stasis field, could do the job right. "It hardly seems possible that a single dose of whatever's in that cup will create a state of near-death that is sure to be reversible. If the dosage isn't calibrated exactly right, Andrei could end up unable to come back." She picked up the goblet and looked into it. The liquid inside appeared thick and so dark that she couldn't determine its exact color. "Besides, without a stasis field and a biomonitoring system, how are you going to know when it's safe to revive him?"

"Usually an antidote is administered when the treatment that the patient is undergoing while suspended is complete," the Zh'ladar answered. "However, since we are uncertain of the nature of the treatment in this situation, it is a matter that I was planning to take up with Commander Savinov."

"No need." They all turned abruptly at the sound of Andrei's voice as he re-entered the room. Dressed in a flowing red robe like the one the Zh'ladar was wearing, Diana noticed that he looked younger, more vulnerable. Her heart contracted with fear for him. "Unity claims that I'll wake up when they're done with me—whenever that is." He leaned over the table and took the goblet from her, twirling it between his fingers. His eyes were unfathomable, as were his thoughts, and she felt a burst of renewed alarm.

"Andrei, wait. Give that back to me," she said quickly. "I'd like to run some tests on it first. It won't take long, I promise. Your Grace, can you describe the nature of this compound to me?"

The Zh'ladar didn't answer her; his eyes were locked with Andrei's. "Andrei, my friend, do you understand completely what it is that you are doing?"

Andrei laughed slightly. "No, Your Grace, I don't."

"Are you afraid?"

"Yes, I am."

"But you will do it anyway? You will accept whatever happens next?"

The smile left his face. "I will do it anyway, but I won't accept whatever happens next. You must all promise me that if it appears that I've been taken over by one of these alien entities and am being used against my will, against the Alliance, you'll do whatever it takes to stop me." He stared intently at each of them. The Zh'ladar and Sylvain slowly nodded their agreement. Diana opened her mouth to protest. What was she supposed to do if that happened? Kill him? But the look in his eyes silenced her, and she also mutely consented. The tension left his body, and he closed his eyes, swaying for a moment before recovering his balance. Just as she was about to scramble to her feet to support him, he opened his eyes again, smiling as he raised the goblet in a toast, and emptied its contents.

* * *

He felt numbness that started with his feet and worked its way up. At least he wasn't cold. He hated the cold and had been worried that dying would be like freezing. *Not dying,* he thought. *Suspension isn't death, so there's nothing to be afraid of. No fear allowed. Don't think about Ashahr, what Ashahr Sent …*

"Can you hear me?"

Diana's voice. Her face flickered in his fading vision. He tried to nod but didn't know whether he'd succeeded or not. The numbness was moving higher.

"Squeeze my hand if you can still hear me."

He tried to comply. His fingers twitched slightly, but that was all.

She kissed his forehead. *Come back to me soon.*

He wanted to hold her, but he couldn't make it happen. The ceiling had dissolved in a haze, and he couldn't feel the bed beneath him anymore. He felt a flutter of panic as he thought of all the things left undone, left unsaid. But there were still the messages he'd recorded.

"Syl." He could barely whisper; Sylvain leaned all the way over him to try to hear him. "Final instructions …"

"I know where they are, Andrei. I have the access codes." Sylvain's voice sounded thick and shaky. "Not going to need them."

"Messages for you, Corie, Nick …" He stopped. He'd never deleted the one he'd done for Kylara. He certainly didn't have anything for Diana. He'd known that he could die doing this, but he hadn't wanted to prepare for it. He couldn't see or hear anything anymore, and finally, finally, he stopped caring.

Eternity passed, in darkness and silence. No dreams. The first peace he could remember in … as long as he could remember. Just darkness, and silence, and a pair of golden eyes watching over him.

Chapter 20

Nick couldn't sleep, so he swam.

Moonlight coming in through the high-ceilinged skylight silvered the little pool and limned the curving, cobalt-blue walls. The warm water caressed his skin as he moved through it. He thought about Darya Ardelle's comments about the haves and the have-nots. T'lar's population lived in small, unadorned domes, but the planet's leader lived in this big, beautiful palace—with a pool, no less. Sure, the Zh'ladar told him that it was left over from a continuous-cycling water project ,and yeah, he'd said that anyone on T'lar could use it. But it was deserted now, right?

It's the middle of the night, his more rational side reminded him. *Get a grip. She's got a point, but that doesn't mean everyone who has some power is evil. Otherwise, what'll happen when we have power?*

He was a strong swimmer, though it wasn't something he got to do often, and the rhythm of his movement was relaxing. It helped him think more clearly, which was good, because there was a lot to think about. That was why he couldn't sleep. He couldn't stop going over and over the whole situation in his head, trying to figure out the next move in the game.

After dropping off Ravat, he'd thought he was going to figure out whom to recruit and how to approach them, but the news about Andrei meant he'd had to put that off. He set up a shadow presence on Kitrian, the other Free Raider outpost out by the War Border, so Darya and company would think he was there trying to find people for the strike force and waiting for further instructions. If they contacted him there, he had friends to cover for him, and the message would be routed to him wherever he was. If they sent someone to look for him, he'd find out about that too … hopefully before they realized he wasn't really there.

That done, he'd taken off for T'lar. It had taken some doing to talk his way into Sanctuary—it wouldn't have happened if Sylvain and Diana hadn't vouched for him—and he'd been hanging around here ever since. Two totally wasted days, watching Andrei lie around looking like he was dead; then this morning, he'd awakened and … Nick shuddered, lost his rhythm, and came up with a mouthful of water. *Forget about Andrei right now,* he thought. There was nothing he could do about that, and thinking about it wouldn't help. What the hell was he going to do about his own situation?

At least he was still alive; that was a nice piece of luck. Well, not just luck—they hadn't decided to give him a job out of charity. They'd obviously needed someone like him to get the weapons and let the Zoryans in, so why not just let him do it, since he already knew about it? They didn't know how big a mistake they'd made in choosing him, because they didn't know about his connection to the Peacekeeper.

He thought about that, as he had repeatedly since the whole thing started. If Andrei wasn't his brother, would he have been so quick to sell them out, or might he really have gone along with the whole thing? They could do what he'd been trying to do for years and couldn't: bring the PAs to their knees and free his people.

He flipped over underwater and started back the way he'd come. Yeah, but he couldn't stomach the price tag. Just the thought of being a Zoryan collaborator sickened him. Sure, he was willing to live with violence. He didn't agree with Fiona, and those like her, that making change happen on Logos Prime could be painless—that people could simply be educated into being different. That they would somehow, someday, see the light of reason. Bunch of crap. He sure as hell didn't agree with Diana and Coraline that PNs could win by becoming telepathic. He thought of Andrei; now that he was telepathic, he was no more sympathetic to the PN cause than he'd ever been. He was still obsessed with Zoryans and now some crazy, psychic demon from hell named Ashahr …

So, yeah, sure, there had to be violence, but this went way beyond that. This was mass murder, plain and simple, because the Zoryans sure as hell weren't gonna bring the PAs back to Logos Prime once they were done sucking the thoughts out of 'em. And he knew he couldn't just send them all to their deaths that way … not to mention whatever was going to happen on Sendos and, in time, to the other Alliance worlds.

He turned over on his back and floated, gazing up at the night sky through the open skylight. So what did he really want, and how far was he willing to go to get it? The more he thought about it, the more confused he got. He knew he wanted the weapons on Selas, in order to give the Challenge something to bargain with. But what were they bargaining for? Control of Logos Prime? Who'd run it—PNs instead of PAs? He grinned at the thought of those high-handed PA bastards doing manual labor and his friends hanging out at Lake Glass. Or would it be PNs and PAs together? Hard to imagine.

Hey, as long as it's not me, he thought, flipping over and swimming again. He didn't want any part of organized anything; didn't really believe much in government. He'd been kicked out of his mother's house because he wasn't having any part of his work assignment. He'd been kicked out of the Alliance Military for chronic insubordination. As a Free Raider Captain, he made enough money to live on doing whatever he damn well wanted to do, and he'd spent most of the war as a smuggler of both weapons and prisoners across the War

Border. Yeah, he'd killed some Zoryans along the way, but not enough to really count. Not like Andrei.

It wasn't worth spending a lot of time figuring out who was gonna run Logos Prime while it wasn't yet theirs to run, he concluded. He needed to get back to work on his own situation. He had to hire his own team, figure out someone he knew who'd be able to go along with the double-cross. Even though there were lots of Logos Prime PNs who were Free Raiders, most of them didn't give a damn about the Challenge; like Andrei, they'd just ditched the homeworld and all its problems. Would money be enough to persuade them? Raiders who double-crossed their employers usually had trouble getting another contract—they became outlaws even among outlaws. Who'd be willing to go along with that? And what would happen to him when it was all over? It wasn't like he was independently wealthy and could afford to be blacklisted. *Ah, hell, that's the least of my problems, right?*

Footsteps, and a shadow in the doorway: a small female shape. "Hello?"

He swam over to the side of the pool and looked up at Diana. "Come on in," he answered. "The water's great."

She shook her head. "I'm not exactly dressed for swimming."

He laughed, gesturing at himself. He wasn't wearing anything. "Neither am I. Don't let that stop you."

"Thanks, but even if I was willing, I don't know how to swim."

"Really?" He was surprised. "A big-shot PA, unlimited access to Lake Glass, and you don't know how to swim? Why not?"

She shrugged. "No one ever bothered to teach me when I was a child, and when I got older, it didn't occur to me to learn." She turned to leave. "I couldn't sleep. I was just taking a walk. I don't want to disturb you."

"Well, obviously I couldn't sleep either. Want to hang out for a while?" He jumped out of the pool, shook the water out of his hair, and went to grab a towel, chuckling to himself as she quickly averted her eyes.

"You wouldn't make a good Raider with that modest attitude," he commented as they sat in a pile of cushions—the usual T'larian seating—next to the pool.

She snorted. "And you wouldn't make a good PA."

"Why? Because I have a great body?"

She laughed. "Among other reasons."

"Unlike my brother."

"His body's just fine."

"Cute. That's not what I meant, and you know it."

She sighed, amusement erased. "You don't waste too much time on small talk, do you, Nick?"

"I don't have time to waste," he replied. "So tell me, what do you make of all this?"

She didn't answer right away, and he took her silence as a time to study her. She didn't look too happy. She'd spent the two days mostly hovering around Andrei, monitoring his vital signs and pretending there was something she could do if those vital signs failed. It hadn't taken long for him to figure out that she had a relationship with Andrei—or at least thought she had one. It was pretty obvious from Andrei's behavior today that he had other things on his mind. Or should he say, *in* his mind?

"He's not PA in the normal sense of the word," she finally answered. "PAs have never had the mindpowers he has now. In all the work the Think Tank has done, we've never been able to prove the existence of even the potential for humans to have those mindpowers. And to use them so easily, so skillfully! I think he's telling the truth—that he is now mindlinked to a highly evolved, very powerful telepathic entity that calls itself Unity."

"Yeah? Do you really know who Unity is and what they want?" Nick asked.

"We know what Andrei's told us."

"What if Andrei hasn't been told the truth? How the hell would he know?"

Diana sighed again. "We have to assume that he does know, and that whatever agreement he has with them will work … for him and for us."

"But what if it doesn't?" Nick pressed her.

She shook her head, exasperated. "We'll deal with that if it happens, won't we? Besides, don't you have more immediate problems of your own?"

Nick leaned back and gazed at the vaulted ceiling. "Yeah, I do. I sure as hell do. Thanks for reminding me, Diana." He didn't say anything else, and the silence lengthened.

"Do you think Ardelle and Saalovaarian really believe you're going to work with them?" Diana finally asked.

He nodded. "Neither of them are telepaths, so they can't Read me to find out for sure. I don't really get what the Sendosian is all about, but I've certainly met PN fanatics before, and that's Darya Ardelle—so sure she's right that she isn't going to pay close attention when someone agrees with her. She'll just assume they've finally seen the truth. Her truth."

"Now that they know you know about the weapons, they'll be more heavily guarded in the future," Diana said.

"Yeah, but not from me or the team I put together."

Diana frowned. "What are you going to do about that?"

"I'm gonna do it," Nick replied. "The only difference is that it'll be my team, not Darya's."

"So what is it that your team's going to do that they wouldn't do if they were her team? Or what are they not going to do …? You know what I mean."

Nick laughed. "You know, I can't get used to the idea that someone who can just pull the thoughts right out of my head is asking me what I think, and what am I am going to do, and what do I mean, as if you don't really know."

"I don't," she replied evenly. "I won't Read you without your permission, and you know that." She looked thoughtful. "Though I guess you've been away from Logos Prime for so long, you haven't had much contact with the Bridge, have you?"

He didn't answer.

"There are PAs who have ideals, Nick. Who believe in social justice."

Nick couldn't help but laugh. "PAs and justice. PAs willing to give up their privileges. What exactly is it that you're willing to change, Diana? Is there room for all the PNs in the uppermost levels of the Outer Core, or do you plan to put up new viewscreens in the lowest levels of the Inner Core to pretty it up? Are you gonna open Lake Glass to everyone? When there's an agripod failure, are *you* gonna go hungry? And what about advanced medical care? There's not enough of *anything* on Logos Prime for *everyone*. Someone's gotta win, and someone's gotta lose. Or can you and your fellow dreamers just shut your eyes to that reality because you know that nothing's really gonna change, and you can just feel good about yourselves for thinking you would do things differently if you got the chance?"

He was surprised at his own vehemence, and he felt a little bit guilty as a brief look of pain passed across her face. She really didn't act much like any PA he'd known outside his family. She sat looking at the water, not speaking, but she didn't make stupid excuses or run away, either. He admired her for that.

"I would have thought that my work on the implant speaks for itself, but you don't agree with my theories or my methods," she finally replied. "I don't think I could convince you of my sincerity if I sat here all night and debated you point by point. So let's get back to what you're going to do about the weapons on Selas. Just because I won't Read you doesn't mean I can't figure things out. And what I think I hear you saying is that you're going to raid the prison and use the weapons in your own private little war against the Core."

"After getting rid of the Zoryans, of course," he answered with a mocking grin.

"Of course. And Darya Ardelle?"

"Well, we'll have to see what happens to her—and her Sendosian friend—when they don't do what the Hegemony wants."

She frowned at his light tone. "You still haven't answered my question. How are you going to pull this off? And if you use weapons against the Core, how is the result going to be different from what Ardelle is planning?"

"There won't be any Zoryans involved when I do it."

"What makes you think they're going to let you ruin their plan so easily? What about Ashahr?"

"Ashahr is Andrei's problem," Nick answered sharply. "And assuming he can solve it, we can work together to defeat the Zoryans."

"And take over the Core? I don't see Andrei doing that."

"It's not up to Andrei what happens to Logos Prime when the Zoryans are gone. I have my own plans for the Core." He stood up abruptly and gathered his clothes, getting ready to leave. "And no, I don't care to tell you what they are."

* * *

Diana watched him go. She didn't try to call after him; there wasn't anything more to say. Whatever he was planning wasn't that important to her right now. If Andrei could deal with Ashahr and the Hegemony, his brother wouldn't be that much of a problem. Or would he? What if Nick was as determined to get what he wanted as Andrei was? She shook her head, dismissing the thought. Though it was easier to worry about

Zorya's plan to occupy Logos Prime than to think about what happened—or didn't happen—between her and Andrei, and what their relationship was going to be …

I'm not going to let this get to me, she told herself for the hundredth time. *If it turns out that we can't be lovers, we can still be allies.* But things were different now. For one thing, what was her role now that Andrei said that the experiment was over? Had the implant become inert? What had Unity done to create the changes she'd observed?

She didn't know what was more astonishing, the change in Andrei's physical condition or the change in his mental state. He was far more telepathic—and far more comfortable being telepathic—than he had been with her device. Or was it Unity who were enjoying themselves—a disembodied mind once again anchored in reality? *Robert Jaxome would leap from the beautiful windows in his office if he were to find out that there are aliens out there whose mindpowers are so far ahead of humanity's that we can't even begin to understand their nature,* she thought. Studying Unity would be the chance of a lifetime, but when she'd mentioned it to Andrei, he'd rejected her request. Rejected her. Which hurt, no matter what she tried to tell herself. This time she'd thought she had finally found someone who was right for her, but once again she'd chosen the wrong lover. Or was this only temporary? What would happen to Andrei once Unity was gone—would he want to be with her again? More to the point, would she still want him? Did she really want him now?

The truth was, she wasn't sure what she wanted, because she wasn't sure that the person looking at her through Andrei's eyes was really Andrei.

Chapter 21

Andrei wasn't sleeping either, but he wasn't tired. He was Searching for K'ril I'th.

He wasn't tired. It felt so good not to be tired: to be strong and sure of himself again. It felt great not to be walking around fighting off panic. He knew the others were afraid of him, but they were wrong; they didn't understand. He had the power now to fight their enemies and have a good chance of winning; he couldn't have said that before Unity joined him.

The holo-model was a good likeness of K'ril I'th. It hadn't been Unity's idea to make a physical representation of whom he was Searching for, but the process of Searching for someone, if he didn't know whether that someone still existed (not to mention that he didn't have any idea where kri was), was so complex that he thought it might help him focus. Besides, making holo-models was so much a part of Andrei Savinov that it reminded him that he was still ... himself. With modifications, to be sure, but still himself.

He'd been doing this for hours, but he wasn't discouraged. Maybe K'ril I'th truly was dead; but hopefully, as kri had suggested, the Zoryan was deeply hidden away, waiting for ... what? *For me to find kri,* Andrei thought. *For us to destroy Ashahr and its militant Zoryan puppets together.*

Even as part of his mind was Searching, another part had registered the presence of Sylvain, Nick, and Diana as each of them separately passed by his door earlier in the evening, wanting to talk to him privately—to see who he was to them now. *You really don't want to be here,* he had thought, and they had turned back, having changed their minds. This wouldn't last long, but hopefully by the time they remembered that they'd wanted to see him, there would be something else to divert their attention. He didn't have anything against any of them in particular; he just needed the privacy in order to do his work. If that was hard on them, well, as Nick would say, they'd get over it.

But when the Zh'ladar came by, he hesitated. The fact that he was a Head of State was a good excuse for letting him in, but he knew it wasn't the real reason. Ever since he'd met the Zh'ladar, Andrei had felt a bond with him. The Zh'ladar had both taught him and helped him at various times in his life, and he greatly valued the relationship. If there was anyone who could accept him the way he was now, it would be the T'larian leader. "Come in, Your Grace."

Andrei motioned briefly, and the door opened. T'lar didn't have electromechanical doors operating with motion sensors; they had to be opened by hand. The Zh'ladar walked through the door, peering with raised eyebrows as it opened and closed behind him on its own. He crossed the room to study the holo-model of the Zoryan negotiator. "Still drawing, I see. Though I must say I prefer the models you've done of T'lar. I even prefer the one you did of me."

Andrei performed a flawless T'larian bow. "Would you like a drink, Your Grace?" When the Zh'ladar nodded, Andrei gestured to the decanter on the sideboard, which rose and filled two empty glasses. As the decanter settled back onto the sideboard, the glasses rose and sailed gracefully into Andrei's outstretched hands. His hands curled around them easily, the scarring faded to a few barely perceptible silver lines. He handed one of the glasses to the Zh'ladar, who raised it in his direction and drank.

"What can I do for you, Your Grace?" Andrei asked, swallowing half of his own drink and gesturing for what was left of the food to come and join them, followed by two empty plates. He offered the platter first to the Zh'ladar, who declined, and then took a generous helping for himself. He'd been hungry ever since he woke up; it seemed that his appetite had expanded along with his senses. Sylvain would be pleased about that, if nothing else.

"I assume that you already know the answer to that question," the Zh'ladar responded.

Andrei didn't like the edge he'd Sensed in this reply. "I'd rather have you tell me. I have no interest in having a conversation with myself." He leaned back against the pillows on the floor and gazed at the skylight. "I haven't become some kind of alien, in spite of what Nick and Diana think."

The Zh'ladar looked directly at him, and Andrei knew that he was taking in the green irises of his eyes, which were now ringed with gold. *So superficial,* thought Andrei. *Why should a little thing like that bother anyone?* But it did. He blinked slowly, and the gold faded out—at least in the mind of the beholder.

"Is that what they think?" the Zh'ladar asked quietly. "Did you Read them to find out, or did they tell you?"

"I didn't need to Read them, and they didn't need to tell me. Their fear was in their eyes when they looked at me. It was what they didn't say that counted." He shook his head, struggling again with his impatience and resentment at the reactions of those whom he'd thought were closest to him.

The Zh'ladar was staring at him intently. "They're frightened of what you have become, Andrei. Aren't you, even just a little?"

Now his impatience turned on the Zh'ladar, and he pushed it down as hard as he could. "No, I'm not," he answered calmly. "Not at all. I feel fine. I feel better than I've felt in a long time.

I'm not going to turn on them, or on you. My work is still the same. I'm just going to be better at it now."

"Your work?"

"My cause. Our cause."

"Is it?" The Zh'ladar's voice was gently probing. "Is Unity's cause the same as yours?"

"Our alliance serves us both. Serves us all."

"Unity is a complex entity whose nature you are only beginning to understand. How can you be so sure that your feelings haven't been created by them to make it easier for you to serve them?"

He stared hard at the Zh'ladar. "That sounds like something Ashahr would say."

Stalemate. Neither spoke. Andrei tried to shrug off the feeling of betrayal. He'd expected support from the Zh'ladar, but maybe even a sentient as evolved as the T'larian couldn't get beyond a basic fear of the unknown. But it really didn't matter; what mattered was the work he had to do. He stood up, but the Zh'ladar didn't move. "Your Grace, I must get back to work. I don't have time to waste."

The Zh'ladar looked up at him, but without any indication that being seated put him at a disadvantage in their argument. "I did not realize that you considered conversation with me to be a waste of time."

"This one is."

"This is not the behavior of the Andrei Savinov that I have come to know. This also is not the behavior that I would have expected of Unity."

Andrei felt restless. He circled the room. He noticed the Zh'ladar following him with his eyes, but he still didn't move. Andrei swung back toward him. "What is the behavior you would have expected of Unity?" he demanded.

"Unity exists in our legend as one of the Gatherers of Sacred Light. Since Sacred Light is the source of wisdom and compassion in the universe, I would have expected that behavior from them ... and from you, as their mindlinked partner."

This piqued Andrei's curiosity and diverted his attention from their brewing argument. He sat down again. "They haven't told me about this yet. What is Sacred Light?"

"Do you remember our discussions about faith?" the Zh'ladar asked him.

"Not well," Andrei admitted. "It wasn't my favorite subject."

"I have always had difficulty understanding your hostility toward religion."

"I'm not hostile. I just don't believe in it. I'm familiar with the stories, but that's all they are—stories. Myths from the fragments of recorded ancient history that still remain."

"How can you be certain of that, Andrei? Perhaps human faith has merely been suppressed."

Andrei shrugged. "I suppose it's possible, but we'll never know, will we? Anyway, what does religion have to do with Unity?"

"Our legends claim that the Creator of the universe—the Source of all life—formed vessels through which the Creator's energy would flow out of mind-space and form what we think of as reality. Our worlds. But there must be balance in reality. Even the Creator has a shadow side—its aspect of destruction, which is revealed as evil in all its multitude of forms. The combining of the energies of creation and destruction was too powerful for the vessels, so they shattered, scattering the Creator's Sacred Light.

"In the universe, there are forces of both kinds—those attempting to regather the Sacred Light and repair the vessels as well as those attempting to advance the patterns of destruction. If our legend is true, Unity is one of the former, while Ashahr—"

"I understand," Andrei interrupted. "While it's an interesting—and rather poetic—explanation, I just don't believe it, at least not in the form in which you present it. I suppose I could ask them … but this is your world's legend, Your Grace. They probably wouldn't see it the same way. Unity was formed from the combined minds of a destroyed planet's population. Who's to say that they don't exist just because that's how they managed to survive, or just to help others being attacked by Ashahr, instead of for some larger purpose?"

Silence. "There is no proof either way, Andrei," the Zh'ladar finally said. "But what I do know is that your attitude toward those who are concerned about you is out of character—both for you and, I believe, for Unity. I would not have expected an entity like that to be something so convinced of its own superiority. The perception of superiority fuels many of Ashahr's patterns."

Andrei suddenly felt lightheaded, and he found that he'd accessed the mindlink … or maybe it had accessed him. His eyes once again glowed green and gold together. "You are correct about our nature, Your Grace, and so is the Peacekeeper. Repair is indeed one of our sacred purposes. Another is creation, and the third is protection. This is also the primary purpose of the Alliance's Peacekeeper, which is why we will be able to work together. But that does not mean that those whom we are protecting are always able to accept us. We will see what sentients in this place and time are capable of."

"Who is speaking?" the Zh'ladar asked.

Andrei blinked, surprised. "I am."

"Who are you? Unity or Andrei?"

Andrei closed his eyes, sighing with frustration. "We are together."

"An ordinary human would find that idea intolerable," the Zh'ladar pressed him. "As I recall, you were extremely distressed about merely becoming telepathic. And now you are mindlinked to an entity whose powers far exceed anything that telepathic humans can do, or even imagine doing."

"It isn't intolerable. Not at all."

"What is it like, Andrei?"

Again Andrei took a deep breath. He really didn't know how to explain, and he really didn't want to try, but he couldn't refuse to answer. "After everything that's gone wrong in my life in the past year, it's like I've been given a second chance." Once again, he locked eyes with the Zh'ladar: his own green eyes this time. "Unity fixed my heart, Your Grace. The pain is gone. I've got my normal lifespan back. I've got the use of my hands back. I'm not a damned invalid anymore! And for the first time since Kylara died, I have a strong, capable partner again. Unity understands what we need to do."

The Zh'ladar was silent, but the T'larian's concern and skepticism resonated in Andrei's mind. The Zh'ladar was afraid that these feelings of newfound strength and power were all an illusion. Could he have a point? Or was he was just like the humans, simply afraid of what he couldn't understand? Andrei didn't know the answer, but the conversation convinced him of one thing: he had to be more careful, if not about what he thought, at least about what he said. The only one who really could understand what it was like was Unity.

The Zh'ladar finally left him alone, and Andrei went back to Searching for K'ril I'th. He needed to know what was happening in the Hegemony, and his spy network had completely disintegrated. Reports over the recent weeks had become sparse and disorganized, until they finally stopped coming—meaning that most of his spies were likely dead. The information that had arrived indicated both increased unrest and increased tightening of security measures, both on Zorya Prime and on the slave worlds. After regaining consciousness (or was it finally becoming conscious, Andrei thought, savoring the memory of that ecstatic first moment of awareness with his expanded senses and new mindpowers), he'd gone over the reports again, trying to see if there were any patterns that he hadn't noticed the first time around.

And then he found it: Ashahr's pattern of chaos and self-destruction. As Ashahr consolidated its hold, the power struggle between members of the ruling class on Zorya Prime diverted attention away from the continuing resource problems of the slaveworlds, which were growing more and more desperate. While the planets closest to Zorya Prime still appeared to be under central control, the outermost slaveworlds were undergoing uprisings and rioting. It was nothing big enough and organized enough for rebels to take over the colonial governments, just enough to create the kind of damage and destruction that hurt the rebels rather than the rulers. This was perfect for Ashahr's purposes. And with Zorya preparing for renewed war with the Alliance, the situation would no doubt get worse. So, like the Alliance, the Hegemony could end up with a war on two fronts, Andrei mused, inside and outside its borders …

That's where K'ril I'th has to be if kri is still alive, Andrei concluded. *On the least well-controlled slaveworlds.* He focused his Search on Devra and Corval. Devra was an industrial center, a hive of activity, while Corval was an isolated mining outpost. Which was the better hiding place? A place with lots of sentients, where there would be support systems in place? Or a place with fewer sentients who could possibly betray kri—but fewer resources for creating an opposition force, which Andrei knew K'ril I'th had been attempting to do?

All the minds pressing against his as he Searched Devra were beginning to drain him. He felt as if he were falling, and the delicate mental thread he'd sent dissolved. He stood up, stretched, and rubbed his eyes. He noticed a wash of color through the window; the sun was beginning to rise.

Rest now, Unity Sent.

I thought I didn't need to rest anymore, he Replied, still feeling cheerful in spite of his temporary lack of success.

Of course you do. You are still human. As it needs food, the human body needs sleep.

But I feel so much better.

That did not make your body superior to a human body. Nor is your brain superior to a human brain.

He almost laughed out loud. *I find that hard to believe.*

No. Unity's Reply was strong; they pushed hard against his consciousness for emphasis. *Your Logos Prime PAs fall into the same trap. Their brains are constructed with the specific differences that allow them to experience telepathy, but this does not mean that they are superior. This is something that you have always known. Why do you forget it now?*

His good humor faded. *If all humans could do the things that this mindlink allows me to do, you would be right. But the truth is that I am the only one who can do them.*

And do you believe that these abilities make you a superior human being? Or will any superiority that you possess be based on what you decide to do with those capabilities?

Andrei was silent. He felt as if he were in an out-of-control transport tube: first climbing high in a blaze of pure energy, then plunging into free fall.

To go from Psi-Null to Psi-Active to mindlinked with us in such a small span of human time is difficult beyond measure, Unity Sent. *It could take years, the way you measure time, to truly understand and accept the consequences.*

I don't have years. I have to return to the Peaceship and start countermeasures against Zorya and Ashahr now.

Not now, Andrei. Soon, but not now. Now you should rest. Let us help you. The entity whispered in his mind, and his brainwaves smoothed into patterns that Ashahr couldn't penetrate. It wouldn't be so bad to take a break, he thought, leaning back on the floor pillows. He closed his eyes and let himself drift into a deep, dreamless sleep.

K'ril I'th's voice in his mind snapped him back to consciousness. "Is someone here? Who called my name?"

Unity had finished the job for him, he realized. They'd taken what he'd been working with—the image of K'ril I'th, translated into a mental signature through Andrei's experience of kri, and his speculations about the two Zoryan slaveworlds—and found K'ril I'th, alive, on Corval.

He thought for a minute. How was he going to explain this?

K'ril I'th, it's Andrei Savinov. I'm not there. I'm on T'lar. I'm Sending thoughts to you.

"Impossible. Andrei Savinov is not telepathic, and neither am I. What kind of a trick is this?"

Listen to me. Ashahr isn't the only telepathic entity out there. I have an ally now who is also telepathic, and who knows Ashahr and is trying to fight it. He tried to convince kri, reminding kri of their secret meeting and of the message kri had sent him.

No response.

He tried telling kri some of the things that only he, among humans, would know about kri. He could Sense kri's disbelief and suspicion beginning to be replaced by curiosity and hope that this might be real, but kri wasn't there yet.

Do you understand what I'm saying?

Silence. Andrei hesitated. What would he do if K'ril I'th didn't believe him?

K'ril I'th, I have a question. Why did you fix it so I couldn't make a copy of the message you sent me? It would have made things a lot easier if I could have played it for the members of my government. No one believed me.

K'ril I'th made a hissing sound that Andrei recognized as the Zoryan equivalent of laughter. "You are still the enemy, Commander. Why would I want to make anything easy on you?"

Andrei was briefly stunned; then he laughed as well, more out of relief than anything else. *So what now, my honorable opponent? What have you been doing with your time while I've been learning how to be telepathic?*

"Planning a coup. The outer colonies are rebelling, and my associates have been collecting arms and collaborators. I still have some contacts back on Zorya Prime, and we think that some well-placed assassinations will work with the rebellions going on out here to throw the Central K'rilate into chaos." Again the hissing sound. "I will not miss G'al or S'lat. And I imagine that you will not either."

Andrei thought about this. If the leaders of the militant Zoryan faction fell, who would the Alliance collaborators have to work with? Their plot would fall apart at the same time. Could Ashahr be stopped simply by killing a few key Zoryans? *But haven't large sections of the population on Zorya Prime accepted the idea of going to war with the Alliance again? Is there still a critical mass of Zoryans who are in favor of the Settlement?*

"That is a problem," K'ril I'th admitted. "There is a chance that these assassinations could trigger civil war."

Are you prepared for that? Do you have enough arms and personnel?

"I doubt it," K'ril I'th replied. "It is very difficult for me to know what progress has been made. Communication between the rebels on the colonies, as well as between the colonies and Zorya Prime, has been extremely difficult, as one might expect. In fact, it has been many days since I have heard from anyone. I am concerned—some of my associates may have been captured."

I can help with that, now that I have this mindlink, Andrei told him.

"Would the Alliance be willing to help our faction secure power? This would be a small price to pay for avoiding another war."

I don't know. I would have to think over how it could be done.

"Do not take too long, Commander Savinov."

Andrei ended contact. He leaned back against the floor pillows and closed his eyes again. He needed to figure out his next move. The negotiation session was now a week away.

Maybe it was time to bring in the Alliance military, but how would he explain all of this to Prime Commander Sesna-Goveril? And even if K'ril I'th got rid of kri's enemies in the Central K'rilate, what about Ashahr? Would this be enough to ruin Ashahr's pattern and send it on its way?

We think you can do better than that, Peacekeeper, Unity Sent.

What do you mean?

Do you want Ashahr to remain in existence? What makes you think it won't return and try again? And what about other vulnerable civilizations? We would like Ashahr to be destroyed, and we think that you are capable of doing that.

How?

You will find a way.

"You think so?" he muttered under his breath. He was finally tired after what had turned out to be only an hour of sleep, and frustrated by all the unknown variables in this game—and alone, too alone in making decisions with consequences he could barely anticipate.

Chapter 22

The last thing Sylvain thought he'd be doing on this trip was hiking down into a cave under Mount Dhaslan, but here he was, following Andrei down this suicidally narrow path, hanging off the edge of a chasm he couldn't see the bottom of. Since there wasn't enough room to walk side by side, as Andrei's bodyguard, was it better to be in front or in back of him? He couldn't figure it out, and then it turned out that it really didn't matter, since Andrei was the one who knew where they were going. He had no idea how Andrei could know the way, since he didn't have a map, but things had gotten so weird lately that Sylvain figured this was just something else he had to accept.

At least Andrei didn't fight him when he'd insisted on going along. That had surprised him, since Andrei wasn't willing to do anything that any of the others wanted. And he wasn't being real nice about it, either. Nick had tried to force him into talking strategy before finally giving up in disgust and leaving that morning for Tiflet, or Kitrian, or whichever Raider outpost he was going to recruit his strike force from; he hadn't told them. He was headed to Kitrian, most likely; there were more Raiders hanging out there, looking for work.

Then Diana had wanted to do her big doctor act, figuring out the changes Andrei had gone through since joining with Unity and maybe even trying to talk to it. (Or them, right?

Didn't Andrei call "it" a "them"?) But Andrei didn't go for that; he'd just told her that her experiment was over and stopped answering her questions. So much for their affair; it didn't seem like they could be lovers now, at least not while there was somebody (something? some things?) stuck in Andrei's head. Unity would be watching the whole time … at least that's what Sylvain thought a mindlink would be like, but he sure wasn't going to ask Andrei about it. It wasn't his business.

Andrei was acting strangely, but Sylvain thought he still knew how to handle him. He wouldn't talk about anything important until he'd sorted it all out for himself, made sense of it all, and figured out his next move. So he needed to be left alone; that was okay, but where was this cold, arrogant attitude coming from? And why couldn't he just do his thinking in the comfort of Sanctuary?

They'd set up a beacon floating in front of them, but it was only one patch of light in the cold, creepy darkness. *Could've lived my whole life without ever setting foot in a cave, and it would've been just fine,* he thought. He tapped his jacket's insignia again to give him some more heat. They moved ever more slowly as the path narrowed, almost clinging to the wall as it became even steeper. Sylvain tripped and stumbled close to the edge of the path as he maneuvered around a tight corner, and the pack on his back threw him even further off balance. He felt himself going over the side, and there was nothing to hold onto …

His body froze in space. Or at least, that's what it felt like—like time itself had stopped. He turned his head and saw Andrei gesture with both hands, and he felt himself float back to the ledge. He landed on his feet, but fear turned his leg muscles to water, and he collapsed onto both knees, shaking.

Andrei looked down at him thoughtfully but didn't say anything and didn't even try to help him get up. It was obvious that he was thinking more about what he'd been able to do with his mind than about how Sylvain felt about his brush with disaster. *This Unity doesn't think much of people,* Sylvain thought suddenly, *because for sure this isn't how Andrei'd be acting if he was just Andrei. Got a real bad feeling about all this ...*

He decided not to say anything. "Far to go now?" he asked, once he could come up with more than a squeak.

Andrei closed his eyes and stood still for a minute, as if he was listening for something. "The pool's at the heart of the cave, which is a long way from here, but the path widens soon. It should be easier going."

"Great." Sylvain tried to rub the darkness out of his eyes, which just made it worse. He *hated* this. He'd had a weird feeling that something bad was going to happen on this trip, and sure enough, it had. It was like one of those bad nightmares he'd been having for the past few days had come true. "Will we get there today? By nightfall?"

Andrei shrugged, still not acting like he cared how Sylvain felt. "What does nightfall mean when you're inside a cave?" He turned around, readjusted his own pack, and started the descent again.

Sylvain stared after him, shook his head in disgust, and followed.

Lucky the survey team had air mattresses, Sylvain thought as he rolled out his sleeping bag. They were already asleep, and Andrei had turned off his beacon a while ago, so hopefully he was sleeping too. Sylvain crawled into the sleeping bag, muttering under his breath about harebrained schemes. "All this work to look at a little pool of water." He rolled around, trying to get comfortable until he was too tired to care, and he slept.

And dreamed.

* * *

Ashahr and Unity. Andrei's thoughts went back and forth between the two telepathic entities as he settled into a hollowed-out part of a wall of rock not far from the edge of the pool. He wasn't trying to communicate with them, just think about them: who they were, what they wanted, what he would do with them, to them, about them …

The survey team finally turned off their beacon on the other side of the pool. After eating, they'd sat talking in low tones with Sylvain. Andrei couldn't hear them physically, but he knew exactly what they were saying. They were still trying to figure out why he'd come out here himself, especially since the rumor was that he was very ill and had gone to T'lar for medical treatment. They were also annoyed and puzzled that the only conversation he'd had with them was to ask for a report—and having gotten one, Andrei had gone off by himself to the other side of the pool.

He didn't care what they thought. Of course he could have just stayed at Sanctuary and Read their minds to find out what they'd discovered, but he wanted to see the reality of his vision of water on T'lar for himself. Besides, it felt so good to be able to exert himself physically again; part of the reason he was doing it was just because he *could*.

So here it was. It was too small to be a source of rehydration for the planet, but just the fact that the pool existed at all meant that there was hope of finding more water. He daydreamed about the planet turning lush and green again, not this barren echo of a once-glorious past …

He thought about damage and about renewal. Even with his beacon off, with his expanded senses, he felt T'lar all around him. The darkness within the cave was intensely alive, not with plants or animals, but with whispered promises of the pure essence of life itself. He could see flickers of life energy in transparent blue, green, and gold; they were only shadows, but they were there nevertheless, and their beauty was exhilarating. He thought of the Zh'ladar's story about Sacred Light.

The planet wasn't dead, as so many in the Alliance believed. He saw the broken connections lying dormant, waiting to be brought back to life again. Unity could fix broken sentients— was it possible that they could fix a broken planet? If so, why hadn't they fixed their own planet when Ashahr laid waste to it?

We became Unity because our planet was dying. It was too late, by then, to heal it, Unity Sent. *But sometimes even a change that appears catastrophic has within it the potential for something better, waiting to be unlocked.*

I know this place isn't dead, Andrei Sent. *Does T'lar have the potential to be unlocked? Can you do it?*

We do not yet know what the pattern will be for this world, Unity Replied. *In some ways, that pattern will be up to you.*

I want it to happen. What do we have to do?

It is not the right time for this question, Unity Sent.

But... Andrei wanted to continue but Sensed that the door was closed for now. He went back to thinking about Ashahr. And Unity.

The important thing to remember, he thought, was that Ashahr had mental influence over its subjects but no physical control. Otherwise it wouldn't have gone through all that trouble to drive him to the edge of madness and suicide— it just would have killed him. Ashahr had to manipulate its victims into doing things to themselves, or to each other. And it was amazingly good at this, he remembered, a chill going through him.

Yet part of him had to acknowledge that it wasn't all demonic skill; Ashahr had found him at a time in his life when he was weary and demoralized ... He shook his head, dismissing the thought. It was over. Ashahr had no more power over him, at least not that kind of power. What other kind was there? And what would it take for him to have power over Ashahr?

Unity, on the other hand, couldn't control anyone's mind. He could have refused the mindlink, and they wouldn't have been able to complete it. Though they couldn't do anything without creating a mindlink with an embodied sentient, once they created that mindlink, the chosen sentient had capabilities that Ashahr could only dream about. (Did it dream? Could he get into its dreams the way it had gotten into his?) But Ashahr could mobilize large numbers of allies, and there was only one of him and Unity. So he had to get Ashahr alone, separate it from its followers. If he could do that, what would he do to it? How could he destroy a psychic predator without a body?

His rage at how the entity had used him against himself was still raw. He felt a burning desire to hurt it as it had hurt him … not just hurt it, but kill it. As a strategist, he knew that he wasn't truly ready to fight it. He didn't know its weaknesses, didn't know how to attack it, didn't know what it would try to do to him now that he was mindlinked with Unity. Right now, though, none of that seemed to matter—at least not enough to quench the fire of his obsession.

Ashahr. He Sent the thought into the darkness. *Come to me. We're not done yet, not by a long shot.* He scrambled to his feet, his breathing rapid and shallow, body tensed as he braced for the physical combat that wasn't coming, but it was the way his body interpreted his mind's desire. *Ashahr, you almost got me when I wasn't ready for you. I'm ready for you now. Come to me, and we'll see who's stronger.* He cast his mind's eye into space, Searching for the entity's mental signature.

Andrei, stop this. Unity's mental voice echoed inside his head, and he winced at the intensity of it. He had the feeling they had been trying to communicate with him for a while but he'd shut them out. *You are far from ready for the encounter that you are attempting to provoke.*

What makes you so sure? he Replied angrily. *Are you afraid?*

There was a long silence. *In many ways, you are the right partner, Peacekeeper. But you have a serious flaw, which could cause our defeat if you cannot master it,* Unity finally Sent.

He really didn't want to know what they meant. *What would that be?*

Part of your soul is so lost that it does not care whether you live or die.

Chapter 23

Diana looked up from her fileviewer at the sound of a knock on her door, but she didn't bother to get up from the nest of cushions on the floor. At least her prison was comfortable. "Come in."

When she saw that it was Andrei, she thought about pretending to ignore him, but that was too childish. She stood up slowly. His eyes fixed on her briefly, and then he looked over at the packed duffel bag and equipment case next to the door. "I've been to see the Zh'ladar, to tell him about the pool. That we found it, and it's real," he said. He looked at her, but she didn't respond. "The Zh'ladar told me that you wanted to leave."

" That's right, she answered. "Since you left without telling me what you were doing, I didn't have time to discuss it with you, and then I found out that I was stranded here until you got back." *Why were they speaking instead of Sending thoughts?* She wondered.

He shook his head. "Diana. I can't win, can I? Can we please just talk?"

She studied him. He was still wearing the clothes he'd set out in, which looked like he'd slept in them. His boots, pants, and jacket, all black, were streaked with rust-red grime. He had a stubble of beard, and his dark hair looked like he'd pushed it out of his way rather than combed it for the last couple of days. She tried as hard as she could to Block her traitorous thoughts, which were all about how attractive she still found him.

He waited for her to say something, and when she didn't, he continued. "So is it the Peaceship you were planning to go back to, or the Core?" he asked.

Since he was speaking, she would, too. "I don't see the point in my returning to the Peaceship with you, Andrei, unless you let me continue my experiment. Otherwise I should go back to my labs so I can try again with someone else. Though I would need to get my implant back, to find out what happened to it." She swallowed hard and moved over to the window, looking out to avoid looking at him. "I may not really want to live in the Core anymore, but it's the only home I've got."

He looked startled. "You don't want to go back to Logos Prime?"

She was surprised too—surprised that he hadn't Read it, and surprised that she'd finally put voice to something that had been on her mind over the last few tumultuous weeks. No, she didn't want to return to Logos Prime. She'd felt alienated from society for as long as she could remember, but there had never been a choice before. Now that she'd lived in space and seen another planet, she thought that maybe there could be something else for her besides the sterility of life in her labs, the twisted politics of the Think Tank, and trying to convince the Challenge to trust her and work with her. Her old life felt fruitless and empty.

But without Andrei … what kind of life could she have away from Logos Prime and away from him? With the exception of the last few weeks of studying Zoryan brains, she didn't have any training in xenobiology, and without it she couldn't join the Alliance Military as a doctor or scientist. She thought of Nick's comment that she wouldn't make a good

Free Raider, and she knew he was right. "If there's no work for me on the Peaceship, I might as well go back," she repeated.

For a while, neither of them spoke. He crossed the room and stood next to her, but he still didn't say anything. She decided to wait him out. Finally, he sighed deeply. "I know I've treated you badly," he said. "What can I say to make things right? I'm truly sorry …" His voice trailed off.

She didn't answer.

He gazed out the window. "I don't know what to do about you."

She raised her eyebrows. "What do you mean?"

"I can't let you into my mind, Diana. Not with Unity there. I believe that the barriers they put in place to keep Ashahr out would damage a human telepath as well. They've rewired my brain to make it possible for me to communicate with them, but I'm afraid that if you tried to enter my mind, you could be hurt, maybe even killed. Unity either doesn't know what will happen or won't tell me. So we can't risk it." He shook his head, obviously frustrated at not being able to express himself more clearly.

"What do you think would happen?" she asked.

"I don't know." He sighed. "I don't understand the mental processes involved, so I'm just going by my intuition. I wish I could be more specific, but I can't."

"What about Reading Zoryan minds?" she asked. "How will that work?"

"I can Read Zoryan minds. I already have, " he answered. "It's PAs that are the problem. Maybe because of the differences between PA and Zoryan brains." She leaned with her back against the wall, finally facing him. "So why didn't you tell me this in the first place, instead of pushing me away without an explanation?"

"I don't know. When I first woke up, I was so shocked by the changes in my mind—and body—that I got caught up in how amazing it all was. How good it felt," he replied.

"The expanded senses that came out of becoming telepathic through the implant were so frightening and …" He hesitated, as though searching for the right word. "Invasive. I felt like I was under attack even before Ashahr came along. But being telepathic through Unity is completely different."

His expression changed; he looked like he was entranced. "Unity's expanded my entire consciousness. There's a whole world of sensation and awareness that humans—PNs and PAs both—don't have any idea about. Everything is alive and has a pattern, and there's so much beauty in the patterns." He sighed. "I'm not explaining it well. It's visual, but no holo-painting or model I could make would do justice to this reality."

She couldn't help but stare at him in astonishment. He didn't sound like the man she thought she knew. Yet when she thought of his holo-models, she suddenly understood. Behind the soldier and diplomat was someone who, in a different world and a different life, might have been an artist of great vision. Unity had managed to bring out that side of him.

He shook his head again, looking embarrassed. "Anyway, I got distracted—and impatient with all of you for not being able to understand, for being afraid, for being so limited …" His voice trailed off again. "At least, that's how it seemed to me at the time."

"And now?" she asked.

He turned his gaze on her again, and her heart caught in her throat at the look in his eyes. "I had time in the cave to think about what I'd been doing, and I didn't like what I discovered. Now I remember that I have flaws of my own. And I remember that there are people who care about me, and whom I care about as well." He reached for her, brushing the fingers of one hand against the side of her face and gently pulling her closer with the other. She'd resolved to stick to her ultimatum (let me continue to run my experiment, or I'm leaving), but once he'd wrapped his arms around her and his mouth found hers, she lost track of her argument. As their embrace became more passionate, she instinctively reached out with her mind to Share telepathic union with him …

And fell into a pit of darkness so deep and so wide that the terror of it was overwhelming. Unlike the time she'd gotten a glimpse of Andrei's inner world in his encounter with Ashahr, there were no emotions, just this chasm. She felt as if she were suffocating in the emptiness, as if she'd been cast out into the vacuum of deep space and there was no end to it. She couldn't think her way through this; she just kept falling and falling …

"*No!*" Finally, a sound, a scream. Her voice. She could feel a barrier of some kind trying to force its way between her mind and the darkness, and then, after an eternity, she was free. When her vision cleared and she caught her breath, she saw that Andrei had backed away from her. He too was breathing heavily, and he looked dazed as he shook his head to clear it. With an enormous effort at self-control, she wiped her eyes, resting her head in her hands for a minute. "I guess you know what happened to me," she said. "What happened to you?"

"I got caught while trying to disengage your mind from the link," he replied, sounding weary. "Are you all right?"

She almost laughed at the foolish question. But there was no point in getting hysterical. "I guess so," she finally answered. "It seems like your intuition was right after all."

"For all the good it does us." He rubbed the bridge of his nose. "Do you think we could shut down our psi-senses when we …"

She shook her head.

"Then, unless things change, we can't be together. Not now, anyway."

"Not until this is over," she replied. "Until Unity is gone."

He nodded. "Unless something changes," he repeated. "But I'd like you to stay on the Peaceship, at least for now. You can work on your study of Zoryan minds."

She gave him a look of disbelief and didn't say anything. Why did he need a study of Zoryan minds now that he could Read them himself?

He tried again. "You can monitor me to study the nature of the mindlink, the way you did with the implant. Maybe I can even figure out a way for you to Read Unity without getting hurt."

He was grasping at straws, she thought. *Why won't he tell me that he needs me? That he could use some support and encouragement as he prepares for the fight of his life?* Even as she thought this, though, she realized how futile a hope it was. He might be able to acknowledge that he cared for her, but after Kylara's death, it would be a cold day in hell before he admitted to anyone, including himself, that he *needed* someone.

"Besides, you'd be in danger on Logos Prime right now," he said. "Who knows how Nick's civil war is going to work out?"

She felt tears coming to her eyes again and blinked them away, furious with herself for her weakness. "So I guess we go back to being colleagues."

He went over to her and carefully brushed the tears off her eyelashes. "We could at least be friends." He moved to put his arms around her again, but she backed away.

"Yes, we could." She couldn't speak above a whisper, and she turned her back on him. It was only after he closed the door behind him that she finally let herself cry.

Chapter 24

Kitrian, the Free Raider outpost on a distant moon of Karellia, had become a tent city over time. The Raiders had paid Karellia to put up a dome over part of the surface, and it served as a place where they could leave their vessels (which is where many of them lived most of the time, ferrying cargo and carrying on a variety of misadventures) and congregate with each other.

But after the war, the settlement grew larger than they'd anticipated, and now it was pushing up against the dome's physical limits. Brightly colored tents and ramshackle structures made of a variety of surplus materials had almost no space between them, and the winding paths that separated the rows were barely wide enough for one human at a time to pass. Nick threaded his way through, kicking aside debris and trying to breathe through his mouth; the dome's air quality had also gotten worse with the extra population. He finally reached an electric-blue tent at the end of the row. *She got herself a corner office,* he thought. "Anyone home?"

"Who's askin'?" A head popped out the flap, and the woman's wary look was replaced by the flash of a grin. "Cap'n Hayden. Come on in."

The tent was a lot bigger inside than it looked; both he and its occupant could actually stand completely upright. Given the size of its occupant, this was especially surprising. Gretchen Vandermar was easily as tall as Nick, and about as large. He knew that she was fanatic about exercise, and her muscular arms and legs strained against her tight-fitting short-sleeved shirt and shorts. She was not wearing the gray jumpsuit that served as an unofficial Raider uniform, so she wasn't working, at least not right now. Her long, white-blonde hair was tightly pinned up, though a few stray wisps brushed her wide face and occasionally drifted into her pale-blue eyes. When he'd first met, her he'd wondered why a practical woman like her would keep all that hair, but then he remembered that her old boss—her idol—Kylara Val had also had long hair.

She was studying him too, and she seemed to like what she saw. *She might be interesting,* he thought, but the nature of the connections between them made life simpler if they kept their relationship strictly business. *Besides,* he thought, *she could probably crush me.*

At the end of the war, there were hundreds of Logos Prime PNs who decided they weren't going home. The problem was that no one wanted to take them. The leaders of the other Alliance worlds were worried enough about what would happen when their own soldiers came home after being at war for so long; they didn't want to add to their burden by taking the soldiers of an alien race. Andrei pushed hard, but most of them stood firm—except, of course, for T'lar, who would do it as a personal favor to him. But the planet couldn't really support even its native population; besides, humans didn't want to try to scratch out an existence in such a hopeless place.

The Free Raiders were the obvious answer: after all, there was no one in charge to refuse. But each Raider Captain with a ship large enough to require a crew had to be approached individually, which was a lot of work. Andrei had needed help to get it done, so on one of the rare occasions of concord between the brothers, he and Nick had worked together. During the war, Andrei had hired Raiders to do spying and guerrilla attacks, and many of the Captains knew and liked him. The two of them, with Andrei pretending to be a client of Nick's, managed to place a large number of Logos Prime humans with Raiders as crew.

Only one Raider knew the real nature of the connection between Nick and Andrei—and Nick was standing right in front of her. Gretchen had been Kylara's Exec until her death, and she'd refused to sign on with anyone else in the Alliance Military. Andrei had gotten her a ship of her own and asked Nick to help supply the contacts to get her business going. At Andrei's request, he checked on her from time to time; she seemed to have made out all right. That heavy, lowest-level Inner Core accent masked a shrewd mind and years of experience of witnessing military decision-making at its highest levels. *Yeah,* Nick concluded, *she'll do just fine.*

"Good to see ya again, Cap'n," she said. She gestured to a brightly patterned rug covering the floor of her tent and went over to a storage locker in the corner. "Have a seat. Can I getcha a drink?"

Still big on titles, he thought, somewhat annoyed. He never used them himself, unless he was forced to. Lying about her age—and getting away with it because of her size—she'd gone into the Alliance Military so young that she probably couldn't get rid of the conditioning. "*Livrash,* if you've got it, Gretchen, thanks."

"*Livrash,* huh? C'mander Savinov's old fav'rite," she remarked, bringing over an unopened bottle and two grimy-looking glasses.

Nick eyed his glass, then shrugged and tossed down the drink. He hoped that the *livrash* would kill whatever was still alive in there. "It's hard for me to imagine Mister Serious drinking anything stronger than tea."

She snorted but didn't reply.

He was curious; *livrash* seemed so out of character for Andrei ... or maybe not. "Tell me something. In all those years, did you ever see Andrei get drunk on this stuff?"

She eyed him coldly. "I ain't tellin' no tales on the C'mander. Haven't ya ever gone out drinkin' with your own kin?"

"It hasn't been that kind of relationship," he answered, trying not to sound bitter. His anger extended from their past into the current situation. When he last saw Andrei, his brother had been so damned preoccupied with the weird alien mind-thing in his head that he wasn't interested in talking about how to defeat the Zoryan collaborators. Nick had gotten fed up with him and left. He wouldn't have stuck around as long as he had if he hadn't been scared that Andrei was gonna die.

There was an awkward silence. "So how's he doin'?" she finally asked. "His heart and all."

Nick stared at her, confused. "What do you mean?"

She looked shocked, then defensive. "Nothin'. Didn't mean anything."

"Gretchen, come on. This is my brother we're talking about. If there's something wrong with him that he hasn't had the decency to tell me about …"

She looked down at the rug and traced the pattern with a finger. "About a year ago, Zoryans almost got him with a flashbomb. New heart, new lungs. New heart don't work so good."

Nick wanted to get up and move around, but there was nowhere to go. Part of him was furious with Andrei for not telling him, while part of him was horrified at the thought of how much his brother had been through and felt guilty because he hadn't been able to help … but how could he help if the bastard wouldn't tell him anything? He fumed silently.

"Look, Cap'n Hayden, I'm real sorry ya had to find out this way. I screwed up." Gretchen was awkward in her apology.

He shook his head. "It's not your fault. Don't worry about it." *Think about the job,* he told himself. "Look, Gretchen, I'm here about a job. For you, that is, as my subcontractor." He shook his head when she offered him the bottle again. Stuff was too powerful; he needed to keep his head. She finished her drink and refilled her glass. It didn't seem to affect her at all; she probably could drink him under the table. If she had a table, that is.

"What kind of job?" she asked.

"I'm putting together a strike force," he replied.

"Strikin' at what? Zoryans?" Her face lit up. "Count me in, boyo—um, Cap'n."

"Damn it, Gretchen, call me Nick, already, okay? No, not Zoryans. At least not directly." It was harder to get into it than he'd thought it would be; in spite of himself, he kept imagining what would happen if Darya and Saalovaarian discovered his double-cross. Part of the reason he'd chosen her was that there was no possible way that she could be involved in this plot: Kylara's Exec wouldn't be caught dead collaborating with Zoryans. Finally, against his better judgment, he took another drink and a deep breath and plunged in, telling her all about the arms cache on Selas and the collaboration between the Hegemony, the ultraradical wing of the Challenge, and the Ilyat of Sendos.

She put down her latest glass of *livrash* untouched; obviously the seriousness of the whole thing had gotten through to her. "For Earth's sake, Nick, that's a killer of a story. I don't think I woulda believed it if it came from someone 'sides you. Who else knows about this?"

"Andrei knows. He doesn't want to go to the Alliance Military, because he thinks that if it all comes out in the open, it'll start the war up again right away, and he says we're not ready."

"We would be if Prime C'mander Val was still around," she said fiercely. "Bloody Sesna-Goveril ain't good enough to lick her boots."

Nick absentmindedly poured himself another half glass of *livrash* and sipped at it. The stress was getting to him. He hated plotting and planning; he just wanted to go kick some ass. Now. "Yeah, well, sorry to remind you, Gretch, but she's not around anymore, and my brother didn't get the job—"

"Didn't want the job," Gretchen interrupted. "Turned it down flat."

Nick blinked. Something else he didn't know about Andrei. No point in pursuing it, though. "So we've got what we've got. Besides, I don't want the Military to take the weapons, 'cause I want them for myself."

She looked puzzled. "Whatcha gonna do with 'em?"

He grinned at her. "I'm gonna take over Logos Prime, that's what." He finished his drink. "With your help, that is."

After he explained the plan to her, she sat back, looking thoughtful, and didn't say anything for a while. Finally, she studied him, and he could tell that he'd made the right choice for a partner. "So ya gonna let those that hired ya think you're working for them long enough so we can get the weapons off Selas, but insteada helping the Zoryans get in, we're gonna go off to Logos Prime and use Councilor Ardelle's setup to take over the place for the PNs."

He nodded.

"Nobody'll be around to make sure ya do what you're s'posed to do? I thought you said the Council members got allies in the Military."

"Yeah, I did, but I don't know what Darya's planning to use 'em for. If some of them come out with us, we'll have to deal with 'em. It could get nasty."

"Yeah, it sure could. What if there's lots more of them than us?"

"I don't think there will be," he replied. "If the plot gets too big, they can't keep it a secret."

"So how many of us are there gonna be?"

"That's a good question, Gretch. There's gotta be enough of us to stay in space with the weapons and hold the Upper Core hostage while some of us are inside the Lower Core helping the PNs take it over and secure it. It's hard to figure out who to trust with this. Too many Challenge members wouldn't give a damn if the Zoryans carted off all the PAs, and too many Raiders would be happy to take the weapons for themselves and just go off and sell 'em to the highest bidder—or turn around and sell the knowledge to whoever they thought might pay 'em for it."

"So ya gotta be real careful who ya tell what to."

"Yeah, it's a really delicate operation," he answered. They both laughed. Neither of them were well suited to delicate operations, and they knew it. "My main contact on Logos Prime is Fiona Callahan." He looked over at her; she shook her head, indicating that she didn't know her. "Fiona's the one I told about the weapons on Selas. She told the Challenge leaders, and that's how Darya found out that I knew. I told Fiona to go along with whatever Darya wants her to do. I assume she's gonna be mobilizing people to seal off the PN levels of the Core so that when the attack comes from space, the PAs can't use PNs as hostages or escape into our levels."

"And the Raiders?" Gretchen asked.

"I've got a couple of ideas I want to run through with you."

When they were done, he felt more hopeful than he had in a long time. It really seemed like they might be able to pull this thing off after all. He stood up to leave and found the floor and the ceiling trying to change places. When had they finished that bottle of *livrash?*

She caught his arm to steady him … and didn't let go. She didn't seem at all drunk, but she had that same look in her eye that she'd had when he first walked in. "Wouldja wanna celebrate our partnership, Nick?" she asked. "I have some free time. Might be fun."

He ran his hands through his hair and looked all around the tent—anywhere but at her. *Sober up, Hayden. Think fast.* "I don't think it would be a good idea," he finally answered. "You

275

know, while we're working together ..." His voice ran down as he ran out of ideas for how to handle the situation.

She shrugged, not looking the least bit upset. "No big deal. No harm in askin', right?"

"None whatsoever," he agreed, sighing with relief at her calm reply as he stumbled out of her tent. He didn't even want to think about what she'd be like if she were angry.

Chapter 25

Back on the Peaceship, Andrei found that he'd developed a taste for mind-travel.

Searching for K'ril I'th had started it, and Sending messages between K'ril I'th and kri's conspirators had sharpened his skills. Soon, though, he got bored with the simplicity of that and began using the mindlink to explore different parts of the Hegemony. K'ril I'th inadvertently helped with this by providing access to the conspiracy members' minds for the messages kri Sent, which gave him their mental signatures. All he had to do was find someone whose mind he could enter and look out at the world from that sentient's vantage point. He learned a lot this way: what was actually happening on the various slaveworlds as well as in the Central K'rilate (where there was an aide here, a junior guard there, who shared K'ril I'th's cause) and where the vulnerabilities were. The information, which he carefully recorded in case anything happened to him, would be highly useful in future negotiations. Which was why he kept doing it ... or so he told himself.

But after awhile, even this wasn't enough. The more mind-traveling he did, the hungrier he was for more. He was hungry for freedom from physical constraints and hungry for knowledge. He wanted to see other parts of the galaxy. He wanted to see where Unity and Ashahr came from. Was it possible that he could find Ashahr instead of waiting for Ashahr to come to him?

He also thought about humans. There were no remaining records to identify the home planet's location, but maybe Unity knew where Earth was. What would it be like after all these centuries? Were the humans there PA or PN, or had they transcended those categories altogether? And no doubt other humans had set up their own communities in space; would it be possible to find them?

Unity's reaction to his questions was frustrating. Their answers were cryptic, and they didn't want him to spend time Searching for anything unrelated to their mission. They didn't know how to locate Ashahr, they told him; Ashahr was as capable as Unity was of hiding its mental signature from its enemy.

There must be a way to figure it out, Andrei Sent.

We have been trying for more years than you have been alive, Peacekeeper, Unity Replied. *You are getting sidetracked. You are letting this infatuation with mind-travel divert you from your work.*

He was annoyed. *Untrue. I'm preparing for Settlement negotiations, helping to engineer a Zoryan coup, and trying to figure out a way to destroy your enemy. So don't tell me I'm not doing anything.*

Nevertheless, your attention is not fully focused on these things. You have such a powerful and restless mind. Flooding it with the sensations of mind-travel is too seductive, Unity Sent. *Mind-travel is draining as well as diverting. You are not spending enough time preparing for battle with Ashahr. Ashahr is not finished with you, Andrei. It will try again, and we do not yet know what form that attack will take.*

Nonsense. I haven't been seduced by anything. But it was a reflexive response on Andrei's part; he knew they were right about Ashahr still being out there, and he knew he enjoyed mind-travel more than preparing for psychic combat. Who in their right mind wouldn't?

Even worse, he knew that eventually Unity would end this mindlink. How in the name of the Six would he go back to life as a PN?

He Sensed someone in the real world trying to get his attention, and reluctantly he left mind-space to return to reality. As his vision of mind-space faded, he felt a wash of dizziness. It was almost like Unity was trying to prove its point that too much mind-travel would drain him, he thought resentfully. Finally his office came back into view—along with Sylvain standing in the middle of the room with his arms crossed tightly over his chest, watching him.

Andrei had been sitting at his desk, and he spun his chair partway around to get a closer look at his Exec. Sylvain looked angry: not concerned-angry, which he was used to, but genuinely grim. It seemed like he'd been that way ever since their trip to the cave on T'lar. "What's wrong now?" Andrei snapped, still caught up in his exchange with Unity.

"Nothing, sir." Sylvain responded. His tone sounded distant and mechanical. He held out a stack of discs. "We just received these from the Zoryan negotiating team. New demands."

Andrei inserted each of them into a fileviewer and scanned them one by one. Sylvain stood stiffly next to his chair, his eyes fixed on the far wall. The tension was easy to Sense, and Andrei knew they were past due for some kind of discussion to clear the air between them. He took two of the four discs out of the viewer and handed them to Sylvain. "Pass these along to Danar's team for research and recommendations," he told him. "I'll handle the rest myself." Sylvain nodded and turned to leave. Andrei touched his arm. "Wait, Syl," he said. "Let's take a break. Want some tea? I'd like to talk—"

Sylvain quickly stepped away from his hand as if he'd gotten a shock. "Sorry, sir, got a lot of work to do right now,"

Sylvain interrupted. "Maybe later." He was gone before Andrei could finish his sentence, making it an order rather than a request. *Sir?*

Diana was coming in just as Sylvain was leaving, but he barely nodded at her. Andrei found his own sense of confusion mirrored on her face. "What's with him?" she asked.

"I don't know," he answered. "I've been trying to figure that out myself."

Diana looked thoughtful. "He's been acting strangely ever since we got back. I know you're not going to like this idea, but maybe you should Read his mind—find out what's really going on."

Andrei shook his head firmly. "Absolutely not. I couldn't do that to him. Besides, he asked me to promise that I wouldn't, and I did."

"When did he do that?"

"On the way back from T'lar."

"Don't you think that's kind of strange?"

"No. No PN wants someone inside his head. I did it a couple of times to him by accident when the implant was active, and I guess he was afraid it would really get out of hand once I became ... well, the kind of telepath I am now."

"But you have control over it now," she argued. "You're not going to Read him accidently anymore."

"Listen, he doesn't want me to Read him, so I'm not going to do it," Andrei said impatiently. "The days before Settlement negotiations are always stressful, and now he has to deal with a telepathic boss. He's probably just feeling uncomfortable with this whole situation. I'll try again to get him to talk about it."

"But what if something's really wrong? You may have promised not to Read him, but I didn't," Diana persisted. "Let me do it."

Andrei rubbed the bridge of his nose, feeling a dull ache starting up behind his eyes. *There are times when I spend more time arguing with my allies than fighting my enemies,* he thought. "Leave him alone, Diana. I'll handle it."

* * *

Diana wasn't the only one who didn't feel bound by Andrei's promise to Sylvain not to Read him. Unity hadn't made that promise either. When they told Andrei about what they'd discovered, his rage reverberated through the mindlink. But when he finally calmed down, he came up with a plan that was like nothing they could have anticipated.

In all their years, Unity couldn't remember ever being linked to a creature as passionate as this one. Passion was not a productive emotion: Ashahr had inspired the passions that had destroyed their world and countless others. Unity had renounced all of that when they became a group mind— otherwise the mindlink that bound them together would not be able to function.

Yet now they were linked to a sentient whose mind was profoundly disturbing to them. Brilliant and relentless, striving toward the light of understanding but plagued by dark memories and unresolved losses and conflicts, Andrei's mental signature set the crystalline harmony of the group mind vibrating with the intensity of his demands. The more they gave him, the more he wanted.

And now this. Unity was a spiritual entity, and Andrei's radical idea evoked a response that could only be described as passionate.

Sacrilege! It would be sacrilege!

That's not a meaningful response, Andrei shot back at them.

Sacred Light is not meant to be used to destroy.

What makes you so sure of that? The Zh'ladar told me that Sacred Light was a mix of creative and destructive energies. If it's so powerful and Ashahr believes in it, it might just work.

There was a long silence.

In all these years you've been chasing Ashahr, you haven't come up with anything else that's worked, Andrei persisted. *If destroying Ashahr truly is your goal, you have to use every resource at your disposal to make it happen. You can't let anything get in your way … least of all your personal feelings.*

We are not referring to personal feelings when we say that what you propose would be sacrilege, Unity Replied. *We are referring to universal law.*

Again, I want to know what makes you so certain you know what that is. Perhaps being able to use Sacred Light to destroy evil is part of universal law. Did you ever think of that?

They had not thought of that. They would think of it now.

Chapter 26

Nick sat in the pilot's chair of his cruiser with his back to the viewscreen and watched the image of Darya Ardelle materialize on the holo-pad positioned in the empty space in back of the passengers' seats. The cruiser was on a launch site outside the domed city on Kitrian. She'd found him pretty easily—but then again, he hadn't been hiding from her.

It was comforting to know that she was far away on Logos Prime right now; most likely she wouldn't check up on him too closely in terms of whom he'd hired for the strike force. After all, she wasn't exactly a professional conspirator. He'd invented a cover story for Gretchen and planted it in both the Logos Prime and the Alliance datanets in case she wanted info on whom he'd picked as his second-in-command, but there was always the remote possibility that she'd seen her with Kylara sometime during the war. He just had to hope she wasn't a control freak who needed to meet every member of the team.

Andrei sat in the pilot's chair with him. Well, that wasn't exactly right; Andrei's body was on the Peaceship, which was in its usual spot on the Alliance side of the War Border until Settlement negotiations, when it would move into neutral space. But Andrei's consciousness was inside Nick's mind, ready to listen to the conversation between him and Darya.

He never in a million years would've thought he'd do this, not even for his brother, but wasn't there some expression about desperate times calling for desperate measures? At least it didn't feel as disgusting as he'd thought it would. In fact, he didn't feel anything unless Andrei Sent a thought, which came out as if he were standing next to him, talking in that obnoxiously calm, quiet, reasonable voice of his. Andrei never yelled; his voice never cracked with emotion. How the hell did he do that, especially given everything he'd been through?

"Nice to see you again, Nick," Darya said. Was he imagining it, or was her voice full of unspoken menace?

Get a grip, Nick, Andrei Sent. *Now's not the time for misgivings.*

Fuck off, Nick thought back at him. "Hey, Darya. What's up?"

"The first payment should be in your account by now," she said.

"Yeah, I got it. I used it to make down payments to my subcontractors."

"So you've put your team together already. That was quick."

"Well, you told me this was gonna happen soon." Briefly he described the skills and assets of his partners. "They want to know what they're supposed to do. What should I tell them?"

"You're going to pick up some of the weapons from Selas," she replied. "From Selas, you'll go to the War Border. I'll give you the coordinates when we're ready to proceed. You'll get codes to access the Alliance defense grid to let in our Zoryan allies, and you'll escort some of them to Logos Prime and help them secure the Core."

"What's all this 'some of' business?" Nick demanded. "Some of the weapons. Some of the Zoryans. What about the rest of 'em?"

"You don't have to worry about the rest of them, Nick," Darya snapped. "You just take care of your end, and not only will you be well paid, but you'll be around to witness the dawning of a new age for free PNs."

"That's all well and good, but how the hell am I supposed to know which weapons are ours? And how are we supposed to get them? If we've gotta fight for 'em, I'll need more help than the team I hired."

"Saalovaarian is mobilizing a strike force of Ilyat members of the Alliance Military and Ilyat Free Raiders to secure the prison, which should be under his control by the time you get there," she answered. "So getting the weapons off Selas should be easy."

"Won't the Sendosian government send troops to get their prison back?"

"We're planning for it to be over too fast for that. By the time they mobilize, we'll have control of the prison, which of course is heavily armed and easy to defend when you're expecting trouble. You won't have to worry about which weapons are yours—they'll be given to you."

"Isn't part of the arsenal already in place, hidden in the Core?"

"That's right. But not enough, and not the right ones."

Nick was about to open his mouth to ask more questions, but Andrei stopped him. *You're supposed to be a Raider doing this for pay, remember? She'll get suspicious if you ask too many questions about parts of the plan that don't concern you.*

So how're we supposed to find out—?

Don't worry about that right now. Just ask about what's supposed to happen on Logos Prime.

"Okay, fine," he said to Darya. "So we take the Zoryans and the weapons to Logos Prime. How do we get through the planetary defense grid, and what do you want us to do once we've done it?"

"This whole thing's being handed to you on a silver platter, Nick," she answered, her image grinning smugly. "I'm an Alliance Council member with top security clearance, remember? You'll have the planetary defense grid coordinates by the time you get to Logos Prime. Your job will be to help the Zoryans secure the PA levels of the Core, take over intra-level communications and transport tubes, and capture and hold key leaders. I've got my Challenge members getting the word out to the PNs and preparing them to help secure their own levels by the time you show up."

"Got it. So how much lead time am I gonna have?" he asked her.

"You and your strike force are on standby as of now," Darya replied. "You may have to wait a couple of days, but your team should be mobilized and ready to move immediately." Her image started to fade. "Good-bye, Nick. Next time I see you, it'll be on Logos Prime, and I'll be the one sitting behind Robert Jaxome's desk."

"So what do you think of all this?" Nick asked Andrei once he was certain Darya's transmission had ended. He felt weird speaking out loud to thin air, but he sure as hell wasn't going to start pretending to be telepathic himself.

Very productive session. We know a lot more now than we did an hour ago, Andrei Sent. *The best part is that now I've got Darya's mental signature. I can use the mindlink to go into her mind and get the rest of the information we need, including access codes to all those files you saw on Selas. We'll also have the names of all the conspirators in the military. I need that for Sesna-Goveril.*

"So you're gonna tell him what's going on?"

I'll tell him what he needs to know, so that he'll do what I need him to do.

"What do you mean?"

I've been working with a group of Zoryans who are trying to get back in power. The key conspirators are spread out across the Hegemony's slaveworlds. They have to be transported back to Zorya Prime and to the Peaceship. I need the Alliance Military to help with this, using captured Zoryan cruisers to disguise themselves.

"You think Sesna-Goveril will believe you?"

I think I have enough evidence to convince him.

"So what *aren't* you gonna tell him?"

I'm not going to tell him about what'll be happening on Logos Prime ... until after it's done.

Nick grinned. Finally, Andrei was on their side. "So the Alliance Military is off ferrying Zoryans all over the place while we take over the Core. Where do you think the Zoryans and the weapons that aren't coming with me are going?"

It's obvious that most of the strike force will be needed to secure Sendos, Andrei Sent. *The rest will go to the Peaceship.*

"Why there?"

Because we start Settlement negotiations in two days. The Zoryans intend to use the breakdown of talks to start the war again. Their first act will be to take over the Peaceship, as well as Sendos and Logos Prime. They'll need the extra troops to accomplish this.

"And what about you?"

They're assuming that I will be dead by then, or be killed during the takeover.

Nick's high spirits evaporated. "So Ashahr's gonna be on the Peaceship?"

Ashahr will have to be there. It seems that Robert Jaxome was right. Zoryans aren't telepathic. They're getting the information from Ashahr, who can do what I'm doing now—communicate telepathically with a non-telepath.

"Do you know how to kill it yet?" Nick asked.

Silence. *I have an idea,* Andrei finally Sent. It was obvious that he wasn't going to share it.

Nick was silent too, thinking about what would happen if Andrei's idea didn't work. "You think you're strong enough? You think your heart can tolerate this kind of battle—a mind battle?"

My heart? Nick could hear surprise in the thought Andrei Sent; a moment later, he'd obviously Read the rest of it. *Gretchen told you.*

"Yeah, she did. Why the hell didn't you?"

Silence. *My heart's fine now, Nick. Unity repaired it.*

"That doesn't answer my question. Damn it, Andrei, we're family!"

Would you have wanted your family to worry about you when there was nothing they could do?

Nick sighed, thinking about it. He found that he couldn't say for sure whether he would've told them or not. He thought about his own reaction if Andrei had told him: he would have gone crazy wanting revenge. Then he thought of Coraline: she was so sensitive, and had been through so much, that he couldn't imagine dumping something like that on her. He didn't say anything.

We still have to work out what's going to happen to Logos Prime, Andrei Sent, changing the subject.

"I've already figured that out," Nick answered.

You think you have, but there are two questions I wonder whether you've considered.

"Such as?"

I know you'll have help from the inside, but since you're not planning on bringing the Zoryans with you, you'll only have your small team of Raiders to take over the entire Core.

"That's why the kind of weapons she's gonna give us is so important," Nick replied. "I know what I need. I just hope she's got the same idea."

Which is?

"That we're gonna have to hold the Upper Core hostage from above. So the weapons I need are the really big ones. Particle beam torpedoes. Long-range laser cannons. You know, the kind of stuff that can blow up big chunks of a planet. PA bastards'll have to stand down, at least long enough to start dealing." He felt smug. Andrei wasn't the only one who could put a battle plan together.

Makes sense, Andrei Sent.

"So what's your other question?"

Once you take over the Core, what are you planning to do with it?

Shit, thought Nick. Had Andrei Read his thoughts about this? "What do you mean?" he asked, trying to sound casual.

What type of government are you planning to install? How will it operate? What laws will it follow, and what are you going to do with all the PAs?

For Earth's sake, Nick thought. "The Challenge'll be in charge ..." His voice trailed off. The truth was, they'd never gotten close enough to even the most remote prospect of a true revolution, and they didn't have a real plan. This was all happening way too fast. But he'd be damned if he'd admit that to Andrei. "We'll figure it out as we go along. What do you care, anyway? You lost interest in what happened on Logos Prime a long time ago."

I care, Nick. Maybe it took me a while to realize it, but I do care, Andrei Sent. *Besides, I told you I'd help the Challenge, and I will. But I need you to open your mind to another idea of freedom for PNs besides conquering the Core.*

Nick was puzzled. What else could there possibly be?

Andrei told him.

Chapter 27

The jeweled Erlandian stiletto had a name: Illusion. Sylvain studied it, turning it over in his hand and watching the midnight-blue blade glitter as it caught the light. Those who made these knives by hand, one at a time, gave each its own name. A long time ago, the Erlandian Council member, knowing of Kylara's rare weapons collection, had presented it to her as a gift, and now Andrei had it. He kept it locked away with Kylara's other personal property, but it didn't take a genius to figure out the code: Kylara's birth date. Andrei hadn't bothered to put in a fancy lock, because who was going to steal anything from him?

Not stealing, Sylvain thought. *I'm not keeping it for myself.* Yet when he was done using it, there wouldn't be anyone left to give it back to.

Unity was evil; they had to be stopped. And Andrei ... Andrei was gone. Sure, his body was still here, but the inside—the soul—wasn't his anymore.

Andrei had warned him about this, and as usual, he'd turned out to be right. Before he took that drugged drink that let the entity into his mind, he had said quite clearly that if it appeared that Unity was using him against the Alliance, Sylvain should do whatever was necessary to stop that from happening. And he'd never failed Andrei before; he wasn't going to start now. He wouldn't let Andrei's body be used by this thing to destroy everything that mattered to him.

Ever since the first moment of Andrei's transformation, Sylvain had felt like there was something wrong. The glowing, golden eyes were the first sign of trouble; he was used to reading the expression in Andrei's eyes to help figure out what he was really thinking, and he couldn't see anything anymore. The cold, arrogant manner, the indifference toward people who mattered to him, the way he hadn't cared when Sylvain had almost fallen to his death in the cave on T'lar—all pointed to trouble. Just days before, he'd told the Zh'ladar that Sylvain was his closest friend! And since then, Andrei hadn't had two words to speak to him that weren't orders.

Yesterday Andrei had said something about wanting to talk to him, but by then it was too late. Sylvain had sweated through enough nightmares by that point to know that it was too dangerous to have a private conversation with Andrei— he'd use Unity's magic to pull Sylvain into the entity's evil spell, and he'd be as trapped as Andrei was. No, the right thing to do at this point was to stay away until he could put his plan into action.

The Zoryans would arrive at the Peaceship the day after tomorrow for Settlement negotiations. Andrei wasn't even making a good show of preparing for them; he'd handed off most of the stuff to Danar and the team to work through, and he hardly even met with them to review what they did. Sat most of the day in a trance. Sylvain knew why: because he wasn't planning to use any of it. Unity was in league with Ashahr to take over the Alliance. They'd carve up the Alliance and the Hegemony between them. They'd just made it look like they were enemies, so Andrei would let Unity in – said they needed a mindlink with him so they could leave mind-space and enter reality. Then they took Andrei's body for their own use. Nightmare come true.

But Sylvain wasn't going to let it happen. He would get rid of Unity by killing Andrei—or rather, killing Andrei's body. His trapped soul would be set free when his body died. Sylvain could barely stand the pain of thinking this, but his exhausted mind insisted that it was true. The man he'd served for so long—who'd given meaning to his life—was gone. Killing the enemy who'd stolen his body would be Sylvain's final act of service.

He sheathed the slender dagger and locked it away again. Illusion was the best choice for the job. The Peaceship was already on alert and in lockdown mode for the move across the War Border, with all known weapons stored and tagged. If any disruptor pistol was so much as touched, it would show up on the Lithras' security boards. The one Andrei had kept under his mattress, since the first of many Zoryan assassination attempts years ago, was still there, but it had also been tagged—they'd know if he moved it. Besides, he wanted something as painless as possible, and death by disruptor blast didn't fit that description at all.

Illusion did. It was made of a special alloy whose outer layer was coated with a numbing agent; the victim would hardly feel anything after the initial impact. Upon contact with the skin, it released a paralytic poison that would first induce relaxation, then sleepiness, then ... nothing, all in the space of about two minutes. Even if Andrei figured it out after he was stabbed, he wouldn't have enough time to do anything about it. The antidote was rare and hard to come by; medlab wouldn't have any just lying around.

Stabbing Andrei in the back ... the thought made him sick to his stomach. But at least he wouldn't have to live with what he'd done for more than a couple of minutes, since he planned to turn the stiletto on himself as soon as he was done with Andrei. Since they'd be on board at the time, the Zoryans would be blamed. With Andrei refusing to let the Military know what was going on—or rather, with Ashahr and Unity blocking him from doing so—the Alliance didn't even know how bad a threat they were. This would alert them …

But that wasn't why he was going to kill himself at the same time. No matter what his tortured brain told him was the right thing to do, he knew he couldn't live with the consequences of his actions. He would die at Andrei's side, like he was supposed to.

* * *

"One-way audio message coming in, Commander. Priority Gold. Origin: Sanctuary."

Andrei looked up, startled by the sudden sound of his desk's voice. More and more, he was living half in mind-space and half in reality, and it took a minute to figure out which was which. Reality: a message from the Zh'ladar. He felt a stab of excitement. "Play it."

The message was short. "What we have hoped for has come to pass. Share it with me."

Andrei's heart raced with anticipation as he imagined what he would see. It took him a minute to calm down and focus his mind enough to access the mindlink, visualize the Zh'ladar's mental signature, and send his consciousness to T'lar.

The Zh'ladar was in the cavernous main audience hall on Sanctuary's ground floor. The walls were tiled with the traditional red and gold abstract-patterned mosaic, while the high, vaulted ceiling was a spangled wash of gold, ivory, and celestial blue. Tapestries showing scenes of natural landmarks in their former state of glory rippled with the breeze. Breeze? The air on T'lar was usually either still as death or choked with dust storms. But this was a gentle, whispering wind.

He looked around the room. Usually empty, today it was full. T'larians in red and gold robes were gathered in small groups, some chanting melodically and moving their bodies in graceful patterns, while others sat motionless, moving their lips in silent prayer. The Zh'ladar was standing in front of a floor-to-ceiling window. He noticed that she'd recently made the change from male to female. He could feel the cool breeze on her face, and he could Sense her thoughts and emotions. Astonishment. Joy. Gratitude.

It was hard to be restrained and formal when he just wanted to grab the information out of her mind. *Greetings, Your Grace,* he Sent.

He Read her lack of surprise at hearing his voice. Obviously, she'd been waiting for him. "Peacekeeper. Look what you have done," she said.

He gazed out the window through her eyes and was stunned speechless. "You have accomplished what decades of terraforming attempts have failed to do," the Zh'ladar continued. "We have rain! The desert will bloom again. T'lar will bear life again."

A soft, silvery rain fell gently and steadily from mirrored clouds piled against the reddish-purple, translucent light of the T'larian sky. It wasn't the type of hard rain that would just erode the powdery soil and leave nothing behind. He could see it sink in; could almost see the rust-colored ground stretch and spread to welcome it. He looked up from the ground and outward across the landscape. More T'larians were coming toward Sanctuary, hands and faces raised to the sky to welcome the rain. He could Sense their elation; it mirrored his own.

I didn't do this—couldn't. It's Unity you should be grateful to.

She shook her head. "It was your plan, Andrei. Your name will be legend on our world for all time."

It *was* his plan, and he let himself feel a moment's worth of sweet satisfaction at the fulfillment of his vision. Immortality. At least now maybe he'd be known for something besides killing large numbers of Zoryans …

He tore his vision away from the landscape and forced himself to think about what came next. *Your people may not feel the same when they find out the price for this miracle.*

"Untrue, Peacekeeper. We have already discussed the plan and voted. All have agreed to it, and we are ready to do whatever is necessary to make it work."

Thank you, Your Grace. It won't be long now. I'll contact you when I need you. Please give the people of T'lar my congratulations.

His consciousness returned to the Peaceship, and he went over to study his holo-model of the Six. With rain that could be counted on to continue, the genetically engineered plants that had failed to take root and propagate in the past would grow now, and the burrowing worms that would open and aerate the soil would survive and breed, all on the accelerated timetable unlocked by Unity. T'lar would support life—its own and that of others who were willing to work the land in order to live free. He brushed his fingers through the model of T'lar as if he could hold the planet in his hands.

"Where's Sylvain?" he asked his desk. Syl would be as happy as he was when he heard the news.

"In his quarters, Commander," his desk told him. "Would you like an audio channel right now, or should I summon him here?"

Andrei opened his mouth to reply but closed it as he suddenly remembered what was going on between him and his Exec—his best friend. It was as though someone had thrown cold water on him. "Neither," he answered wearily. "Forget about it."

* * *

Back on Logos Prime, over the past few days, Coraline's compartment had become a hive of activity as the Bridge and the Challenge finally came together to get ready for the revolution.

The Challenge needed PAs on their side now, in order to Block S2 from getting wind of what they were doing. Security Service usually didn't bother much with the lower levels of the Core—the extreme poverty and self-inflicted violence effectively disconnected them from the rest of society. But the closer PNs got to PAs, the more often they were subjected to both mechanical and mental surveillance.

Mechanical surveillance was something PNs were pretty good at getting around, but the mindsweeps were an ongoing problem for conspirators; in fact, they were the key reason that the Challenge had accomplished so little. Bridge PAs were, for the most part, strong telepaths—stronger than those who got stuck with work assignments in S2. So they took on the task of running interference for the PNs who were smuggling weapons from level to level.

Coraline had another advantage besides her telepathic skill: her relationship with Nick. Nick's part in engineering this coup put her right in the middle of it, creating instant trust from the Challenge members. Also, Nick had taught her everything she knew about smuggling and keeping secrets. Through Fiona, he'd set her up with communication devices that sent and received untraceable signals, and he'd procured the special portable privacy screens that allowed them to store the weapons on all of the different levels.

For all the emphasis on them, the weapons actually were not the first line of defense. That role went to the various jamming and neutralizing devices that would be used to seal off the PN levels from S2 once the Raiders attacked the upper levels. Hand-to-hand combat in the corridors of the Core was only a fallback position—one that Coraline fervently hoped wouldn't be necessary.

It was a huge undertaking, and Coraline worried that they wouldn't be ready in time. She also worried about what could happen to Nick if the PAs managed to fight back. She didn't know whether to worry about Andrei or not. So far, she'd had no contact with either him or Diana since they'd gone to T'lar. The only thing she knew was that the implant hadn't killed him, and Nick claimed that he was helping them. He hadn't said how, though, and he'd convinced Coraline that she had to accept this. Just in case she was arrested, she shouldn't know everything. Reluctantly, she agreed.

Besides smuggling messages, devices, and weapons, she was busy with another project: figuring out how the Challenge would keep the power they took. Bridge members had the best access to databases, and Nick had showed her how to get around the datatraces. She and her Bridge colleagues feverishly searched for information on alternative forms of government, but none of them had ever experienced anything but the so-called psipower meritocracy that had evolved on the generation ship that had brought humans to the Core. She was aware that the other planets of the Six had other forms of government, but she knew nothing of the cultures that went with them. Could the Core handle democracy?

She hoped that they would get the chance to find out.

* * *

It took a while before Andrei felt the touch of a hand on his shoulder, and it took even longer before he recognized his name being called. Surfacing slowly from the trance he entered when his consciousness was mind-traveling, he found that the disorientation he felt on returning to reality was more intense than ever.

The touch on his shoulder was gentle and delicate, like one of those beautiful little flying creatures on Erlande ... what were they called in Standard? Butterflies. He remembered the feeling of one settling in the palm of his hand ...

He was daydreaming. *Wake up,* he told himself. The woman touching him looked delicately beautiful herself, and he knew that he should know who she was—and he would, in another minute—but right now the pieces just weren't coming together.

"It's me, Diana," she said. He must have looked as confused as he felt, if she thought she needed to provide her name. He licked dry lips and squeezed his eyes shut, then opened them again. Reality finally prevailed.

"How long have you been trying to get my attention?" he asked.

"Maybe five minutes," she answered. "Are you all right? You look exhausted."

"I've been practicing defense strategies against Ashahr," he said. "I don't understand why this is so tiring. After all, my body's just sitting here."

She sighed. "You know the answer to that, Andrei. You're human, which means that your body and your mind are still connected to each other. If you push your mind as hard as you do, your body will wear out along with it."

He rubbed his eyes and realized that he would fall asleep at his desk if he didn't move. He went over to the dispensers on the opposite wall. At the medical dispenser, he injected a tube of restorative into a vein on the inside of his wrist. Then he used the food and drink dispenser, where he got himself a glass of tea and a protein bar and took them to the sofa. Diana took the chair opposite him. He had a brief fantasy about pulling her onto the sofa and making love one last time before … who knew what. It was lucky that she couldn't Read him.

"I guess the new door codes work, since you got in," he said.

"They did, and you were right about Sylvain's reaction. He was really upset about the whole thing. When he couldn't open the door, he called the Lithras to find out if they'd changed the codes. They told him you'd done it yourself and instructed them that no one could have the new codes—not even him. That's when he really lost it."

Andrei shrugged. "So he'll have to try to kill me on my timetable, not his."

Diana didn't laugh at what even he knew was a poor excuse for a joke. "Are you sure you're ready for this?"

He nodded. "I may be tired in reality, but in mind-space I'm perfectly fine. I can do what I have to. What about you? Are you sure you're ready?"

She nodded.

"It's very important that you give him the message I recorded, as soon as he wakes up."

"I know that, Andrei."

"He's got to understand that he isn't responsible. That Ashahr's been using him—"

"I know that too. Try not to worry about it. I'll make him understand."

Andrei nodded, trying to reassure himself as much as her. "I'm sure you will. You're very persuasive."

There was an awkward silence. The stress of waiting for something to happen weighed heavily.

"Will you be happy when it's all over?" Diana asked.

He knew what she really meant, but he decided to misunderstand. "When Ashahr's dead? Yes, of course. The Zoryans—"

She interrupted him. "I'm talking about the mindlink, as you well know."

She always managed to cut right to the heart of the matter. He drank his tea and didn't reply.

"You don't want it to end, do you?"

"We really don't need to discuss this," he said as coldly as possible, in order to discourage her.

She ignored him. "It has to end, Andrei. You know that. You still have a body—Unity doesn't. You can't go with them, and it's not likely they'll be hanging around here once Ashahr is destroyed." She waited for him to say something; he didn't. "You can still be telepathic, you know. Maybe the implant will work better for you now that you've had more experience with the psi-sense."

He couldn't help but react. "I don't want any part of the implant." He stood up, turning away from her. "Let's just take it one step at a time, all right? First I have to survive Ashahr. Then we'll see what comes next."

She stood up too and opened her mouth to speak. He didn't hear what she was going to say, though, as two things happened at once: his desk signaled an incoming blackcoded transmission, one way only; and the intra-ship communications link chimed. Returning to his desk, he started decoding procedures for the blackcoded message while speaking to the intra-ship comm channel.

"Yes, Lithras?"

"Commander, we have received a message from the Zoryan negotiating team. They are leaving Zorya Prime. Should we set out for neutral space now?"

There was only one long pass-through point between Zorya Prime and the coordinates in neutral space where the Zoryans were to meet the Peaceship; the trip would take them a Standard day. Andrei wanted as much time as he could get, so that he wouldn't be occupied with the Zoryans—and Ashahr—when Nick needed him.

"No," replied Andrei. "We'll wait until they're at the Zoryan side of the War Border."

"But Commander, we will be late to meet them if we wait that long!"

Andrei snorted. "What are they going to do about it? Go home? Start a war?"

There were brief, indignant noises of protest at the other end of the channel, then silence.

"You have your orders. Notify me when the Zoryans reach the War Border." He closed the channel and turned back to the blackcoded message, instructing his desk to play it when the decoding procedure was complete.

A minute passed that felt like an eternity. Finally, Nick's voice echoed in the room. "Andrei, I just heard from Darya Ardelle. We're to mobilize and head for Selas immediately. Wish us luck."

"Good luck," he said softly.

Endgame.

Chapter 28

When Nick and his team arrived at Selas, they didn't find the well-oiled machine that had been promised. Instead, the energy shield was still in place, and his sensors detected weapons being discharged inside the prison.

"Fucking amateurs," Nick fumed as he moved his little fleet out of the prison's sensor range.

"What now?" Gretchen's voice came over the inter-ship channel.

"We wait and see if Saalovaarian's crew can get their shit together and take over the prison like they're supposed to," he answered. "If not, we have to abort. Without those weapons, this plan goes nowhere."

So they waited. A few minutes later, Nick got a transmission from inside the prison. A Sendosian Free Raider he didn't know told him that most of the place was under their control, but there were a few areas still holding out, including Command/Control. Would Captain Hayden be willing to provide a diversion, so they could finish the job?

He was. The ten ships fanned out and moved directly into the prison's sensor range, peppering the energy field with shots that obviously couldn't puncture it but would at least let C/C know that someone was out there. By moving around continuously, it would seem like there were more of them than there were; this would also make them more difficult targets. They played this game for another half hour or so, until suddenly the energy field shimmered a few times, then winked out.

"Thanks, Captain Hayden. You're cleared for entry."

The loading of the weapons also ran into trouble, but for a different reason. Specifically, the Sendosians wanted to keep almost all of the planet-killer weapons for themselves, on the premise that they were going to need them to take over Sendos.

"What about Logos Prime?" Nick demanded, infuriated. "We're your partners, remember? We've got our own takeover to do, and we can't pull it off with this crappy little stash you're giving us!"

"Nonsense, Captain." An unpleasantly familiar voice interrupted his argument with the Raider Captain leading the Sendosian group. She backed away from him and let Saalovaarian take her place as she went off to deal with the loading.

He smiled malevolently at Nick, his huge, bulging skulls pulsing with pleasure. "I know you already have weapons in place inside the Core. You don't need more than these to finish the job—unless of course you're less capable than my dear colleague Councilor Ardelle believes. Which would make it her problem, not mine."

"You scum-sucking piece of—!" Gretchen grabbed his arm and pulled him away before Nick could finish giving Saalovaarian a piece of his mind. The Sendosian chuckled and sauntered away.

"That's not gonna help us," she whispered. "What about callin' Ardelle and let her deal with it?"

"What the hell can she do for us sitting in the Core?" he snapped.

Gretchen shrugged; he had a point. "Okay, then, what about takin' him hostage until his crew hands over the weapons to us?"

That was better than her first idea, except then they'd have to take Saalovaarian with them when they left Selas, or they'd have to lock up his whole team or knock them all out. This would be tough, especially since there seemed to be a lot of them in a lot of different parts of the prison. Would Saalovaarian's crew let them take him, or would they fight to get him back? No, this didn't sound too promising either.

"Maybe it's time to get some help," he said.

"What kind of help? Do ya have a shadow team out there ya didn't tell me about?" Gretchen asked.

He shook his head. "A shadow operative. Maybe. If it really works."

"If what really works?"

"Shhh. I have to concentrate." He closed his eyes and thought about Andrei, visualizing him as best he could for someone who didn't believe in this mental telepathy stuff ...

What is it, Nick?

He could hear Andrei in his mind. He didn't sound nearly as close as the last time they'd communicated mentally, but nevertheless he was there. *Guess there is something to it after all,* he thought. He tried thinking the situation to Andrei. *Is there anything you can do?*

Yes, Andrei Sent. *I can change his mind, but it won't last long. You'll have to work very fast and get out of there as soon as possible, and hope they don't decide to go after you.*

I don't think they will. They have their own shit to get done before the Sendosian and Alliance military forces come down on them.

Nick turned, ran down the corridor after the Sendosian, and caught up with him just before he got into the transport tube. "Saalovaarian! Time for another little chat."

"Whatever for, Captain Hayden? My mind is quite made up ..." Saalovaarian's voice trailed off. He looked confused; he shook his head. He turned away from Nick and Gretchen, turned back, and finally stood there, paralyzed—seemingly with indecision. Slowly he took out his pocket comm and called his Raider Captain. "There's a change of plans," he said. "I'm sending you a new manifest for the weapons to go with Hayden's team. Yes. Yes, I'm sure that's what I want to do. Carry out my orders, Captain. Immediately!" He didn't look at Gretchen and Nick; in fact, he seemed to be intently focused on the closed doors of the transport tube in front of him. They didn't wait to see what he was going to do next; they just ran back the opposite way, toward the loading dock.

"Now, that's a neat trick, for sure," Gretchen laughed as she helped Nick and the other team members pull the large weapons onto floating loading pallets and send them into their ships' cargo holds. "Imagine if you could just make people do stuff for ya by battin' your eyelashes at 'em."

"Yeah, well, it's not gonna last all that long, Andrei says. So let's get the hell out of here and as far away as we can before Saalovaarian wakes up and declares war on us," Nick replied.

Even with these minor setbacks, they hadn't lost all that much time. They made it through the two pass-through points without incident and soon arrived at the next problem that they would need Andrei's mind-magic for: dealing with Darya Ardelle. They were supposed to go to specific coordinates on the War Border and let the Zoryans slip through the Alliance defense grid, using codes she'd provide. The Zoryans themselves were supposed to provide confirmation that everything was on track for the final part of the plan: the taking of Logos Prime.

The problem with this was that there weren't going to be any Zoryans, which would cause Darya to get in touch with her own people in the Core to abort the takeover—after which she'd likely concoct some story that would set the Logos Prime defense forces on Nick and his group in order to get rid of the evidence. The only way to keep her from ruining everything would be to convince her that Nick had done what he was supposed to do.

This was Andrei's job. He'd Read the name of her Zoryan contact, found him through K'ril I'th, and Read the message kri was supposed to send once they'd crossed the War Border. Luckily, no conversation was involved. So Darya received the "right" message from the "right" Zoryan and gave Nick the codes to the Logos Prime defense grid. And once again, they were on their way.

"What's gonna happen when the Zoryans are sittin' there, waitin' for us, and we don't show?" Gretchen asked. "Won't they try to get in touch with Ardelle?"

Nick grinned. "Nah. Not after Sesna-Goveril's border patrol ships surround 'em and take 'em into custody for violating the rules of neutral space. They're not allowed in there without notifying the Alliance, remember?"

"What about Saalovaarian? He's waitin' for Zoryans too."

"By the time he figures out that they're not coming, it's gonna be too late for him to do anything about it."

Gretchen was still worried. "But what if the Zoryans decide to put up a fight, Nick? Couldn't this start up the war again?"

"Yeah, I guess it could," he answered, "if these were the Zoryans who were gonna still be in power. But they're not."

Then, suddenly, there wasn't any more time to worry about it, as Logos Prime came into view.

* * *

Doctor Jaxome.

Robert Jaxome, Director of the Think Tank and Governor of Logos Prime, whirled around to find the source of the thought he'd Received. His office was empty.

He'd retreated to his office to think about what to do next. He knew it wouldn't be long before the rebels hacked through his door codes, but any time he could have before then was worthwhile. Most of the Core was locked down by the PNs, who'd somehow managed to acquire a stockpile of arms and jamming devices. He couldn't find out what was going on in the lower levels, because of the communication jamming devices; and he couldn't get S2 soldiers down there, because of the transport tube jamming devices. How could this have happened right under their noses? As soon as this was over and things were back to normal, he was going to do a thorough purge of S2.

But when would that be? The lower and middle levels of the Core had been taken over by PNs (with an amazingly small amount of blood and destruction—how could those limited minds have accomplished something like this?), and the Upper Core was being held hostage by some damnable PN Free Raiders claiming to have weapons that would take out the defense grid and slice through the Core structure like a hot knife through butter. S2 (those disgraceful idiots!) assured him that the weapons were really out there and could do what the PN rebel leader claimed they could do.

Would these people really bomb the Core? What about the PNs, whom the leader (a Free Raider Captain named Nick Hayden who, according to the Logos Prime database, did not exist) claimed to represent? What did he think would happen to them if the Core was bombed?

"The lower levels have been provided with atmosphere suits that will help them survive until we can re-seal the Core," Hayden told him. "But you PAs'll be long dead by then. So cut the crap and stand down. You're wasting my time."

"What do you want from us?" Jaxome asked, genuinely curious.

"We want your government," Nick snapped. "We want your living space, your resources, and your freedom."

"PNs wouldn't know what to do with freedom if they had it," Jaxome replied coolly. "Your limited minds can only conceive of violence as the way to solve your problems."

"Oh, yeah, and you would've sat down with us and negotiated without planet killers at your back, right?" Nick's voice dripped with contempt.

"If you stand down, I am willing to devise some mechanism to address your grievances," Jaxome replied. "Perhaps we can meet and have a civilized discussion."

"Sounds like a plan, Bob," Nick said, "at least the discussion part. In fact, I have an idea who might make a good mediator."

Jaxome decided to ignore the affront to his name, at least for the time being. "Who would that be?"

"Logos Prime's Alliance Representative, Darya Ardelle."

"Do you know her?"

"She's a PN, but she's got a high position. She would know how to talk about this type of thing," Nick answered.

Jaxome thought about this. He didn't really know Darya Ardelle. She delivered messages and requests from the Alliance, most of which Jaxome ignored or rejected. However, it didn't seem like a bad idea. There weren't any PAs whom the rebels would trust, and maybe an Alliance Councilor, even though she was a PN, would understand that this type of action was completely unacceptable and put them back in their place. "Your people have barricaded the transport tubes," he said to Nick. "Councilor Ardelle's compartment is in the mid-level section of the Core."

"Yeah, so we'll open up one of them," Nick said. "But understand this, Jaxome. Anyone you try to send down there will be killed. Don't do anything stupid."

* * *

But he had done something stupid, Jaxome thought, still in shock at how he'd been deceived. He'd let them open a transport tube right through to the top level of the Core, and Darya Ardelle and her troops had stormed in and taken over. What remained of the S2 forces was locked up in holding cells; PAs were locked in their compartments, and the leadership (except for him) had been herded into the Think Tank auditorium, where they were being guarded by these treacherous rebels. Hayden and his second-in-command were on their way into the Core, and Ardelle was working on the codes to his office.

And now, on top of it all, he was hallucinating.

No, you're not. There it was again. *This is Andrei Savinov.*

Impossible, he thought. *Savinov isn't PA. And even if he was, he's too far away for me to receive thoughts from him.*

I am now, Andrei Sent. *PA, that is, and I'm on the Peaceship. Not only am I now telepathic, but I can Send thoughts anywhere I want, and obviously I can enable you to Receive them.*

Inconceivable, thought Jaxome.

Really? Why do you think so? After all, you provided the mechanism that made it possible.

Jaxome felt a sick chill. He tried to Read Savinov's mind, but nothing happened. PAs couldn't Read minds from this distance. So how in name of Wisdom could Andrei Savinov do it? He tried Sending a thought to him. *What do you mean?*

Diana Zarev. She's developed an implant that substitutes for the missing sensory organ in PNs. It turns out it's much more powerful than the real thing.

Shock upon shock. *Why in the world would Doctor Zarev, one of our most brilliant scientists, do something like that?*

Haven't you ever heard of the Bridge, Doctor Jaxome?

No. Not possible. *Yes, of course. We occasionally capture renegade, mentally ill PAs who consider themselves part of a movement for equality between PAs and PNs. But it isn't the type of thing a woman like Diana Zarev would be involved with.*

Perhaps you don't know her as well as you thought you did, Andrei Sent.

The whole thing is inconceivable, Jaxome thought once more. That Diana Zarev would do such a thing, that she would be a traitor to her kind … and how did she manage it, anyway? He never would have imagined that it was possible, even if someone, for some twisted, insane reason, would want to attempt it.

Andrei Sent, *What would you prefer as an alternative explanation? That a thought-based entity from beyond our star system found me and gave me these mindpowers?*

He was furious that Andrei had obviously Read his thoughts. *Is that supposed to be funny, Commander Savinov? What a ridiculous idea!*

Indeed so, Doctor Jaxome. Let's assume there is an implant and that PNs can become PAs whenever they choose. The rules of your society say that you would have to treat them as full PA citizens. More people to share your limited resources and privileges—possibly a lot more people. Let's also assume that PNs now have control of the Core. It seems that any way you look at it, you aren't dealing from a position of strength.

Damn him, he was right. *How are you involved in all this, Commander? You are the Alliance's Peacekeeper. Is this how you do your job?*

As a matter of fact, it is.

Andrei had just finished his explanation when Darya Ardelle burst through the door.

* * *

So this Robert Jaxome's office, Nick thought, surveying the room. *Top of the Core. Big fucking deal,* he thought. It actually was big, and the transparent dome structure was pretty cool looking. But this guy had no more right to this space than anyone stuck in the bottom of the Core with no viewscreens at all. Maybe even less right, considering how he'd oppressed them all this time.

The room was crowded. Nick had left a skeleton crew of Raiders in their ships, and the rest were with him, helping the rebels. Jaxome was there, of course, looking dazed and confused. Or maybe he was just pissed off because Darya Ardelle was sitting with her boots firmly planted on top of his desk, looking pretty pleased with herself. *She won't be so happy when she finds out there aren't any Zoryans here to back her new regime,* he thought. Gretchen just stood with her back against the door, looking solid and impassive. She obviously was the type who would wait and see what happened before she got all excited.

Where the hell was Coraline?

Nick was trying to convince himself not worry about her yet. Everyone was still trying to make sure that key locations were secured, and that was probably what she was doing. Or since she was also a medtech, maybe she was helping people who'd been wounded in the little fighting there had been. Maybe he'd send Gretchen out to look for her.

"Nick!" It was her voice on the other side of the door.

He breathed a sigh of relief and nodded to Gretchen to let her in. His second guess obviously had been the right one: she was dirty and bloody but not wounded. Smiling radiantly, she rushed into his arms.

"I'm so glad to see you! We did it! We've actually taken over …" Her voice trailed off and she turned around, staring at Jaxome, who was staring back at her with something like revulsion. He knew she was PA.

"No telepathy here," Nick said in a threatening tone of voice, glaring at Jaxome.

Jaxome glanced briefly at him, then his gaze returned to Coraline. "You look familiar," he said to her.

She returned his look with hatred in her eyes. "I'm Coraline Saint-Claire. Perhaps you remember my mother. People have told me there's a strong resemblance between us."

"Astrid Saint-Claire," Jaxome whispered. He seemed to draw into himself, suddenly looking older. "Yes. I knew your mother."

Coraline crossed the room rapidly to stand directly in front of him. "Really? Did you order her various arrests? Her Reconditioning? Did you order her sons taken from her home? Was it you we have to thank for all that?"

He shook his head. "I wasn't Director back then. I wasn't involved in any of those decisions. It was so long ago."

"Not as long as you might think," she replied bitterly. She looked as though she was going to hit him, but abruptly she shook her head and went over to stand next to Nick. He put his arm around her shoulder.

Jaxome studied her and then Nick. "Is this your brother?" he asked her.

"One of them," she replied.

Darya Ardelle cut in. "All right, all right, already. Nice family reunion scene here, but hey, Nick, let's get down to business. How many Zoryans do we have out there?"

"Zoryans?" Jaxome's voice came out a strangled whisper. "He didn't say anything about Zoryans."

"He who? What the hell are you talking about?" Darya turned away before he could answer. "Nick? How many are out there?"

Nick folded his arms across his chest. "Actually, Darya, there are none. We didn't let 'em in. The message from them to you was faked. The Alliance Military's either chased 'em off or picked 'em up at the War Border by now."

"You miserable traitor! How are we supposed to hold the Core without the Zoryans?" she shrieked, charging at him. It was a good thing Gretchen was there to pry her fingers off his throat, but she wasn't quick enough, and it took Nick a while to get his breath and his voice back. "Y'know, Darya, to my way of looking at things, you're the traitor, selling out the Alliance to the Zoryans," he said. "How could you think they'd really let you run this planet? They enslave everybody they get their fucking talons on. And even though we all hate the PAs, they're human, damn it! How could you send humans to what would probably be an unbelievably horrible death?" His anger rising, he found himself wanting to throttle her in return. "You bitch, did you really think I'd sell out my own brother?"

Darya looked bewildered. "Your brother? What in the Six are you talking about ..." Her voice trailed off as realization hit her. "For Earth's sake. Is Andrei Savinov your brother?"

There was a gasp loud enough to make them all turn as one to find its source. It was Robert Jaxome's.

Nick carried two message cubes with him. Jaxome helped him hook up the spindle that would play them to the central communications control unit in the Director's desk, which would broadcast the images to viewscreens all over the Core. They opened an all-Core audio channel. Now everything was ready.

They stood in a circle around a pool of light and watched the holo-images materialize. The first thing they saw was the surface of T'lar. Jaxome had never been there, but he recognized it from pictures. At least he thought he recognized it. He'd thought that T'lar was a barren wasteland, but the images before him were of silver rain falling on new blades of reddish-gold grass. Even though it was raining, the sun was shining. Into the landscape walked a golden-robed T'larian. He couldn't see how anyone could tell one of these beings from another, but he had to assume that this was their leader.

He was right. "I am the Zh'ladar," she said. Her voice was simple, relaxed, and calm, like her manner, yet power radiated from her. "What you are seeing here are images of T'lar as it is today. Accelerated terraforming has given our planet new life. In a short time, our land will be arable. We welcome you, Logos Prime PNs, to leave the Core and settle here with us. Shelter will be provided for you, as well as the means to work the soil. Those of you who do not choose to do that can go to the mountains, where mining opportunities exist. It will not be an easy life, but you will be able to live on the surface of a growing planet and be free. Think it over. We await your answer." The message ended.

There was no sound in the room. Jaxome felt drained, but at least this was one thing that hadn't taken him completely by surprise; Savinov had told him this was coming. He hadn't Sent anything to Jaxome about the Zoryans, because he'd gotten rid of them. Darya had double-crossed him, and he'd returned the favor. *I can't believe how much I underestimated him,* he thought. *Astrid Saint-Claire's son.* Jaxome looked at Nick and Coraline. *Astrid Saint-Claire's children. Her revenge …*

Nick was putting the second cube onto the spindle. Sure enough, the next image to appear was Andrei's.

"For those of you who don't know me, I'm Andrei Savinov, the Alliance's Peacekeeper," he began. "By now, you've heard the Zh'ladar's most generous offer. All PNs and any PAs who wish to live in peace and equality with PNs are welcome to emigrate to T'lar. The Alliance will provide transportation and help you get started there. The T'larians are a peaceful, spiritual people from whom I believe humans have much to learn.

"Assuming that many PNs will want to pursue this new life, PAs need to consider how they will manage to run the Core without their labor force. Though life may be hard on T'lar, life in the Core will also become much more challenging. For everyone.

"So perhaps it's in both sides' best interests to think hard about how you want to proceed. Perhaps there's something to be said for PAs and PNs trying to find new ways to live together. The Alliance is standing by with a neutral force to ensure that no more fighting takes place, as well as skilled negotiators to work with the representatives of each side that you will choose. If you can learn to stop hating each other and work together, perhaps someday there will be two successful human homeworlds in this star system." His image faded out.

For several minutes after the two broadcasts, there was silence. Then Darya jumped out of her chair. "Forget it! I'm not buying it!" She turned to her followers. "We don't need the Zoryans. Let's start rounding up the PAs ourselves …" Her voice trailed off as she stared into the barrel of Nick's disruptor pistol.

He shook his head. "Forget it, Darya. It's not gonna happen." He signaled to Gretchen, who pulled Darya's hands behind her back and slipped an energy bracelet over them. He studied her followers, none of whom had moved while their leader was being taken into custody by the Free Raiders she'd hired. They shrugged and turned away.

Jaxome felt lightheaded. He wanted to sit down, but the only unoccupied chair was the one behind his desk, and the symbolism of that was … inauspicious. He leaned against the wall instead. Savinov hadn't said anything about PNs being able to become PAs, because that wasn't the offer on the table today. He would keep it in reserve, he'd told Jaxome, in case the PAs failed to cooperate.

"Captain Hayden," he said, trying to sound friendly and cooperative but not quite succeeding. "How do you propose that we proceed?"

"We start thinking about how we're gonna organize these peace talks, while we wait for the Alliance force to show up," Nick replied.

"Will the Peacekeeper be leading the talks?" Jaxome asked.

Nick shook his head. "I think Andrei has other plans."

Chapter 29

Back on the Peaceship, Andrei opened a new bottle of *livrash* to celebrate the events taking place on Logos Prime. The Shield Unity had built for him had allowed him to deal with Jaxome PA-style, without damaging anything but the Director's pride. The Peaceship was finally moving through neutral space on its way to the meeting with Zorya's Settlement negotiators. Word of events taking place on Logos Prime (and Sendos, for that matter, where the Alliance and the Sendosian military were battling the insurgents to retake the prison on Selas) hadn't reached either side yet, so Andrei and Diana were the only ones on board who knew.

They shared a drink together, but after she went back to her quarters, he didn't put the bottle away. It was only after he'd finished most of it—and the room had started tilting in all kinds of unpleasant ways—when he began to realize that he was drinking for a different reason altogether. The time had run out for pretending he wasn't afraid of the coming battle with Ashahr.

Waiting was hard; there was too much time to think. Once a battle had been planned and all contingencies accounted for, there was nothing left to do, and the imagination ran wild speculating on everything unknown that could go wrong and the dreadful consequences of failure. He'd done the best he could to strategize moves and countermoves, but the truth was that he was dealing with the strongest, least-understood opponent he'd ever faced. He had a theory about how to trap and kill it, but he hadn't been able to test it, and he wouldn't get another chance if it turned out he was wrong. Unity claimed they would protect him as best they could, but he knew that Ashahr had destroyed many of their previous mindlinked partners.

He thought about his previous encounters with the entity. He'd never actually won any of their mind battles; the most he could say was that he hadn't lost, meaning he hadn't gone mad or killed himself—though he'd certainly come close enough. The one time he'd managed to build a barrier against Ashahr, it had held—meaning Ashahr hadn't been able to find out what he didn't want it to know—but somehow it had still been able to hurt him. It went digging in the most painful of his memories and forced him to relive them. So the barrier he'd built had protected information, but it hadn't protected him against his own emotions. Could this be the weakness in his defenses?

If it was, he had no idea how to fix it. All his life, he'd been told that he didn't pay enough attention to his own feelings to know how to take care of himself. It hadn't mattered much when Kylara was alive; she'd protected him, and he had done the same for her. With the crushing depression following her death, he'd tried to get away from his life as a Warleader by resigning his commission and going to T'lar. But it hadn't lasted; he'd been pulled back in before he'd had any chance to heal.

He shook his head, frustrated. *This is nonsense,* he thought. *There's no room for emotion when you're fighting a war.* Or was this the flaw in his thinking? All the losses he'd suffered— Kylara's death being only the most recent—and the feelings he'd refused to acknowledge about the losses he'd caused, were buried as best as he could bury them. But his encounters with

Ashahr had showed him that it was all still there, just waiting for him to stop being so damned busy … to pay attention.

If he paid attention, he wouldn't have the strength to keep fighting. He would be paralyzed by all of it, or so he believed. But even as he resolutely stoppered the bottle of *livrash* and dialed up an antidote from the medical dispenser, he knew something was wrong. He just had to hope Unity could keep whatever it was from working against him.

* * *

The door buzzed over and over again. He didn't have to be telepathic to be able to tell that whoever was on the other side was angry. Andrei knew it was Sylvain without Reading his mental signature. He swallowed a panicky urge to pretend he wasn't there, then let him in.

"Sorry about the door codes," he said in as casually disinterested a tone as he could muster. "I thought it was safer to change them so no one could walk in on me when I was mind-traveling."

Sylvain didn't respond. He stalked across the office without even looking at him and went into his bedroom to assemble the various parts of the formal Peacekeeper uniform.

The Zoryans were finally on board, with loud, angry protests for the late arrival of the Peaceship. Andrei could Sense their ugly mood: they were out for blood. His. He didn't try to Sense Ashahr's presence. He didn't have to; he knew exactly where the entity was.

Right there in his bedroom.

He rose slowly, looking around at his office. He'd already remotely stored, black-coded, or deleted everything he didn't want the Zoryans to get their hands on, just in case he didn't come back. *Don't think about that now,* he told himself. He'd thrown everything out on the bed so Sylvain wouldn't have to go searching through the room, but he hurried in just to make sure.

Sylvain was waiting for him, frowning as he sorted it all out. First came the lightweight shirt threaded with sensors to monitor and control skin temperature. Andrei wished he had it on already so Sylvain wouldn't notice him sweating. Then came the long coat with built-in body armor, the formal pants, and finally the gauntlets. Andrei took off his own clothes and tossed them on the chair in the corner. He pulled on the pants and the high, black boots lined up next to the bed. That done, Sylvain finished testing the sensors on the shirt and handed it to him. He put it on and tugged it into place. Sylvain stood by with the coat. Neither spoke, acting out the usual routine.

The black coat was heavy and tight-fitting, especially the sleeves, as the gauntlets had to fit over them. Andrei stood with his back to Sylvain, waiting for him to drape it over him and adjust the silver side buckles while he pushed his hands into the sleeves. The silence, his heart hammering, the seconds ticking in his head …

Even though he knew it was coming, the pain and terror of the exact moment of being stabbed were absolute. A sharp, icy tearing of flesh, cold quickly mixed with the wetness and warmth of flowing blood … then the pain stopped. Time slowed as his limbs turned to gel. He sensed rather than felt himself falling to his knees, then lowering as his hands couldn't support his arms. After his initial uncontrolled cry, there was silence. No, that wasn't true. There was a sound, but he couldn't understand it.

Turn around, he thought. Damn it, he had to turn. He had known that he wouldn't be able to move, but he'd thought he would have time before that happened. *Turn. Roll.* He summoned the last ounce of his rapidly fading strength to roll on his side and face Sylvain.

That was the source of the noise. Sylvain was sobbing, his tears running down his cheeks as he drew the blade across his own wrists. Through the numbness and encroaching lassitude, Andrei felt a sudden stab of guilt. He'd let this happen; no, he'd made this happen. What a monster he was.

No. The monster was in Sylvain's eyes—malevolent, rabidly hungry, burning with desire, the need to devour his life energy, released by murder and Sylvain's life energy, released by suicide. No better meal for the entity called Ashahr.

Andrei breathed in deeply to send oxygen to his brain, to try to wake himself up. The room faded out and faded in again as he took another breath. He locked eyes with Sylvain, Read Ashahr's mental signature, and left his body behind to follow it into mind-space.

Ice. He was locked behind walls of translucent ice. Curved walls. A sphere; this universe was spherical. He stared out at what was probably the closest thing to the real appearance of Ashahr that he would ever see.

It was a roiling mass of darkness. Various shades of black existed within barely defined, constantly shifting boundaries. The blackness boiled with rage and hatred: negative energy taken shape. The chaos of the twisting shapes was nauseating to Andrei's mind's eye, which, because of his human essence, translated what he was seeing into human emotions. He saw rage, hatred, disgust, terror—they weren't Ashahr's feelings; they were what Ashahr's aspects engendered in him. Unity had told him that it would happen this way, and he had prepared for it by trying to maintain a separate self that could preserve some mental distance, but it wasn't working as well as he'd hoped. Even with no body attached, he had the same feelings he would have as a human who was going to be sick.

No good. Block. He calmed himself, and the nausea faded. Tentacles of boiling darkness reached out at him. Like the dream he'd had, they were razor-sharp, and they sliced at the ice globe around his consciousness. It held through one strike after another. Andrei could hear shrieking—howling wind, madness, intolerable pain. Terror. *Block.*

Your skills have improved since we last met, Ashahr Sent. *And that was quite a clever trick you played, using your aide against himself. It was truly worthy of me.*

Andrei didn't Reply. He'd already decided that he wasn't going to talk to it. It would use interaction to gain insight into his emotions, which it would then turn against him. As long as he stuck to the plan, he'd be safe. At least, that was the theory …

In fact, the better I understand you, the more I think you are more like me than you could possibly imagine.

As Ashahr Sent this thought, it also Sent an intense mind-strike. The thought rattled Andrei, so while the strike didn't pierce the barrier, it bruised his mind … which rattled him even more. He tried to refocus his consciousness as Ashahr continued working on cutting through with the thoughts it Sent.

Ah, yes, that prospect frightens you, doesn't it? It frightens you because in that place you humans think of as your inmost self, you've wondered whether it could possibly be true that you're a killer, Peacekeeper. Ashahr Sent a grotesque imitation of mocking laughter. *How many have suffered because of your plans? How many have died the types of horrible deaths that feed me? One of your schemes even killed your own lover, and now you have killed your closest friend.*

He's not dead. Andrei's resolve not to speak to Ashahr snapped with the sudden fear that it was telling the truth. What if Diana hadn't gotten to Sylvain in time? Or what if she had given him the antidote, but he'd bled to death or died some other way? He tried to Read Ashahr to tell if it was lying, but he couldn't. Instead, the distraction left him open to attack. The hole in his defenses was small, but it gave Ashahr something to work with. A tentacle poked through, reaching into Andrei's mind. He shrank away from it.

You want Unity to help you. I have destroyed Unity's mindlinked partners in just this way. But that would be a pity in your case. You could join me. Ashahr's tentacles started reaching around the spherical barrier, not striking any longer, but exploring. *You would make a worthy partner. What I could give you in return is what you want from Unity, who will never give it to you—a mindlink that will last forever. Unlimited mind-travel. Unlimited power. Immortality.*

Andrei had known that his defenses wouldn't last forever, but he'd counted on them lasting longer than this. He'd have to change tactics and engage with Ashahr directly, to buy time for Unity to finish the trap they were creating. *Hurry,* he thought.

What makes you think I still want to be mindlinked? he Sent.

Again came the horrible sound of metal on metal: Ashahr's representation of laughter. The writhing darkness was beginning to surround Andrei's globe. Light flickered red along with black, and he began to get a perception of flame. If cutting didn't work, would fire? No. *Block.* If he thought about it, surely it would happen.

Of course you do, Ashahr Sent. *You crave the power of higher thought, but Unity will never let you keep it. You are an agent of destruction to them. They are using you to attack me and will get rid of you as soon as you have served your function.*

You'll say anything to try to make me submit to you, Andrei Sent. *I've no reason to believe any of it. Enough nonsense. You think you can destroy me? Go ahead and try.* He shut his mind to the thoughts Ashahr was Sending and put every ounce of energy he had into his defenses, blocking out the sounds of roaring flames, of Sylvain's despair, of Kylara's death screams, the death screams of thousands upon thousands of Zoryans from the baseship he'd destroyed ...

Ashahr surrounded the globe and began to invade it from all sides. The tentacle that had gotten through first finally touched his consciousness. Andrei braced for pain but felt none, only a spot of cold. He didn't have time to think about it, though, as Ashahr broke through and wrapped him in a whirlwind of darkness.

Now, he Sent.

And Unity surrounded his consciousness and Ashahr's consciousness—which was its whole self, unlike Andrei, who still had his body left on the Peaceship—with another sphere. Only this one was made of glowing, perfect light.

Sacred Light.

The sphere was a tightly woven lattice of Sacred Light. It was so bright that Ashahr's darkness turned the color of ashes; the sharp tentacles compacted back into a solid mass under the pressure of containment. Unity formed no thoughts to Send; all of their energy went into holding the light together as a form. Flooded with relief, Andrei used the mindlink, which was wrapped in Sacred Light, to pass his consciousness through the sphere and away from it. But Ashahr was held firm.

Unity had told Andrei that since he had designed Ashahr's prison, it would be up to him to create the final act of destruction. He had thought he was ready, but the interaction with Ashahr made him hesitate. Not that he had any ideas about letting Ashahr go, but he had questions ...

Forget it, he thought. What could Ashahr tell him that would make him change his mind and let it live? He created the mental image of the sphere cupped between his two hands ... then he brought them together, crushing them into one fist.

The sphere collapsed inward.

Ashahr's death scream ripped through Andrei, and the implosion of Sacred Light obliterating the entity's darkness seared his mind's eye. For a while—he didn't know how long—he was nowhere: neither in mind-space nor in reality. He was beginning to wonder if he was dead when he opened his real eyes and found himself in his body, in his bed on the Peaceship.

He couldn't move, and for a brief, panicked moment he thought he was paralyzed from the knife wound. But no; he could feel his fingers moving, and he lifted his arm. It was too heavy, though, and he let it fall back to the mattress again. His back hurt where he'd been stabbed, and he gave a sigh of relief.

"You're awake." Diana sounded surprised. He looked up at her and tried to speak but couldn't. She lifted his head and gave him some water. He struggled to sit up, but she pushed him back. "No, don't even think about it. I got the poison and patched the wound, but you've lost blood, and whatever you did out there sent your body into shock." She brushed her hand across his forehead. "By the way, is Ashahr dead?"

"Yes," he whispered, but he didn't explain. He was still dazed with reaction. "Sylvain?"

"Right here," she said, gesturing. Andrei turned on his side to look at the medfloat next to his bed. Sylvain lay on it, regen gelpacks covering his wrists, eyes closed.

"Why isn't he awake?" Andrei asked.

"He did wake up after I gave him the antidote. I spoke to him and gave him your message, and he seemed to be coming around, but at the same time your vital signs collapsed, he sort of went catatonic."

"Sort of?"

"Well, not in the technical sense, but he just seemed to fade out. Staring into space. I needed to work on you without worrying about him waking up insane and trying to kill you, so I decided to sedate him until I could figure out what was happening."

Andrei nodded, thinking. "I wonder …" He pushed himself onto his elbows, then tried again to sit up, waving Diana off when she moved to restrain him. "What's going on with our Zoryan friends?"

"I don't know," she answered. "The new door codes, the energy field, and the privacy screen—plus the message the door kept sending that you weren't to be disturbed—may have kept your staff from breaking down the door, but every light on your message board is lit, and I finally shut off the audio on your desk when I couldn't listen to it say 'You have a new message' for the zillionth time."

He laughed slightly, then swung his feet over the side of the bed. "It's time we found out." Ignoring her protests, he stood up. He would have fallen over if she hadn't caught him, but he righted himself, threw on a shirt, and made his way to the door.

The corridor was crowded with guards and Mission staff, whose minds were so filled with frantic confusion that he couldn't make out what had happened by Reading them. They stared at him like he'd risen from the dead.

Everything will be all right, he Sent, changing their minds. They quieted. He signaled to the bodyguard unit assigned to him while Zoryans were on the Peaceship, and they followed him to the main conference room.

He studied the Zoryans sitting there, waving a hand in front of K'ril G'al's face. There was no reaction; they too were catatonic. Apparently Ashahr's death had thrown those under its spell into temporary mental confusion.

The door to the conference room opened, and Lithras A and B burst through it with a team of security guards. "Commander Savinov! There has been a revolt on Zorya Prime! With Alliance assistance!" Lithra A said.

"Alliance assistance! We have been instructed to take the negotiating team into custody …" Lithra B added. Her voice trailed off as both Lithras noticed the frozen Zoryans for the first time. "What has happened here?"

"I don't think they're going to give you much trouble," Andrei remarked "But you'd better keep them under armed guard anyway. At some point, they'll come out of it, and they may be unhappy at the turn of events."

A few hours later, Andrei found himself looking at a different Zoryan face: one he knew well and was very pleased to see back on the Peaceship again. K'ril I'th stood before him. In front of a viewing screen watched by Alliance Council Members (with the notable exception of Darya Ardelle and Saalovaarian-sar-Ilyat) and members of the re-formed Central K'rilate on Zorya Prime, K'ril I'th gave him a full Zoryan military salute, followed by a low bow.

"All honor to you, Peacekeeper," kri said. "You have saved us from interstellar war."

"It's good to see you again, K'ril I'th," Andrei replied. "I'm glad you were successful in regaining power. And now, about our agreement ..."

"We will honor it."

"What agreement is that, Commander Savinov?" the Alliance Council Chair asked.

"K'ril I'th agreed that if the Alliance helped kri's group regain power, the Central K'rilate will take up the question of the responsibilities of Zorya Prime to its colonies," Andrei answered. "Which reminds me. Given the recent events on Logos Prime and Sendos, I think it's time—no, it's actually past time—the Alliance Council took up the question of the rights of minority citizens on its own homeworlds. In fact, I believe future Settlement negotiations will require it."

There was silence, then pandemonium. Andrei laughed and cut the channel. Then he turned to K'ril I'th. "You know, I've had enough excitement for one day."

"Perhaps longer," kri agreed. "And I am not prepared for this round of talks. I have been busy with other matters and have no briefing papers."

Andrei grinned. "Indeed. So let's say we adjourn and start up Settlement negotiations again after the dust settles. Take your prisoners home." They bowed to each other, and Andrei turned to leave. Suddenly, he swung back again.

"We had another agreement, K'ril I'th. Do you remember it?"

"Yes, Commander, I do. I hope you will change your mind and continue to lead Settlement negotiations for the Alliance, but I will accept another Peacekeeper in your place if necessary. It is hard for me to imagine anyone else with your sense of humor and your interesting way with words. I will miss you."

"I won't leave until I have turned my successor into a most honorable opponent for you," Andrei replied.

"What do you plan to do when you are no longer Peacekeeper?" K'ril I'th asked.

Andrei shrugged. "Truthfully, K'ril I'th? I have no idea."

* * *

High on triumph and adrenaline, Andrei felt like he was flying as he practically ran back to his quarters. When he got there, he dismissed his bodyguards and went in alone.

He checked the bedroom briefly. Diana and Sylvain were gone. Back in his office, he re-activated all the door locks and changed the door codes once again so Diana couldn't get in. He thought briefly about the not-quite-empty bottle of *livrash* from the day before. It might slow his racing heart and mind, but he decided against it. He would need all of his concentration for this final move in the game.

He sat in his desk chair and slowly looked around the room, as though seeing it for the first time —or the last. The holo-models were nicely done for what they were, but his mind's eye could see so much more now, that they seemed pale and uninteresting. His whole life in human reality seemed pale and uninteresting. He'd grown beyond it. He'd done what Unity had requested of him, and he was going to demand his reward.

He thought briefly of what he was leaving behind. There were a few people he would miss, but not enough to keep him there. Nick and Coraline would be busy helping to create a new life for Logos Prime's PNs. Sylvain could work with them, or stay with the Mission, or even join the Free Raiders, if that was his choice. Diana …

He drew a sudden breath, thinking about Diana. There was a part of him that had fallen in love with her, but it was a lost cause. If he got what he wanted, he wouldn't be able to have a relationship with her, and if he didn't … She was telepathic to her very core, he thought, and would have no interest in being with him if he was Psi-Null again. She deserved better.

He leaned forward, rubbing suddenly cold hands against his crossed arms as he was caught by doubt. What if …? *No,* he thought. *No use speculating. Just get it over with.* He straightened up again, focused his consciousness, and left reality for mind-space and Unity.

Congratulations, Peacekeeper, Unity Sent. *You have successfully reshaped the destiny of two star systems and destroyed a source of evil in this universe.*

I had a good partner, Andrei replied. *We make a good team.*

But the patterns were yours.

We are effective together, Andrei repeated. *Together, we could accomplish so much.*

Silence.

Andrei tried again. *I wish to remain part of you. I can't go back to my old life—it's too limited. If you make me part of you, or even just let me stay mindlinked with you, I'm sure we can do great things.*

Silence.

Andrei began to feel desperate. Once again he reminded them of how well he'd served them, how the skills he'd acquired as both Warleader and Peacekeeper would be at their disposal.

Finally, he ran out of ideas and just waited in silence for them to pass judgment.

They did. The answer was no.

He would be removed from the mindlink, they told him, but he would be able to keep the repairs they'd made to his body, plus a few additions that he might like to take advantage of sometime in the future. Unlike becoming part of the mindlink, detachment would be quick and painless.

Why?

They explained. They had set a killer to catch a killer. Their previous mindlinked partners had failed because they were too much like Unity: agents of creation. They could not have conceived or executed the plan that destroyed Ashahr. Andrei, on the other hand, was an agent of destruction. He was capable of creating a pattern of death, while Unity was not.

Liars! Hypocrites! I couldn't have killed Ashahr without you. You are equally responsible. Besides, Ashahr was evil. Your sacred task is the destruction of evil.

No, Unity's sacred task is the act of creation. It required something other to perform an act of destruction. You were the catalyst.

I am capable of much more than destruction! As you said, I've created peace for my worlds.

But destruction has been your primary purpose for so long that it is part of your nature.

Andrei didn't reply. He couldn't. He was numb with shock and misery.

Unity continued, *We cannot have one such as you become part of us. Your individuality is too strong. You could never be part of our group consciousness. And now it is time for us to go our separate ways.*

No, wait! The thought he Sent was barely a whisper. He was so stunned by what they'd told him that the elegant argument he'd prepared dissolved into meaninglessness. They saw him as something evil, unworthy of their light and harmony. Perhaps they were right. *Wait. Please don't do this.*

Unity didn't answer. Darkness like a soft, gentle wind spread through his consciousness until it covered his thoughts. Painlessly he slid into unconsciousness, and when he came back to himself, he was on the Peaceship, and they were gone.

The light hurt his eyes, so he turned it off. The holo-models still glowed in the darkness, so he turned those off too. All of the systems on his desk still blinked, so he turned them off, one by one, until the only light in the room was the soft blue glow of the privacy screen over the door. No light, no sound, no sense of anything, anywhere. He was alone.

Almost alone. The last remnant of Ashahr, the seed it had planted in the back of Andrei's mind, fed by his negative energy, stirred and came to life.

He had no idea how long he sat there, staring at nothing, but after a while, his mind started working again. He was Psi-Null. Null. Nothing. There would be no more celestial light, no more celestial music. He was trapped in the body of a killer—someone who wanted to pretend that he had some value in this life, but he couldn't escape the truth of his existence any longer. His pattern was destruction.

He felt empty and tired. Used up. Even when he was fighting Ashahr, he'd never felt as tired as this. He felt worthless, utterly defeated, and sickened with self-hatred. He was done with all of it; he had no desire to go on. If his true pattern was destruction, he would complete it. He stood up, gripping the edge of the desk. Dizzy and weak, his whole body shook with exhaustion. Finally he pushed himself away from the desk and turned toward the bedroom.

It seemed to take hours to reach it. He kept wanting to lie down on the floor and just disappear. The bedroom was also dark, but he didn't need any light to find what he was looking for. He got to the bed and sat down heavily, then leaned over and reached under the mattress for his disruptor pistol.

It wasn't there.

A thread of surprise cut through the fog in his head, and he knelt by the edge of the bed, pushing both hands under the mattress as he searched. He checked under the bed and on either side of it as well as in the night table, but it was gone.

He lowered himself to the floor and sat with his back against the bed, his knees drawn up to his chest and his head resting against them. He had no idea what to do next.

"Looking for something?"

Raising his head was next to impossible, but he managed to look up. Even in darkness he could see Diana's pale hair and silver-gray eyes. She came over and sat down on the floor next to him. She didn't touch him or say anything, but he could feel her warmth at his side.

"How did you get in?" he finally asked.

"I never left," she replied. "I'm just glad I don't suffer from claustrophobia, with all the time I've spent hiding in that damned closet." She reached out to touch him, but he drew away from her, so she put her hand back in her lap. "After you came back from mind-space, I tried a mindtouch, but you didn't respond, so I realized what had happened."

He squeezed his eyes shut, dropping his head back to his knees again.

She continued. "You've been sitting out there in the dark for an hour. I tried speaking to you a couple of times, but you didn't even look at me, so I Read your mind to find out what was going on. I'm sorry—I know it's a violation, but it seemed like a matter of life or death." She paused, but he didn't say anything. "It is, isn't it? A matter of life or death. Or at least that's how it feels to you right now."

"Don't play therapist with me, Diana," he said, but there was no force behind his words. He was in too much pain to talk.

She shook his shoulders. He winced and tried to draw away from her again, but he was too weak to move. "Andrei.

Listen to me. In your whole life, you've never blindly accepted anyone else's judgment of you. Why start now?"

"Because they're right," he whispered.

"You don't have to believe them," she insisted fiercely. "You can think about what existence would be like for the Six, for Logos Prime, if you hadn't stopped the war. You can think about what this universe would be like if you hadn't stopped Ashahr.

"Think about Ashahr, Andrei. Think about what sustained Ashahr—the energy of self-destruction. It left a piece of itself behind, inside your mind. Fight it. Don't let it win."

She got to her knees and pulled him toward her, holding him tightly. "Andrei, I love you. I don't give a damn if you're telepathic or not, as long as we can be together. If you can't think of any other reason to stay alive, think about how lost I'd be without you."

With a cry, he took her in his arms and kissed her passionately. There in the silent darkness, they made love, and he found his way back.

To her.

Chapter 30

Sanctuary on T'lar, nine months later. Diana, Coraline, Nick, and Sylvain were in the sitting room in Diana and Andrei's suite, finishing the evening meal. The air was warm but not hot, and it was comfortable and lightly scented with flowers.

It was supposed to be a surprise thirty-sixth birthday party, but the guest of honor was missing. Even though he wasn't officially part of the Peacekeeping Mission anymore, Andrei had taken off for the Peaceship three days ago, summoned to help put the finishing touches on the final peace agreement. He'd told Diana that he'd be back today, but he was late.

Coraline leaned back contentedly among a nest of brightly colored pillows. "Too bad Andrei missed this feast. Or do you always eat this well here?"

"It's actually not that fancy," Diana answered. "It's the fact that it's real food, not reconstituted from a dispenser, that makes the difference. When the human settlement is fully established, it'll grow its own food."

"The settlement seems to be coming along well," Coraline remarked.

Diana nodded agreement. "Are you thinking about emigrating?"

She shook her head. "No. There's so much left to do on Logos Prime. I think the negotiating team could work all day and night for years, and we still wouldn't be finished."

"Andrei thinks the process is going well, all things considered."

"He's been a big help," Coraline replied. "Talks would have broken down a long time ago if not for him." She studied Diana. "How is he, really? When we're together, I've tried to ask him, but he still doesn't stray far from the subject of what we're working on." She sighed. "Some things never change."

Diana didn't say anything and didn't Send anything. Coraline knew she wasn't using telepathy much anymore, so she just waited for an answer.

"You know what Andrei says—some days are better than others. There are times when I can see he's still wrestling with demons I don't understand, but there are fewer bad days now. The Zh'ladar's helped him a lot, and this project he's working on has been really good for him."

Coraline caught Sylvain nodding his agreement, and she turned to him. "What do you think of your new life here on T'lar?"

"I like it," he replied. "Having fun building my own house."

Diana grinned. "And sharing it with a certain newly arrived Logos Prime settler."

He looked away, embarrassed but also pleased.

"Do you think you'll go with Andrei when the ship is completed?" Coraline asked him.

He nodded. "It's going to be a big ship," he answered. "Lots of automated systems, but it still can't run itself. Won't be done for a while, though. Gives me and Hannah plenty of time to get used to each other before taking off for ... who knows where." Sylvain turned to Nick. "We could use a guy like you with us, Nick. I know Andrei'd never ask you himself. Wouldn't want you to feel obligated."

Nick snorted. "Since when would I feel obligated to my kid brother?"

Coraline rolled her eyes. She knew how Nick really felt about Andrei, and she knew that if Andrei wanted him to, he'd gladly go with him.

"Besides, I like having my own ship. I like my freedom."

"But there isn't as much for Raiders to do these days," Sylvain pointed out. "Not much thrill left to it. The adventures of the future are out there, where Andrei's going. Into the unknown."

Nick shrugged. "Maybe. We'll see."

Coraline looked fondly at her brother, still wild after all these years. If it meant adventure, he'd go, for sure. Then she turned back to Diana. "What about you?"

Diana raised her eyebrows. "What about me?" she echoed. "Are you asking if I'm going too?"

"No, of course not," Coraline replied. "I know you're going. I was just wondering what you were up to these days."

"I have a project of my own, but it needs work before I'd want to tell anyone about it." Diana rose. "Andrei called just before you all showed up, to tell me he was on his way. I didn't want to spoil the surprise, so I agreed to meet him over at the warehouse where the ship's being built. Enjoy yourselves here at Sanctuary. We have a swimming pool, you know." She and Nick exchanged glances, and she was laughing as she left.

* * *

Andrei stood in the shadows, gazing at the beginning of his future.

The ship was a parting gift from Unity—or at least the knowledge of how to build it, and where it could go, had come from them. When he had resigned from the Peacekeeping Mission and moved to T'lar, both Diana and the Zh'ladar kept asking him what he really wanted. He'd thought that what he really wanted was closed to him, but when he started to heal, he had discovered that a different version of it—to explore beyond the boundaries of Alliance and Hegemony—was actually still possible. So he had commissioned the building of this deep-space exploration vehicle.

The skeleton of a crystal-shaped hull gleamed in the gathering twilight. The design and materials were unlike anything the Alliance had ever seen before, and he and the builders struggled with them. There were times when he knew that the scientists and engineers working for him doubted the ship would ever be able to be completed and go anywhere, but Andrei knew it could be done.

He knew he was going into space. Unity hadn't given him the exact coordinates for Earth or any human outposts, but they'd left enough information in his mind to show him where to look. Maybe he'd find other humans, or maybe he'd find something else—something he couldn't even imagine right now. Thanks to Unity, he had a normal human lifespan again, and he planned to live it to the fullest.

With Diana, who appeared at his side. He drew her into his arms, and they stood quietly together, looking at the ship.

"How did things go on the Peaceship?" she asked.

"Fine," he replied. He took a last look at the ship. "I haven't had dinner. Let's go back."

He turned to go, but she put her hand on his arm. "Wait a minute, Andrei. There's something I want to tell you."

Surprised, he turned back to her.

"I've finished all my tests, and they proved that my initial theory was correct," she began. "In order to create the mindlink, Unity had to change you down at the cellular level. Which means your DNA has been changed."

He didn't know what to make of that, so he chose the most bizarre thing he could think of to ask her. "Are you telling me I'm not human any longer?"

"Not a Logos Prime type of human. A new type. And given Unity's nature as a highly evolved telepath, all the extrapolation scenarios I've run point to the likelihood that the DNA you're carrying would create a new race of—for lack of a better word for it—super telepaths."

Andrei stared at her, stunned. "But I'm not telepathic."

"Not you, love, your children. Your descendants."

"But I don't have any children …" His voice trailed off as he saw her face change from serious to almost laughing. "What are you trying to tell me?"

"I want to have children with you, Andrei," she said. "We could start a new race of human telepaths unlike any that came before. And we could raise them to be the kind of people I believe advanced humans are capable of being." This time, she did laugh. "Hey, if it was a good enough experiment for your mother …"

For once, he was absolutely speechless.

THE END